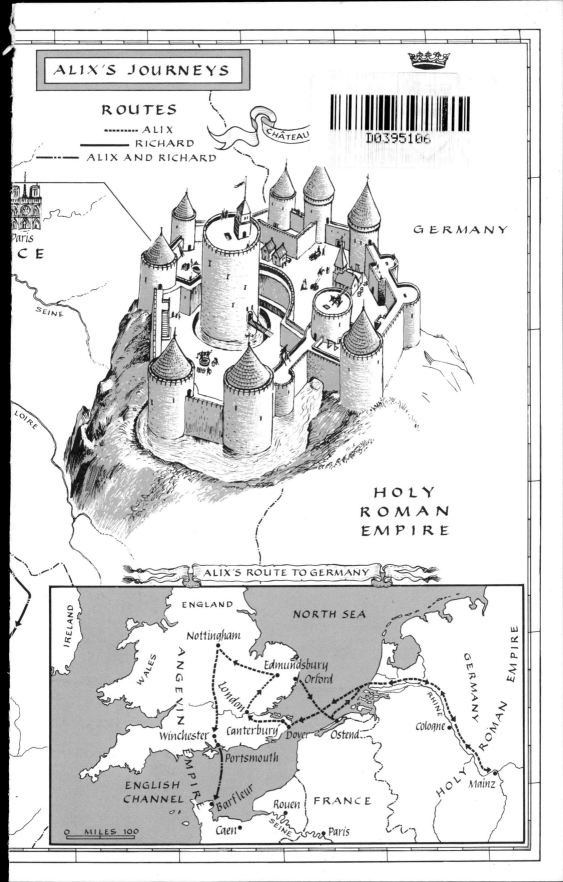

# ALIX'S JOURNEYS

## ROUTES
- ---- ALIX
- —— RICHARD
- —·— ALIX AND RICHARD

CHÂTEAU

D0395106

Paris

CE

SEINE

LOIRE

GERMANY

HOLY
ROMAN
EMPIRE

ALIX'S ROUTE TO GERMANY

IRELAND

ENGLAND

NORTH SEA

WALES

ANGEVIN

Nottingham

Edmundsbury

Orford

London

GERMANY

RHINE

Winchester

Canterbury

Dover

Ostend

Cologne

Portsmouth

HOLY ROMAN EMPIRE

EMPIRE

ENGLISH
CHANNEL

Barfleur

Rouen

FRANCE

Mainz

0  MILES  100

Caen

SEINE

Paris

# BANNERS OF GOLD

*By the same author*

Shield of Three Lions

# BANNERS OF GOLD

## PAMELA KAUFMAN

CROWN PUBLISHERS, INC.
NEW YORK

*Copyright © 1986 by Pamela Kaufman*
*All rights reserved. No part of this book may be reproduced*
*or transmitted in any form or by any means,*
*electronic or mechanical, including photocopying, recording,*
*or by any information storage and retrieval system,*
*without permission in writing from the publisher.*
*Published by Crown Publishers, Inc.*
*225 Park Avenue South, New York 10003 and represented in Canada*
*by the Canadian MANDA Group*
*CROWN is a trademark of Crown Publishers, Inc.*
*Manufactured in the United States of America*
*Library of Congress Cataloging-in-Publication Data*

*Kaufman, Pamela.*
*Banners of gold.*

*I. Title.*
*PS3561.A8617B3   1986       813'.54       86-8908*
*ISBN 0-517-56133-6*
*10   9   8   7   6   5   4   3   2   1*
*First Edition*

*For my mother, Marcella McKeddie*

*My banner is love.*
*Stay me with flagons,*
*Stay me with apples,*
*For I am sick with love.*

—SONG OF SOLOMON

# NOTE

Chroniclers of the last decade of the twelfth century failed to account for the activities of King Richard of England for as long as a year and a half, and, as men of the Church, continued to exclude women and Jews altogether from their observations. Scholars in the intervening centuries have attempted to fill these gaps in knowledge with varying success. Often, later historians reveal more about the nineteenth century's interest in Constitutional law, or the twentieth century's fascination with depth psychology or assorted liberation movements than they do the period in question. In short, anyone seriously interested in this span of time is forced to speculate or to revise according to the accepted wisdom of the moment.

In my case, since fiction takes precedence over history, I have used the scanty records as the basis of my tale, have invented almost no new events, but have felt free to enlarge my research to art and architecture, music and literature, and the events which preceded and followed the brief years I cover. The only liberties I have taken with known incidents are chronological and then by only a few months. The tragedy of Bristol and the papal bull, however, both came a few years later than I have indicated.

Most of the characters in the book actually lived, though we know almost nothing about them as people, but those I've created are based on types we know did exist. An instance of the latter is Robin Hood, a folk hero rather than a real person. Yet Robin Hood, as Andrew McCall remarks in his fine study *The Medieval Underworld*, illustrates a point where fact and fiction merge. Better born than the peasants around him, champion against unjust Forest Laws, corrupt officials and a rich, indolent clergy, his historical prototype lived in the persons of several recorded men; the fiction, unfortunately, is that any of them robbed from the rich to give to the poor. The character Tib comes from the concept of the old Trotula, an almost mythic healing prostitute known since Roman times, a woman who treats women. Sister Hilaria owes much to the real Abbess Hildegard of Bingen and other religious women of the era.

The historical people are almost as elusive as the invented types, for they left little beyond their names in the records. Queen Berengaria, whose marriage to King Richard was in name only and who never saw England, is described once as a "prudent lady," which is usually interpreted to mean religious and plain of appearance. I have made her a typical, medieval, religious bigot, with all due apologies to the real Berengaria. Even Queen Eleanor, a perennial favorite of our own time, was never described as a person, was ignored in the records for years even when she was a ruling queen, and was not mentioned at all during the last years of her life. In her case, for example, I have applied modern knowledge of dominant and recessive genes to reconstruct her appearance from the evidence of her sons, who were described. King Richard, by comparison, was fairly well documented, and whenever possible I have seamed his own vocabulary and set speeches into my fictional invention.

Most of all, I have tried to present a "real" young woman, Alix of Wanthwaite, as she might have lived and thought. Therefore I have rounded the other characters so that they can interact with her as living people. In so doing, however, I have tried to be true to a world view very remote from our own, to lives lived close to nature and God, to rigid social

attitudes based on feudalism, but I've assumed that these
profound differences in perception between then and now
do not preclude normal human emotions and the fallibilities
thereof.

Pamela Kaufman
Los Angeles, 1986

# BOOK ONE

# KING RICHARD

~~~~~~~~~~~~~~~~~~~~~~~~~~~~~~~~~~~~~~~~~~~~~~~~

*That stink you breathe is a world that stinks to heaven.*
*The stench was painful yesterday?*
    *Smell it today!*
*Since the Emperor broke from God's goodness*
*We have not heard of his power increasing,*
    *nor his honor,*
      *nor knightly prowess. And now*
*if the fool leaves Richard to rot in prison, the*
    *English will have their say.*

    *let no man think I am humbled by them!*
*I am led by a precious joy that is born in me,*
*holds me rejoicing.*
    *Her life sharp and certain,*
      *clear coming in pleasure,*
        *arms wide in rejoicing.*
*You're curious?*
*Do your asking in England.*

          —PIERE VIDAL, TWELFTH CENTURY

# 1

BITTER SHAFT BLEW FROM THE FIRTH.
Cold as a bone, it whipped the last of the
leaves off the wands, turned turnips in the
field a bright blue, keened around our castle
towers while inside we labored frantically to
hang hides across arrow-slits. I was dragging a ladder to my
second window when I heard a familiar scratching.

"Dingwall?" I called suspiciously. "Where are you, Dingwall?"

My hound pup's rump wiggled from under my bedmat.

"If you take . . ."

He faced me with a vellum in his jaws, tail thumping the
rushes in anticipation.

"Give that to me, you wallydrag!"

He darted out the door as Gruoth lumbered in.

"Catch him, Gruoth! He's got Enoch's letter!"

She stood back as I flew past her. Through the courtyard
and gate, across the moatbridge, down the steep spinney
where I fell on rime-coated grass. I would kill that no-good
brute, slice him small and put him in a saucepan. Wind
howled, branches splintered and shot past like arrows, but I
picked myself up and plunged after Dingwall where his tail
disappeared in the brush. I found him crouched by the
Wanthwaite River, the vellum spread under his splayed
paws as he licked it with slow savor. He was too cowardly
to swim, but he would dash up and down the banks for a
week if I chased him.

Feigning indifference, I swung on a low branch, then hoisted my heavy cowhide boots over my head and let go with my hands, dangling upside down so my hair brushed the ground; Dingwall couldn't resist my hair. From this view, the sky was an alarming chaos of flying gray cushions; the earth thumped and shook, as if its heart beat in panic.

"Come, Dingwall," I called sweetly.

He growled, let flee a series of excited yips.

Puzzled, I turned my head and gazed into the pup's spiked tail, and beyond the tail to a horse's leg, and up the leg to a black boot in a gilded stirrup.

I put my hands flat and wheeled to an upright position.

A stranger looked down on me from an enormous chest-nut destrier. Behind him stretched a line of soldiers and packed mules. *Benedicite*, how had they stolen so stilly through the wood? Then I recalled the beat I'd heard— horses' hooves.

The stranger pricked the vellum with his broadsword and held it forth. "Is this what you want?" As if he were offering the letter to a monkey.

"Aye. Thank you."

"Perhaps you can help me, lass. I seek Lady Alix of Wanthwaite, and the villagers in Dunsmere told me that this was the path. Are you one of her villeins?"

I hesitated. He was elegant as a black swan, swathed in dark furs over fine black wool and scarlet sendal, wore a crushed red hat on black crulled hair, but I didn't like the army behind him. Why would they travel to our remote Northumbrian estate with swords and heavy crates?

"Who seeks the lady?"

His lips tightened in irritation. "Bonel of Rouen, the king's man."

I studied him for insignia. "What king? William of Scotland?" Though he spoke with a Norman accent, not a brogue.

"King Richard of England!" he snapped, then pulled his reins as if to pass me.

*King Richard.*

Fighting a rush of fear, I leaped into the center of the path, fixed myself firmly.

His horse shied. "What are you doing? Be careful!"

By now I'd counted sixteen soldiers. "All the way from London, sir?"

"Yes." Snow began to fall in flakes big as rabbit tails, and I could hardly see him, but his voice threatened. "Please step aside before you get hurt."

I could think of no further delay. "I'll lead you, sir."

Abruptly I scooped Dingwall into my arms and scrambled up the slippery path half on my knees, the stranger following close at my heels while his men struggled with the laden mules. Before us, Wanthwaite's louring black walls and square towers pulsed in and out of vision behind whirling rings of snow.

When we reached the courtyard, I shouted over my shoulder, "Wait here, sir, and someone will come for your horses."

I dashed ahead into the great hall, where Dugan was climbing down a ladder from the highest arrow-slit.

"Dugan, armed men! From King Richard!"

He jumped heavily before me. "Keep your wits. Do ye ken their purpose?"

"Maybe from the king's Exchequer," I replied. "They have heavy crates."

"They canna dig silver from our ears, Alix," Donald assured me. "I'll tell him sae. Let summun elsit pay fer the Crusade."

"How many are they, Milady?" Dame Margery asked.

Before I could answer, the door blasted open behind us and Bonel swept in, a black mountain of a man in his swirling furs.

"For Goddes' sake, spare us!" Gruoth screamed.

All of us stared, stunned. In the wood, half of Bonel's face had been concealed. Now I saw that the right side was blighted by a webby scar centering on his eye, a huge magnified blue orb like polished ice with the eye painted on the underside. Then the door slammed behind him, and we were in semidarkness—the only illumination coming from the fire—and he was an incorporeal voice, dripping with honey and faint menace.

"I'm Bonel of Rouen," he announced, unperturbed by our reaction. "I represent King Richard on business with Lady Alix of Wanthwaite."

All of us drew slightly closer to one another.

"I'm Lady Alix." I tried to match his dignity, though my own voice bleated. He stared at me, transfixed, as if my face were as astonishing as his.

He recovered quickly. "I should have known at once, except that you're so . . . young."

So besmottered, he meant, so poor I took you for a villein.

"I'm fifteen." Let him think as he liked. I was proud of my tattered bliaut, bearskin vest, sheepskin cope, short plaid kilt with straw and feathers in the woof, bare raw knees, muck-covered boots—proud to look like the good Scot that I was, by marriage anyway. "Do you have proof that you represent King Richard?"

Bemused, he reached into his drafsack. "I carry the royal seal."

My heart squeezed as I held the heavy metal plaque in my muddy palm, pretended to weigh and study it. The seal gave Bonel an ominous authority far beyond his eye or voice, for few men carry the king's seal. Dugan leaned over my shoulder and muttered that it looked genuine, which it did. Richard rode with upraised sword on its polished surface, like himself yet different from when I'd last seen him in Acre.

I almost dropped the odious object as I returned it. "For the king's sake, welcome to Wanthwaite. Please let me take your cloak, and then join us by the fire."

Dame Margery dragged two faldstools close to the hearth while Donald crept quietly halfway up the stair and Dugan signaled to the women to draw close.

I caught the heavy furs as Bonel released two gold broaches. His crimson tunic had high, puffed sleeves with tight forearms; belted with jewel-studded leather, it flared just below his knees where it met fur-lined boots. Around his neck hung a gold Byzantine cross big as a horseshoe and encrusted with rubies. With his splendid dress, magnificent jewels, and viewed only on his good side, he was an impressive man. Yet, even discounting his uncanny eye, he was strange, a perplexing choice as royal officer; he might be a sultan from the east, or a Venetian, for he had the exotic and sinister aura of the orient.

"Thank you." Bonel appraised my face again, almost with wonder, then noted the positions of the Scots.

I unfastened my sheepskin to put with his cloak.

"You wear the Crusader's cross!" he remarked, pointing to my old Plantagenet bliaut. This time his shock was plain to see.

I tried to cover the stained emblem with my hands.

"It's not . . . ."

Gruoth blabbed proudly, "Alix were on the Crusade wi' King Richard."

"But women weren't permitted on Richard's Crusade."

I shot Gruoth a warning look. "The fact is . . ."

"She went dressed as a boy," Gruoth boasted.

*Benedicite.* My face heated, I stared at Bonel's narrow boots.

"Quhat's wrong wi' yer eye?" Gruoth clattered on.

"Gruoth!" I jerked her braid. "Apologize to Bonel."

Our guest waved a bejeweled hand. "That's not necessary, Lady Alix. Everyone wants to know." He bent over Gruoth and lowered his voice. "I received my blue eye under peculiar circumstances, young lady. One stormy night four years ago I was struck by a thunderbolt which changed my life. I fell into a swoon, and when I recovered, I was marked by my scar and my eye. Ever since, I've had special vision; I can see directly into men's minds and hearts—especially into the evil that lurks therein." He straightened, touched his cross significantly.

Gruoth was entranced. "Did it cum from the Devil? Be it the Evil Eye?"

"No, God revealed Himself to me with His mighty bolt; I call this my Christian Eye."

"A miracle forsooth," I commented skeptically, not appreciating his gulling poor Gruoth. "If it please you, I would like to introduce my household, Bonel."

As I was presenting Dugan, Donald, Thorketil and Archie, Gruoth, Matilda, and my old nurse, Dame Margery, Bonel's men entered and quietly lined themselves against the walls. The Scots squinted at them suspiciously.

"Tell yer men to put doon their swords," Dugan ordered brusquely.

"They're always armed—a caution against thieves along the road."

"There be no robbers in Wanthwaite."

But the swords remained unsheathed, and the atmosphere chilled. The Scots turned slowly to count the wights; then Dugan threw me a subtle signal.

As I walked to a faldstool, my household moved as well, each person placing himself to oppose Bonel's soldiers if need be; Donald managed to slip up to the balcony. When Bonel sat on the stool opposite me, three mercenaries gathered close behind him, their faces pinched and surly, their hair plastered like tree fern on low foreheads.

Bonel bent forward like a conspirator, enclosed my hands with his bejeweled fingers.

"Lady Alix, I've come to take you to London."

THE WORDS exploded.

"*London?*" I echoed faintly. "That's a woodly jape, sir."

"No jape at all. Surely you've heard that two hundred hostages are being sent to the Holy Roman Empire in exchange for King Richard. Your name is on the roster."

I jerked my hands free and my movement permitted the firelight to catch his Christian eye: it glowed like a malevolent jewel.

"I'm sorry we couldn't give you fair warning, but your castle is remote, and we've had little time ourselves to prepare."

"You speak in riddles, sir. I know nothing of hostages or the Holy Roman Empire, and King Richard is leading a Crusade against Saladin in the Holy Land."

"Good God, can you be so ignorant?" Bonel cried. "Everyone in England knows that Richard left Acre almost two years ago, that he disappeared on his homeward journey and was thought to be shipwrecked until he was discovered as a prisoner in Austria!"

His insult brought a mighty roar from my household to the effect that they were not ignorant and that Wanthwaite Castle was in Scotland, not England. I let them rant as I watched Bonel; he was not a lunatick nor a scoundrel nor a sorcerer, but much worse: he was soothly an emissary from the king. I wondered how much he knew.

"That's enough!" I stopped Dugan. "Let the man speak. I want to hear more about these two hundred hostages and the roster."

Bonel's blue eye fastened on me like a spider. "King Richard is being held by Emperor Henry Hohenstaufen of Germany and Duke Leopold of Austria," he resumed, "and they demand a handsome ransom for his release, one hundred and fifty thousand silver marks."

Again the Scots interjected a loud groan of disbelief.

". . . of which England has raised one hundred thousand. For the rest, we are sending two hundred hostages with their English estates as security; many volunteered and the rest were carefully selected."

Selected? The word jarred my fantastick cells. "And I was one of those selected?"

"Yes. I can understand your confusion, since you're so

isolated, but we have no time to jangle further. I'll answer
questions along the road; now I suggest you begin your
preparations."

I didn't move.

"You've made a long, hazardous journey for no purpose,
Bonel. I can't possibly be a hostage."

There was no audible sound, but I was aware of the collective sigh of relief behind me. Bonel, the brow over his
brown eye raised, gazed at me as if I were an irritating dolt.

"Your name is on the roster, and I was sent most particularly to accompany you to London."

"You can explain that I refused to come—that it's not
your fault. Perhaps you can find someone else—someone
more important—as you ride to London."

He rose, looked over his shoulder at his men, then stood
silhouetted against the fire so that little flames darted around
his black form, a Byzantine icon. "You have no choice in the
matter, Lady Alix. England has been invaded."

The shocked Scots demanded details. King Richard's
younger brother, Prince John, wanted to seize England, and
King Philip of France was his ally. John's mercenaries had
landed close to Sandwich—they held Windsor Castle.

I went weak with apprehension. "As a woman, I can
hardly fight an invasion."

"No one is suggesting that you do so, but Philip and John
are trying to pay Richard's ransom themselves. You see why
the hostages are vital to our national weal."

"Aye, but . . ."

"There can be no buts."

"There are reasons I can't go, *won't* go."

"You have no choice. To refuse is tantamount to treason."

"To accept is tantamount to death!" I cried.

"No one will die. The king has sworn to redeem all hostages within seven months of his release."

"With what? If you couldn't raise the money, how can
he?"

"He promised . . ."

"And if he doesn't, what then? The hostages are forfeit! Will die!"

"You have a female morbidity, Lady Alix, and don't understand . . ."

"Spare me your flattery," I interrupted angrily, "and let me think. I need to confer with my household."

He shrugged elaborately. "As you like, so long as you're prepared to ride at dawn."

He walked to a shadowy corner followed by his loathsome mercenaries. The Scots huddled close around me.

"I have a plan," I whispered feverishly. "We must say that Enoch's expected at any moment."

Gruoth stretched her stied lids. "But he be wounded, Alix."

"Don't mention his wound," I warned and quickly outlined my scheme. I would insist that I couldn't leave without Enoch and try to persuade Bonel to wait one more day. Meantime, Archie would sneak away to Dunsmere to rouse the villagers. As soon as Bonel left Wanthwaite, with me in his company, the Scots would join the rustics and prepare to fight.

"Aye," Dugan breathed, looking like a mad bull with his horned hat and red eyes. "We'll ambush them by the river quhere the big bend gi'es cover. They'll be too surprised to fight, and too weighed doon wi' silver."

We honed our strategy as well as we could do in our brief time, then called to Bonel.

"I should explain my refusal, Bonel. If you know my name's on the roster, you must know that I'm married to Lord Enoch Angus of Dingle-Boggs. He was called to Edinburgh by King William, but returns at any moment—we thought today, but certainly tomorrow. I must await his pleasure in this matter."

Bonel's smile unnerved me. Did he know I was lying?

"Queen Eleanor will leave London on December tenth, and you will be with her."

"Not December tenth!" Dame Margery shrieked so loudly that we all jumped.

"Be ready tomorrow morning, Lady Alix. You're wasting precious time."

Dugan stepped between us.

"Bonel, ye doona appear to be a fightin' man. The rules say that a husband decides yif his wife be hostage; betimes the husband goes in her stead."

"But Lord Enoch isn't here, so the point is moot."

"He will be here, tomorrow at the latest," I insisted. "If you tell us your route, we may join you. If not, we could ride straight to London. At the very least, he'll want to accompany me."

So rooted in truth was this statement that I almost believed my own lie.

Bonel spoke curtly. "You'll go with me, Lady Alix, and your husband can follow—if he so chooses."

Dugan's short temper snapped. "Ye hear the harp boot nocht the music!" he roared. "Alix canna gae no place wi'outen Enoch. That's my last word."

"I won't go," I confirmed. "My husband is my lord in this matter."

"King Richard is your lawful lord, and you are his vassal," Bonel said impatiently. "In return for your title and lands, you owe him fealty. If you refuse to leave now, then I'll simply reclaim your lands and title forthwith. That's one reason I carry the seal."

"Wanthwaite's mine!" I cried in panic.

"If you go, yes."

"But I can't go! You just heard that my husband won't permit it!"

"Loyalty to the king takes precedence over marriage vows. Do you concede or shall I begin an inventory?"

He waved derisively at my great hall and for a moment I

saw it from his view: the chickens and pigeons scratching in one corner, snow falling through a leak in the center, rotting carrion and dog messes besmottering the rushes—for we'd had no time to clean. His scathing glance enraged me as much as his demand.

"Do whatever you like! You can't harvest the beans! Can't carry Wanthwaite away on a mule!"

"I grant that you're easier to transport than your estate, which is the point of being a hostage. However, the king is riding north the moment he's freed. Do you want your household to face his wrath?"

His words struck like mallet blows.

"All he wants is revenge!"

"*Revenge?*" Bonel was brought short, gazed on me as if I'd tinted my reason. "The King of England wants *revenge* on a paltry baroness?" He hooted in contempt. "My God, the absurdity—if you think . . ."

The Scots were equally astounded, as none but Dame Margery knew anything of my former relationship with the king. Much as I was appalled by my blunder—especially to Bonel with his smirk—it was the truth. Certainly Enoch would agree that the king sought revenge . . . no, I couldn't let Richard ride north, couldn't let him fight Enoch. *Benedicite*, it was the collapse of my plan.

Dame Margery shook my arm. "Alix, I must speak with ye prively. 'Tis most urgent."

"Aye," I said, in a trance. "Bonel, I'm going to my chamber with my old nurse so we may be alone; there's no exit from the room, so you need not worry."

Before he could reply, I took a firebrand and led Dame Margery up the narrow stair.

I FELT I WAS STEPPING into the past as we entered the memory-haunted room. There was the bed where I'd been born, where my mother and I had slept together the night before she died, where Enoch and I had first . . .

I held the torch high. A faint alarmed rustle in the eaves revealed that some canny animal or bird had found a home; snow blew across the center from the open window and covered the furs on the bed. I led Margery to a corner protected from the wind where we huddled close, the flame a waning flicker before us. I put my arm around my shivering nurse.

"December tenth, Alix." She clutched my wrist with an icy claw. "Do you take the meaning?"

"It's when Bonel said Queen Eleanor would be leading the hostages from London."

"Aye, and what else?"

She asked with heavy significance, but I couldn't answer.

"December tenth in 1174 my own sister Annie were taken hostage by the Scots, and we never saw her more."

"Aye," I breathed, impressed.

She then repeated a tale I'd heard all through my childhood but had never found so real before, how Scots, painted with woad and berserking like savages had raided Wanthwaite and captured forty prisoners. The hostages, among them Annie, had marched naked through the snow to their deaths.

" 'Tis a warning, Milady, and ye must heed it."

"Aye, it couldn't be coincidence."

I shouldn't have agreed. My doughty nurse, who is tough as a wild boar, waxed to a morbid frenzy, sobbing and groaning in ever louder wails until I became alarmed. I tried to undo the mischief.

"Be brave, Margery. Remember that I was only eleven when I left before and came back safely."

She blew her nose on her barmcloth and gradually gained control.

"I'm sorry, honey-lips. I'll take hold in a moment, but . . ."

I stroked her thin hair.

"But it's different, Alix. Last time ye were forced to flee

Wanthwaite for yer life. But why should ye go now? To rot in prison fer that worthless king? Look how he abused ye before. The whole scheme be daft."

"Aye," I agreed forlornly.

"Last time ye had Enoch to protect ye."

I couldn't deny it.

"Fer yer sake—and fer his—I hope ye're together soon."

Wind yowled at the base of the tower, and suddenly I saw my mother at the snow-rimmed window as she'd stood that last night, moaning and praying for my father—both of them dead the next day. Where was Enoch now? How grave was his wound?

"I love him!" I cried vehemently, and my voice echoed like a thin shadow.

"Of course ye do, sweets."

The firebrand went out, leaving only a glowing ash, but we didn't move. I felt the power of her argument, though I needed no omen to strengthen my resolve, but what could I do? My few Scots against sixteen armed mercenaries, the weight of that seal . . . King Richard. Who could have anticipated the long reach of the king's wrath?

At the foot of the tower, the wind growled ominously; higher, over the turrets, it was a haunted shriek. I listened, and a second plan took shape. I clutched Margery's arms and began to whisper rapidly, though there was no one to hear. Bonel's mules and their load of silver had been taken to the stable—and that silver would save me as well as the king. I would go back to the great hall and argue with Bonel. While we talked, Margery would sneak down the steps, out the door and to the stalls. There, with the help of our villeins, she would load the mules and lead them to our labyrinth and thence to the cave by the river. If Bonel wanted to retrieve his treasure, he must agree to leave without me: silver would be *our* hostage.

Margery pointed out that he might torture me, but I was sure I could withstand any pain he might inflict. He wouldn't dare mutilate or kill me in the king's name—to that extent I trusted Richard—and his insistence on speed indicated that he wouldn't tarry long.

Dugan shouted my name from below.

"Coming!" I answered.

I pulled Margery to her feet, and we embraced in the dark. Whatever the flaws in my scheme, Margery was not one of them. We'd conspired before in our time, and I knew she would get the treasure out of sight—if only all else went well.

I walked alone onto the balcony, looked down on anxious Scottish faces. Bonel didn't even glance upward as I ran lightly down the stair to his side.

"My mind is set, Bonel. I'll not be going as hostage."

A lusty cheer rose around me. Bonel let it die.

"Are you sure?"

I heard the menace, but paid no heed.

"Please give my regrets to the queen. I appreciate the king's danger, but . . ."

"I don't think you do."

Above me the door creaked; Margery had begun to move. Dugan stepped between us. "The lady ha' made up her mind, Bonel, and that be that. Ye're welcome to sleep the nicht, but they'll be namore blether about hostages."

Bonel made a slight gesture with his gold cross, and two mercenaries leaped up the stair and grabbed Margery's arms. A hiss of metal followed and swords gleamed.

"I'm sure you don't want that old woman harmed, Lady Alix."

I was dazed. "Why are you holding her? Tell them to release her at once."

"She's our hostage until you agree to come peaceably as ordered."

"But you said—you said—I was given a choice!"

"Never. You wanted to talk and I let you, but I told you plainly from the beginning that you had no choice. We'll leave at dawn."

"Let them kill me, Alix!" Margery shouted. "I don't care! But ye mustn't go! Remember December . . ."

One of the mercenaries struck her face.

Gruoth burst into sobs.

"Stop them!" I cried. "I'll go! Only tell them to release her."

Bonel called in a foreign tongue and the mercenaries dragged Margery down the stairs. Her eyes were wild with fanatic hate, but her bones rattled with fear when I held her.

"It's all right, Nurse, I'll be all right," I whispered. "I'll be back, I promise."

She drew away. "Mayhap."

I clutched her again, spoke to Bonel over her shoulder. "I need money for myself and two retainers."

His voice was conciliatory. "The king's coffers will provide, and we carry tents for emergencies. However, my orders are to bring you alone—I'll look after you."

I turned away, unable to face his suave duplicity.

FROM THAT POINT ON I didn't speak to Bonel, though I had Dugan ask when the king was going to be released—the date of my imprisonment—and was told that he would be free in early January. I calculated swiftly: if the king redeemed the hostages in seven months as promised, I would be back in Wanthwaite in August at the earliest. I had no preparation to make for my journey, none for my sojourn in Germany, but I must plan my absence from Wanthwaite.

With Matilda and Dugan, I pored over my records and listed plans for the spring planting, for the rotation of cows in the field to avoid hoof rot, the purchase of more swine. Matilda took notes, for Dugan wanted to go for Enoch at the first thaw.

By daybreak we were weak with weariness and appalled at what hadn't been done, but time had run out. My friends now gathered in predawn murk to present farewell gifts. Dugan gave me a leather band for my arm, Archie his own quiver, Thorketil a horseshoe, Donald another horseshoe,

Matilda a bag of herbs against spells and diseases, Gruoth her best squirrel hat.

Dame Margery pulled me outside the great hall and marched us to the kitchen court. There, in the dark crevice of the chimney, she handed me a rag containing a long object within.

It was my father's dagger.

I looked up, startled. "Are you suggesting . . ."

"Ye don't need suggestions, Alix," she reminded me. "Ye killed a man once."

But under different circumstances.

"And ye may do so again. Keep it close."

"Soothly I don't think Bonel will harm me."

"Mayhap not," she replied grimly, "but what about his army? What about the hundreds of ravening wolves along the road?"

Remembering her panic the night before, I tried to comfort her. "I know how to look after myself, dear. After all, I was in much greater danger when I went as a boy. Suppose my disguise had been discovered?"

"Ye miss my meaning. Ye're a walking honey-pot among bears." She put a hand to my lips to stop my protest. "Even that sorcerer slavered at the sight of yer bonny face, like he was bespelled. I've ne'er seen yer match: ye don't walk as other people, but float and bend like a swan; yer hair be yellow as gorse, yer eyes gray as heather, yer lips, pearly teeth and dimples enough to tempt a priest to ragery—even my old blear-eyed Tom can rise fer thee."

"You'll make me vain. Suppose what you say is half-true, remember that I'm a married woman. Any man can see my virtue."

Her eyes bore hotly into mine. "Nay, Milady, ye don't know yerself as I do—as any sharp man will know as well. Ye cry out in the night from hot dreams, betimes stroke yer breasts, lick yer lips and sigh most bewitchingly."

"Stop!" My cheeks burned.

"Enoch lit a mighty fire in yer bedstraw."

"What are you suggesting?" I cried, incensed.

"That ye've been alone too long—that ye're ripe to be plucked."

"Only by Enoch!"

"Enoch be a phantom riding yer sweet mound. Married three months and away near to three years . . ."

"No more," I beseeched, not wanting to part in anger. "Enoch can't help that he's . . ."

"Called to be a soldier? Is wounded? No, 'tis no one's fault, but take care."

Promising that I would, I held her tight, noting how frail her frame had become, how precarious her balance. Seven months—would she last so long?

"I'll not see ye again, sweet lamb," she wept, answering my thought.

I fought tears myself, not wanting that one-eyed mooncalf to know how I suffered. Then we walked swiftly to the courtyard where the line waited, where my horse Thistle was saddled and ready. For the last time, I embraced each of my friends and servants.

"You dally too long, Lady Alix," Bonel scolded. "We have a long ride today."

Dugan helped me mount, put my mule's rein in my hands to pull the beast behind Thistle, and I took my place beside the king's man. I dug my heels. "Hoyt!"

We clopped slowly over the slippery boards of the moat-bridge, down the spinney and into the wood. The last thing I heard was Dingwall's unearthly howl of grief.

# 2

LOP-SUCK, CLOP-SUCK, CLOP-SUCK. THE HEAVY weight of the treasure forced the mules' hooves deep into mud and impeded our progress. We'd turned off the Roman road of Dere Street at a stone marker, but had quickly lost our way. Now the sun was low in its run, dusk descending, a gale off the firth whipping upper branches and fast turning dripping water into ice. Our line was a confused serpent dragging sluggish coils through a riddle of trees.

"Where are we going?" I asked, my first words to Bonel of the day.

"Malbysse Manor."

Bad-bitch manor, I translated.

Bonel dismounted, fished in his saddlebag and brought forth a flat dish and needle. He placed it on the ground, floated the needle in wine and studied, then got on his horse again.

"This way."

"I see smoke," I offered, pointing in a different direction.

He stared, and followed my finger without a word of thanks.

Any pretense of courtesy had disappeared, now that I was firmly his captive. I wondered who the victim at Malbysse Manor might be.

Soon we entered a clearing before a large, timbered hunting lodge. Grooms rushed from the stables to harangue with the head mercenary, a dour, long-jawed churl called Bok, about the disposal of the treasure as Bonel and I dismounted. He might have forgotten me for all the attention he paid, but I followed close to his dark furs as protection against the wind.

The great hall of Malbysse Manor had high vaulted ceilings and a balcony; saddles and sour-smelling arms were piled against the shadowy walls, a smoking fire rose from a pit in the center and stung my eyes. From the far side of the pit, four men watched us silently, crackling flames and smoke obscuring their lower parts so that their disembodied heads hung eerily in the fluttering orange underlight.

"Well, Bonel, we meet again," spoke a thick, husky voice.

Bonel stared. "Sir Richard Malbysse."

Our host was redder than the others for he had copper hair and skin; his head was squashed from top to bottom, his nose almost meeting his chin, ferret eyes gleaming under low, bristling brows.

"I'm flattered that you remember me." The flat monotone managed to convey heavy sarcasm.

"One remembers an arch-fiend, if you consider that flattering." Bonel replied with equal vitriol.

"So the worm has found a tongue along with a royal benefactor. Well, worm, on my right is Sir William de Fauconbridge, on my left Sir Robert de Cuckney and Hugh, Bishop of Durham and Lord of Northumberland. You did request their presence?"

"Yes."

The menace was palpable; I edged closer to Bonel. Fauconbridge and Cuckney hardly acknowledged the introduction. The former had dark brown hair, a slack full mouth, a cleft chin, the latter no hair, a jutting nose and tiny mouth, but they were alike in their own choleric humor.

I was most intrigued by the Bishop of Durham, however, a famous man. He had a sanguine complexion, face round and red as an ashberry, watery green eyes. Then he came around the pit and revealed a ponderous belly, on which lay a cross and a sword.

"Greetings, Bonel, and welcome to Malbysse Manor. I've looked forward to meeting . . . Holy Saint George! Who's that ragged wench?"

"Did you bring a whore?" Malbysse snarled in outrage.

He leaped across the pit and threw me to the floor. "A common strumpet, by God!"

"I'm not a strumpet!" I protested hotly. My knee was bleeding.

Bonel grabbed Malbysse's fustian. "She's a lady! Apologize!"

"You're nothing but a Jewish whoremonger!"

"I'm Christian! *Per Jesu Cristo qui generare facet orbem per coelum et terram.*"

"Blood-drinking Jew!"

A Jew? I forgot my injury at this stunning revelation. No Jews lived in Northumberland, but I'd heard . . . what had I heard? Great wealth, strange practices . . .

Bonel struck Malbysse's chin a sharp blow with his cross. "Jews don't carry weapons, Malbysse. Does my cross make my point?"

Blood gushed from Malbysse's chin. The other knights quickly muttered prayers against this miracle, but from my angle I'd seen a blade snap from the cross.

Malbysse's breath sounded through the hall; his rasp dropped to a whisper. "Your conversion was false!"

The cross slid to Malbysse's throat.

"Apologize."

Bonel's soldiers were now in place, swords ready. After a long tense period, Bishop Hugh stepped from Malbysse and Bonel.

"In the name of our Lord Jesus, *pace*. Malbysse, you witnessed Bonel's conversion; apologize."

"You're a Christian," Malbysse muttered as a thin line of blood trickled from his throat.

Bishop Hugh turned to Bonel. "Make memory cold, Bonel."

Bonel slowly withdrew the cross.

And that was all? What about *me?* I knew naught about Jews or conversion, but I knew about strumpets and Malbysse should apologize to me.

Belatedly, the Bishop remembered. "Now, tell us about this child, Bonel. Who is she?"

"Lady Alix of Wanthwaite."

"Then I'm King of the Jews!" Malbysse scoffed. "Send your filthy baggage to the stable."

"King of ostriches," Hugh rebuked him sharply. "Come close, dear, so I may see you. I knew Baron William of Wanthwaite before the tragedy, and I think I would recognize a daughter."

I looked fearfully at Bonel but he didn't stop me. Hugh knelt down clumsily, for he was ancient as well as fat, and put his hand under my chin.

"With Saint Denis as my witness, this has to be young Alix. The father had the same peculiar silver eyes, like shattered ice. See? And that delicate face, a jonette-pear blossom. You've fallen on hard times, haven't you, dear?"

"Aye, Your Reverend Sir."

"What is a northern lady doing with a jackal like Bonel?" Malbysse asked. "Is he abducting you?"

"Aye!" I cried.

"She's going as hostage for Richard," Bonel countered quickly. "That's hardly abduction."

Cuckney joined Malbysse, incensed. "You're going to send one of our noble women to die for that monster?"

"Die?" My own fears were confirmed.

"You're hirpling to your grave," he told me.

"Traitor!" Bonel accused. "Richard is still king!—She goes with the cream of England!"

"All to their graves. Henry dangles Richard as bait, and the whole English court sails into his net!"

They then exchanged insults with accelerating heat about fleets, Queen Eleanor, Prince John, treasure and I know not what. They couldn't be this exercised simply because of my fate.

"Where's Richard being held?" Malbysse demanded.

"In Speyer."

"Balls. Why don't you admit you don't know? He's probably in Hagenau."

"Which means he's dead," Cuckney concluded.

Malbysse took my arm. "You don't have to go, Lady Alix."

"By law she does."

"In the north, Malbysse is law."

Bonel fingered his cross. "So you believe, but your law is treason."

Malbysse shoved me toward Bishop Hugh. "Lady Alix, we'll return to you later."

I sank onto a large log beside Bishop Hugh; my fantastick cells whirled with the upward draft of sparks. "Hirpling toward your grave," ominous words, but true. Margery's sister Annie had died of exposure to the cold, and that was only one hazard. Even if the hostages for Richard were great lords and bishops, as Bonel claimed, that wouldn't guarantee good treatment. If Emperor Henry put Richard in some remote dungeon where it was assumed he was dead, what would he do to lesser Englishmen?

Or suppose Richard didn't pay the silver within seven months? Aye, that was a hazard of which I had some knowledge. The week before I'd run away from the Crusade, Richard had awaited payment from Saladin to redeem three thousand Saracen hostages. Enoch and I had seen the emirs led to a sandy field to wait, had seen the sun pass its zenith with no sign of Saladin. In midafternoon, Richard had ordered: three thousand unarmed men had been ruthlessly massacred, and soon the sandy plain seemed the Red Sea.

Or if death were not swift . . .

My head jerked. I'd almost fallen asleep. The heat, choking smoke, the wine the bishop had put in my hand, the tension and loss of sleep . . . I blinked, pinched my thigh to wake myself. I must watch Malbysse; he was now my only hope.

"The Jews are the thieves!" he shouted at Bonel.

"What Jews?" Bonel demanded scornfully. "There are no Jews in the north."

"Yes, there are Jews, millions of them. No one you know, but they fly from the Devil's ears thick as bees from a hive. He populates the earth with his minions to prepare for the coming of the Antichrist at the millennium."

"*Commota est et contrummit terra; fundamenta monitum conturbata et commota iratum est!*" Bonel chanted, waving his cross in a series of strange motions.

"Sorcerer! Take back your spell," Malbysse rasped in sudden fear.

Fauconbridge squeezed the hilt of his sword; Cuckney's neck ran with sweat.

Bonel tapped his blue eye. "I see Richard with upraised sword, your bloody heads at his feet."

Using my shoulder to hoist himself, Bishop Hugh again entered the fray. "Malbysse, you bray like a jackass. The year 1200 is a turn of the century but not the millennium; let those in 2000 worry about the Antichrist. Furthermore you take Bonel's simple Latin prediction of the end of the world to be a heathen spell."

Malbysse relaxed warily, but kept his eyes on Bonel.

"Bonel, you're even worse with your pretended incantations," the bishop huffed, "preying on superstition in order to get confessions. Leave such nonsense and stay with the theme."

He glanced over his shoulder. "Lady Alix, dear, why don't you go to the balcony and sleep. The heat rises there."

"Doesn't Malbysse want me near? In case . . ."

Malbysse barked gruffly, "Tomorrow, for God's sake! We'll take care of you, but now . . ."

"No!" Bonel placed his hand on my wrist. "Don't interfere as you value your lives. Her presence has been ordered in high places."

The men turned as a body, much intrigued; I tried to move and was held.

"Who wants her?" Fauconbridge asked.

"For what purpose?" Cuckney added.

I watched Bonel closely.

"Queen Eleanor. She sent me on a special mission to bring her, 'the wildflower of the north.' "

How could that be? I'd never met the queen.

Bishop Hugh nodded sagely. "Naturally, if it's Eleanor. You're fortunate, Lady Alix. Richard's mother is better than that catamite Longchamp who was supposed to accompany the hostages."

"Go on above," Malbysse told me.

Did he also signal with his brows? The light was dim; I couldn't be sure.

Reluctantly I took my drafsack and dragged it up the ladder. Looking down, I saw that Bonel gave quiet orders for two soldiers to guard the bottom, as if I would be luna-tick enough to run in the night. I lay my mat at the edge and peered under the rail. Fire shadows leaped eerily around the dark foreshortened figures, as if they were demons in hell. *Devil-Jew, Jews from the ears of the Devil.* That must explain Bonel's sinister aura. Vague slurs about Jews heard on the Crusade drifted back, and I may have seen a few on the London streets.

I rolled to my back and watched orange and black shad-ows dance on the timbers. Queen Eleanor, wildflower of the north . . . high places. The foreboding I'd felt when I'd held the king's seal in my palm returned. I was no ordinary hos-tage, but had been specially summoned.

By King Richard.

Who else had reason? For that matter, what was Richard's motive? I turned once again to my stomach, still exhausted but too agitated to sleep. Richard must harbor a deep anger, and I knew well that he wouldn't rest until he'd punished his adversary. Yet I'd been the innocent victim, in my opin-ion, guilty only of trust, while he . . .

I turned again, flung my arm over my eyes to shut out

firelight, tried not to hear the loud voices below with the repeated words, *Richard, John, Jews, debts*—Bonel was trying to collect debts and had duplicate records. I flipped to my other side.

Malbysse had promised . . .

My eyes were grainy, my nostrils dry from smoke. The fire was only ash, orange shadows gone, and wolves flung themselves against the walls, howling in hunger. Bonel climbed the rungs and rolled his mat close to mine. His licorice scent replaced the smoke and he lay absolutely still —too still to be asleep. His presence added to my sense of being in an eerie nightmare; Wanthwaite was only a day's ride away and remote as a pale winter moon. I was hirpling to my death in a frozen waste and lying next to a former Jew and present scoundrel.

Yet I slept deeply, too exhausted to worry more.

I WAS WAKENED by angry shouts. Richard was invoked again and again as Bonel threatened the northerners with the king's vengeance, but they weren't as easily cowed as I had been. Bonel lost, and his wrathful face confirmed that he was a son of Satan. We dipped a little bread in sour wine and prepared to depart. I looked desperately at Malbysse, then at Bishop Hugh; both avoided my gaze.

Then the horses were ready. Breath rose in plumes against the morning chill, but no one spoke or called my name. I pretended to lose control of Thistle so I could circle close to Malbysse.

"Goodbye. Thank you for your hospitality."

"Goodbye, Lady Alix." He blinked one eye and I paused. Bonel took my bridle. "Ride next to me, Lady Alix."

Bishop Hugh blethered incoherently about his sweet lord, Richard, the most amiable of queens, Eleanor, the saint of all time, Walter of Coutances, on and on in a confused garble to prove loyalty despite his actions.

The instant we were out of sight, Bonel pressed us to

move faster. We all called "Hoyt" and used our whips as the mules strained under their heavy burdens. The weather was against us for, though the wind had dropped, the cold had increased, causing layers of mist to rise from the ground and hover at eye level. Every step was a hook in my heart, and the wound grew larger as bells in the distance struck hour after hour. I mustn't go to Germany, not after hearing Cuckney confirm that I would die, must get back to Wanthwaite this very day. I fondled the dagger in my drafsack.

As we finished our midday dinner, we heard the beat of hooves in the distance. Bonel signaled silently, and we began to ride again, everyone tense. The pounding grew closer. My breath hurt my lungs.

"Heigh-ho, Bonel, wait!" Malbysse called.

There were three of them; Bishop Hugh was missing.

Malbysse cantered easily to the front of our line and stopped in Bonel's path.

"We had a talk after you left, Bonel, and want to send a message to the king."

"We've changed our minds!" Fauconbridge shouted from the rear.

Bonel turned suspiciously, hand to his hilt.

"We admit we owe the treasury, and we'll pay our debt when Richard rides north," Malbysse took up, "but we want to hear exactly what you know."

"I told you," Bonel said.

"We'd like more details," Cuckney called, then rode through the center of our line, forcing the mules apart.

I had to edge Thistle back to make way.

As he passed, Cuckney muttered, "Into the mist."

Startled, I watched him, not sure of what I'd heard.

"Damn, if you'd only told us about those duplicate records when you summoned us, we would have brought the amount," Malbysse said.

Cuckney raised his hand slightly. Fauconbridge galloped to the opposite side of Bonel, distracting his attention.

Looking beside me, I backed into a heavy bar of fog.

When I emerged on the other side, Malbysse and Fauconbridge engaged Bonel in argument and incidentally stood so
he couldn't see me; Cuckney gestured again.

The next bar was several yards distant. Heart pounding,
I forced myself to back slowly, soundlessly, and disappeared. Gauzed in mist, I considered swiftly what I was
doing. An enormous risk, but worth it.

Cuckney was watching for me when I came out on the
other side. Bonel was still screened from my sight; I could
hear voices but no longer distinguish words. Cuckney nodded.

I dashed headlong into the forest.

PRESSED FLAT to Thistle's neck to avoid low flying branches,
I rushed through brambles, past trees, over rocks and gul-
lies. Torn or whipped, I didn't care! I was free!

Yet I mustn't go in circles.

Panting and sweating, I paused to take stock. Damn the
sun. In winter it sneaked along the horizon like a furtive cat,
and today it hid behind a thick gray lid altogether.

How to tell the direction? Patches of pebbly snow clung
to one side of the trees, one side of the crevices, an arrow
pointing north. I turned Thistle's muzzle and plunged.

In spurts of speed across clearings countered by tortuous
twisting through thorns we galloped toward Wanthwaite. In
the slow spots, I tried to listen. Once I heard my name called
in the distance, and my breath ceased. It didn't repeat—
probably my fantastick cells. If I could just put distance
between us. Bonel had sounded determined about his ren-
dezvous with the queen on 10 December, less than two
weeks distant; he wouldn't waste much time searching for
me.

I came to a wide, fast-moving stream flowing from east to
west and studied its murky center to see if I could ford it
here.

"Alix! Lady Alix, can you hear?"

*Deus juva me*, how had they found me? Because I'd gone due north! Idiot, I berated myself. Quickly I turned to follow the river toward the east and Dere Street.

Like a game animal on the run I fled, my rage spurring me ever faster. Sick of wars, crusades, kings and would-be kings. I flew swift as an arrow.

So weary I was near tears, I finally slipped to the ground. Thistle's nose dipped while I cupped scarlet palms in the freezing liquid to drink.

And was struck by a clod of dirt on the back of my head!

"Stop it!" I screamed.

A huge golden eagle clutched my head and beat his wings in an effort to lift me. My squirrel hat!

"Take it, you wallydrag!" I fended his talons with my elbow and tried to loosen my thongs, but they were in a snarl and I must protect myself. His ferocious saffron eyes were close, his beak closer, and his feathery legs strong. I bent double and made myself a ball. Thistle reared and crashed through the trees.

The eagle left. But not far and not for long. Directly above me he circled upward to pause for his second stoop. And dropped like a stone!

Again we tussled. A sickening crunch and a hard beating on my head. My hat was both lure and protection, for he couldn't get to my skin.

He rose once again, but this time I flung the squirrel hat downriver and watched him snatch it from the current.

"I hope you're not hurt, Lady Alix," Bonel said from behind me.

"I won't go!" I screamed.

From my crouch, I lurched along the bank, falling and scrambling on hands and knees, my heavy hide boots slipping in the crusted mud. A horse followed and passed, then blocked me. It was Bok. I veered into a small copse and battled my way through.

"Thistle!" I yelled.

"Stop her!" Bonel snapped.

Steeds pounded on all sides and I ran under bellies. Once a hoof almost struck me and I saw blood on my sleeve.

I doubled back.

A deadly game with the circle closing. I was struck and struck back just as hard. Held by my hands so I must use my teeth, was beaten about the head.

"You make your own whip, Alix!" Bonel warned. "Stand still before you get hurt!"

By now he was on his feet along with two others. They had Thistle and I knew I couldn't get away but by Holy Saint George they'd wish I had! They wrestled me to the black sod.

"Grip with your claws, tiger!" I spat into Bonel's face. "Beft me! Sturt and strife all you like, but you'll never get me!"

He locked my arms from behind and held me tight.

I raised my heavy boot, slid it like a razor the length of his shinbone and stamped to break all his toes!

"Bitch!" He clutched his foot.

As I hurled forward, my sheepskin was pulled off my shoulders, then my kilt ripped from my waist and I was down to my leggings. So much the better for running. I was tackled and fell with a heavy thud on my face, my breath knocked out.

The hands that held now were not kind.

Straps cut my wrists, someone draped me in skin and tied my skirt in place.

"I'll not go!" I cried. "Take some other patrick to the king!"

"You'll go," Bonel said through his teeth, "and there is no one else."

"Fiend!"

"Look to her ear, Piers. How bad is it?"

They turned me to my side and jerked up my hair. Piers jabbered and Bonel replied. I was on my back again.

"Evil Eye! Cyclops! Spider-face!"

His scar stood forth. "Get me my bag, Bok. I'll use the poppy."

It took four of them to spread my jaws so that Bonel could pour a heavy, sweet syrup down my throat. I tried to spit, but he closed my mouth and held it till I was forced to swallow.

"Augh—ah—you poisoned me!"

"When you're calm, I'll dress your wound," he said hollowly as if he stood inside a clinkenbell.

My lips tingled and my tongue was big as a quince, but I struggled to speak. "May you drown in your own vomit, Devil-Jew!"

And had the satisfaction of seeing him flinch.

# 3

AN YOU HEAR ME, LADY ALIX?"

"Uuhh."

"The eagle ripped your ear and I've given you a drug to stop the pain."

I couldn't answer.

"Your ear is mauled, Lady Alix, and must be sewn."

I tried to touch my ear . . . couldn't find it.

"I'm going to clean the area, Alix. It may sting at first, but the poppy will soon take effect," he said with the same hollow echo.

A feather spread liquid fire along the rim of my ear and only my pride kept me from shrieking. Then gradually the pain turned to a tickle and I began to giggle.

"Dooon't," I choked. "You're making me laugh."

"Hold still."

Eye like a serpent's egg, stench of sweet licorice.

Prick, prick, prick.

Hands so delicate, so kind. I kissed long elegant fingers.

Startled voice. "All finished, Lady Alix. We're going to help you mount, then tie you to your horse . . . Piers will stay close in case you start to fall."

At first I rode in a stupor, but gradually the strange elixir mortified my senses in most peculiar fashion and I was in a different world than the churls around me. I knew they were still there, could hear and see them through a misty curtain, but at the same time the place and the time were transformed into something both remembered and new.

Snow fell aslant like gleaming stars and caressed my face with moist kisses. Then, before my wondering eyes, the flakes changed to glowing, geroldinga apple blossoms; the pewter sky became blinding blue, and the movement of my horse the cradle of love.

Movement was all. Rapturous. Warm. Building to incredible bliss. Only one person could make me feel so . . . I lolled my head back and watched the tangle of bright branches dance by. Sure enough, the skein took shapes, began to grow solid, melt away and reform in tantalizing patterns. Then a face appeared and rode with me.

Enoch.

His glinting head shut out the unbearable dazzle as he leaned over me.

"Let me luik in yer lyart eyes, honey-lips."

I opened them wide, swooning with delight at his square-toothed smile, his beard rough as a houndfish on my cheek.

"Ye havena changed, bairn. Eyes clear pools under shifting clouds."

His own eyes were as blue as ever, as if the sky shone through them, as if his face were a mask held against heaven. I yearned to touch his ruddy cheeks, his bronze elflocks, but a small voice prohibited me: he's real, but masks are not.

"Are you soothly here, Enoch?"

"Dinna be sae wan, youngling. I've cum hame to ye."

"But are you here or at Wanthwaite?"

"Mayhap both, mayhap neider. Close yer swate lips sae I may kiss them."

A warm pressure against my mouth made me moan with joy.

"Quiet, luv."

"I can't help it—I'm so happy."

"Dinna worry about them frekes none. Willy ha nilly, I mun tak my lemman, my luv."

The unbearable ecstasy I recalled so well filled my chest-spoon, all of me, and I turned my head this way and that.

"Are you in pain, Lady Alix?" he asked in French. "Shall we rest for a bit?"

"No! No! Don't stop!"

The movement was sweet agony—then the awaited stab and my body was transformed. I began to dread his withdrawal.

"Don't leave me," I begged. "They'll say terrible things if you go."

"Their wordis be nocht worth a herring. A youngling mun ha'e her fleshly lust."

"But are you soothly here? Am I dreaming?"

"I'll gi'e ye a cockstone to prove I'm wi' ye."

He pressed a gem into my palm and laughed joyously, then fainter and fainter.

I searched for him in the branches, a heavy grid between me and the snowy sky as if I looked up through a dungeon lid.

"Come back!" I screamed.

Arms held me down, and another draught of the sickly syrup was administered.

WONDROUS BIG STARS hissing and pulsating in a tilting sky, trees writhing like black snakes.

"We're going to lift you down, Lady Alix."

They tried; I crumpled helplessly in laughter.

I was draped across a strong chest, fur-smell and licorice, faint cast of brine.

"I love you," I said, putting my arms around Enoch's neck. "Love you so."

Inside a tent, on the soft earth, familiar, Enoch's leather tent. And he was on the mat next to me. I rolled close and cuddled against him.

"Kiss me, Enoch, kiss me, kiss me."

Sweet Scot was already asleep. I rose to my elbow and brushed his cheek with my lips, then slept myself.

WE RODE in a forest so dark that the raindrops seemed black. I held my head back to catch the ebony liquid on my parched, furry tongue; the lower half of my body had turned to stone. I toppled into the tent the instant we stopped. The next day I still had a pounding megrim, but my cod had regained sensation and I was able to eat. That night Bonel said he must change the bandage.

With no aid from the poppy, I fixed my eyes on three drenched sheep clinging to the shaley steeps above me and let him work.

"No infection," he announced with satisfaction, "and I think you'll cure without a scar."

"You can't take credit for sewing a wound you caused in the first place," I said grimly.

He cleaned with his hot feather again. "I don't bite ears, Lady Alix."

"Good thing or I'd be dead. You probably have poison fangs."

He started to walk away, but I held his tunic.

"You abducted me!"

"I forced you to obey a royal order. Abduction has a different purpose."

"Why didn't you tell me I'd been ordered as hostage by some wight high in the court?"

"Everyone was ordered by a committee of lords, bishops and the queen."

"No! I was ordered especially and my friends at Malbysse Manor were not to interfere. I want to know who and why."

"How many times must I tell you that Queen Eleanor . . . ?"

"Until you tell me the truth!" I cried. "I don't know the queen! Why don't you admit that King Richard gave the order? That he wants me to die?"

He jerked himself free. "I deny that he wants you dead."

"But not that he gave the order."

"If he did, he'll regret it!" I'd finally pierced his thick wall and he lapsed into choler. "You're not fit to serve with the other hostages."

"Then release me! I'll get back to Wanthwaite somehow."

He bent close. "Nothing would please me more. You're a vicious, bigoted slut with the morals of a rat. Just like your murderous 'friends.' "

He walked into the wood, leaving me stunned. Not one of those words applied to my character, not one! Unless by "slut" he was referring to my lickerous dream about Enoch.

"It's his fault; he shouldn't haven given me the poppy," I said to the munching sheep.

They gazed calmly from vacuous eyes and then climbed upward into midnight gorse.

WE RODE in hostile silence through drear, dun countryside. Some nights we stayed in hovels marked by their alestakes as inns, but hardly as snug as our tents and certainly not as clean. Three times the mercenaries and I were placed in such hostels and told to wait; Bonel then went to collect more treasure. We were forced to buy another mule.

A week passed before Bonel said he must remove my stitches. The process was more tedious than painful and I sat with my face buried on my knees. Snip, snip, snip, as opposed to the prick, prick, prick before, the same heady scent of licorice, the same long elegant fingers, except that before I'd . . .

"Don't move."

Before I'd turned and kissed . . . was it possible? My heart thundered in my injured ear.

He finished and left without comment as I put hands to my burning face. Giggling, being carried, saying . . . and in the tent . . . *Deus juva me!*

*"Fire in yer bedstraw, Lady Alix."*

I'd rather kiss a dead tunney fish than Bonel! Aye, and probably would, too, if one were in the tent. What must he think?

*Slut. You're a slut.* Not because of my dream, but because of my acts. But he must know it was the poppy speaking, not I. Hadn't I made it clear how much I despised him?

As we rode through the milky mist, I tried to clear my addled head. Slut. Very well, he had some reason to call me that, albeit unfairly, but he shouldn't have said "vicious" or "bigoted." I'm never vicious, have been told all my life what a kind, generous bairn I am. How could I be vicious just because I'd said he abducted me when he had? Should I ask him? Not that I wanted the approval of this lizard, but I deserved fair judgment.

The fog was so thick that I couldn't see him across the fire that night which was good for neither could he see me.

"My ear feels fine, Bonel," I mumbled.

He was frying bread and seemed not to hear.

"I'm glad you didn't have to use the drug this afternoon. It"—my voice went thin—"it makes me toty."

He flipped the bread.

"Did you hear me?"

"I know its effect," he said dryly.

I breathed easier.

"Do you think it sometimes makes a person vicious as well?"

"No, it can't create character, just releases what's already there."

He took his bread off and started away. Suddenly I could see him, his scar glowing white pearl, and was jarred with a second memory . . .

"It's odd, Bonel," I said hurriedly, "that I hardly notice your eye or scar anymore. I think they're fading. I mean your scar."

He stopped very still.

"In the wood—by the river—I called you names I didn't mean. I was angry and . . . I'm sorry."

He didn't move, seemed deep in thought, then raised his head and spoke with slow venom. "Possibly you weren't responsible for your acts when drugged, but you meant every word in the wood, and your hypocrisy adds to the offense. My scar appalls you, my Christian eye is an abomination, my former religion Devil-worship."

He disappeared in the mist and once again I was left to absorb his insults, which were much graver this time because they were considered. They were also unjust. I had become accustomed to his scar and eye; I had no opinion whatsoever about the Jewish religion.

But so be it. I still resented his abducting me and lying about the king; he still judged me vicious and bigoted.

It was not a good plit for a journey.

WE WERE ALL FRIGHTENED. Riding south on Dere Street was a descent into a sulfurous pit. The white bars of the north closed to a solid impenetrable mist, and we had difficulty staying on the pavement. Our horses frequently stepped into pits where the stones had washed away, or stumbled over fallen trees.

Yet we were not alone.

In the distance we could hear the thunderous thump of stones cast from the mangonel, occasionally the clash of steel and men's voices. We were riding through country held by

John and challenged by Richard. Over and over we pulled off the road to permit horsemen the way, never sure whether they were friend or foe. Even I looked forward to the safety of London's walls.

Nights were the worst. The renegade army around us apparently didn't follow the rule of no fighting after sunset, and they rode like ghosts howling and pounding in the wind. We were afraid to build fires and huddled in a pile for warmth.

We tried to sleep in towns. The loom of a gate, the call of a guard meant security for a few hours.

Our last night was particularly treacherous. The mist had become thicker than ever, cutting off visibility and distorting sound. Even though we tried to ride close, we kept losing one another and circling to connect again. Finally Bonel suggested we divide into pairs and tie ourselves together so that not one person got lost, for that was the greatest danger. He tied my arm to his.

He wouldn't let me lead, but I should have because of his poor vision. His Christian Eye might see evil in men's hearts, but it couldn't see the road ahead of us. Never had I strained harder to peer through a fog.

"I think we're close, Bonel. A town wall—someone's on top with a torch."

"Where?"

"Straight on."

The flare bobbed in and out of sight, casting shadows along the road.

"Who goes there?" a distant voice called.

"Bonel, man to King Richard!"

"Proceed with caution! There's a . . ."

But he was too late. Directly in front of Bonel, the light reflected on a thin, wrinkled tissue like scum on milk. Ice!

*Benedicite,* I was tied to this blind wallydrag! And he was going to drown me!

"Bonel, stop!"

"What?"

He turned and tried to see me, but his horse kept moving.

There was no more time for talk—let him drown if he list, he wasn't going to take me with him. I roiled Thistle to rear and deliberately crashed down on Bonel's stallion, knocking the horse to its side. I then tried to turn Thistle and succeeded—but Bonel's fall jerked the rope and I lost my seat.

And plummeted into deep icy water!

I was stopped by the rope on my arm and dangled in liquid black, my feet skirting pulpy objects on the bottom. *Deus juva me* that Bonel not tumble after me or I was surely lost. Instantly I swallowed putrid water, began to choke, swallowed more, lost my sheepskin, struggled for the surface. My arm tore from its socket as someone pulled from above, and finally I gasped air, went under for another load of liquid to my lungs and was thrashing against a slippery edge.

"Go limp, Alix! Let us do it!"

I fought harder than ever.

Was scraped along a rough stony surface, felt my feet catch on the rim of the pool.

"Put her on her stomach."

Someone sat on my back and began to pound. I retched up gallons of slime, couldn't breathe.

"Harder. Bok, kneel down."

I was draped over the mercenary's rear, head falling upside down to the ground.

"Harrow! Alas! Here lies a dead fellow!" shouted a stranger.

"She's not a fellow, and she's not dead," Bonel grunted as he pounded my back.

"She be the fourth to drown in the stank," the voice insisted with ghoulish glee. "I voted to punish the miller, but the others . . ."

"Where's the nearest shelter?" Bonel snapped.

"Boose and Gerland have a cot just inside the wall, but they . . ."

"Take her to the inn," said another.

"Or to the church so she can confess afore she dies," added still someone else.

"Lead us to the cot," Bonel ordered. "Alix, can you hear me?"

"E—noch!!" I sobbed.

I was rolled onto a blanket.

"Cold," I said, teeth chattering.

Then a fur fell atop me.

"You're all right, going to be all right. Nothing's broken, but you need care."

There was more plather. I was lifted, drifted into a stupor. A torch flickered above and we'd reached the door of a narrow cot. A woman haggled ferociously.

"Aye, I want to do my Christian duty, but first we mun douse her. That stank were used fer a shit-pit afore it filled with water."

*Benedicite*, no wonder I hated to breathe: my own stench mortified my nose.

"We'll bathe her inside where it's warm," Bonel insisted. "You'll be handsomely paid."

"Naturlich ye'll come into our home," a man whinnied. "Gerland, shove Malkyn and Talbot to one side and make room."

"Aye, My Lord," the dame simpered to Bonel. "'Tis a mean hut and we mun keep our cow and sow within agin robbers, but ye're welcome to enter."

Without further palaver, my improvised bed was squeezed through the jambs into a sooty bower that reeked of smoke, singed bacon and animals—the pig being uppermost—which would have offended except that I carried a stench to rival a filmart's spray.

The instant I hit the floor, I retched into the rushes for I'd swallowed half the foul stank I trowe.

"Poor lass," the hostess lamented without touching my mess. "She do stink most pungent. Be she yer wife?"

"No. Get me water at once; I have to clean her."

Bonel knelt beside me and fumbled with the laces on my bliaut, made me sit so he could pull it off my head, and again I puked most shamefully all over myself. Then came my kilt and my boots, my leggings, my chemise, and I was naked as the day I was born. As Bonel worked, Boose and Gerland argued as to who should fetch the water, but Bok was there with a pail before they finished.

Bonel dumped the cold water over me without ceremony and sent for more. The process was repeated three times so that I lay once again in a puddle of icy liquid, but I didn't care: I was fighting a great flood which threatened to drown me from within. Bonel took advantage of my lethargy most grievously, flipped me til and fro, slapped me in the face.

"Her legs and toes be blue as the sky," Gerland remarked with awe.

"Is the kettle hot?" Bonel asked. "Alix, this may seem to burn your skin—your temperature has fallen—but it's only tepid."

Again liquid was poured over me, and this time I screeched protest. They were boiling me alive! Then I was lifted—by Bonel and Boose?—and placed in a tub where strong ash soap was added, most of it to my weeping eyes. After that I lost track of the times I was dunked and dried, dunked again, scrubbed as if to remove my skin, poked in ears and mouth, pulled by the hair and I know not what. I wasn't always sure who applied the torture, but our host and hostess were fighting too hotly to do much. It took at least three rinsings for me to realize that they were blaming me for falling into the pit and that Bonel was defending me.

"Your town should be fined for criminal negligence," he said grimly. "This isn't Germany."

"Nay, it be St. Albans," Boose agreed. "But folks here-abouts manage to avoid the pit."

"Except for the glovemaker from Minster Lovell," Gerland reminded him. "There be some as say that Pert the Miller dug the hole a-purpose to trap the glove-maker."

"He dug it, dame, to get ramming clay to fix his wall. Why would he kill the glovemaker?"

"No one e'er found the pannier of gloves the varlet car-ried, did they? Though many fished fer days. In my opin-ion, Pert would murther fer a thimble, let alone a pannier of gloves."

"He still murders innocent travelers!" Bonel cried, in-censed. "He should be hung by the neckbone along with with every citizen who permits the deadly hole!"

Boose waxed choleric as well. "It were fine until cumen the winter rains. Yif ye pushed the piss and dong cart as I do, ye'd be grateful to have yer dong-land close by."

"The stranger be right," Gerland said. "Mayhap the glove-maker were murthered, but not the six swine and two sheep that lie on the bottom. That were a real loss. Ye voted wrong on the council."

Boose shouted like a fiend in Hell. "Aye, that's a woman's opinion! 'Twas yer advice that brung us our first woe and . . ."

I fell into another stupor, only this was filled with melan-choly dreams of nightearth, black bulls and bears.

When I woke I was under a heavy fur and Bonel was shaking my shoulder. He forced me to sit upright.

"You've swallowed polluted water, Alix. I have to purge you."

"Open you mouth and drink," Gerland ordered. "Laxa-tyfs mun be swilled in swich cases."

I pushed the cup away feebly.

"Drink, or you may die of tertian fever."

"Noooo bobby."

"It isn't the poppy."

"Nay, love, 'tis a mix of laurel, fumetore and hellebore, guaranteed to drain ye above and beneath," crooned the dame.

I drank, vomited instantly into a bucket that was held forth, was told where the pot was when I was ready to use it, and fell back onto my furs already asleep.

I was up frequently throughout the long night. Bonel slept upright against the door and as far away from the sow as possible; he may have witnessed my shitting into the pot, which looked to be a cooking vessel, but I didn't care. Never had I been so filled with woe and waste.

So far my attempts to save myself had led only to disaster. A mighty self-pity waxed in my chestspoon as I considered my sufferings, especially my fall into the stank. How vexing that I'd actually saved my captor instead of myself. There he sat, smug and perfumed, while I writhed in a puddle of half-digested animal rot.

It wasn't fair. While my enemy thrived, Fortune's Wheel rolled back and forth to be sure I was properly crushed. Furthermore, he wasn't even grateful. After all, he didn't know but what I'd tried to save his life.

*Save his life* . . . an idea wiggled like a torpid worm in my fantastick cells. Grew livelier. Why not? Nothing ventured, nothing gained, as Dame Margery oft said. Tomorrow I would try.

IN THE MORNING I faced a second disaster. The hostess had washed my clothes to rid them of the foul infection and they'd shrunk so I could hardly get them on. She had to split my bliaut at the back so I could breathe; worse, my kilt had a large scorched hole from the fire so that I must wear it sideways for modesty. My boots, which had been emptied but not cleaned, smelled like dead rats. The eagle had long since taken my hat, my sheepskin lay at the bottom of the stank. I would probably freeze by nightfall.

Bonel was doing business in the town. When he returned, I awaited a derisive comment but was surprised. He carried a fine hooded cloak of gris fur which fitted me perfectly and covered my rags.

"Thank you," I mumbled.

His face looked different somehow, though I was too groggy to define the change. Younger?

"How do you feel?"

"Hungry."

"A good sign, but let me be sure."

Before I could avoid him, he lay his cheek on mine. "No fever, thank God. You'll be all right now."

Yet he permitted me only a crust before we rode, saying my cod might be tender from the elixir. Indeed the medicine had a strong effect which, combined with the shock of my plunge, put me in a malaise. Good English air seemed redolent of decay and the balls of my feet carried the imprint of dead swine; I constantly brushed my face against gossamer webs. Even Bonel's announcement that we would reach London by afternoon didn't penetrate; my fantastick cells floated in gray ether.

Drifting in my own haze, much as if I'd drunk the poppy, I nevertheless was aware that Bonel watched me intently. I pretended not to notice, but straightened my furs across my meager bliaut, cleared my throat nervously. What was wrong? Then it struck me. *Benedicite*, Bonel had seen me naked! Had washed me with his own hands which I could still feel as vividly as if a snake had slithered my length. My cheeks heated. Had I said anything untoward? I tortured my wizened brain trying to remember, but nothing came, a fact which didn't reassure me. Why else would Bonel take this dour interest in my person?

The weather cleared at midday. We sat on a wall warmed by winter sun to eat our dinner. The mercenaries gulped a poisonous stew made nearly a week ago, for they'd not been able to hunt, but Bonel offered to share his staple diet, jarred

Rouen fish. So bitter with salt that every bite had to be washed down with Burgundy red, it nonetheless tasted fresh, and my head began to clear.

Bonel continued to watch me. "We'll soon say goodbye, Lady Alix."

"Aye." *Deo volente.* But not in the manner he intended.

I reached for another fish. He touched my hand; I jerked it away, startled.

"I'm sorry. Aren't there enough?"

"Take them all," he said.

*Benedicite*, there were four fat herring swimming in brine. I lifted one delicately, let it drip.

"Our last chance to talk."

The bones were soft enough to swallow.

"This has been a perilous trip for you."

Wiping my mouth on my sleeve, I admitted honestly, "The worst weeks of my life."

"Yes." He continued to study my face as if he'd never seen me before.

I had no place to hide, but I lowered my eyes, was tempted to take another fish but was afraid I would choke from mortification. What could I have blathered while in my shocked state? I must find out before I made my plea.

"You could have escaped yesterday."

"How?" I asked, jarred out of my preoccupation.

"By letting me fall into the stank. You couldn't have been blamed; it would have been an accident."

He was right. How could I have been so daft? I tried to keep my face ordered, for it was a dreadful thought, yet it led beautifully to my plan.

"Oh no, Bonel, you misread my character. I wanted only to save *you*. Don't you recall?"

He spoke slowly. "You mean that you let yourself fall in order to save me?"

"Didn't *let* myself," I protested. "I jumped with all my force. All I could think was that you were about to die. Oh, it was terrible." I shivered prettily.

He sat absolutely still, as if stunned, then repeated. "You saved my life?"

"Aye, though anyone would have done the same."

"True," he conceded, "by calling out a warning, but you risked your own life."

"Well . . ." I hesitated, not wanting to miss this opportunity, "perhaps I did since I can't swim." At least not with heavy boots and a sheepskin. "Anyway, to not move would have been a greater risk. And you would do the same for me if . . ."

Before I could make my point, he interrupted.

"It's not as if you cared for a 'Devil-Jew.' "

"I already apologized for calling you that," I reminded him tartly.

"But I didn't believe you," he answered quietly. "Tell me, had you ever met Malbysse before?"

For a moment I didn't know whom he meant.

"How would I meet him? He's never come to Wanthwaite."

His brown eye had emerged from its lair and made me hot, uncomfortable.

"Soothly, Bonel," I repeated, "I'm sorry I called you Devil-Jew. I knew it would rile you, but I know nothing of Jews." I considered; that was still vaguely insulting. "I mean —I'm sure there are nice Jews. You must have been one, and your father . . ."

"What do you know about him?" His voice was a whip-crack.

Now what had I said that was wrong? "Nothing. How would I know anything? I just . . ."

"Because he was a famous man," he replied tersely. "Or infamous, depending upon your beliefs."

"What was his name?"

"Benedict of York. Along with Joce of York, two of the richest, most powerful Jews in the nation."

My curiosity was titillated, though I wavered, knowing we were drifting from my point. "What happened to him?"

Bonel stared at the outline of London on the distant horizon.

"He was murdered at King Richard's coronation."

It was a doubly shocking statement because Bonel worshipped Richard. "How could that be? Surely the king . . ."

"Didn't know. Though he'd forbidden Jews to attend. Joce and my father simply didn't believe the edict and took rich gifts to the door of the palace. There they were attacked by knights who *did* take the edict seriously; Joce escaped with his life, my father didn't."

The note of finality in his voice prohibited further questions, but it was my turn to stare at him. Bonel rode wrath like a wild horse to be curbed, but his brooding face now revealed a deep melancholy under the rage. But why? The loss of his father? I'd lost mine, too. No, it was something more: a mystery lurked behind his every utterance.

"Are you married, Bonel?" I blurted.

He seemed less appalled by the question than I was—it wasn't what I'd intended to say at all: I wanted to know why he idolized King Richard if his father had perished at the coronation.

"I was going to marry, but she died."

"I'm very sorry," I said hastily, hating my unruly tongue for throwing him into a deeper despair. He sat in a trance, sans movement or speech. This time I waited respectfully.

Finally he turned back to me. "I want to know more about you, Lady Alix. You've been alone for three years?"

"Aye." I let out a relieved breath. Better to talk about me where memories could be carefully selected than to open the abyss behind his face.

"Who managed your estate during that time?"

"I did. Dugan and the Scots helped, but I made the decisions."

But you were—are—very young."

"Not in experience, Bonel. I was an only child and my father brought me up more as a boy than a girl. And I'd been on the Crusade. Then Enoch . . ."

"Where's your father now?"

I caught my breath. "Like yours, he was murdered."

"Hardly like mine," he said with heavy irony, "but go on, tell me."

Well, I'd asked the same of him, hadn't I? Now I must answer. I gazed across the long, hazy valley before us and began my sad recital. It had been a glorious spring day in May when my little friend Maisry and I had sneaked away from Wanthwaite against my father's orders to see a fair in Dunsmere. During that day, Wanthwaite had been sacked, the bailey swaled, my friends and household piled in the courtyard, my mother . . .

"At least my father still lived, though he was bleeding to death where he lay sprawled in our moat. He told me that we'd been attacked by our overlord Northumberland and . . ."

"Bishop Hugh?" Bonel interrupted incredulously.

"No, the earl before him, called Osbert."

"But why?"

"He wanted to marry me for our lands."

My father had instructed me to dress as an ordinary boy and make my way to London to see King Henry, the only lord great enough to overrule Northumberland.

"But Henry was in Normandy and . . ."

"Richard became king. I begin to see the pattern."

"Aye, and took me on the Crusade, thinking I was a boy." I waited with dread to be asked why I remained in disguise, what had happened later, which I would never tell, but Bonel simply studied me as he had since early morning.

Then he moved closer and took my hands in his. I grew rigid as an oak, but that was all he did.

"Lady Alix, I've misjudged you. You look so young and . . . Please forgive me."

"Of course." I tugged gently on my hands; his grip tightened till his rings cut into me.

"We had a bad beginning, but that changed last night. You saved my life, which creates a special bond between us that, as any knight could tell you, can never be broken. Henceforth I'm your friend."

For the first time since I'd known him, he smiled, a remarkable transformation, revealing a sweet, sensitive young man behind his many masks.

"As your friend, I'll protect you, be loyal at all times."

At last he'd given me an opening to present my scheme. "The bond of saving lives goes two ways, Bonel, as any knight could also tell you. I risked myself to keep you from drowning; it's your turn now."

"Go on."

"Send me back to Wanthwaite."

He released my hands.

"I can't."

"Why not?" I cried with passion. "Would you sentence me to die in the Holy Roman Empire after we've become friends? After I saved you? You owe it to me!"

"I admit my debt, but I owe still greater ones."

"What's more important than a life?"

He licked his lip. "Many lives . . . and the dead."

"Then you lied!" I was close to frustrated tears and wished he were floating with the swine in that murk. "You won't protect me or you'd let me go! Otherwise, I'll join the dead."

"Alix, I promised and I meant it. Listen to me: I've given you my oath to protect you; I've given another oath to fulfill my duty to the royal house. I can assure you on my very life, however, that there's no contradiction between oaths. You will be safe on this journey."

"How do you know? I demanded.

"Say I had a revelation. You're much more than a pretty face; you have a natural superior . . . that is, I see why Richard . . ."

He never groped for words like this.

"Why Richard what?"

"Why Richard must be king and not John."

Which didn't follow at all from my "natural superiority." Now thoroughly alert, I tried to cut through his maze of evasions.

"What are you trying to tell me, Bonel?" I asked directly. "Do you have special orders from the king that you've kept from me? Did you make an oath to him personally?"

"No one has seen the king for months."

"Before, then, since you know him so well. He must have said something."

"I've never met the king."

"What? I don't believe you! With your high position . . ."

"He was on his Crusade before I joined the Exchequer. Few people know him unless they reside on the continent."

"But you live in Rouen."

"Now. I haven't always."

"But . . ." I stopped at the expression on his face, again clouded, sad. Still, I was shaken by his disclosure, astounded even. All of his positive assurances turned ephemeral, based as they must be on Richard's reputation rather than his character.

"If you don't even know the king—haven't even met him —you can't possibly predict his actions. I could tell *you* . . ."

"I don't agree. I know his policies, am well acquainted with his closest advisers. I repeat, Alix, you will be perfectly safe."

And I wished I *had* let him drown in the stank. He wasn't saying anything new—albeit he said it with softer cadence —and I wasn't likely to get such an opportunity again. Not that I wanted him dead, but he would probably have been rescued as I had been and with the excitement, the fog, I could have escaped. For all his pretty words, I was still a prisoner.

I ate the last herring, wiped oil from my chin. We mounted our steeds for our final spurt and by Nones could see scarlet Plantagenet banners fluttering on London's walls. Suddenly I was terrified. All the angers and arguments of the past two weeks had been dandlepuffs compared to the reality of those banners; the formidable power of the absent king was manifest in every approaching sign, the sound of city bells, trumpets, men shouting, even the mill wheel whirling over the bourn.

"Will I never see you again?" I asked Bonel, for his proffered friendship suddenly loomed as my last hope; it was more than I could expect from Queen Eleanor, King Richard, or Emperor Henry.

"I'm accompanying the treasure to Germany. I promise I'll watch out for you." Again the open, reassuring smile.

And we wound down to Aldgate to show the king's seal. Once I'd entered these gates to seek the king with the innocent optimism of a child; now the king sought me with the cynical pessimism of a great warrior accustomed to discarding *enfants perdus* like so many fish bones.

# 4

ONDON WAS A MILITARY CAMP.

This was Richard's capital and reminders of his presence were everywhere. The Plantagenet red and gold floated from spires, hung from rooftops, and most of the knights wore the Crusader's red cross. From left and right came the snarl of fanfares as great lords of the kingdom rode to Westminster. Templars led parades of chanting monk-knights toward the tolling bells of St. Paul's.

In the midst of this Plantagenet panoply, rooting pigs, snapping curs, kine and chickens combined with horses to turn the streets to piss-stained muck, while less fortunate beasts hanging from butchers' hooks dripped slow puddles of blood. Hawkers sold everything from roots to stacked wools; freaks and rogues conned the unwary; jug-bitten harlots and their customers staggered blithely til and fro, dropping their own flotsam into the general stench. Small squares served as open gaols where some scurvy drunkalewe prisoners snored on cucking stools while others shouted curses from stocks and pillories; at one corner, two men hanged with bloated black tongues, their eyes long since taken by daws.

Bonel ordered the mercenaries to close ranks and ride with swords outstretched to guard our cargo. One rabid dog threatened and was swiftly dispatched, but otherwise everyone gave way, awed by Bonel's magnificent robes and fierce routiers. We rode directly to the Thames, which flowed sluggishly as pale yellow cheese under the winter sun. At port in Queenshithe, Bonel pointed out Queen Eleanor's barge carved in the new grotesque Gothic manner. All too quickly we reached Westminster Palace, actually two palaces joined by a narrow passageway.

Prelates, knights and guards surrounded our train and fought to make space for our treasure in the crowded courtyard. Among the most interested were a company of foreign soldiers with tall pointed helmets, representatives of Emperor Henry sent to count the ransom.

For the first time, I grasped the scope of the operation. I was a midge on the body politic, could expect to be slapped away if I became too demanding. Yet even a midge has a right to live; I must try.

"Come, Alix, the groom will care for Thistle." Bonel offered his hand to help me down. "I'll take you to the queen."

I slid to the ground and went with him into the palace. Low ceilings intensified the contentions within to an echoing roar and Bonel fought his way with his elbows through the press of bodies, up steps, down corridors, more steps, more corridors in a maze of small chambers. When we'd reached the end, he pushed me flat against a wall.

"Wait here. I'll see the queen first."

I pressed tight, closed my eyes and listened to the jumble of languages linked by the litany of *Richard, Richard, Richard.* Time stretched interminably; then Bonel was back.

"You can wait inside the queen's chamber, Alix, where you'll be more comfortable. She's eager to greet you but has several people to hear first."

"Are you going to wait with me?"

"No, I can't."

He pulled me through crowds of anxious jabbering men, past a guard, into a small anteroom, with another guard and a door.

"Farewell, I'll be watching for you." He touched my shoulder, smiled to reassure me, then smiled in earnest as he had on the wall outside London, sweetly and openly. "Queen Eleanor protects her favorites."

"Favorites?"

But he was gone; I was inside the queen's chamber, alone among strangers. An usher led me to the back of the room where I sat on a bench against the wall.

At least this crowd was quiet. Each person strained to follow the proceedings at the dais where the queen was dispensing decisions, in her son's name, critical to the kingdom. I couldn't see her at first, but her clear carillon voice carried to the farthest reaches of the chamber, youthful and confident.

"No, Guillaume, we can't trust the truce beyond the Nativity. Take your own men to the beaches and ask the burghers and farmers to help."

Next: "The danger is in Normandy, not with Ademar in the south. The king wants Aquitanian lords to meet him in Rouen."

Then: "The king thanks you. Where should I sign?"

And sharply: "Tell him to desist. Prince John is in the king's purview; he will do the king's bidding when he's free of evil influence."

One by one, prelates and lords moved forward to present their cases, then left the room. As the crowd thinned, I caught glimpses of the queen. Dressed in Plantagenet scarlet —even her wimple was scarlet, though bound by an intricate round of gold—her sleeveless surcoat was embroidered with gold thread and studded with flashing jewels. A few more dismissals and I could see her face, from this distance a perfect chisel of arched brows, high round cheekbones, firm chin. I'd never before appreciated that bones could be beautiful, but the balance and proportion of Eleanor's face transcended age.

As the business continued, I formed a quick estimation of her character. Her intelligence and talents were formidable; she had vast ranging knowledge of governance and could make fast decisions; she knew everyone of importance in all of Europe; although her manner was feminine and charming, she thought like a man, had the same interests as a man. Perhaps because of her age, she was unsexed; she would not be swayed by my dimples or blandishments, which might succeed with a man, nor would she identify with me as another woman. I doubt if she'd ever invoked her own sex for special treatment. My only possible strategy must be played on the board of wits; a bleak prospect, for the queen was acute.

"Lady Alix of Wanthwaite, are you there?"

Startled, I realized that I was the last person in the room. My plan was still unformed, but I would have to improvise as best I could.

"Aye, Your Majesty."

I walked to her dais and bowed to the floor.

"You may stand."

I looked into the face of a glowing, vigorous woman with dark brows, fringed blue-green eyes, rosy taut skin, lips pursed in speculation. Behind her sat her ladies-in-waiting, probably her contemporaries, though they appeared a decade older.

"Welcome to our court," she said most cordially. "You've had a difficult journey, Bonel reports."

"Storms made the way hazardous, Your Majesty," I re-

plied cautiously, not knowing if Bonel referred to my attempted escape as difficult.

"To be expected on this putrid isle in the sea. However,
he also reported that you saved his life most heroically."

"Anyone would have done the same."

"Modest as well," she approved. "Now, Lady Alix, my
clerk Fitzroy would like to write certain vital information for
our records, if you don't mind answering my questions."

"Of course, Your Majesty."

"You have no children?"

"No, Your Majesty."

"Why not?"

A small flame shot in my cod: it was none of her affair,
queen or no.

"My husband and I were together only three months before he was called to war and God chose not to give us a
bairn."

"Was God the only instrument?"

How dare she ask such a question? And to what purpose?

"Answer me, please."

"I was not quite thirteen and Enoch had lost two sisters
in childbirth because they'd conceived too young," I muttered angrily.

"In short, he spilled elsewhere."

I looked away.

"Don't be embarrassed, Lady Alix. You will no doubt be
a mother in a more suitable season, and at least your husband was faithful. Now I need to know your bloodlines."

Still simmering, I didn't hear.

"Your ancestors."

Bewildered by the illogical shift, I thought of the Bible.
"Eve was my mother . . ."

"No, your family."

"My father was Baron of Wanthwaite," I said hesitantly.
"My grandfather as well."

"Go on."

"Are bloodlines writ somewhere, Your Majesty?"

"Probably not, but your father must have told you unless you come from thieves. Think of tales he repeated when you were a child; that's how I first learned."

"My mother told me many stories about her family in the west country."

"We're interested only in male seed, not female earth. Were there no great deeds? No heroes?"

"Aye," I answered with more confidence. "My grandfather fought with King Henry in the wars of 1154, and my own father helped take the King of Scotland at Alnwick, July thirteenth, 1174. King Henry sent a commendation because it happened the very day he shrived himself for the murder of Saint Thomas à Becket."

"A murder he didn't commit," she said sharply.

Why was she defending her husband? After all, he'd put her in prison. *Benedicite.*

"Can you go back a little further? It's important."

"We descend from the Vikings," I began. "My father came directly from the Viking Rognvald, but Malbridge the Bucktooth is our greatest hero."

"Malbridge the Bucktooth?" she repeated doubtfully.

"A great hero in the north," her clerk confirmed.

"Go on."

"Malbridge the Bucktooth, so called because this tooth"—I pointed to my own—"stuck straight forward like a fang, fought a series of battles with Sigurd the Dane." I grew excited, hearing my father's voice recount the vivid tale. "Bucktooth fought fiercely, but lost. Sigurd scooped up Bucktooth's head and hung it as a trophy on the curve of his saddle bow. As he rode back to his camp in victory, the slain head bounced up and down against his thigh. Some say Bucktooth still lived, for his bucktooth penetrated Sigurd's skin and the Dane died of blood poisoning."

The ladies behind us laughed and applauded. The queen turned her turbid green eyes on me.

"Most original, if true." Then, with irritation, "This light is too dim. Come to the window that I may see you."

She walked around a table where her clerk was transcribing our session and took my arm. She was tall and straight as a man, her breasts pointed as pinecones, and her robes were scented with attar of roses. At the foliated window she turned me so the last rays of the sun played on my face while she stood in shadow, yet I could see her as well and amended my first impression. Her skin owed its pink radiance to paint, a cunning gloss betrayed by a faint fuzz on her skin; her eyes penetrated to my thought, as Bonel claimed his Christian Eye could do, but masked her own feelings in a dense green opacity, like moss under water; muscles around her mouth, trained by a lifetime of courtesy, held her petal lips in a perpetual smile. Like King Richard, she wore a mask; unlike him, however, she couldn't entirely conceal the anguish of her son's imprisonment which lay behind her bland public expression. She was distraught beyond measure, fevered, angry, determined. In that respect, she reminded me of Bonel.

"Wildflower of the north, precisely. Do you know how delectable you are, young Alix?"

"I hope I have good character, Your Majesty," I answered carefully. So Bonel had been telling the truth when he quoted this phrase. But where had she heard it? She hadn't seen me before, indeed implied by "precisely" that she was confirming a report.

"I hope so too. Are you as delicate as you appear?"

"I'm very strong." I hesitated, then made my first move to discover the source of the description. "Is that what you meant by calling me a wildflower? Our northern weeds have to be strong to flourish in rock and ice."

"Yes." Her eyes caught the thrust, feinted. "That and the exquisite beauty of the bloom."

"Thank you, Your Majesty." The gambit had failed, foiled by a pretty turn.

"Please take off your furs."

I untied Bonel's gift to me.

"Lord help us, what are you wearing?" the queen exclaimed. "Lady Mamile, come see this savage garb, worse than a Russian's."

The old ladies converged around us and commented rudely about my blouse which crushed my breasts, my burnt skirt, my boots still reeking of dead rats.

"She appears to be the same size as Lady Castellux," the one called Lady Mamile judged. "I'll look in her trunk and find appropriate robes."

"Make haste then. She can't go on like this." Queen Eleanor continued to stare. "Turn around slowly."

I did so, felt a quick touch to my hips.

"Am I to carry an excessive weight, Your Majesty?" I asked with elaborate innocence.

"No, of course not. Why do you ask?"

"You examine me for soundness as if I were a horse. Would you like to count my teeth?"

Her eyes were filmed ice. "The wildflower grows thorns."

"Nature's protection against being picked."

"You surprise me. Flowers rarely develop such wit."

"My wit is too thin to understand why my name was put on the roster, Your Majesty. Despite my thorns, I was picked. But why? I'm poor compared to most lords, am the only surviving member of my family and a vulnerable woman." My voice trembled at my own audacity, but what worse fate could befall me than going as hostage?

" 'I'm so-and-so, I'm such-and-such, please release me from this service,' " she paraphrased angrily. "I've heard these words a hundred times, but there is no release. Are you so afraid? There's no danger."

I took a deep breath. "Aye. I'm afraid, Your Majesty, not of being a hostage, but that someone doesn't want me to exist." I dared not add that "someone" was King Richard, but she would know.

She stopped performing, showed true outrage. "Are you accusing me?"

"No, Your Majesty, I'm asking your help! I mean no harm to the Crown, indeed want the king's release with all my heart, but I sense that something's amiss. Either my name was put on the roster by accident, or someone schemed for his own reasons to summon me in this manner."

"You cultivate Byzantine complexity, Lady Alix."

"I cultivate spontaneity," I said truthfully.

"Cultivated spontaneity is a contradiction in terms." Then she flicked a lock of my hair and smiled as if we shared a secret. "However, your thin wit has discovered us. Your name was listed as Lord Alex of Wanthwaite on the Chinon Pipe Roll, and we summoned you as the greatest heir in your region aside from Northumberland. When we were informed that you were an heiress, there seemed no reason to change the roster. To that extent, your case was special."

Outwitted. She waited now for me to explain the error, as if she didn't know. What was her game?

"My disguise was not Byzantine, Your Majesty. That, too, was a spontaneous error on my part."

"Your spontaneity apparently doesn't include telling the truth."

"I don't tell the truth without good reason," I admitted artlessly, then smiled as well. "Do you?"

Her lips smiled back, not her eyes. "Truth is its own good reason. You should learn that."

*I'll not learn it from you,* I thought angrily.

"What charming dimples. Once you're properly dressed, you'll have no peer." She took my arm again and walked me back to the clerk's desk, then sat on her dais. "One final question you must answer that supersedes all others. Do you love King Richard?"

Her clear voice thickened on his name and her eyes bored into mine.

"I love my lord king," I answered solemnly, "and pray for his safe return to our land."

"Good." Her eyes held. "Very good. Fitzroy, close the book; we know all that's necessary. I like you Lady Alix. You're indiscreet, rude and unpolitic, but you have passion —an essential and unteachable quality. Welcome to our great enterprise. With God's help, we shall prevail."

I bowed, defeated.

"You will travel with my household as handmaiden to Lady Mamile who will look after you in return for a few services. We'll talk again."

Her scarlet robes slithered silkily past my lowered face and I could have bitten them in my frustration. It's hard to outwit a python when you're in its coils.

When I rose, I was surrounded by her ladies.

The prettiest of them spoke. "I'm Lady Mamile and hope we'll be friends. It's a pleasure to have a young woman in our midst."

Her still-dark hair curled from under her wimple, her eyes were wide-spaced and a startling violet in color, her smile sweet, her teeth complete and even, albeit somewhat yellow. She went on to say that she was crippled with severe arthritis which advanced each day so that she faced paralysis in the near future. Her hands were useless, her hip in constant pain, her neck "frozen" in one position. All this was presented as an embarrassing vexation, in the same order as bad breath, for which she apologized.

The other women were Lady Toquerie of Bouillon, Lady Faydide of Toulouse, Lady Florine of Burgundy, Lady Sybelle of Flanders, all with deep bags under their eyes, throats stretched and withered as dead lilies, but with lively expressions and voices that belied their antiquity. They were tough and wise; as Dame Margery would say, sisters to dragons, companions to owls.

THE CONFUSION in getting started the next morning made our most abysmal day on the Crusade seem a marvel of organization by comparison. The treasure alone created a massive problem, for it was loaded in longcarts which tended to bog in the mire or tip on the stones. Over and over the weight was redistributed, the mules changed fore and aft, as bishops prayed over the Church's contribution, calling the Germans "children of perdition" for stealing from the patrimony of Christ, the pitiful substance of the poor, the tears of widows, the dowries of maidens, the substance of scholars, the spoils of the Church. I agreed fervently, but wished they had mentioned the lives of the hostages, which must surpass the treasure in value. Bishops and lords mingled in a chaotic pattern with servants, folk, hawkers, knights and the ever-present Germans.

Lady Mamile and I watched from a window above.

"Which are the hostages?" I asked.

"Almost everyone you see. The Archbishop of Rouen, Walter of Coutances, there beside the second cart, he's going."

An astonishingly old man to make such a fearsome journey.

It was my first view of the hostages and I studied them with morbid intensity. One by one, I forced Lady Mamile to identify them. There were many prelates and knights, lords, small boys who were heirs to great estates.

"How many volunteered and how many were forced to come?"

"I'm not sure, perhaps half and half. The children didn't volunteer, but most of the others did. Such a weighty responsibility—it makes me weep." But she didn't weep.

"Are they all here?" I turned to Lady Mamile's smiling countenance.

"Not all, for a few *preux chevaliers* from the Crusade volunteered at once and must be in Germany already."

I looked again.

"Lady Mamile, am I the only female going?"

Her lavender eyes widened. "I don't know. Bless my skull, it would appear that you are. What an honor!"

An honor I would gladly forgo. Transfixed, I searched the

male company below for a single heiress to contradict me, but to no avail. No longer could I ignore the nagging worry I'd had from the beginning, no longer accept Bonel's pretty speeches about safety and "the roster," not even accept the queen's assertion that they'd thought I was a boy; they could have changed their minds.

I must find Bonel at once.

THREE DAYS LATER I sat on the beach at Orford Castle, still desperately hoping to see him. There was little time left; the ships were waiting to take us to Germany.

Another hostage called Sir Crispin pushed beside me on my log. "Good morrow, Lady Alix. You're abroad early."

"Aye. I heard that we would sail this morning."

"Yes, the weather looks clement."

He edged closer and I wished I still wore my rags, my malodorous boots. Lady Mamile had outfitted me in an elegant tunic of pale-blue Flanders wool, embroidered with silver days-eyes. I was warmer and more comfortable, but I attracted attention. Sir Crispin reminded me of my dog Dingwall when he's found a prize to chew, and the fact that I was married merely titillated his interest.

"Have you seen a wight called Bonel?" I asked.

"With the strange blue eye?"

"The very one!" I cried. "Oh, Sir Crispin, I would be so grateful if you could find him for me. It's a matter of life and death."

He rose reluctantly. "Anything to serve you, My Lady."

"I'll wait here," I promised.

The morning passed and the beach became thronged. The chapel bell had rung twice from Orford Castle behind me; men whipped beasts to haul the heavy treasure through sand; the pale, ghostly ships lay at anchor in the shallows, their holds open to receive the cargo, and still no Bonel or Sir Crispin. Then the hostages gathered on the rise behind me, their faces pinched and anxious, and the Archbishop of

Canterbury led the *Te Deum*. I stood awkwardly: one foot
was asleep, the other wrung by my fancy pointed boot. I
walked up and around the hostages to join the queen's company.

And we sailed. After all my protestations, my oaths not
to go, I stood at the rail of my ship and watched Orford
Castle diminish in size, its octagonal shape reflect golden in
the Alde, then fade in the mist that hovered on the shimmering sea. There was no sound but the slapping of oars,
for the sails hung slack and no one spoke; already we feared
King Philip's ferocious fleets awaiting us off England's
shores. *Off England's shores*, impossible words, impossible situation. Now I lost the shoreline and could see only the top
of cliffs, then nothing.

By afternoon I strained in the other direction to see Flanders, though I knew we must be far at sea. Then I caught
the scent of roses: the queen. She stood beside me, hands
gripping the rail, profile agonized. Without a word, her right
hand reached and hugged me close to her sables. I didn't
breathe, felt smothered, tried not to resist. What was her
purpose? To seek sympathy? Whatever her motive, I resented the gesture. She might play a constrictor's game with
the victim in her grasp, but she had no right to caress me, to
act as if we shared the same fate. After she left, I paced the
deck until sundown to give vent to my vexation.

Three days later, we entered the Rhine with two vast
fleets of busses that had joined us at Ostend. Pulling hard
against the fast current, the oarsmen stayed to the middle of
the river and away from the treacherous shores which floated
like ominous ice sculptures on both sides, their crags lined
with bear-like creatures who shook their fists and shouted
obscenities. Runners were sent ashore at every port, but the
message was always the same: no one knew where Richard
was being held.

The Bishop of Cologne greeted us most cordially to celebrate the Nativity, but he couldn't abate our fears. No, he

didn't know where the king was; no, he couldn't say where Emperor Henry could be reached; no, he couldn't guarantee that King Richard was still alive.

Our first afternoon in Cologne, one of our sailors was attacked and flayed to death, accused by the uncouth locals of falling from a ship in the sky that brought bad weather.

We left at once. A few miles upriver, we dropped anchor in a wilderness while royal counselors climbed aboard from other galleys to discuss our plight. Was all England sailing into a trap? Would the hostages, treasure and court disappear together into the continent's maw? We would go to Mainz and no further, said the sage men, and there we would demand that Richard be delivered on January seventeenth as had been promised.

Or what?

Even I could hear the hollowness of our bombast. I looked desperately for Bonel. I had wanhope that he would give me aid, but he'd assured me unequivocally that I'd be safe and he owed me a life. The plunge into the stank loomed as a most fortunate accident, a debt to be collected forthwith.

THE BISHOP of Mainz greeted us 2 January 1194. Yes, the king would be exchanged for the hostages and silver on 17 January as promised. Emperor Henry would alert us.

For the first time the full *mesnie* from Britain crowded onto German streets: earls and bishops—most of them destined to be hostages—a special retinue for the crowning of Richard as King of Provence, which was part of his bargain, Templars, Crusaders, the royal household of chaplains, stewards, clerks and servants. I followed the queen and her women from meeting to meeting with potentates and princes of the German Empire, many of them sympathetic to Richard. Again I looked for Bonel, but Lady Mamile suggested that he was assigned to the royal coffers.

On 16 January, we'd still had no news, but the queen ordered that Richard's royal regalia be prepared for his

release the following day, the promised day of his freedom. The servants complied with grim faces; two weeks
among chilly Germans had frozen our hopes more than
winds off the Rhine. But the queen was vindicated; the
following morning the Bishop of Mainz invited us to the
cathedral for a momentous occasion. The phrasing was coy,
but it must have meant that Richard was to be released. The
hostages attended evening Mass in preparation for the coming ordeal.

The ladies left without me in the morning. At the last
moment, Lady Mamile and I had a sharp exchange about
what I should wear. I claimed it made no difference, so long
as it was warm enough to keep me alive in an underground
dungeon; she argued that it was important that the English
Court appear rich above all others: "As we are seen, so are
we esteemed," the motto of the Plantagenet house.

After she left, I rummaged through the trunk of the dead
Lady Castellux and finally selected a rose wool tissue lined
with silk and warm gris, a compromise between the elegant
and the practical. I then combed my hair viciously against
the snarls caused by the wind, using Eleanor's ivory comb,
and slipped Bonel's hooded gris cope over the whole. If I
were still in prison when the weather became hot, I would
just have to suffer.

Everyone was seated by the time I reached the cathedral,
and I cast about in vain for a place close to the queen. Then
I saw Bonel. Fast as a ferret, I squirmed in beside him.

"Greetings, Lady Alix," he said warmly.

"Bonel, I must talk . . . have you been avoiding me?"

"Not at all. I've looked everywhere for you." His face
flushed with pleasure.

Immediately some of my tension dissipated. *Deo gratias*
that he was my friend. Yet what could he do? My eyes filled.

He turned to regard me. "What's wrong?"

"Have you seen all the hostages together?"

The Bishop of Mainz entered the sanctuary from a far side
portal.

"They're all here, I believe. Why?"

"Quiet, please." The priest in front of us glared over his shoulder.

The bishop began to speak.

"Your Majesty, esteemed company, fellow bishops, welcome to our cathedral on this happy occasion." He stood on a large platform which had been constructed to welcome the king. His face twitched, his voice trembled. *Benedicite*, one would think he was going to be a hostage. "This is a harrowing time for my English friends, a time when distraction must come as a relief. Therefore I've asked our cathedral players to perform a play written here in Mainz, *Ludus de Antichristo*."

He was down the steps and out of sight before the purport of his announcement struck. The queen rose in fury from her first-row seat and her face would topple nations; she cried after the bishop, but was drowned by thunderous music from the rear. Kettles rolled, trumpets blared, bells rang, and children's voices shrieked in shrill chorus.

Dazed by the sudden turn, the din and babble of voices around me, I clutched Bonel's sleeve. "What does it mean? Isn't Richard going to be released after all?"

Bonel's face was ashen. "Quiet! I want to hear!"

The queen rose from her place in the front row, her ladies with her.

The chorus of children with sconces held high marched up one aisle while a motley group of characters came up the other on our side. When the lines of vision cleared, I saw the queen—now surrounded by her personal guard—stepping into the aisle to make her exit.

"The queen's leaving!" I cried, "Richard isn't here, won't be here! *Benedicite*, perhaps I'll be free!"

Bonel was studying the row of characters across the front of the platform as if seeking someone he knew. While children lighted tall metal candle trees with their torches, others sang out the cast of performers: representing the three great religions were Christianity, Paganism and Synagoga or Judaism; the Antichrist in shepherd's guise; three living rulers, Henry of Germany, Philip of France and Richard of England.

At the word Richard, Queen Eleanor stopped on her royal route and looked back. Instantly her face filled with martial fury. Henry, magnificently garbed in black and gold, was played by a singer fit to be a Roman god; Philip, in French blue and gold, was likewise handsome; whereas Richard was a caviling comic buffoon, a shriveled carrot, and his three lions looked distinctly like rats.

The queen raised an imperious hand. "Cease this din at once!"

Her bell tones penetrated the cacophony, and gradually the music came to a rest as the confused actors gazed into the audience. Eleanor confronted the seated bishop.

"Isn't it enough that you break faith with England? Must you add personal insult to a Christian king? You deliberately flaunt your contempt for both country and God. To desecrate your cathedral with this demeaning display is beyond comprehension or redress."

The bishop rose, said something we couldn't hear.

"Don't speak to me of Rome!" The queen answered bitterly. "Send your players to the eunuch pope who lets the sword of Saint Peter rest in its scabbard between his impotent thighs while princes ravage our lands, hold our monarch in captivity. Let them sing out that England will not stand by!"

Again the bishop made an effort to speak.

"No!" the queen cried. "Such excuses cannot suffice. You make a travesty of justice, of honor among nations. Remind the pope that England once saved the Church from schism, but I promise you, as I am queen, that unless my son is released at once we shall rend the tunic of Christ in twain! And this time universal Catholicism shall be dissolved forever!"

She gathered her sables and marched with majestic grace from the church, her guard behind her.

Instantly the music resumed, and when several hostages rose to follow, a German imperial guard stopped them at the exit. We were all hostages of the bishop's entertainment.

"Please, Bonel, let's follow her," I begged. "They'd let you through and I must talk with you."

He was deaf to my protestations. In all the audience, he was the only one watching the stage and he did so with total concentration. Accompanied by the dulcimer, bell carillon and kettle, the three religions now stood forth and sang their respective dogmas. They were played by countertenors dressed as women, their pendulous cods drooping like slipped breasts, their jowls showing blue under white paint, but Bonel listened to every word.

"Did you know that I would be the only woman among the hostages?"

"Quiet!" The angry German priest half turned around.

I waited until the religions had left the stage, then tried again. "Answer me," I whispered.

Bonel didn't respond even to my sharp tug.

The kings now dominated the action. Each was approached by the shepherd-Antichrist; Germany and France resisted his wiles, but Richard instantly succumbed.

In a voice too weak to prevail, Walter of Coutances stood in the audience and tried valiantly to speak. However, his effort signaled the hostages to roar and stamp their feet in dissent.

Now France and England both wore As plastered on their foreheads as signs of their weakness, and the German king was the only monarch who kept true Christian faith. The climax came when Synagoga swayed forward followed by a host of Jews. They made hideous grimaces and licked Antichrist's feet in fawning idolatry. Instantly the cathedral shook as if in an earthquake, as the true Antichrist slithered up the aisle to claim the lapsed souls; he was a dragon big as three men with claws that clutched into the audience as he lurched from side to side, his tongue flicking, jaws pouring forth smoke. The creature lumbered onto the stage, then climbed a painted mountain at the rear. I grasped Bonel's arm in terror as God struck Antichrist with a thunderbolt and the mountain collapsed.

An angel sang out: "Oh Judah and Jerusalem, fear not, and be not dismayed!"

Synagoga ripped the blindfold from her eyes, knelt and accepted the true Christ as every voice in the Ludus rose in triumphal chorus. Christian kings advanced on the weeping Synagoga with swords held high. As they were about to smite her prostrate form, King Richard threw himself into the fray to save her. There ensued a mock battle in which the English king ran howling up the aisle with the German emperor in pursuit.

"God damn them in Hell!" Bonel shouted.

His cry was lost in the general melee: the audience screamed; the remaining kings hit Synagoga and the Jews until blood spouted in all directions. The play ended in a climax of gore, with kings triumphant, Jews sprawled in obscene death.

Now Bonel needed no urging to leave. He was the first up the aisle, was caught by a crush at the exit where I clung to his furs as he shoved his way through. Once on the street, he shook me off and ran into the maze of the city and away from our ships where I belonged. I plunged after him.

"Bonel, wait, I must talk . . ."

He'd rounded a corner and didn't hear.

I stood uncertainly at the top of a lane, not liking the surly faces of the Germans, then ran to the bottom where I glimpsed his black fur swirling around still another corner. I slipped and slid, clinging to walls and shutters, and found him in an open square gazing blankly at the frieze above an arch.

"Bonel, why am I the only female among the hostages?"

"Why did they kill Synagoga after she'd converted?" he retorted angrily.

"I don't know! Does it matter? That was only a play—this is my life!"

He gripped my arms and shook me as if I were an ungovernable child. "The play was *my* life!"

"But you're not . . ." I was going to say "dead," then "blindfolded," but became confused. Was there a connection between Synagoga's blindness and Bonel's Christian Eye?

"Suppose they made a Ludus of your experience at Wanthwaite," he went on bitterly, "where you were the villain and Northumberland the hero."

"You're evading my question. Why am I the only female?"

"Those that are brought up in scarlet embrace dunghills," he said enigmatically, and dropped his hold.

"Are you calling me a dunghill?" I shouted, incensed.

"I'm talking about the Ludus, damn it! Did the eagle ruin your ears?"

"I can hear very well, but you talk in riddles."

"What riddle? Christians torture Jews into conversion, then kill the Jews. What puzzles you?"

"Don't be sarcastic, Bonel. I know that your father was murdered, but he wasn't tortured into conversion first."

"Yes, my father!" he shouted. "Exactly my father's experience! And others." He pounded a fist into his palm.

"What others?" Let him talk out his fanciful obsession—and then he'd have to answer me.

"Go back to the ship; they'll be looking for you," he ordered angrily. "I want to be alone."

"Answer me and I'll go."

I meant about being the only female, but he misunderstood. "No—it's not your concern." Then he laughed a dry mirthless hack. "No, I'm wrong. Let a good Christian hear the truth for a change, especially you." He turned and fixed me with his uncanny eye. "My father's death caused a riot in London . . ."

And he launched into a tale so vivid and immediate that I

lost all sense of Mainz, the Ludus, King Richard and my
own peril. We were in London at Richard's coronation once
more. Joce ran blindly through the milling mob, while Benedict lay supine in his own blood. Someone shouted that the
new king wanted all the Jews in London destroyed. *Kill their
women and children! Strip their homes of their unholy wealth which
they'd stolen from good Christians! Greedy Hebrew swine with their
foul usury!* The mob descended on the unsuspecting and
unarmed Jewish quarter and set thatches ablaze, burned and
hacked screaming people when they ran, looted until there
was nothing left. Only then did the madness subside, a full
two days later. Most of the attackers fled the city for the
Crusade before the king could act. Benedict, who had converted to save his life, was released of his forced conversion
by the furious king, but died of his wounds. Joce went back
to York.

Exactly like the Ludus, I thought, stricken by my own
callous assertions. *Deus juva me.*

In York, Bonel, a lad of eighteen—only seven years older
than I had been in 1190, which surprised me—and his
brother Isaac heard that the riot was spreading like the Black
Death from city to city with no one to stop it, for Richard
was already in Europe preparing for his Crusade. First
Lynn, then Stamford and next . . . York. Except that none
of the Jews in the north would believe it. York was rich,
safe, remote, and Jews had been good friends with the
Christians since the Conquest. Bonel and Isaac pointed to
the First Crusade a hundred years ago when Jews of Rouen
had been massacred; the few survivors had tried to warn
Jews in Speyer and Mainz, but the German Jews had
claimed that their situation was secure among their Christian
friends; they had died for their stubbornness.

"You mean Jews were murdered here in Mainz?"

"Why are you surprised? You just saw that virulent tract
performed in the cathedral."

Even Rabbi Yontob—the Jewish equivalent to a priest,

Bonel explained—claimed that York was safe. Then came Easter Week 4952, always a dangerous time for Jews.

"When?" I interrupted.

"Sorry, 1190 by your calendar. During Holy Week, drenching spring storms blew through York accompanied by thunder and lightning, and the lightning set fire to houses all over the city. Even Isaac and I didn't suspect arson when we volunteered to fight the flames. We came home at dawn to find our house looted and burned. Among the ashes lay dismembered, charred pieces of our mother and sisters. *May the murderers' bones be ground between millstones!*"

Our lives merged: I, too, had found my mother dead and dismembered, and the stench of burned flesh would be with me forever. I reached for Bonel's hand—he didn't notice.

At last the York Jews saw the peril of their situation, but it was too late. In a series of deperate moves, they sought to regain lost time: Joce appealed to the town warden for sanctuary, and soon all the Jews, carrying their personal treasure —the huge amounts collected from debts and their records were sequestered in the York Minster—took refuge in Clifford Tower.

"Why did they delay so long?" I asked, unable to bear that "too late." "How could they ignore your warnings?"

His mouth twisted bitterly. "Are Jews the only people who deny danger? Did your father know that Northumberland might attack?"

The answer was too painful. Aye, he'd known, and waited just one day too late to get my mother and me to safety. "Go on," I said.

"It's human nature to deny, but the York Jews were also lulled by years of peace, as they were here in Mainz. It is hard to believe, even now. After all, Jews and Christians have coexisted in relative harmony for over a thousand years —until the Crusades; most of the worst rogues were Crusaders who could rob and run."

"But there's no Crusade now," I pointed out, "So perhaps the Ludus has no significance."

"Crusaders simply responded to increased invective against the Jews, coming from ignorant priests and wandering zealots. That verbal poison now infects the entire populace."

"What happened in York?" I pleaded, for I had to know.

"Clifford Tower was instantly surrounded by a howling mob: ordinary citizens and the youth joined the rabble and rabid monks of the Premonstratensian order from an abbey in Welbek—endowed by the Fauconbridge and Malbysse families."

"The men we met at Malbysse Manor?" I interrupted.

"The same—they were there directing the attack."

Anger choked me as he continued. To think I'd accepted these men as friends!

"A hermit called Norbert incited the mob to riot: 'Crush Christ's enemies and you'll go straight to Heaven! Stop their generation, disembowel their women, stone them, behead their men, strangle the old!'

"As Isaac and I leaned from the window to hear his ranting, a stone fell from above us and crushed the hermit dead. The mob, crying revenge against us for the act, demanded that the sheriff bring forth his siege machines.

"For those of us inside the tower, the heavens suddenly darkened, the stars lost their radiance as we faced our doom. It was to be our last day on earth, and our final act was to elect a noble death, worthy of God.

"Rabbi Yontob advised mass suicide: 'God to whom none shall say *Why dost Thou so?* orders us to die for the Law. Death is at our door. Let us remember the example of our forefathers and follow *Kiddush-ha-Shem*, death rather than conversion. Let us willingly and cheerfully render back to our Creator the life He gave to us and not wait for the hostile jeering mob to tear us like wolves among sheep. BLESS THE LORD, YE ALMIGHTY IN STRENGTH THAT FULFILL HIS WORD.' "

Bonel's cry attracted the attention of a few passersby. Abruptly he rose and strode away.

"Wait, Bonel, you must tell me . . ."

We walked in circles before he stopped on a rise overlooking Mainz. The blue-hazed city could have been the smoking ruins of York. Bonel's hood blew back and his black hair rose like a storm cloud in the breeze.

"My brother Isaac, God rest his soul, argued with Rabbi Yontob that we should have a choice without recrimination: Jews who wanted to survive, even if it meant conversion, should do so as they had done here in Mainz; let others die. The Rabbi agreed and advised those who chose to live to crowd to the right side of the tower. Without hesitation Isaac and I elected life."

"Why?" I knew I would have as well, though perhaps not for the same reason.

"To see justice done—no matter how long it took—and to prevent any more massacres. But . . ."

For the first time his voice faltered; anger turned to anguish.

"Joce's daughter, Anna, my dear . . ."

Intended wife, I thought.

". . . chose to die with her family. Rabbi Yontob instructed us to pull our treasure to the middle of the room. When he put the flame to the pile, Joce drew his shearing knife across Anna's throat, white as a swan's . . ."

He stopped, the muscles in his face taut.

"I turned away, unable to . . . . The turn saved my life, for the roof collapsed above me, and I was set afire. Isaac put out the flames. I lost my eye."

His account moved swiftly now. A hundred and fifty Jews had perished that night as fathers slew their families, then themselves; those who still lived shouted down that they were ready to accept the horizontal-vertical sign.

"The what?" I asked.

"The cross."

"The rabble claimed that it was a trick, that they were only pretending that most Jews were dead. The living were forced to drop the bloody corpses from the parapets before the Christians permitted them to come forth.

Isaac, Bonel and a friend called Aaron were the last to descend. The Jews knelt in a row as a priest moved before them, baptizing and giving each the wafer.

As the *conversi* stooped in penitence, Malbysse made his first open appearance. Before the Jews could raise bare hands to protect themselves, Malbysse and his men attacked them most savagely, and soon a second grisly lake of Jewish blood soaked the ground.

Paralyzed with horror, Bonel watched in a trance until Isaac fell beside him—then he was inspired.

"I know where the treasure is hid! Spare our lives, and we'll show you!"

Malbysse grinned and agreed.

Bonel then led the Pudsy, Malbysse, the Fauconbridge and Cuckney families—and Aaron who was dazed—to York Minster and pointed to the treasure chest.

"Though I didn't say that the records were duplicated, or that Isaac and I had hidden vast hoards, sent other chests abroad. Malbysse beat us unmercifully and left us for dead. His greed kept him from completing the act, however, and Aaron and I were rescued in the morning by a laundress."

They'd departed from Aborak—York—that same night, had passed Clifford Tower with its stench of charnel rot, had tasted gall and wormwood. In the next village, a Jew had affixed crosses around their necks and a Jewish goldsmith had made Bonel's Christian Eye.

"But you said that God had given you your eye."

"God made the goldsmith's hand, did He not?"

"Aye," I granted, unconvinced. "But then you can't see through the eye, can't pierce the evil in men's hearts."

"Perhaps not," he admitted, "though a blind man has divine visions, as the legends say."

"Do you?"

He turned his face in profile so that I could regard the hard, dry orb, now sickening in its implications.

"Yes, Alix, I do. After escaping the blade's swift kiss, I crossed stunned fields toward the sea and safety. At the edge of the Channel, I lay alone one night bathed in the stardust of the Pleiades and cried aloud to God to instruct me as to why I lived. Night parted in a brilliant clap; a whirling eclipse shaped like a wagon wheel turned red, green and black, and out of the eternal swirl thundered the voice of God: *The sun burns red, herald of the sword at hand. Lives have been shed as a bride-price for the future triumph of the Law! You are summoned to fulfill the prophecy, to save the Chosen People in their calamitous situation; you are epilogue to darkness and prologue to light!'* "

Bonel's clarion passion was awesome. Frightening. I drew away, not knowing this possessed blaze of a man as my suave friend. He stood transfixed, gazed across the city. The breeze stirred hair and clothing but made no sound, a voice from the dead.

After a long time, I shivered and tried to speak in a normal manner. "And then you went to Rouen?"

"Yes." He became himself again. "That's the only reason I live, Alix, to save the Jews."

"Did you convert to Christianity in order to save them?"

He gazed at me somberly. "Some Christians can—do—help the Jews, but I converted to save myself for God's will."

"Why didn't you kill Malbysse when you had the opportunity?" I asked bluntly. "I would have."

"You're a better Christian than I am," he mocked.

"Perhaps I am. I stabbed Roland de Roncechaux to death."

I met his surprised brown eye without flinching.

"You astound me—you couldn't have been more than a child."

"Aye, or God instructed me as well. All I know is that Roland raped and decapitated my mother, which seemed reason enough."

"I want Richard to move against Malbysse," he said quietly. "I want him to avenge all the Jews, and I'll help him in every way I can."

"Is that all?" I cried in disbelief. "You let the king do your work?"

'I'll order new *Memorbuchs* to warn my people, but Richard is my real strength. Remember that in the Ludus he was the only king who protected Synagoga. Your Roland was a single individual against you, another single individual. Malbysse is mere drummer boy to a vast army against the Jews —not just me, but all Jews—and it requires the power of a deified king to stop its march."

King Richard. The name brought me abruptly back to my present woes, though I no longer dared broach the trivial subject of being the only female, in the wake of Bonel's tragic disclosures. He reached and took my hand.

"You're chilled. Come, I'll walk with you to your ship and you can tell me why you were so upset."

Within a few heartbeats I'd asked and he'd reassured: the queen had been accurate about the confusion of my sex— which Bonel had known from the beginning—but I'd still been taken because of my strategic position on the Scottish border. The selection had something to do with the Canterbury Quit claim, the meaning of which eluded me, but I pretended to be satisfied.

When we came within sight of the royal cog, I stopped Bonel.

"Bonel, I'm soothly sorry," I said, the words ringing hollow in the wake of his tragedy. But what would suffice?

"Don't apologize—it's hardly your fault."

"I'm not apologizing—I knew nothing of the whole affair
—but I meant I was sorry for your suffering. Your desolation."

Impulsively I cupped his scarred cheek in my hand, held
it so for several heartbeats. He turned to look at me with the
same intensity he'd shown in his account, folded my hand
in his.

"I accept your sympathy, Alix," he replied softly, almost
with menace, "but it counts for little unless you turn it to
action."

"What can I do?" I faltered. "It was a long time ago."

"And you were ignorant. But now you know, and with
knowledge comes responsibility."

Bewildered, I couldn't fathom his enigmatic words or his
equally enigmatic face.

"You mean the whirling eclipse and turning darkness to
light?"

"Something like that."

"But how?"

Now he reached and cupped my face. "I'll tell you exactly
how in good time."

"If there are any Jews left when I'm released from my
dungeon," I said bitterly, "provided I ever am released, or
that I live through the experience."

He smiled and withdrew his hand. "Go now, before the
queen's guards come looking."

I ran across the cobbles to the gangplank and onto the
deck. When I looked from the rail, Bonel had disappeared
into the city.

ON 2 FEBRUARY we again convened in the cathedral to celebrate Candlemas. A thousand tapers bobbed in the gloom to
make *Nunc Dimittis,* and the bishop intoned the famous
scripture: *Lord, now lettest Thy servant depart in peace, according
to Thy word.* He then added his own message: "The emperor
has seen fit on this holy occasion to announce the release of

King Richard of England in the Hall of Justice two days hence."

# 5

 HIS TIME THERE WOULD BE NO ERROR. LADY Mamile borrowed the queen's silver-backed mirror so I might view the gilded chaplet she'd placed on my aching head. I gazed upon the face of a stranger, not having seen my own reflection ever before except in bits and pieces in glass shards: lucent skin of palest rose, hair a golden cloud, dark winged brows over luminous gray eyes, upper lip perfectly bowed, lower now held by teeth of pearl. A fair damsel, soon to be a shade. I gave the mirror back. The sweetness in that face had naught to do with me; I was a roiling cod, a hot liver, fantastick cells gone tinty.

The walk along the slippery street was a march to the gallows. A kite pecking at the slops was better off than I was. Yet a blessed numbness separated me from the reality of my situation; I was outside my own body watching this doomed stranger in her borrowed splendor.

The railed platform at the front held the queen and her advocates, several bishops and the Archbishop of Rouen. On the other side sat a king in black and gold, Emperor Henry of the Holy Roman Empire, a thin-faced man with a jutting jaw and small hazel eyes, not nearly as imposing as his counterpart in the Ludus. With him was Duke Leopold of Austria who'd captured King Richard in Vienna, a bloated lord with hooded blue eyes and streaked blond hair who talked with extravagant gestures to the noblemen surrounding him; he openly relished his importance in the drama. All of the German contingent glanced from time to time at Eleanor, surprised, I trowe, to see her so strong. I'd learned from Lady Mamile that she was seventy-two years old, but her antiquity added to her eminence, as with a Roman marble.

I tried to find Bonel, saw him in the distance, but he didn't turn. My eyes did catch those of the hostage Sir Crispin, who waved and smiled faintly. I nodded back. I doubted if I would be imprisoned with the men, but no harm maintaining his friendship.

Time dragged. Knights coughed. Bishops straightened their robes. A voice cried out: "It's a ruse!" Queen Eleanor looked to Emperor Henry, who avoided her eyes. One hostage coughed nervously, then another and another.

Outside, a faint neigh and snort of horses, then the clamor of male voices. The queen turned pale, strained forward to hear. Slowly the double door groaned open; heads turned to see, all except mine. Then the pound of boots and the alien sound of metal dragging—the king was in shackles!

Disbelief ran through the hall like wildfire. How dare Henry bring Richard forward as a common criminal! I watched expressions shift and fill with wrath as men beheld their monarch pulling his fettered feet heavily along the stones like the meanest Arab slave. Then the king passed close enough for me to touch, and I still didn't look, but could hear his labored breath, smell his sweat mixed with sweet woodruff, feel animal emanations of heat—a dangerous, trussed lion. Wrath gave way to awe in the faces around me; Eleanor watched with anxious, radiant relief. Now he'd reached the platform, refused help to drag himself up the steps, and continued his heavy metallic progress to the very center, where he finally turned to face us.

He was magnificent!

Supreme ruler of the universe without peer! Fit as the most practiced chevalier, bursting with health and vitality, he gave forth light like the sun. Nor did he slight the Plantagenet motto, for he was draped in dazzling scarlet and

green robes emblazoned with gold and pearls. His pured
ermine shone like snow; his close leather hat reflected myriad colors in its diamonds, rubies and amethysts as he turned
his head. Despite his chains, he was unconquered. He
smiled, and the whole crowd melted, all differences, fears,
sacrifices succumbing to the confident blaze of his smile.

"Long live the king!"

He raised his chained arms over his head.

"Long live Richard!"

The queen and counselors all wept and laughed together.
Then she moved to his side; he bent and kissed her, said a
few words.

The audience stood and began to chant: "We love Richard! We love Richard! We love Richard!"

His lips formed silently: "I love you!"

*I love you.* My thought flew back to Acre and that same
glorious head bending close.

"*Alex, I do love thee . . . swear that you love me.*"

"*I love you.*"

"*And you'll be loyal?*"

"*I'll be loyal.*"

"*Forever?*"

"*Forever.*"

The wild cheers continued. Richard was hailing friends
in the audience though no one could hear. The queen
watched adoringly, her face transfigured by love. I hid behind the bronze tangle of hair of the wight in front of me.

"*You are frightened,*" he'd said to me that last night in the
dark. "*Your heart strikes like a stone caster.*"

It was striking so at this moment.

The exuberant chanting ired Emperor Henry. He tried
repeatedly to speak with no success and finally approached
Richard to bask in his reflected glory. The contrast was
striking: Henry, a still-young man but already grayed in
spirit, a shadow to Richard's stalwart glow with his hot blue
eyes and flashing smile. Henry touched the English king's

arm, then reached to give him the kiss of peace. The ceremony had begun.

People finally returned to their places. Someone called out, "Quiet," so that Henry's thin, reedy voice could be heard. Richard continued to smile and paid little attention to his captor.

Henry accepted a scroll from his clerk.

"I want to read you a letter I've just received from King Philip of France."

The quiet turned ominous; Richard's smile froze.

Eleanor's hand went to her lips.

Reading swiftly in his breathy voice, Henry delivered a vicious diatribe at King Richard, claiming that he was a tyrant who'd committed heinous crimes against Church and state, that he'd insulted Count Leopold of Austria by tearing his banners from Acre's walls, that he'd backed the usurper Tancred in Sicily and then unseated a lawful king, Isaac Comnenus, in Cyprus, that he'd murdered Conrad of Montferrat, on and on . . .

" 'Worst of all, he deserted his sacred mission in Jerusalem and left the task undone, was bribed by his enemy Saladin into submission, accepted rich gifts and robbed captured bounty for his own coffers. He left a record of unparalleled brutality and deception.' "

The letter ended with a demand that King Richard be handed over forthwith to Philip and John in exchange for one hundred and fifty thousand marks of silver.

Signed by Philip of France, John of England.

An angry mutter swept the hall.

"I must consider accepting this offer," Henry announced. "Therefore our present transactions will be deferred until a later date."

I sought Bonel. This was the Ludus, only worse, a betrayal of the first magnitude. I saw consternation in his taut profile, though he didn't look my way.

The former protestation was nothing compared to the outcry that followed Henry's perfidy, and the rustle of swords promised a swift bloodbath.

The good humor on Richard's face congealed to the famous Angevin rage as his blue eyes hardened to agate, his jaw thrust forth and whelks appeared along his cheek.

Well did I recall the fury of that temper in the dark and his hands at my throat. *"Who put you up to this? As you value your life, answer me!"*

Queen Eleanor and his advisers clustered close to the king.

Archbishop Walter emerged from the group and said, "The king will conduct his own defense."

A roar of approval. I listened with mixed feelings, understood the treachery, but also understood that if John and Philip captured Richard I would be free.

King Richard took the stage with an authority to make all actors envious, and his sinewy voice rang strong as a trumpet, each word enunciated with sharp bite.

The roar abruptly stopped.

"Your Imperial Majesty, fellow Englishmen, good friends who've come so far to help me in my travail, I protest that as an anointed king I am accountable to no one but God!"

His cadence rose to an angry shout on the word *God*, and his audience stormed approval.

"But I voluntarily and cheerfully answer all charges, that the world may know my innocence."

He stamped his shackled foot, and the English stamped too.

His countenance twisted in scathing contempt; he then turned to the Duke of Austria. "You're a spoiled child in a tantrum, Leopold; your charge is unworthy of a count of Austria. The truth is, you came late to the Crusade with a tiny force, did nothing but dodge the crocodiles, then arrogantly raised your banners after my hard-won victory in order to steal a share of the spoils. Of course I ripped them down, would do so again. If you objected, why didn't you face me then? Because you were afraid! You prefer the coward's way of capturing me against holy edict, of putting me in Durrenstein Castle. In all men's eyes, you're an unchivalrous scoundrel, unworthy of your title or our concern."

There was delighted laughter. As the king went on, disproving every charge with wit and grace, I sank into memory again.

*We'd been in bed as man and boy, until his searching hands had discovered my true sex. The moment appalled, but I was the one in danger. I'd insulted the king, demeaned him by cheap deception, and my only defense had been the truth. With nothing like today's eloquence, I'd argued for my very life. I'd assumed that he knew my gender. Hadn't he said often that he "knew"? How could I dream that a man would love a boy?*

My defense had been truth and innocence; oddly enough, that was Richard's defense as well.

He stooped so that his nose almost touched Henry's. "I have a letter from the Old Man of the Mountain completely absolving me of the murder of Conrad of Montferrat, but I protest that proof should be unnecessary. Such a charge is unworthy between princes of nations." He dropped his voice to a sinister low. "And when I'm no longer in chains, will you dare repeat the accusation?"

He stood tall again, his mien deadly, and addressed the chamber with measured wrath. "The most unforgivable charge, however, impugns my conduct on the Crusade. I was the first monarch in Europe to take the Cross and the last king to leave the Holy Land; I fought alone against formidable odds. King Philip deserted, his French lords followed, then the smirking Duke of Austria; I was left with less than half an army to lead against the Saracen hordes. Philip and Leopold are the traitors! With God as my witness, they'll feel my revenge!"

Indeed. There spoke the true Richard, a man of intractable hatreds who never forgot an injury, the man I feared more than death. I pitied King Philip; I pitied myself. I didn't know why King Philip had deserted, but I'd had no choice.

The king's other pages had threatened my life if I didn't leave, for I impinged on their relationship with Richard.

Confused, I could hardly accept my discoveries of that night. Richard might be embarrassed and angered; I was frightened and shocked out of my wits. I'd never dreamed such a thing could be—wondered even now as I gazed on the great warrior king.

"Forget the calumnies of my foes!" he roared. "Put faith in my actions! *With God as my witness!*"

His voice reverberated in the vaulted dome, his hands reached high, his head went back.

The crowd became a howling mob demanding justice—screamed out that Henry had English silver in hand and only French promises. Then one after another bishops shouted that Rome would impose the interdict on Germany; princes and counts of the Empire clustered to Richard's side as Henry was left alone. After an hour of pressure and ominous turbulence, the Emperor succumbed—but with a barb. Richard must kneel and do homage for his lands in England, thus making himself Henry's vassal, England a province of Germany. It was a mortifying condition and one that Richard obviously wanted to fight. His counselors advised him otherwise, and he knelt before Henry, handed him his leather hat, then turned back to his audience a free man.

The shackles were unlocked.

Everyone on the platform embraced the liberated king. Lords and bishops rushed forward to join Richard, hoisted him on their shoulders, from where he reached down to touch fingers as he was carried from the room with his royal train behind him, then the hostages. The entire hall emptied remarkably quickly. I glimpsed Bonel as he followed to supervise the transference of the treasure.

"Well, it's over," I said forlornly. "What do I do now?"

"Stay with me, dear," Lady Mamile fussed. "The queen instructed me that we were to follow her and the king wherever they went, for he'll want to thank all the hostages before you're . . ."

Thrown into a dungeon. After seeing his chains, I could have no doubt as to my fate. I rubbed my wrists nervously.

We found the English in a cold, high-ceilinged chapel, the hostages and courtiers in line to meet with the king and queen. I started to join them, but Lady Mamile held me back.

"No, dear, stay." She touched my arm with her knobbed hand. "Queen Eleanor wants you to wait till last."

I stood on tiptoe to count: two hundred and sixty-two people ahead of me, the more important hostages to the front. I had a half-day left of freedom. I watched the ritual of words exchanged, embraces, the kiss of peace, smiles and tears. I observed Bonel's first meeting with the king, longer and more intense than that of the others, ending with a warm embrace and the kiss of peace, after which Bonel stood close.

"Come, dear, he's ready for you," Lady Mamile whispered.

The hostages were being accompanied by German soldiers through a side door. I was alone before the royal party: king, queen, Bonel watching from behind, others in a blur. Seen close, Richard's features were bigger than life, vivid skin made more so by a high patina as if rubbed by wax, eyes not clear at all but myriad layers of smoke and glints, muscles and bones chiseled to inhuman hardness. He was an actor of overwhelming physical presence, and hidden character.

Taking a deep breath, I lowered my eyes, raised my chin, stepped forward proudly, then flourished to the floor and stayed there.

"Lady Alix of Wanthwaite." His dark vibrant voice required a hall.

I bowed my head. "Your Majesty, we are delighted at your release."

"Rise that we may see you."

I stood, met his eyes, like looking into the sun.

"You've changed," he said quietly.

Unprepared for his simple directness, or the searching concentration in his look, I became apprehensive.

"Aye, it's been three years, Your Majesty." I moistened my lips, glanced at Queen Eleanor. Everyone was staring, motionless as figures in a frieze.

"A lifetime."

Signifying what?

"So it must have seemed in your prison. All England suffered for you, Your Majesty."

"You've made a long, difficult journey to offer yourself as hostage."

Was he being sarcastic? Again I glanced at the immobile queen. "Everyone has traveled a long distance, Your Majesty. We're honored to serve you."

"Except that the others aren't young women. My chivalry can't permit your sacrifice."

The frieze around him resumed life. Eleanor smiled and glanced at Bonel, who nodded at me.

"I truly don't mind, Your Majesty," I said uneasily, then tried to bring dimples. "After all I, too, was a chevalier on the Crusade."

"But now you're obviously a young woman. You can't be a hostage."

His eyes glowed as with a fever. Was it possible that he meant it?

"I don't think I understand, Your Majesty."

"You will return with us to England, and thence to your home. I herewith release you from your vow."

I'd made no vow, still didn't know what to say, suspected a trap, felt I was being forced to protest my willingness.

"You don't have to," I stumbled. "I mean, I knew I was the only female—it's all right."

The queen's lips curled.

"Not with me. Now, the kiss of peace."

He bent forward, brushed my lips lightly, and began to move in the company of his mother, his chaplain, physician and magnates, both English and German, and Bonel.

Leaving me a tranced bird.

At the door, Bonel turned, smiled, raised his hand. *See*, his gesture said, *I told you to trust me.* And he was gone. Trust him to do what? Was this journey an elaborate jest? I was utterly bewildered, so much so that I felt actually *deprived* of my dungeon.

Lady Mamile twittered that we must return at once to our ship because Henry Hohenstaufen might still change. Docilely I followed her to the street. Only when we had to stop to permit the hostages—now marching in pairs and accompanied by mounted knights—to pass, did I fully realize I wasn't with them.

WE LEFT MAINZ that same night, for no one trusted Henry's commitment to Richard and all thought it best to get away quickly. Indeed, spies confirmed that Philip had sent the French navy to waylay us wherever possible, probably at the group of islands at the mouth of the Rhine called the Scheldt. We shot down the river like an arrow, wind and current both with us.

On the third day, I began to believe I was free.

At the same time, I realized that the hostages were now in dungeons, and I could hardly bear to think of their fates. I prayed and fasted and promised God to give whatever silver I could spare for their ransom to relieve my guilt—though I'd done nothing against them. Then guilt dissolved in joy again, and I ate to make up for lost sustenance. *Benedicite*, at this rate I'd be home before Enoch.

I WAS ON the royal smack—Bonel was not. The forecastle was too crowded to accommodate me, however, for Richard and his chaplain joined with the queen. I was told to bed below deck with the other passengers, but I preferred a private spot under a small bark that leaned against the mast. There I pulled furs around me and slept warm and snug, except that my teeth became cold from constant smiling.

Neither the king nor queen showed any interest in me.

They were absorbed in making policy at various stops along the river. Richard made appearance after appearance and turned to a legend before our eyes. He was a martyr, a saint, a model prince with his fabled humor and generosity. On board he labored like Hercules with his ministers and generals. Therefore, I was free to indulge my own dreams of reunion with Enoch, which I did night and day, mixing memory equally with anticipation.

We finally reached the ice-strewn Scheldt and anchored off a small island for the first night. As I lay under my boat in early evening gazing on the fiery sea, voices approached; then feet and long tunics passed slowly by, as the king and queen talked in low tones.

". . . came down from his nuptial bed looking like a ghost. They never consummated," said the queen.

*Benedicite,* was she speaking of Richard's own wedding night with Berengaria? Well I recalled his stricken mien, her remote indifference the morning after their marriage in Cyprus. It had almost made me swear off marriage forever. But surely Eleanor wouldn't speak so to her own son, and call him and his wife "they."

"What else could she expect from Philip?" Richard asked bitterly. "Look how he treated his own mother, treated me. He's incapable of love."

"So his record would indicate. Nevertheless, the golden arrow found him. Within the month, he cast off his untouched wife and took the lowly Agnes of Méranie as mistress. His ecstatic moans from the bedchamber scandalize all France."

"And for that he's been excommunicated?" The king was interested.

"Worse, the interdict . . ."

They moved out of earshot. It might seem remarkable to them that Philip could love; I found it incredible that anyone could love him, king though he was. He was a mean, milky-eyed varlet who always imagined he was an invalid. They turned and paced my way again. Now the king was speaking.

". . . a military advantage if he's fighting with Rome, for the French cherish their Church. Have you sent a proctor to Pope Celestine to exacerbate his difficulties?"

"Not yet. I await your decision."

"I should think my decision was apparent."

"Only the first stage. Will there be a second?"

"Frankly, yes, but there are obstacles."

"Not for a king."

"And other priorities."

"That could be argued."

His voice chided lightly. "We're not speaking of a battle. I must form my own strategy in this matter."

"When will you move?" she insisted.

"In the . . ."

And I lost them again. War was fought on many fronts apparently, and King Philip's unfortunate passion was an Achilles' heel. I recalled when Richard had called me an Achilles' heel because of his affection for me, only then I hadn't known what it meant.

"How is she changed?"

"She's no longer a child."

"Though very young."

"And her female dress enhances her."

"So it does," the queen said with quiet satisfaction. "Lady Mamile reports that she's stubborn and willful."

"Virtues, if properly directed."

"And she saved Bonel's life."

The king was intrigued. "Tell me about it."

I heard the beginning of my action in the stank, greatly exaggerated for dramatic effect, and they walked away.

I lay rigid as death, not breathing, but they didn't return.

At first I was hurt by Lady Mamile's opinion of my character, and I'd thought I helped her so much, that we were friends. My bruised feelings quickly gave way, however, to the larger issue. Everything they'd said indicated that the conspiracy still thrived.

What else could that "first step" and "second step" of the king's mean? The first step must be releasing me. Then what?

Was my fate connected in some fashion to King Philip's? Twist though I might, I couldn't discern any similarity in our situations.

By dawn, I was still grappling; there was no evidence that the three fragments were one continuous conversation, though they might be. The king and queen had discussed Philip and his difficulties with Rome, caused by his putting away his lawful wife; the second fragment speculated about how Richard might benefit from France's difficulties; the last fragment had been about me.

But why discuss me at all? After our adventure on the Crusade, Richard might be somewhat intrigued by my fate, but not enough to speak of me as a matter of policy. No matter how I twisted the words into new patterns, the very fact that the conversation had taken place was sufficient reason for dismay.

For the rest of the voyage, I determined, I would try to make myself invisible.

# 6

 NGLAAAAND!"

I squirmed sleepily from under my boat as everyone ran from below to point and shout. A horizontal line crossed misty gray—land! Then Kentish farmers drove a team of white oxen along the line, wherrymen rowed from the mouth of the Thames. Sunday, 13 March, we were home! As we knelt to pray, a huge fiery globe crept over the horizon and hung motionless in the sky, exactly the height of a man's head. Everyone remarked on the strange phenomenon, and the priests declared it a miracle of good omen.

Once we were ashore, the entire country rushed to welcome us. For three days we could hardly move at all as the Archbishop of Canterbury stopped us on the road to rejoice, then at Rochester lords of London came forth to greet the king, then London itself.

After the conversation I'd overheard between Richard and Eleanor, I stayed carefully to the sidelines during the celebrations. I was especially cautious in the company of Lady Mamile, noting now a sharp watchfulness in her violet eyes, an acerbic edge to her bland judgments. Henceforth she would be able to report naught except that I was docile and quiet. As we entered London, however, I was drawn into the parade to give the queen's contingent greater importance. Once she'd had over forty ladies, but one by one they'd died; now I must ride behind her to increase her dignity.

The procession into London was carefully staged. At the head rode heralds in lines six deep, their silver trumpets hung with scarlet oriflammes emblazoned with golden lions *en passant*, their hats sprouting swan feathers like earthborn clouds. Long clarion blasts alerted the world of the king's approach. Then came a small Crusading army of knights encrested with coats of arms, red crosses proclaiming their holy purpose, pennants on high. Between the knights and the cheering crowds walked lines of pages dressed in gaudy silks and velvets.

Even this splendor faded before the dazzle of the king riding with arm upraised, a moving splay of crimson and weld glints in the winter sun. Hasped in an armor of gilt from gorget to sabots, knee-plates and elbow-cups cinched in pure gold, gloves and spurs jeweled with topaz, a crimson-looped ceinture at his saddle, he rode without helmet or crown, his hair a blowing halo. His great courser, Fauvel, was likewise caparisoned in brocheed velvet, forelocks and tail pranked with glittering gold. From Richard's shoulders and trailing over the horse's rump almost to the ground fanned a scarlet velvet cape embroidered and painted with peacocks, parrots and doves in many colors, lined in pure white furs, all lached and looped with gold. His passage aroused a moving roar of wonder and delight that mixed with the wild bells of London.

I was deeply stirred by the spectacle; I was also glad I wasn't a hostage. There was enough gold on the king's person to pay half the ransom.

THE ROYAL PARTY rode directly to Westminster Palace, arriving just in time to avoid a rising spring storm. The ladies disappeared to rest, the king went I knew not where, and I quickly changed to plainer garb so I could rush into the garden to watch the approaching blow. How my mother and I had loved the prelude to a gale, the roiling anticipation of the skies, the whistle and groan, the rumble and crash, fanfare of a cosmic tourney.

Squatting happily under a budding beech, I gazed to the saffron west where the wind pushed unruly clouds like a border cur herding sheep, this way and that, stupid little puffs blown widdershins across their shining field. No wonder God had created the world in March, the most toty and glorious month of the year! Now the boughs began to bend and snap as the gale gathered force, and I bit my lip in delight.

"Charge!" I cried to the west wind.

The invisible breeze reached the ground and flattened new grass to silver sheets. I stretched onto the miniature world of blades where wood lice rolled resentfully against the invasion of wind and one lady beetle clung desperately to a thistle.

I was not alone. Crouched before me in the grass, a cat

watched from black-sluiced yellow plates, his tongue hanging roguishly from one side of his mouth, his sable fur riffling.

"Heigh ho, Tom," I said softly. "Will you dance with me?"

He stretched, arched his tail, reached a soft paw in greeting.

Flattered, I held out my hand in response and tickled the grass to entice. He stiffened his legs, leaped backward.

"You lead, I follow!"

I rose, he ran, I chased, he turned and chased me in the hurly-burly of bending limbs. I laughed, he meowed, I meowed, he laughed and all lines dissolved—I was the cat, the trees, the sky and wind.

"My turn, cat!" I shouted into the billow. "You follow me!"

I grabbed the beech, swung my legs upward and let go, my hair brushing the ground as it had in Wanthwaite. Blood rushed to my toty head, and I heard the warning roar of thunder. I sprang upright again.

"Now you do it!"

The grinning tom leaped lightly to the branch and down again.

Suddenly the heavens darkened and the breeze bit with wintry teeth. I raised my face to drink directly of heaven and turned round and round in the fast-falling drops.

Drunkalewe with spinning, I stumbled headlong into King Richard.

Fell to my knees. Aghast. All lines reasserted themselves as the trees stayed trees, the cat disappeared, and I tried to hide my embarrassment by staring at the king's gilt toes.

"Quite a pagan bacchanal," he said pleasantly.

"I'm sorry, Your Majesty; if I'd known that you were near . . ."

"You would have stopped? That would have been my loss."

I rose and looked through the drench at his wet smiling face. Behind him a train of nobles waited discreetly, but the king seemed in no hurry to join them.

"Did you enjoy our ride through London?"

His eyes flicked downward, and I became aware that my tunic must be clinging in most licentious manner. I folded my hands across my breasts as if I were cold.

"Aye, Your Majesty. Your subjects are overjoyed to see you again on English soil."

"Yes, I would like to linger in the capital, but we'll leave at dawn for the north."

I forgot the rain and my appearance. "Will you be taking me to Wanthwaite yourself, Your Majesty?"

"Hardly." His face closed, but he reached his hand to my dripping hair when he saw my disappointment. "I must fight at Nottingham, but thereafter will meet with the King of Scotland at Clipstone. Perhaps we can put you in his company for your return."

"Oh thank you, Your Majesty!" I forgot my mortification at his witnessing my mad gambol, forgot my concern for the overheard conversation on the ship—I would soon be home!

"I think you should put on dry clothing," he said gently.

But he still held my hair. By bowing swiftly to the ground again, I forced him to let go. When I rose he had returned to his party and I ran quickly toward the palace.

RICHARD POUNDED toward Nottingham with revenge in his heart. Nobles who had backed Prince John and King Philip quailed at his approach, or even the news that he might be coming. A constable at St. Michael's Mount in Cornwall died of fright on hearing he was in England; from the castle of Tickhill where Bishop Hugh directed the siege, two knights came to check whether Richard had returned in truth, and once they saw him, they surrendered the castle and threw themselves on his mercy. The castle of Nottingham became the last bastion of John's challenge.

With my vested interest in Richard's victory there, now
that I knew the next stop would be Clipstone, I loved our
speed, loved stretching daylight at both ends, loved the
crush of knights joining us at every stop. The faster we
moved, the more martial our company, the sooner I would
reach Clipstone and home.

Yet the king diverted his huge train to visit the holy shrine
at Edmundsbury to give thanks for his release. At first I
fretted, then decided that I too should show gratitude to
God. We entered the holy city in late afternoon.

The men accompanied the king to the Benedictine monastery, while the ladies followed Queen Eleanor to a small
hospice. Lady Mamile informed me that there was a chapel
dedicated to Our Lady in the city and I soon found it, a
small, exquisitely constructed edifice. The doors alone were
so arresting that I tarried half an hour or more to study
them. Carved of bronze, they were covered with myriad
figures depicting scenes from the life of Jesus. Finally I
pushed them aside and entered the small, dark interior.

It smelled of sweet incense, was wreathed in smoke illuminated by candles along the altar. I was all alone, *Deo
gratias*. Slowly I walked to the altar, knelt and folded my
hands. My prayer was long, for it included Enoch's safe
journey home and a fervent plea for the hostages' swift release, a request that Richard win at Nottingham—but with
a minimum of bloodshed—so that I might go to Clipstone.
My knees ached by the time I finished, and I had to hold the
altar in order to rise again.

As I did so, I saw that the ivory cross was carved in the
same intricate style as the doors, but I couldn't make out the
tiny scenes in haloed light. Glancing over my shoulder to be
certain I was still alone, I picked up the holy rood. Carved
at the center was a medallion in the likeness of a lamb; a
woman beside the medallion stood with her spear upraised
to slaughter the Lamb of God. How odd. This was a chapel
devoted to Mary, yet the cross depicted Our Lady killing
her own Son? I looked closer; she wore a blindfold.

A blindfold—my heart thumped.

Synagoga? Yet, in the Ludus, Synagoga had converted to Christianity; she certainly hadn't killed Our Lord. There was something written very small in Latin under the medallion: *Synagoga ruit molimine stulto.* "Synagoga collapses after stupid effort." A crude inscription, in my opinion, to be found on an altarpiece.

And wrong: Christ had been speared by a Roman soldier. I used to drowse through my Bible lessons as a child, but I recalled that much. Yet this was a great Christian center; surely they couldn't be mistaken. Or—my heartbeat accelerated—deliberately lie.

I looked further. Below Synagoga, men with hooked noses leered upward as if cheering Synagoga: a crowd of Jews. There was another inscription: *Cham ridet dum nuda videt pudibunda parentis iudei risera dei penam mor.* "As Cham laughed at the naked genitalia of his parent, so Jews laugh at the agony of God." Worse than crude—obscene!

The cross slipped from my hands, and I barely caught it.

I put it back quickly and ran from the sanctuary. Once outside, I continued to run until I found a quiet spot behind a copse on the River Ouse. There I mused and brooded until the sky turned deep mulberry and I was forced within. Next time I saw Bonel, I would ask about the cross's significance.

AS IT HAPPENED, I saw him the very next day as we entered Huntingdon during market. He and his mercenaries skirted the booths and hawkers, and I started to call his name, then thought better of it. That afternoon, however, I found him as he left the king's pavilion.

After an exchange of courtesies, we walked away from the army to a quiet square.

"I haven't had the opportunity to congratulate you on your release," he began.

"Thank you." I recalled my perplexity. "How did you know I would be freed?"

"I didn't—at least in that way."

"But you must have. How else could you guarantee my safety?"

"I trusted the king." He gazed at me intently. "Has he spoken to you at all?"

"Aye," I said happily.

His curiosity deepened. "Tell me, are you pleased?"

I laughed aloud. "How could I not be pleased?"

He visibly relaxed. "I'm relieved that you feel so. I was sure that you would."

"Aye, I switch from one royal escort to another, and with this fine weather I should be home within days."

"What do you mean?" He straightened again, alert.

"What we just said, that I'm to join King William in Clipstone and thereafter travel with him."

"King Richard told you that?"

"Aye, in London. Why are you surprised?"

"I'm not." And he launched into a long description about how he, too, would be in Clipstone to confront Malbysse, Cuckney, Fauconbridge and Bishop Hugh once more.

But that was not what he'd meant to say—he'd been shocked to learn of my plans. *Benedicite*, how had he thought I would get to Wanthwaite alone? I waited politely for him to stop his jangle, then introduced the Edmundsbury cross.

". . . Synagoga was stabbing our Lord as the hideous Jews looked on," I finished.

"Tell me the inscriptions again. Can you recall the Latin? Perhaps your translation is faulty."

I repeated them as well as I could. He sat very still, frozen in thought, his brown eye as fixed as his blue.

"Is it important?" I asked after a long time.

"Alix, you don't know how important. You remember the Ludus? There was no mention of Christ's death; this is a new development. Bishop Samson of Edmundsbury is a declared enemy of the Jews, but I hadn't expected such a vicious lie, even from him."

I then assured him that everyone knew the Romans had

killed Christ under the direction of Pontius Pilate and that, in any case, the cross was remote, virtually no one saw it.

"You sound like a Jew," was his bitter response. "You're right insofar as a cross is hardly a papal bull, but the idea is planted, like a torch set to a hayfield. Jews should be warned."

He then repeated with more detail and greater vehemence his theory that sermons, plays and stone carvings prepared men's hearts for violent acts. To fight fire with fire, Jews should speak out, should create artifacts themselves representing the truth and should write books for each other. His agitation rose to such a pitch that I almost wished I hadn't told him.

He ended with his own Latin quotation: *"Cuius regio eius religio."*

I translated to show my accuracy: "He who rules the region controls religion." I tried to turn it to a pleasantry. "Are you suggesting that the Jews should rule England?"

"Perhaps not England," he replied solemnly, "but certainly the Jews are in double jeopardy because they fall under neither religious nor civil law. As the king's men, they're protected by the royal house, but on the books they're still subjects of Rome—which has ceased to exist."

Bonel's erudition about the Jews didn't confound me so much as his interest. He was a Christian now, but he seemed unable to forget his origins.

ON FRIDAY, 25 MARCH, we marched into Nottingham with such a loud blare of trumpets and such a multitude of men and arms that everyone within the city was frightened into a panic. We rode directly to the camp of the besiegers, where Richard pitched his tent at the base of a cliff within plain sight of the castle wall.

The queen led us to the opposite side of the River Trent, close enough to view the battle but far enough distant for safety. I watched most of the day as the awesome army gathered around the king with war machines. According to the queen's clerk, there were twenty-two carpenters and twenty slingers from Northampton, forty-nine chains, four thousand arrows, bolts and Greek fire from London. There were the usual assault towers called cats, catapults with stones weighing fifty pounds or more, and a new invention called a trebuchet with a sling on the end of a pole, which the clerk informed us had more power and accuracy than tension and torsion machines. Urric the engineer and Elias the carpenter came from London to supervise the complicated mechanisms.

Early the following morning, I perched in a tree and therefore saw the king emerge from his tent with six of his men. Richard stretched in the early sun, then froze in position. Arrows whizzed from the castle walls, and four of the six men writhed on the ground at the king's feet, their cries audible across the river. Instantly the king rushed back into his tent and I dropped to the ground to report to Queen Eleanor. I interrupted her prayers before her folding altar, but she didn't hesitate; she hurried outside to see for herself.

The king again came from his tent, this time fully armed, and his horse was held for him to mount.

"But he's going alone!" Eleanor cried. "How can I stop him?"

In an excess of rage, Richard spurred his charger up the tortuous rock with knights shouting in his wake. Trumpets blasted tardily and banners were hastily unfurled as the king's army tried to catch its leader. Archers dipped arrows in flames to hurl over the walls and a battering ram slowly crept into position to strike the gates.

The din alone would defeat the staunchest enemy in my opinion, as the horns, drums, shouts of the berserkers mixed with the deadly thump of machines, the crash of stones, the whir of arrows and the shrieks of the dying. We couldn't see flames, but we could hear the crackle, and soon ashes drifting in the early spring air forced us to tie scarves across our faces. The main gate burned and gave way, then the outer works and towers, the bailey, everything to the curtain wall.

Richard rode back in late afternoon. Before he dismounted, he took a bow and carefully picked off an archer as revenge for the morning's attack.

Sunday, 27 March, machines were placed for maximum effect, and Richard had a long gallows built as close to the wall as possible. There, in blazing midday, eighteen prisoners from the castle were paraded under the wall to be sure they were seen and identified; then they were hanged.

That afternoon Bishop Hugh of Durham arrived from Tickhill Castle with captured weapons and prisoners; King Richard rode to greet him. As the great men were assembled to eat their dinner inside Richard's pavilion, two knights came from Nottingham Castle to verify that Richard was indeed Richard.

"You see me with your own eyes," the king answered curtly. "Tell those within that they'll join the ropes one by one."

Nottingham surrendered the next day. The castellans Ralph Murdoc and William de Wenneval led the entire garrison to the English camp, among them several women warriors, the most famous being Nicholaa, wife of the Sheriff of Nottingham.

No one could believe the swiftness of the collapse, least of all I. I deducted a week from my time to wait, for surely the king would move as hastily as ever, but there was no immediate sign of our packing our supplies to go to Clipstone. I bathed Thistle, then myself, in a fret of frustration. With this fine weather, Enoch must be in Wanthwaite.

In late afternoon on Monday, the queen summoned me to her new headquarters within Nottingham Castle.

She was negotiating terms with various important prisoners. I waited discreetly for her to notice me.

"Lady Alix, how have you fared these last weeks?"

"Well, Your Majesty. I'll soon be home." She already knew it, but I couldn't restrain words or smiles.

"Indeed. To the point. After the strain of travel and battle, the king has decided to linger here a day to refresh himself with the hunt. As it happens, a ruffian came yesterday to view the siege and made his way to my pavilion. He introduced himself as Black Bob or Merry Bowman or Sherwood Archer—he wasn't sure which alias you knew."

"Alias?" I hedged carefully. "I don't recognize any of those names."

Her clerk Fitzroy looked up. "Robin Hood?"

"Aye, Robin Hood!" I cried without thought.

"Yes, he claimed he was your friend. Who is he?" the queen asked curiously.

"I believe he's a loyal subject of King Richard's; the Sheriff of Nottingham persecuted him, or so he says. In any case, he lives in the forest outside the law and wages battle from a hidden lair."

The queen's emerald eyes sparked with interest. "How romantic—if true. In any case, he's been waiting many years for the king to return before he would wed. His lady—Marian?—insisted that you attend the wedding."

She then went on about the hazards of riding into Sherwood Forest where renegades might still lurk. Recalling Lady Mamile's report that I was willful, I didn't comment.

"Do you want to go?"

"It might be diverting, Your Majesty," I replied meekly, "but I have no preference. I wouldn't want to cause you anxiety."

"Robin Hood says the way is exceedingly labyrinthian, so he's sending an old friar to accompany you. If I add the king's page, Hamo, who has a good sense of direction, and an armed knight, it might be all right."

"Yes, Your Majesty." I couldn't control a smile.

She stood and paced. "The weather's unseasonably warm,

almost like summer. I'll see if Lady Mamile can find a lighter tunic for you to wear."

"Please don't bother, Your Majesty. I'm quite comfortable."

She put her arm around my waist and squeezed me affectionately. "Permit me the pleasure of dressing you, my dear. You're the only one of my ladies who can profit from such attention anymore."

"Thank you, Your Majesty."

I bowed low and left. She stood quiet as an icon and watched me, her smile bemused.

THE KING'S PAGE, Hamo, was a pretty boy with a girlish face and voice, yet unlike the odious pages in Acre insofar as his eyes were warm, his manner open and direct. Our guard was an elderly knight with poor hearing. We met at dawn and soon Friar Tuck materialized beside me, a swaying, blear-eyed ancient. Although he spoke my name, I don't think he recalled me at all.

Already drunkalewe by Prime, burping and farting as he swayed in his saddle, swinish folds emiting myriad foul odors from the gullet and below, the fat friar hummed and hiccoughed in happy abandon. Too jug-bitten to respond to my queries about Robin and Lady Marian, he led a haphazard way while the knight, Hamo and I followed, all of us trying to avoid the downwind.

We rode in pellucid light through an awakening wald. April was near, birds chirped on greening wands, new grass hazed the ground. Sap pounded in my veins in rhythm to Thistle's pace and I made no effort to control my lickerous fantastick cells. After all, my animal spirits were safe with Friar Tuck, and certainly from the handsome Hamo.

It was well past Haute Tierce before we reached the rustic hideaway of my friends. A brilliant sun shot arrows between the branches, but poured solidly in meadows, so that I became uncomfortably warm; yet I kept a gossamer gold shawl tight to my shoulders. I know not what licentious taste the Lady Castellux had in her choice of wardrobe and doubted if the queen could have held my tunic aloft before she chose it, for it was indecorous to the extreme. A charming light green color to be sure—much as the tiny buds on today's boughs—and rich in its orefois, it nonetheless was cut off the shoulders, supported only by tight upper sleeves and my bosom. Unfortunately my breasts were not equal to the task. Furthermore the sleeves were heavy with long points trailing the ground and the skirt had a train, which gave the gown a downward tendency. I hitched and pulled upward to little avail.

By the time we reached the clearning where Robin and Marian lived, the birds were stilled. Various cutthroats dressed in tattered green were placing blossoming branches across a new-raised canopy to form an altar, and the cunningly disguised lair was covered with greenery. I leaped from Thistle, promptly tripped on my train and went tumbling, snarled in my shawl. A feminine hand reached to help me.

"Alix, is it you?"

"Marian? *Deus juva me*, this is the first time I've ever worn a train."

Soon we were hugging and laughing at my toty garb, the occasion, the joy of being together on such a day.

"Prettiest bride I ever saw!" I claimed, not lying since I'd not seen another bride except Queen Berengaria, the plainest wench in Christendom. Though, soothly, time had not been kind to my friend.

I figured quickly: She must be over thirty by now, old enough to be a grandmother. The sun and winter winds had drawn all juice from her skin, leaving a dun parchment, and her brown hair appeared sparse. Yet her teeth were sound, her smile radiant.

"Will you stand with me?"

I nodded.

"Let's go where we can talk. We have over an hour—banners must be hung, the feast prepared—and there's much I want to learn about the outside world."

"And I about you. Will you be returning to civilization?"

"What time shall we come for you?" Hamo asked from behind me.

"Aren't you going to stay?" I was surprised.

"No, the queen needs us."

"Late afternoon, when you will. Take refreshment before you ride."

With arms around each other, Marian and I entered her rustic bower which was much as I remembered it, a curious blend of furs, mounted trophies of the hunt, carved tables and stolen silver plates of great worth. We sat together on a mound of soft hides and appraised one another again.

"Your skin is shells and peaches, Alix. Does your glow come from happiness to be reunited with the king?" Her brown eyes sparkled with prurient glee.

"The king?" I echoed, not knowing what she meant.

"Have you forgotten what you confessed to Robin?"

Soothly I had, but her question brought it back: to secure my freedom from the rogue, I'd told him I was the king's beloved.

"Oh, well, you see . . ."

"And has he seen your bairn? Was it a girl or boy?"

"Bairn!"

*Benedicite*, in the stable at night when Robin had tried to seduce me, I'd protested that I carried the king's child which must be guarded. What could I say?

"Oh, it—I mean he—died. This putrid island in the sea, you know. He had the tertian fever."

I touched my eyes and looked away.

"What a tragedy! Oh, Alix, I'm sorry I asked but . . . Perhaps next time . . ."

"I think not, Marian. The king and I are no longer . . . together. He's returning me to my husband in the north."

Her interest flagged. "A husband. Oh."

Momentarily resentful, I soon collected my wits and turned from this dangerous subject to the more interesting topic of a criminal and his bride. Could he still claim to be the Earl of Huntingdon when the real earl, David of Scotland, rode not a half day away with the king? I wondered—but I didn't ask. Instead I queried how they would live. And where.

"Robert—that's Robin's true name—and I will stay for a time with my father, at least Robert believes my father will now accept him. Alas, Alix, I must confess, we had high expectations that if you attended our nuptials the king might come with you. We both feel, you see, that if King Richard knew how Robert had protected his kingdom while he was away, how he raised over fifty thousand marks for his ransom, the generous king would certainly give a reward."

Unflattering as her admission was to me, I sympathized. She was despondent, close to despair at her lot, and I wondered anew how she'd been trapped in such a strange liaison. She must have a dim middle brain to believe that Robin Hood had collected a farthing for altruistic cause, unless lining his own coffer be counted altruistic. As for his protecting the kingdom, Queen Eleanor's ignorance of his very existence answered that.

Our conversation turned now to her toilette and soon I was trying to puff her hair to hide her shining scalp, then instructing her to bite her lips while I pinched her cheeks to make red spots. There was little we could do for her gown, which was white and simple as a nun's, until I had the happy thought of flowers. I left her alone and went to seek blossoms to relieve the severity.

Outside the sun shone almost directly down and only modesty kept my shawl in place. The preparations had progressed remarkably in a small time, ropes between trees now

blowing with bright banners with heraldry of the hunt, fes-
tooned with rich tapestries—stolen, no doubt—and bloom-
ing with flowers. I began to gather a bouquet for Marian to
carry as well as small pink bells to tuck in her locks.

"My Lady!"

Robin Hood bowed to the grass, his head tonsured by
Nature as if he were a priest.

"Robin Hood?"

He stood and grinned brazenly, one tooth less than I remembered.

"Sir Robert Locksley, if it please you. Is the king attending as well?"

"He's coming for me, of course." No harm in keeping the
churl happy, or in assuring my own good treatment. "I
urged him to relax with the hunt. You understood—poor
dear has had so much fighting, so many ceremonies."

I sighed with domestic concern.

His hooded eyes glittered as he bent to kiss my hand, his
glance flitting over my shawl to glimpse my bosom. I pulled
my garment closer.

"I must go back to Marian. She's lovelier than ever."

"Aye, that she is." But his indifferent tone, his wandering
eye revealed only too clearly what Marian's fate was to be.

The company was assembled; hunting horns announced
the bride. Slowly Lady Marian and I walked a flower-strewn
path to the improvised altar, there to face the most motley
collection of rogues in England. They were all male, all past
their prime, all besmottered and torn in costume, and all had
sinister expressions as if they dined each morn on abducted
babes. There was not one official to record the event, nor
children with long memories to give witness. If Robin declared tomorrow that the wedding had been a dream, no one
could gainsay him.

To my dismay, Friar Tuck staggered forth to conduct the
ceremony. Now there was no escaping his foul gases, but I
practiced holding my breath and believe I inhaled not more
than a dozen times during the entire wedding.

At the same time I was vastly entertained. There was no Mass, no mention of God or His Son; the only holy person invoked was Our Lady Mary, and I recalled how Robin and Marian had built a small chapel in Her honor. Mostly, however, the old friar was personal.

"The wedded state be hard to sustain, Marian," he growled.

How would he know?

"Men be men and women be . . . what air women, fellows?" He rolled a lewd eye at his audience.

"Curious creatures wi' the smell of fish, the brains of sheep, and a hole in the middle!" called one wag.

"Get on," Robin said between his teeth.

"Robin be a man," the fool continued, "wi' a man's faults. What be a man's faults, boys?"

"That he's lickerous for the hole!"

"Nay, lad, he licks the hole!"

There was more bawdy exchange, and the ceremony threatened to be abandoned. I took Marian's hand and squeezed.

Friar Tuck belched and produced a flask. After a long drink, he went on. "What I mean to say, Marian, be that ye mustna heed Robin's faults for he be yer lord and master. Men serve God, women serve men. Ye're husband and wife."

Robin Hood reached for his bride to kiss and grabbed me instead. I turned my cheek fast, but still received such a long suck on my ear that I couldn't hear for the next hour. Finally, the bride was properly embraced, and all was well.

Now came the festivities in which Marian and I could take no part. There was wrestling, swordplay, a competition among archers, chasing a greased pig, a rolling of balls and much eating and drinking. Drunkalewe as they were, the men remained boisterous rather than belligerent, and they were most chivalrous to Marian and me for we were their ladies, as if at a tournament.

As the men tired, Robin relented and devised a game we

could join called hot cockles. To escape the unseasonable heat, we moved to the verge of the forest, where the rules were explained: one person was blindfolded and put in the center while the others had to touch his hand and cry out "Hot cockles!" If the blindfolded wight could grab the hand, he then touched the face and tried to identify his adversary. If he guessed right, he gave his blindfold to the loser. Marian and I were under great handicap as our voices gave us away, but we were also sober and much faster than the men.

One after another, Little John, Robin, Friar Tuck and others were caught. Laughing, dodging, running backwards, I discarded my cumbersome shawl and danced around the silly frekes. Then I was caught. *Benedicite*, if I could only remember all the names.

But they cheated. After half a dozen passes, they all fell silent. I turned and darted where I thought I heard movement, only to grasp empty air.

"Unfair!" I grucched. "You have to touch my hand!"

Becoming vexed, I charged too fast, stumbled over my train and fell, I tried to rise, pulled on one of the long points of my sleeve and felt a breast pop free. Now thoroughly vexed and humiliated, I struggled with my blindfold, my exposed bosom, my train and my legs all at once.

Then I felt a hand at my elbow and grasped it.

"I have you!" I cried. "Say, 'Hot cockles'!"

A long pause.

"Go on, you have to!"

"Hot cockles."

Another long pause. With my free hand, I tucked in my breast, then used the hand I held to stand upright.

"I'm permitted to touch your face," I said uneasily.

I reached slowly up the soft sleeve to the shoulder, smelled sweet woodruff and dropped to the ground.

"Your Majesty!"

Instantly my blindfold was released and I stared at King Richard's feet, which seemed to follow me everywhere. Had

I invoked him by unknown magic when I'd said he would come? A frisson troubled my skin.

"Where's her cape?" the king asked. "Give it to me."

Swathed in my golden shawl, I dared look upward. He had changed utterly—relaxed from his hunt, more the hunter than the angry warrior—in that his face glowed a healthy pink, his eyes sparkled like jewels, his whole person took on a lambent ease. He smiled.

"Come, Alix, and I'll escort you back to Nottingham."

I stood, saw a small army of hunters in the lengthening shadows with Hamo and the old knight among them. Had Hamo led the king here? Was it planned?

Robin Hood put a hand on my shoulder and arched his head upward.

"Your Lady Alix would make a dead man fizzle, would she not?"

The insolent tone produced thunder in the king's eyes, but Robin went heedlessly on.

"Sorry you had to miss the wedding. However, we're always happy to receive the greatest monarch in Christendom, especially since we've devoted our life to your cause."

"Indeed," the king remarked frostily. "Would you bring Lady Alix's horse, please."

Someone scampered to obey while Robin chattered his way to oblivion.

"All my merry men have fought valiantly against Prince John and the Sheriff of Nottingham, as well as against the holy fathers who support them. We collect silver and give to the poor."

By now Thistle was in place and the king offered me his hand. *Deo gratias*, I managed to swing into place without more disasters to my modesty. The king mounted his ebony hunting steed and we turned to leave.

"I'll write a ballad about your visit!" Robin called to our backs.

I looked over my shoulder and waved at Marian whose

gaiety collapsed to desolation; the frolic was done, her future descended.

Deliberately I held Thistle back so the king could proceed, but he chose to ride next to me.

"That was blithe company, Lady Alix. How did you come to their celebration?"

"I met them on my way back from the Crusade, Your Majesty. They helped me through the wood."

"When you *ran* from the Crusade," he reproved. "You must explain yourself sometime."

It was the reprimand I'd long been expecting and, though delivered with jocund cadence, ended with the significant word "sometime." When did he expect me to confess? I would be gone tomorrow. Protocol forbade my asking him, but I twisted my reins nervously as I awaited his next statement.

"I do believe this is the most pleasing wood I've ever seen," he continued brightly. "Or am I enthralled because I've been away so long? Do you find it particularly enchanting?"

"Aye, I do," I agreed fervently, giddy from relief that he wasn't pursuing the subject of my desertion in Acre. "There's a sweet, thin fire in the air."

"Intoxicating," he enthused. "Mystery in the gnarled trees, slanted sun a golden confusion of dust."

"You're a poet, Your Majesty!" I smiled in spontaneous delight, waxing more and more at my ease. *Benedicite*, I must quit my suspicious bent. This was a great and complex monarch with myriad responsibilities who nonetheless had taken time to show me kindness.

"If so, you're my muse," he replied gallantly. "A wood sprite—how do you call it in English?—a forest deity who seduces the prince."

"An Elfin Queen?" I replied with less delight, not liking the word "seduces."

"Exactly! You're a 'Nelfin Queen.' Dangerous eyes, like water-pale diamonds."

I met his torrid gaze briefly, then changed the subject. "I see you took two deer, Your Majesty."

With great detail, he described the strategy of his party's hunt much as if it were a battle. When he'd finished, one of his knights began to sing a stirring *sirvente* in langue d'oc, which I couldn't follow. The king joined in the chorus and waved his arm to punctuate the strong rhythm.

We then rode through the dappled light in silence. The distance seemed greater than it had in the morning. I turned my head to search for Hamo; he was chatting with a young squire at the end of our train and didn't guide us at all.

"We won Nottingham quickly," the king remarked casually, as if noting the weather.

"You were magnificent, Your Majesty," I complimented him sincerely. "All England is grateful to have you home again."

"And you?" His eyes scorched. "Are you grateful as well?"

"Well—yes. Yes, I am." For the first time, I realized that I was. "I'll soon be in Wanthwaite, and I owe it all to you, Your Majesty. Your chivalry and now your skill."

His smile faded. "Yet your home can't be happy. If I didn't have so many official tasks, I could assign you to a husband. Would you like that?"

Appalled, I twisted to see if he japed, had to readjust my gown. "You have subtle humor, My Lord, for you know that I'm wed to Enoch. I can't be assigned two husbands."

"And marriages are never dissolved," he mocked solemnly. "Except for consanguinity, or reasons of state, or reasons of religion, or reasons of inheritance."

"None of which applies in my case," I said, then tried to soften my tone when I saw his expression. "Soothly, Your Majesty, I'm deeply touched by your concern."

"My concern is based on my vow to you. I never forget my word."

*I love you, I'll be loyal to you,* I heard again, but he'd made no vow about my marital happiness. Or was he reminding me of my vow to him? No, I was permitting my fantastick cells to run wild.

"All your subjects are aware of your chivalry, Your Majesty. In my case, you have surpassed yourself, for I couldn't imagine myself happier than I am with Enoch."

I spoke honestly, but also deliberately. The king's beneficence was taking a disconcerting turn.

A faint line of whelks appeared along his jaw. "I believe you fear to tell me the truth, Lady Alix. Perhaps you've forgotten how I value plain speaking."

I fought to keep a straight face.

"But I recall well the cruel character of the Scottish brute. I should never have assigned him as your husband—a disparagement of your rank among other things."

"You've forgotten, Your Majesty. Enoch offered you one thousand marks for my hand. He loved me . . ."

"Loved your lands, you mean. He deserted you most heartlessly on the Crusade. Now it appears he's done the same thing again." His tone was no longer flippant, but hard.

A spasm of dismay constricted my chest. How did he know about Enoch's absence?

"You surprise me, Your Majesty. With all your duties, how have you learned about me? I should think you would be weighed down with your impending war."

He couldn't be deflected. "I'm interested in all of my wards, especially if I fail my responsibility. Especially toward you."

"You mustn't think that you erred in choosing Enoch for me. He *does* love me—and I love him."

I was determined to clarify his misconception, but his jaw set stubbornly.

"You have courage, I grant you, but he's not worthy of your defense. He left you."

"I can manage my estate quite well alone," I argued lightly. "I hunt, adjudicate grievances, buy and sell, plant the fields, improve our structures as well as any man, I trowe."

"Which could be expected," he approved, "since not too long ago you were a boy."

Seeing my way out of this dour subject, I smiled to show my dimples. "I hope you've forgiven me, Your Majesty, though the offense was heinous."

"Are you apologizing for your poor performance as page? I admit that I had to discard several garments where you flung the wine."

His jocular tone and hot eyes reminded me that I'd had to bathe him after one such instance, but I continued to smile.

"I apologize for the deception."

"Except that I was never deceived."

He reached across and touched my cheek. I stiffened, but managed not to flinch. *Benedicite.*

"Even the prettiest pages cannot emulate such sweet blushes, young Alex/Alix, and you gave me some of my happiest times by your droll escapade." He laughed softly, then sobered. "Especially when I was imprisoned at Durrenstein and later in the dungeon at Hagenau where few ever leave. There my guards oft remarked on my good humor and now I must give credit where it is due: my memory of you. I was able to savor slowly your innocent affection, your loyal service, your comic pretensions."

This time he took my hand and held it as we continued our way through Sherwood Forest which was, I now saw, indeed an enchanted place. Dark bird shadows darted through the arrowy light; pale luminous flies, born of the sun, sparkled in the trees; the animal odor of new lilac filled my breath. I was happy, aye, happy at last. The king forgave me, and soon I would see Enoch. I rode in a lickerous dream of love.

When we approached Nottingham, I turned to the king, wanting to tell him how I'd misjudged him, how I'd forgotten the good parts of the Crusade when he'd treated me with incomparable kindness, loving me as a father, but his face was preoccupied. He released my hand and rode ahead to greet a group of knights who met us.

THE NEXT FEW DAYS were torture. Instead of moving northward to Clipstone as he'd promised, the king called a great council to be held at Nottingham in the heart of John's country.

On the third day I happened on Bonel as he left the castle's great hall.

"Bonel! Here, it's Alix!"

He turned uncertainly in the dusk to seek my form.

"Why is the king tarrying?" I demanded without preamble.

He laughed. "Hardly tarrying. The taking of the castle and this council are Richard's prime objectives in England."

He then explained that King Richard was bitter toward the English and determined that they would pay for the rest of the ransom as well as finance his coming war with King Philip. While the king and his men had endured untold privations in the Holy Land, and later in captivity, the English had grown fat and self-indulgent. Now he planned to trim the fat.

"What privations?" I scoffed. "The king and his men always lived in comfort; only the foot soldiers suffered."

"You left after Acre, I believe," Bonel chided me. "He told of such thirst in the Holy Land that they were forced to drink their horses' blood and each others' urine, of hunger, storms. He claims that his spirit withered, that he changed from a man of hope to one of hatred, now his driving force."

I thought of his laughter in Sherwood Forest and doubted it, but that wasn't my point. "How long will it take?"

"Our agenda is crowded, but we proceed rapidly. We have to dispense with the prisoners and decided only today that Prince John must report within forty days or lose all claims for the succession."

"I don't care about that. Just tell me how long."

"I don't know. I, too, look forward to Clipstone where we're meeting Malbysse again. Let's say Palm Sunday, about a week hence."

I groaned aloud.

"Calm yourself, Lady Alix. I heard someone say that a contingent of Scots will arrive tomorrow. Perhaps you'll hear some news."

"Tomorrow! Oh, thank you, Bonel."

Ten Scots arrived the following afternoon and pitched tents in the courtyard. I approached their camp shyly, then stopped enthralled: a tall Scot stood in half profile, his auburn hair glinting under his horned hat, the *breacon feile* of the MacPherson clan blowing around his shoulders.

"Enoch! I screamed, and began to run.

"Quhat say?"

I stopped just in time. *Benedicite*, he was a complete stranger. I muttered that I was sorry and hurried away.

The following day Queen Eleanor called for me in her chamber, and when I arrived, the MacPherson Scot was standing beside her. I bowed quickly, then stood and smiled at him. He was a red-faced taciturn warrior with a sour face. How could I ever have thought he was Enoch? Because I wanted him to be, that's why.

"Lady Alix," the queen began somberly, "this is Laird Callum of Dunbar, one of your husband's clan."

"Aye, Your Majesty." Again I smiled to no effect.

Eleanor walked toward me and put her arms around me. The tension in her body alerted me.

"Is something wrong, Your Majesty?"

Her earnest green eyes probed deeply into mine. "Prepare yourself, my dear; I have bad news."

"I don't mind waiting a short time longer," I protested quickly.

"Your wait is finished, Alix. Laird Callum brought news about your husband, Enoch."

Forgetting protocol, I wrenched from her grasp and

turned to the Scot. "Is he with you in Clipstone? Oh tell me, I beg you! When will I see him?"

His flat eyes looked over my head at the queen.

"Alix," she said. "Alix, listen to me carefully. My heart breaks to be the one to inform you: Enoch is dead."

The words were foreign, sans meaning.

She held my shoulders tight. "Enoch died of a battle wound. He developed gangrene and . . ."

"No!" The queen, her chamber, everything bleached to empty outlines.

"Quick, call Bonel! She's going to faint!"

I didn't faint; I died. I spoke through an echoing hollow to the Scot. "Did you see him?"

"Aye, My Lady. Suffrit most dreadful, he did."

His voice was gravel on stone.

"When did he . . ."

Laird Callum ran a finger around the neck of his sark. "I doona knaw the date. In winter."

"You're mistaken," I said distinctly. "He wrote that it was a slight wound. He would have come if it hadn't been for winter—the wound didn't stop him."

"Are you absolutely positive, Laird Callum?" the queen asked from behind me.

"MacPhersons doona make mistakes!" he roared with sudden choler. "I sayed the mon be daid. I saw him!"

Queen Eleanor remained calm. "Even Scots can be in error, sir. Was he dead when you left him? Could he have recovered? For Lady Alix's sake, I ask again: are you certain?"

But I no longer cared for his answer. I grabbed the queen's arms. "Queen Eleanor, as you love me, I beg you, let me leave right now to go to Wanthwaite. Dugan and I can ride to Scotland and learn for ourselves what happened. This laird saw Enoch die, but Enoch is a common name. It could have been someone else."

She held my face, her eyes infinitely pitying. "My sweet

child, why destroy yourself this way? I know it's a terrible blow, but you're young, your life is still ahead . . ."

"No! No, not without Enoch!" I began to weep in long, ugly sobs. "I have no future without Enoch! Please, please . . ."

Someone else entered the room.

"Alix," the queen continued, not permitting me to wipe my eyes or nose, "you're now the king's ward and will soon have a new husband. I'll take you with me to Normandy and nurse you back to happiness. Then you'll see . . ."

"No!" I screamed. "Never! I'll never wed again! How can you be so unfeeling? Enoch . . . Enoch . . ."

I tried to run, but other hands held me. I saw Bonel.

"Bonel, help me! Explain that . . . Bonel!"

He held an oriental flask of silver filigree encrusted with round jewels like scabs.

"Bonel, you're my friend!"

He held the flask to my lips. "Drink this, Alix. It's only to calm you, but . . ."

I knocked it from his hand, tore myself from the queen and dashed to the door.

The Scot attacked me. Then I was on the floor, turning my head wildly from side to side to avoid the odious drug. The last thing I saw before finally going numb was Bonel's Christian Eye.

*7*

~~~~~~~~~~~~~~~~~~~~~~~~~~~~~~~~~~~~~~~~~~~

 ONEL'S EYE WAS A MIRROR SHARD REFLECTING the coming storm. Fat gray clouds scurried like wood lice across his blue iris; fireflash jagged like an erupting vein. Eye of the storm, storm of the eye.

"The king's second coronation here in Winchester will establish his authority once more," he explained, "and send a message to Emperor Henry that England is not a vassal state."

The first drops of rain. I closed my eyes, lifted my face, tears from Hell.

Bonel's urgent voice came close. "Alix, I know you can hear me. Why do you insist on withdrawing? I'm your friend, want to help you."

I opened my eyes and gazed into my own shadowed reflection. Clouds now rolled in gray fur balls across the sky, and the ivy on the wall behind Bonel's head rose and fell in green waves.

He moved back, sighed heavily. "Very well, I can wait. Let's return to the castle before you get soaked."

"If the king is being crowned, why aren't you there?" I asked. "Do his knights guard the gate against former Jews?"

"Jews and women," he returned, "which is why you're not there either. I'm glad to hear you speak, Alix. I've been worried. I sympathize more than I can say about Enoch, but . . ."

"I'm deaf and dumb to hypocritical pap," I interrupted angrily, "which is all I've heard for two full weeks in Nottingham or Mobray or Woodstock or here in Winchester. If you want to speak honestly, I'll listen, then reply."

<p style="text-align: center;">

120
</p>

"Is it dishonest to say I'm sorry about Enoch?"

"I don't know. Is it?"

He took my shoulders in his hands.

"After what I've told you about my loss in York, you must know how keenly I sympathize."

I pulled free. "I see no one scampering and kicking heels on Enoch's grave, but I think several would like to. He died most courteously, didn't he? Just in time for the king and queen."

"What do you mean?" He turned sharply. "Is that an accusation?"

"Soothly, it would be if the Scot hadn't seen him die. Laird Callum was a dour character, but not a liar."

"But the rest of us are? How can you be so cynical?"

"I speak only the truth—and the truth is sinister, not cynical. The king and queen never intended that I should be a hostage; now I believe that they never intended that I return to Wanthwaite. Enoch's death was their good fortune, but they would have annulled my marriage in any case. I told you that Richard wanted revenge on me. Anything else is crambo-jingle."

I waited for another denial.

"Their motive in wanting you is not sinister," he said quietly. "They've taken your castle."

"Wanthwaite?" Such a thing had never occurred to me. "They've seized my home?"

"They'll return it once the border quarrel is resolved. Richard's parley with William, King of Scots, did not go well. Scotland claimed all the castles in Northumberland and Durham based on the Canterbury Quit; Richard refused and sent an army to occupy those that couldn't defend themselves. Under the circumstances, Wanthwaite was vulnerable."

"First Enoch and now Wanthwaite? Then I have nothing." Hot tears mixed with the cold rain; for the first time I believed him. This explained the root motive of royal perfidy, why they were taking me to Normandy, which had perplexed me most sorely.

"You have the most powerful friends now living!" Bonel contradicted me. "They may not express their condolences as you would like but they sympathize, and they want to help you find a new life. You should be grateful."

"Should I be grateful to you as well?" I mocked. "Twice you've drugged and abducted me, like an Arab slave trader."

"I tried to dull your sorrow, nothing more."

"You followed the queen's order, nothing more, and she doesn't care a bean about my sorrow!"

"For a young damsel who hasn't even seen her husband for three years—and separation is the beginning of death—you rail against God's will as if you were the only wife who ever suffered. An end is a beginning, and you're young."

He had a sheep's tod where a tongue should be. This kind of cant had made me dumb in the first place. I turned abruptly to go down the hill toward the city.

Suddenly bells rang out wildly. Clarions muffled by rain blew forth, and the faint *Te Deum* rose from the Cathedral.

*Enoch is dead! Long live the king!*

WE REACHED PORTSMOUTH, there to sail to Normandy.

I wandered in the muddy streets like a cur sniffing garbage. I poked into piles of rotting foodstuffs, kicked at rusting armor, prowled among empty buildings for the town was new, constructed by Richard specifically to launch his military fleets. I ended where all streets led, by the harbor. There I counted one hundred and two ships, all heavily armed. Grunting sailors loaded war machines and round stones fore and aft, as if preparing to invade Normandy.

At the largest buss, King Richard stood indifferent to rain or wind and shouted orders in a hoarse voice. Canvas flapped in mysterious permutations behind him, making him god of war instead of the sun. Now stern, grim, angry and old, he'd shed his shining role of the last few weeks: England had been gulled, and now he could be himself.

I wandered among dockyards and storage stations, walked along the raging Solent, entered the cruciform church of Thomas à Becket, and finally returned to my quarters, drenched and chilled to the bone.

On 2 May we were ordered to sail.

This time I ran to the streets to escape and Bonel rushed after me.

"I won't go!" I shouted.

He seized one arm as a soldier grabbed the other to tug me like a recalcitrant mule to the ship.

We arrived at the dock to find Richard's captain, Alan Trenchmer, arguing that the Channel could not be crossed. He cited terrible wrecks from the past and begged the king to reconsider: he would lose time and probably his life if he attempted such a foolhardy feat. Richard listened impatiently, then ordered everyone on board at once. He would brook no more caviling, no delay. Yet we must wait. Horses —more intelligent than their masters—returned to native savagery in the face of the lashing sea. Each destrier had to be trussed in ropes and dragged up slippery planks, more than one hanging perilously over the surf before being pulled into the hold. Each owner suffered vicariously as he watched, including me with Thistle. My loyal mount's dappled sides blended with the colorless surf, and he threw his head back in a desperate effort to find me, I was sure.

"Holy Mother of God, stop!" I screamed.

For hours we watched while the sea grew ever wilder. Ships pitched dangerously back and forth, round and round, helpless against the cruel spray. Teeth bared to the wind, sailors cried into the crash and shriek around them. Yet the king insisted. Bonel and I were assigned the royal cog, the last to load, the first to sail, and the most seaworthy. Thistle and the other steeds stamped in terror in their stalls below decks. I tried to get down the steps to secure the ropes, comfort my poor beast, but I wasn't permitted.

Inching hand to hand in a human chain, depending on the sailors' strained sinews for our very lives, we couldn't stand

erect but must cling to ropes stretched in a giant net from
rail to rail. Sailors pounded side-planking against side-
planking to reinforce the rails, then daubed with pitch and
unguentum, tied cross-weaving and wattling. Finally Bonel
and I sat heavily under the forecastle where the queen was
already lashed hand and foot and were tied to giant iron
rings bolted to the boards.

Richard wove his way expertly through the rope skein
and looked down on the queen.

"Are you all right?"

"This is madness, Richard. For God's sake, wait a few
days!"

"And let Philip devour another province? God will protect
us."

As he turned, his fanatic eyes passed over me but didn't
linger.

Bonel shouted something though he was not more than a
foot away.

"Louder!"

"We should pray for his success!"

I heard snatches as he closed his eyes: *"Shem'a yisre'el
'adonoy 'elohaynu adonoy 'ehod."*

I closed my eyes and whispered two hundred Hail Marys
fervently, then switched to random songs from my mother:

> "Handsome is the yellow horse,
> When any horse will do—
> But in trouble take the creamy steed,
> Swift as a sea mew . . ."

Which had to do with charming a horse in a race on the plain
of Rhiannon where King Maelgwn lived, and I wished I had
a charred holly twig for luck.

I felt such a convulsion for my lost mother with her
cloudy hair, her sweet dimples, that I must stop.

*"Avant le hel!"* a sailor called from the dipping mast.

Men worked furiously to pull the lines taut and their slow,

inexorable activity made us ready. Canvas bellied with a sharp crack and turned us round on our anchor.

"Bowlines ready!"

"Clew lines!'

"Fast brail to the mast!" the king howled.

And we were off in a whip of ropes into the vindictive sea. For one brief moment I glanced at England, hogbacked and louring in the mist, and it was gone. Enoch—Wanthwaite—memories of my mother and father—gone. Our buss shuddered and turned helplessly, pitched on the crests and troughs of waves big as castles, no more seaworthy than a leaf.

The side-planks ripped off like rotten teeth and hurled dangerously across the deck. People struggled against one another to avoid the slashing boards. Already we were foundering. Bishops tried to lead us in prayer, but no one had stomach. Only Richard kept steady on the capricious deck, a madman riding to doom.

"Down the sail!" he shouted. "Hurry, you bastards!"

Breathing in desperate grunts, three sailors bent to the ropes. Raked with increasing fury, we would surely sink before they got the killing sail down. Everyone screamed and prayed, the queen's women sprawled helplessly in their own foamy vomit. We were chewed in the sea's maw, as salivating carious teeth rose higher and higher over our decks. I cursed the king! Damn him for his arrogance! For his indifference to anything or anybody except his own woodly ambitions! Then the huge sail collapsed, sweeping ropes, kegs, arms, everything on deck except the people with it.

Now we were riding atop chaos. Tossing, slipping up and down steeps of death, sucked faster and faster into a maelstrom. I watched the dizzy sky and the busy sea with detached wonder, for this was my last glimpse of the world. Vast, empty, angry.

"Enoch," I whispered. "Enoch."

A new sound fought the crash and shriek around us. Richard pounded a mallet on a hollow metal drum.

"Dip your blades! Row!" he shouted.

Bang! Bang! Bang!

"Heavier on the port!" he cried.

I watched his manic face in awe. Never had I seen such fanatic will.

"Dip! Pull! Dip! Pull! More to the starboard! We're almost there!"

The sea calmed. Suddenly, miraculously, tamed by the king. We'd crossed the squall, emerged safe on the other side.

Dull, streaked with slime, we stared at one another, sailor to queen, king to oarsman, Bonel to me.

"Thank God for King Richard!"

Richard was King of the Sun once more. He danced over the boards, crowed in triumph. The sky smiled—the rest of us watched dully.

Lines were painfully released for they stuck to our bloody arms; we stood only with help. Bonel unfastened my ropes.

"Let's go check on your horse, Alix."

We did. Thistle had been washed overboard.

I let fly a bellow against the odious king that overwhelmed the serene heavens and everyone within earshot! No one knew what to do with me nor I with myself, except that I was determined to plunge into the surf and rescue my horse! Twice I almost made it, dangling over the hungry sea with Bonel holding my tunic.

Later and after stiff struggling, I lay on the slimy deck and pounded with feet and fists, screaming, sobbing, laying every curse I could think of on the king's head. He was a serpent! Wicked! Selfish! A killer! He'd murdered my steed.

Lady Mamile thrust cloths under my face to catch the drippings and I pushed her away. Bonel knelt at my side, his hand on my hair.

Then the queen. "Stop her screams—the king will hear."

"Let her weep," Bonel snapped back. "She's been holding grief too long."

I shrieked that I wasn't crying for Enoch—this was for Thistle!

"She's mad," the queen judged. "A horse is replaceable."

Never! Thistle, my poor plain beast with his noble heart, such a good friend for so long, the last living remnant of my journey with Enoch. And it was my fault! I should never have permitted him to be taken—hadn't he signaled that he wanted free?—or I should have gone down to fasten his ropes. I could picture him vividly, swimming valiantly in waves that slammed him like falling houses, his mouth filling with salt, mane streaking . . .

In the forecastle, King Richard laughed heartily with his counselors, the struggle forgotten.

Again I delivered a bitter volley against him, putting it in good French so the queen should understand.

"She doesn't mean it!" Eleanor cried in shock.

Bonel was cryptic. "Of course she does."

The queen's rose perfume came close. "Ah well, Richard's shoulders are broad enough to bear her calumny, but only if he never hears about it. Keep her quiet."

Finally, exhausted, I slept.

THE FOLLOWING AFTERNOON we sighted the faint line of Normandy, but the king ordered that we put down anchor until morning, a more auspicious time for him to make his entrance.

We woke to premature summer and Queen Eleanor insisted that I don the green and gold gown again. It was most impractical since I would now be walking, but what choice did I have? Everyone was garbed as they had been in London, lacking only the furs, and the king had donned his sun-god raiment and smiles. Finally dressed and groomed, I gazed on the pretty port of Barfleur, its crescent harbor sparkling in the sun, its tiled roofs glowing pink, and hills in the distance dressed in bright green. Small barks bobbed all around us and fishermen tossed yellow blooms on the water. We were lined up to disembark as soon as the horses waited for us on the sand. The beasts, too, were spruced in silks, gold, belled bridles, and I had to blink rapidly to hold back tears for Thistle. We walked the plank in order of our rank, the lowest first, the king and queen last.

A stranger addressed me courteously. "Lady Alix of Wanthwaite?"

"Yes."

"The king offers you this mount from his royal stable."

I stared in disbelief at a magnificent war courser, a glossy cream color with mane and tail of pure snow. The set of his eyes, arch of his neck, marked him as a rare breed.

"There must be some error," I demurred. "This beast is . . ."

And I became aware of King Richard. Already mounted, he nodded and smiled. I bowed slightly in return. The king rode forward. If Thistle weren't lost, if Enoch lived, I would have gloried in this beast. Then I recalled my prayer on the ship—"a horse of cream"—and became uneasy. Nothing is accidental; the web of fate holds us all in its cast. What now? Where would this noble horse carry me?

London's crowds seemed a thin scattering compared to the solid floor of heads in Barfleur. Soothly, I could have tossed an apple in any direction and not hit the ground. Everyone wept and called to the king in French, threw yellow and white blooms.

A priest held up a bouquet, tears flowing down his face. "God has come again in his strength!"

And later a group of Norman knights in full armor, swords held high: "The lion has come—the wolf will be caught in the net of his own conniving!"

Richard threw them the bouquet he'd just taken from the prelate.

Bells rang from all over the countryside, sweet and sour, near and distant, sharing a steady cacophony of joy.

We turned northward with the tranquil sparkling sea on our left, salt flats on our right blending into orchards and thick forest. The people of Barfleur followed us for miles, chanting their approval as the gracious king turned and waved farewell.

Now we were on a forest path with only occasional clearings where black and white cows grazed in verdant fields. As the crowd dwindled, our pace increased. Soon we were moving at a canter and I marveled at the smooth stride of my new horse. What should I call him? Something significant.

Aye, the name was important, might affect my future, even as my saying that Celtic rhyme had affected my getting a cream-colored steed.

"You came from my mother's charm. I'll call you Sea Mew and we'll swim back to Wanthwaite."

BY PURPLE TWILIGHT, we rode into the narrow streets of Lisieux, again facing thousands of people who'd waited since dawn for a glimpse of Richard. Lady Mamile informed me that we were to sleep in the home of Archdeacon John of Alençon, and at last we reached a pleasant, timbered house surrounded by a spring garden.

"Lady Mamile!" I tugged on her sleeve. "I'm going to the stable to be sure my new horse is cared for properly. I'll join you soon."

"Uhhhh," she groaned, unable to look over her shoulder.

I ran back down the steps, happier than I would have thought possible two days ago. Surely it couldn't be entirely because of Sea Mew—and I throbbed anew with guilt for Thistle—but I admitted that my new steed thirled my heart strings. He was all I had to love and he was magnificent. However, the summer skies of Normandy also contributed to my sanguine humor. The dreaded journey was a *fait accompli*, my fate decided, and my liver had started to bubble again.

"Lady Alix, wait."

Bonel stepped from the shadow of the stair.

"You shouldn't go outside alone; I'll accompany you."

"Thank you."

We stepped together into the gloaming and walked to the long stable adjacent to the house where we found three boys admiring Sea Mew; they'd already cared for him like the prince that he was.

"It's good to see your spirits recovered," Bonel said as we walked back.

"Aye, I'm sorry I've been so churlish. I can't help how I feel, but I shouldn't have vented my spleen on you."

"I'm accustomed to being a scapegoat," he said dryly.

"Which reminds me, you spoke of how the king fared in Clipstone and we both know my bad fortune there, but did you prevail over Malbysse?"

"Not as I would have liked. As universal legate, the king received the duplicates, fifty-one citizens were fined three hundred forty-two marks for complicity. Among the leaders, Bishop Hugh was stripped of his title in Northumberland for other reasons, but Malbysse and fellow scoundrels went free. However, the king hasn't forgotten their treason; we'll continue to work."

We entered the house again, and I asked shyly if Bonel would talk a bit; I wasn't ready to go to my bed. As we sat at a trestle, loud shouting in the courtyard interrupted us and the door banged open. A short, plump swagger of a man confronted us rudely.

"Is King Richard in residence?"

Bonel stood. "Who asks?"

"His brother, Prince John."

"He's in his royal chambers."

"Louvecaire, announce me!"

A mercenary captain bounded up the stairs and along the upper corridor as John paced. He didn't look at Bonel again, but he paused to stare at me. When he began to walk, I studied him as well. What a revolting figure, with his soft cod, pouched eyes, full wet lips, casual movements of his hand toward his crotch. He was far from regal, but he exuded royal vanity if not authority, a popinjay of a prince.

"You can come, Your Highness," Louvecaire called from the top step.

John straightened his tunic and waddled upward.

"So you've now seen the infamous John," Bonel commented grimly, "a man so noisome that buzzards avoid him."

"I don't understand why the king gives him an audience. Or the queen. I should think that he belongs with the prisoners in Nottingham after that letter he wrote to Emperor Henry and his insurrection in England."

Bonel agreed. "I'm sure that Richard wishes he could throw him in a dungeon, but he has to consider the kingdom's weal."

He went on about John's army which could be turned over to Philip, about split loyalties in England. "Most important, John is the only acceptable heir to the throne."

"You call him acceptable?"

Bonel shrugged. "Would you prefer the boy Arthur of Brittany? Already so diabolic of character that rumors spread that he was born with a tail and yellow eyes."

I couldn't answer.

"Unless, of course, the king produces his own heir."

I glanced at Bonel to see if he were japing. Richard was attracted to no woman, but least of all to his queen, Berengaria. As I recalled, he actively shuddered and drew back when she passed close. Certainly, they'd never consummated their marriage. Bonel met my eyes innocently, yet I could swear that there was particular significance in his look.

Then John appeared at the top of the steps again, his face now wreathed in jovial smiles.

"Sorry to break your tryst," he said jubilantly. "I'm to be served a fresh salmon here."

He sat on the bench opposite Bonel and me.

"You can help me celebrate my reinstatement."

"Congratulations, Your Highness," Bonel said with heavy sarcasm.

John's smirk acknowledged the tone, but he continued to grin. "I'm only a babe, you see, too close to the swaddling board to know how the wicked Philip influences me. So, if I just take Évreux from France—which should be easy, since I gave it to Philip in the first place—I'll be the hope of England again. Louvecaire, order wine for my friends! Tell me your names so we can toast."

"Bonel of Rouen, the king's man, and this is Lady Alix of Wanthwaite, the king's marriage ward."

John emitted a great guffaw. "So I'm to drink with a Jew at my restoration! That's rich. If I ever get wine, that is. Louvecaire!"

"Bonel is a converted Christian," I said with asperity. "Notice his cross."

"Aha, the peach can talk. Don't defend a lost cause, darling. What did you say your name was?"

Bonel answered for me. "Lady Alix of . . ."

"Yes, the king's marriage prize. Or does he bed you himself?"

"Sir, watch your words," Bonel warned.

John winked at me. "If you have lands to go with your tits, you'll make some man very happy."

He reached across the table and thrust his hand into my cleavage.

I slapped his exploring fingers with all my strength, which brought more laughter. Then Bonel whipped his cross, and laughter ceased.

"What the Devil?" John gazed in astonishment at his bleeding hand, then rose in outrage, reached for his sword.

"John!" Richard stood at the top of the stair, his face visored in wrath.

"Your Jew wounded me, My Liege," John whined. "I was defending myself!"

"Bonel protects Alix at my orders," the king replied coldly. "Now come to my chamber. Your salmon will be served upstairs, and I must talk to you about Évreux."

John left without argument, but the king remained.

"Thank you, Bonel."

"I fear my cross has a rough edge, Your Majesty."

"A Saracen edge with hidden point." Richard smiled gently at me. "Lady Alix, I suggest that you retire soon. You ride tomorrow to Fontevrault where I hope the tranquillity will heal your recent sorrow." His tone expressed sympathy, his first acknowledgment of Enoch's death.

"Thank you, Your Majesty." I bowed my head.

When I looked up, Richard was gone and Bonel rose to his feet.

"The king's right; you should rest."

"Where's Fontevrault?"

"In the south. An abbey where the queen often retires and where she prepares the king's wards for their future assignments." He hesitated. "I'm sure you'll like it. As the king said, it's tranquil, and your instruction should be superb."

"Are you coming too?"

He laughed with sudden joy. "No, I'm returning to Rouen—to my own life. This is farewell for a time."

He pressed my hand and departed. I didn't move, surprised at my reluctance to see him go. Our relationship had hardly been smooth, but except for the poppy Bonel had been courteous, and he was my self-proclaimed protector. Even more, now that Thistle was dead, Bonel was my last link to Wanthwaite.

I dragged up the steps, passed the king's chamber where loud voices argued battle strategy, and found my mat in the queen's quarters. Tranquil Fontevrault, but it could hardly be tranquil for me if I were to be assigned a new husband.

A new husband to live where? Wanthwaite was my dowry as well as my home, the reason John had called me a "marriage prize" with "lands to go with my . . ." Without

Wanthwaite, who would want me? Was I to be assigned to some rough mercenary, perhaps, and be sent to a foreign land? Be given to one of Richard's loyal, but landless soldiers? To live a brutal, penurious existence?

No, I couldn't bear it. My sensibilities, my pride, everything I valued and yearned for argued against such a fate. My recently acquired sanguine humor flowed away as if through a sieve. *I must not marry.*

But how could I avoid it?

# BOOK TWO

# COURTLY LOVE

*If I sit here in this state
of mind and find I'm hoisted up
to ambiguity's rack,
by this girl who tortures me, who
keeps me in balance,
forward, backward, back, but toward
her with just the final weight,
it is that with soft savour
she primes her hook,
using soft words for bait.*

*This love of mine
loves to complicate things—
It'd take an engineer to ravel them out.
It's with unworthy desire, estrangement,
knockdown and drag-out
that love repays lovers who are over desirous.*

—MARCABRU, TWELFTH CENTURY

8

〜〜〜〜〜〜〜〜〜〜〜〜〜〜〜〜〜〜〜〜〜

*O viridissima virga ave
que in ventoso flabo sciscitationis
sanctorum prodisti.*

OD HAS BROUGHT ME TO FONTEVRAULT. I cross its threshold with deep emotion."

Gone were all signs of cynicism; Eleanor's voice trembled, her eyes swam with tears as she embraced Abbess Matilda at the entrance of the abbey. Following her tall swaying figure through the portals, even her ladies were awed, as if each was being metamorphosed to something new and strange. Indeed, Fontevrault was an enchanted land with its mellow tiled buildings set in its flowery park, the sound of birds mingling with voices raised in lyric worship, fragrance of honey and hum of bees. A place of sublime tranquillity, as King Richard had said.

At my own request, I was permitted to sleep in a dorter with the nuns. I eyed my narrow pointed board with satisfaction; I might have to sleep with my feet crossed, like an effigy on a tomb, but I was entering the holy life. If I didn't want a husband to spirit me away to some remote fort, this was my best alternative. Although there were many nuns in the room when I arrived, no one spoke or even seemed to notice me. When they formed a line at the door, I joined them and marched in silence to the refectory where we had bread and milk, then to the chapel for Vespers, a long sermon with much repeating of psalms, questions and responses. I fell to my narrow perch exhausted and pleased that I'd made a good beginning.

Only to be rudely awakened by a violent shaking. Bells were ringing Matins, and again the nuns were forming a line. I was just beginning to wake when I went back to bed. Three hours later, the same horse-faced nun woke me again for Lauds, then another three hours until Prime and the day began with more prayers. No one else seemed tired, so I set my jaw and prayed silently to Our Lady for the power to sleep in three-hour increments.

Breakfast was bread and milk again. After our long ride the day before and the meager supper, I quietly sneaked an extra piece of bread under my skirt, promising Our Lady that I wouldn't do it again—I would learn to love hunger.

Groggily I stumbled at the end of the line which wound through gardens and past pretty houses to a tiled edifice called the chapter house. Here I met the queen's party and Lady Mamile informed me that we were to hear the business of the day. I sat beside her on a bench in the front and tried to be alert. The Abbess Matilda, a kind-faced, handsome woman, conducted the meeting about grants, leases, rents and I know not what because I drowsed in my upright position. Then Lady Mamile gave me a sharp poke; guiltily I blinked and smiled, but no one had noticed that I slept. Lady Mamile wanted me to see a trial.

A small brown-skinned nun with a withered frightened face stood before the abbess; next to her was the nun who woke me. My nun, her pale eyes blazing, her skin mottled with excitement, lips trembling, muttered some long, complicated accusation I couldn't understand, followed by dialogue between the accused and the abbess mixed with many prayers. Abbess Matilda called for a novice named Agnes; a girl no more than nine or ten, to judge by her breasts and teeth, walked forward. Nevertheless young Agnes towered over the brown nun, and her muscles strained the seams of her tunic; she was all brawn. The brown nun knelt; Agnes took a leather whip and struck her back relentlessly thirty times that I counted. The accusing nun's tongue flicked in rhythm to the lashes.

When the punishment ended, the horse-faced nun turned and looked directly into my eyes, her tongue now quiet but still lolling on her nether lip. My heart froze—I thought of the bread resting in the folds of my skirt. Had I committed a sin against God? I promised Our Lady fervently to drop the odious crust at first opportunity and my prayer must have been answered because the dreadful nun smiled slightly and said naught.

Therefore I was free of sin, but more hungry than ever, when we walked in file to the refectory. The Abbess Matilda, sitting next to our smiling queen, picked up a book and began to read. I kept my hands away from the baskets of bread, pinched my thighs viciously to stay awake and tried to listen to the long tale of how the abbey was founded by a monk called Robert D'Abrissol. He had wandered hither and yon looking for the perfect spot for his abbey and so forth—then suddenly I listened in earnest. Had I heard aright? This Robert D'Abrissol was convinced that women were superior to men and that they were much abused in our society, even the greatest ladies. Therefore he'd created Fontevrault ". . . for even such ladies have no refuge against beatings and rejection. We shall make our establishment suitable for them, however, by housing each lady according to her rank."

Could it be true? Had such a man ever lived? Eleanor's rapt face convinced me. I looked along the rows; all faces were equally enthralled. These women then had once been wives or unwanted daughters or . . .

"A concubine," Lady Mamile whispered, pointing to a drab lady at the end. "Discarded by King Philip."

A lady of love—I stared with interest at her stolid profile

and wondered when the rule of silence would be lifted, for I would like to ask all these ladies whence they came and why. In any case I could take comfort in the knowledge that their primary reason was not a religious calling, but refuge, the same as mine, though they all seemed happy now in the holy life. If a concubine could become a nun, why not me? Again I prayed silently to Our Lady, who immediately tested my sincerity by placing my least favorite vegetable before me—turnips, prepared in a watery mash. Holding my breath, I dipped my bread in the ferrous ooze and ate.

After dinner, the nuns went to their appointed duties for "Idleness is the enemy of the Soul." Queen Eleanor and Abbess Matilda approached me where I stood uncertainly by the door; together they had decided that I would work under the guidance of Sister Hilaria, the novice mistress.

"She isn't here because she's fasting," said the abbess, but I'll take you to her. She goes to the fields for solitude."

I bowed to the queen and thanked her, then followed the abbess, my head pounding most grievously from an approaching megrim and my cod protesting the turnips. The noon sun beat unmercifully.

"You'll like Sister Hilaria, Lady Alix," the abbess said without missing a step. "She's a remarkable woman, a true *religieuse*."

A small frisson pierced the heat.

"I'm sure I shall."

"She noticed you in the chapter house and asked for you particularly."

My heart sank. The nun who woke me, who'd testified against the brown nun, then guessed uncannily that I hid the bread. *Benedicite*.

"There she is!" Abbess Matilda said, pointing to a figure kneeling in prayer.

To my great relief, Sister Hilaria was a stranger and appeared at first glance more a stout peasant than a *religieuse*. She rose when she saw us, a big lumpy boulder clad in rough sackcloth, topped by a small round head and a face like a peeled apricot. Sun-bleached lashes fringed wide startled eyes and her dry lips cracked in the stretch of her smile. She had teeth like gray pearls and only two were missing.

When she approached us, we were smitten by the stench of pigs. Was it possible that she worked as a swineherd?

"Lady Alix, welcome," she greeted me in a voice close to laughter. "I've been hoping you would be assigned to me."

"Thank you, Sister."

"I sense in you a gift for God's love. It shone in your eyes this morning in the chapter house."

My heart thirled. The Blessed Lady had heard my prayers, and this talented nun had recognized my religious desire.

"And smoke rises from your loins."

"Soothly?" I tried to shift away from her noxious fumes to test myself. Perhaps a spark had fallen on my tunic to give the impression of smoke; no, I could smell nothing, but I trusted the sister's nose more than my own.

After Abbess Matilda left us, Sister Hilaria, grinning broadly, took my arm and suggested we go find her dear friend and former novitiate, Sister Damiana, who now was a cellaress.

"She supervises the home farm and may be in the garden by the river."

I followed her purposeful sway, noting that she swung her arms back and forth in front of her instead of at the sides, planted her feet in two lines as if straddling a bean row. We discovered Sister Damiana on the verge of the Vienne staring at another abbey on the far side. I was instantly impressed by her person with its transparent delicacy, her sweet wild face. Dressed in the same rough cloth as Sister Hilaria, she wore her garment proudly, moved with light elegance; her face was dark, her eyes smouldering black jewels, her lips plum-pulp. Sister Hilaria kissed her, then introduced me.

Awed by her ascetic beauty, I almost bowed.

"We noted you in the meeting," she said softly. "You're fortunate to be selected by Sister Hilaria."

Speechless at my good fortune, guilty for fooling these kind women, for soothly I didn't deserve to be selected, I leaned close to Sister Hilaria as she pointed to low buildings of the far side of the Vienne.

"That's our sister institution, a Benedictine monastery of St. John, which we govern in all matters, since women are better administrators than men. Of course we never see the brothers."

Taking a deep breath of her armpit, I almost choked. "Except when a priest conducts a Mass, or for confessions," Sister Damiana added, her cheeks faintly magenta.

I couldn't stop staring at the beauteous nun. Was she an abused wife? Or discarded? If I were a man, I would take her as a concubine.

"Oh, I've seen a few of the monks when I come to study the river," Sister Hilaria boomed out. "I'm composing a treatise on the power of waters, Alix, as a manifestation of the Heavenly Spirit."

"Except that her work may be lost because she can't write," Damiana mourned.

"How does a river manifest God?" I asked.

Sister Hilaria waxed enthusiastic. Salt water was venomous and full of worms—and I vowed to study the sea more carefully when I had opportunity—and southern waters made men fat and black. All water should be boiled before drinking, with which I could agree since Bonel said the same. Rivers came from the sea, God's heart, and like veins in the body carried His wonders to all the lands.

"Oh no, Sister Hilaria," I contradicted. "Look at the current."

"This knowledge came to me in a heavenly vision," she said pleasantly, "and can't be refuted."

"But all rivers flow to the sea," I argued, sure of my facts. "Look at the Seine, the Thames . . ."

"Evidence of the eye deceives, God's Revelation never." There was no rebuke, just sweet conviction.

Her sweating freckled face was transformed with unearthly ecstasy as she gazed at the trickle before us, definitely headed toward the sea. I stared until my eyes bleared, trying to make it reverse direction, then I closed my stubborn eyes and prayed to Our Lady.

"Sister Hilaria has had visions since the age of five," Sister Damiana explained breathlessly. "If you will open your heart to her teachings, you may experience heavenly visitations of your own. That's how I began."

I shook my head. "I'd like to, but I don't have the gift."

Again I was pulled into Sister Hilaria's armpit, which seemed a little less rancid, perhaps because it was her other arm, and she stroked my bare head most kindly. "Of course you will, child. Your gift is love; you are filled with love. You must learn to give it to Christ, that's all."

Sister Damiana put her arm around me as well, so we stood like a single figure, our own tight trinity under the blazing sun.

"Trust Sister Hilaria," Damiana whispered. "Her love encompasses the universe."

Tears came to my eyes. How I yearned to please them, to be worthy; until this moment I hadn't realized my own loneliness, my desolation. I was grateful to the queen for bringing me to this marvelous place, though I quickly prayed to Our Lady above for I could see that my coming was no accident of fate, but God's will.

Our magic moment was interrupted by the call of the bell. Sister Damiana's movement contrasted sharply to Sister Hilaria's solid thump; she walked forward reluctantly as if tugged by something behind her and her eyes moved from side to side. If she were a horse, she would require blinders.

"Are all your visions about Nature?" I asked Sister Hilaria shyly.

"I have a modicum of the natural sciences," she replied modestly, "but my true gift is my direct intercourse with

the loving God. My love wins the kingly kiss, brings me to
a bed of exquisite joy where God and I unite."

*Benedicite.*

"Do you share that kind of vision?" I asked Sister Damiana.

"I can't pretend the same marvels, but in a small way,
yes."

"Go to," Sister Hilaria chided. "Tell your last vision to
Lady Alix."

"I felt pricking in my heart and loins, then a mighty voice:
'On you falls the dew of heaven; the Holy Ghost sows His
seed in you.' "

Her vision sounded familiar, but I must be wrong. Again
my heart thirled. Was it possible that I would ever know
such ecstasy?

As if she read my wish, Sister Hilaria placed her slab-
hand on my arm. "You, too, will have visions one night,
Alix. Do you ever dream?"

"Aye," I admitted, politely refraining from pointing out
that to dream it was necessary to sleep. Or perhaps it wasn't;
perhaps these visions came in a waking state. "Do you do
something special first? Is there a prayer?"

Sister Damiana smiled furtively. "Don't feel impelled to
dream, Alix. God will move when He's ready. Meantime,
listen to Sister Hilaria each morning and try to remember
her visions. We must all try to memorize them, or they'll be
lost to posterity."

"Why don't I write them for you?" I asked Sister Hilaria.

Both women stopped on the path.

"You can write?"

"In the Latin tongue?"

"Aye." Flattered by their stunned expressions, I added
humbly: "I'm no scribe, don't know fancy letters, but my
hand can be read."

"They can teach you in the scriptorium," Sister Damiana
said firmly. "They can't argue that you should be occupied

with the Psalters because you're not part of the order. You're free to be Sister Hilaria's personal clerk."

Sister Hilaria's pale flecked eyes shone like deniers. "God moves in mysterious ways. He told me to approach you for His Purpose—you see? Oh, Alix, you're in God's hands whether you know it or not."

I believed her. Hadn't He led me to her? I could see that she was immersed in a deep communication with Our Lord now as she stood, transfixed, and I tried to reach Him as well, to no effect. It will take patience, I thought; many are called but few are chosen. I'd been called—that was enough for one day.

THEREAFTER I LABORED in the scriptorium every afternoon, scrupulously recording Sister Hilaria's vision of the night before, every day improving my elongated tails on letters, the forms that reflected the architecture of Fontevrault. I saw little of the queen, nor did I want to. The visions entranced me.

"God's love binds my blood and bone," I wrote to Hilaria's dictation. "His vapor enters my heart, His liquid my loins, and I am His forever. His love is a mad spasm . . ."

I lifted my stylus. "Do you see Him? What does He look like?"

Her eyes were closed. "He's a dark shadow, a substance, a sweet weight on every part of me. Oh, Alix . . ."

The ecstasy etched on her plain face moved me profoundly, made me determined to experience it myself. Each night I tried, by prayer, by torturing myself with pinches and scratches, by staying awake or by sleeping. I fought despair at my failure. Was it possible that Sister Hilaria was mistaken about my character? Perhaps my role in religion was simply to be a scribe for someone else's visions but to have none of my own.

I grew to love Sister Hilaria's stench, the brush of her dry lips against mine, her infinite kindness and attention. I also

grew possessive and resentful of her duties, for all the nov-
ices worshipped her and followed her as ruthlessly as a col-
umn of ants. When she wasn't available, I turned to Sister
Damiana. Her visions, though frequent and vivid, moved
me differently than Sister Hilaria's. I listened but didn't
copy as she chanted.

"He called me His sweet thing, His handmaiden of ecstasy, the stone in His sling, and His spear entered my . . .
heart."

Her thin face convulsed; then she controlled herself and
asked if I'd yet had my own visions.

"No." I fought weak tears.

It occurred to me that perhaps I didn't have enough privacy. After all, God didn't speak to them when they were
in a crowd; both sisters sought solitude in long walks. One
afternoon after I'd finished in the scriptorium, I rushed to
the stable and saddled Sea Mew, then skirted the far edges
of Fontevrault to find privacy.

The long twilight had begun when I detected Sister Damiana where she walked on the river's edge below me. I
jumped to the ground and hurried to greet her, but then
stopped short. A shadow preceded me, came from a bush
and wrapped Damiana in his arms. A monk!

I rushed forward to aid her, but saw just in time that she
didn't resist his advances. With shortened breath and painful
heartbeats, I watched as they tore at each other's robes in a
frenzy of desire, kissed and kissed again, fifty-four kisses
before they fell to the ground and he mounted her. Afraid
to move, ashamed to watch but unable to control myself, I
sat very quietly until they finished. Yet it was still a long
time after that before Damiana walked sedately away. She
passed close, but her usual preoccupation kept her from
noticing me.

I then watched the monk push a small bark across the
river.

Dazed, I tried to absorb the significance of the scene, but

couldn't shake myself from a thralled trance of sensation. My hands trembled, I swallowed and licked my lips, and I was too weak to mount my horse. Gradually I was able to see the seriousness of the situation. *Deus juva me*, what should I do? My main concern was that Sister Damiana shouldn't be caught and punished, or perhaps sent from the convent. I now knew that the nun who'd testified against the brown nun on the first day was called Sister Ursula, a most repugnant and dangerous woman. If she should learn . . .

I agonized over the problem all the way back to the abbey, wondered if Sister Hilaria knew, decided she didn't. Since I wasn't a nun, I wasn't compelled to tell anyone, and I wouldn't—unless it was to warn Sister Damiana herself to be more careful. Then I vowed to follow the love-smitten sister and guard her as best I could. If anyone approached during a tryst, I would speak in a loud tone to alert the lovers.

In turmoil and hardly able to meet Sister Damiana's eyes during supper and Vespers, I went to bed in agitation, my fantastick cells racing. The nuns around me fell into a chorus of snores; in the cloister a nightingale began to sing. The moon cast eerie shadows through the foliated windows, and I hummed under my breath with the bird. I crossed my legs for comfort, turned on my stomach, but the hard board hurt my breasts until I cupped them in my hands. My heart pounded so hard that I thought it would wake someone. I must sleep—it was almost Matins. The song grew louder . . .

The next day I couldn't wait to find Sister Hilaria.

"Sister, you were right!" I cried. "God sent me a vision!"

Her face was transfixed. "Tell me!"

I could hardly get the words out. "The shadow entered with a frenzied fit into my bower of bliss! Worked my jewel with His heavenly tool, hurt me with His craving, wrought the gold inside me to His own likeness!"

"Beautiful!"

She kissed me most sweetly.

I could have screamed with joy! It was so easy to have visions once you gave yourself to God. I had them every night thereafter.

"WAKE UP, sweet Alix, it's time to pray."

I buried my head under my arm and snuggled deeper into my dorter.

"Our Lady awaits you in the choir."

"I'm sick," I grucched feebly. "I'll pray on the next hour."

"What is your infirmity, child?"

"My great toe throbs unmercifully."

Gentle fingers reached for my ribs and I convulsed in laughter.

"Come, I'll help you hobble to our service."

Sister Hilaria tugged me from my board and forced me to stand. With eyes half-closed, I smelled more than saw her, a sweet stench, half rancid, half spicy, which I now loved as ambrosia. She hugged me furtively and we walked slowly toward the tolling bell of Fontevrault Chapel.

Sweet female voices chorused in summer air laden with jasmine. From afar other bells rang: the chapel at St. John's, a lesser toll from the lazar house beyond the orchard where the women lepers lived, and a bare clink from the tiny prostitutes' chapel where reformed whores were given sanctuary.

"Sanctuary," that was the proper word for Fontevrault, not "tranquillity." Never had I lived anywhere so exciting. Tranquillity was the ideal to be sure, but the congregation of divers female passions guaranteed constant drama. I loved Fontevrault.

More, I loved Sister Hilaria.

I loved the scrape of her skirt on the gravel path where she walked in front of me, loved the waddle of her ample hips, her deep bosom, her twinkling Celtic eyes. I deliberately swayed my own backside, hunched my shoulders in devotion, planted my feet to punish the ground, practiced crinkling my eyes in mirth.

We entered the nave of the chapel, always an awesome experience but never more so than at this hour. Through large, arched windows a saffron moon floated low on the black horizon; narrow lavender columns reached for heaven, and candles cast golden circles in the greater circle of the choir.

Sister Hilaria was right; we were late. We slipped in at the back as Abbess Matilda conducted the prayer in her strong singsong voice. Queen Eleanor and her ladies knelt in the front row, close to the effigy of King Henry II, who slept in ironic tranquillity at his queen's feet, the only male permitted in our nunnery; he'd gained acceptance through death, for Eleanor couldn't abide him alive.

Sister Hilaria reached for my hand, which she placed under her robe. "You are sweet as the grape," she whispered, "fragrant as balsam, bright as the sun."

I knew she addressed Our Lady, but the pressure of her fingers made her message personal as well, and my heart leaped in religious ecstasy. Yet as the hour droned on, I dozed through her whispers. Day and night blurred in an extended yawn as I fought to stay awake.

Sister Hilaria pinched my wrist to wake me at the finish of the service. I rose to watch the queen walk by, then meekly followed. Outside, red dawn spread behind the eastern wood and the nuns scattered to their appointed chores. Eleanor stood on the path waiting for me.

"Lady Alix, if you please." Then, courteously, "Don't let me detain you from your duties, Sister Hilaria."

I watched the nun's gray habit as she strode to the scriptorium.

"Lady Alix."

Belatedly I bowed. "Your Majesty."

"I'm told that you haven't appeared for your fittings."

I spread my haircloth skirt. "I had the sister make me a tunic more fitting for my station, Your Majesty."

"What is your station?" Voice alert.

I flushed with pleasure. "I help Sister Hilaria in the scriptorium, which is dirty labor because of the inks and paints."

Should I say more? No, this was not an opportune moment; wait, at least, until the queen had supped and was in more receptive humor.

"Yes, I noticed a similarity in your odors. I would like to hear more of your occupation. Come to my house after Haute Tierce and talk with me."

I bowed, smiling to myself. As Sister Hilaria told me every day, if you aspire to holiness, God will provide the way. I'd wanted to talk to Eleanor for at least two weeks.

When the queen had passed, I hurried to the scriptorium. After their labors over Psalters, the nuns were dismissed for dinner, and Sister Hilaria and I knelt again, hand in hand, as both of us were fasting. For me this was the prime moment of the day, for Sister repeated a new prayer from her visions of the night before.

> "I can dance only if You lead me,
> With You I leap joyfully,
> I leap for love
> From love to knowledge,
> From knowledge to conception,
> From conception beyond all sense
> Into the circle of your arms."

A frisson shook me from head to foot, and tears came to my eyes. She turned her exalted face, leaned forward and kissed my wet cheek.

Most of the nunnery slept by the time I made my slow way to the queen's house; she had been given her own small palace on the abbey grounds, in deference to her greatness and her donations over many years. From afar I heard a woman screaming, then the queen's angry voice, more screaming. Intrigued, I hastened my pace.

"You don't seem to hear me! I love him!"

All screams tend to sound alike but I thought I knew that voice. I pulled the bell.

Lady Sybelle opened the door and cautioned with a motion to her lips that I should be quiet. Her bagged hazel eyes sparkled with youthful glee, and she took me by the arm to lead me to the queen's chamber, where all the ladies were watching a drama unfold.

The shriek came from Queen Joanna, Eleanor's youngest daughter and my companion—though she wouldn't remember me—on the Crusade. Now in high fettle, she was more beautiful than ever, virtually Richard's female counterpart, but I recalled her voice as low and throaty. When I entered with Lady Sybelle, she burst into sobs.

"Take me to Richard—he'll understand. You're too old and too bitter to sympathize with love."

The queen's steely eyes gazed over Joanna's golden head to Lady Toquerie; both women shrugged. Then she looked again at her wretched daughter.

"Fortunately, my infirmities don't extend to my ears; suppose you tell me what attracts you to Count Raymond of Toulouse, although he's much your junior and has been married thrice before, is married at this moment, I believe."

"You were married when you met father," Joanna flashed, "and he was ten years younger than you!"

I slid next to Lady Mamile whose lips were parted in delight.

Queen Eleanor remained calm. "Eleven years, my dear, and remember the putrification of that union which ended in my own imprisonment. My spies inform me that all of Raymond's former wives now dwell in towers, stripped of their lands and dowers."

"Because he didn't love them!" Joanna shouted.

"I would hope not. And does he love you?"

For the first time Joanna faltered. "He will, if you make him get rid of that cow from Bourguignon."

"His present wife?"

Joanna grew more confused as she tried to clarify Raymond's passions. She, Queen Berengaria and the Princess of Cyprus had returned home from the Holy Land, and they'd met the handsome Raymond in Toulouse. In their company as well was the Lady of Bourguignon; the count had been smitten by Bourguignon—and sent his present wife to a remote tower—and Joanna had been smitten by Raymond. While he was between wives—and before the Bourguignon affair could be made legitimate—Joanna wanted to seek him as a husband.

She ranted on and on about love as the ladies made moues at one another and rolled their eyes.

"Joanna, you're overwrought," Eleanor said. "Please cease this unseemly caterwauling as if you were a maid of twelve and behave with dignity. You've had sufficient training to know that your arguments have no weight whatsoever; I have nothing against love, contrary to your opinion, but love is irrelevant to the marriage contract. Personally, I would hate to see you committed to such a grievous union, but there are political arguments in its favor if you insist. I promise to speak to the Great One."

Great One was her name for Richard.

"No!" Joanna screamed, forgetting her former demand to see him. "Richard's off fighting, and by the time he returns, it may be too late. You can do it!"

"He'll be in Chinon within a few days. Please retire now, and think upon the gravity of your proposals."

Joanna started to protest, then collapsed before Eleanor's hard face. She ran into me as she rushed from the chamber, but didn't bother to apologize.

The queen emitted a long sigh and shrugged her shoulders at her court. But she hadn't forgotten me. Within three heartbeats, her pear-shaped face was curled in smiles and she opened her arms.

After she'd kissed me, she wrinkled her nose. "Ah, the stench of sanctity. You must tell me about your new vocation, Alix."

"Aye, Your Majesty," I said eagerly. "My heart is so full of joy that I can't sleep at nights." Which was not exactly true, but I hoped it would be. "Sister Hilaria is teaching me how to reach perfection."

"A most worthy goal," the queen approved. "Can you enlighten me as to her methods?"

"Well, I can never be a virgin again, but absolute chastity in widowhood is the next best state, so naturally I've vowed to be celibate."

I was aware of sudden significant silence. My vow countermanded Eleanor's plan to find me a husband, I knew, but surely she couldn't deny a religious calling.

"That's most interesting," she said dryly. "You sound like my daughter Berengaria."

"Oh no!" Then I blushed. Richard's wife, Berengaria, was deeply devout, I knew, but I'd never seen any sign of the ecstasy I felt. Besides, she wasn't a widow.

"No?" Her brows raised. "Ladies, we have a convert in our midst. Suppose we seek some quiet place where Alix can confide her innermost feelings. What say you to taking our dinner away from the abbey tomorrow?"

"I'll make the arrangements," Lady Toquerie said quickly.

Lady Faydide added wistfully, "Perhaps we can find a bit of flesh; I yearn for good meat."

"If we take our repast by a stream, we could fish," Lady Mamile suggested.

"Or even bathe," the queen finished, sniffing delicately of my person.

I'd vowed never to bathe again, but remained prudently silent on the subject. The arrangement was marred by the presence of Eleanor's ladies, a garrulous lot, but it gave me the opportunity to announce my intention to become a nun. Already I anticipated an argument, but I was determined to prevail.

THE OLD LADIES LAUGHED, struck wildly at fruit flies, hiked skirts in the heat to reveal pale, black-veined legs. Lady Florine burst into deep, guttural song.

> "I must hold my knight
> Naked in my arms
> So he may suck the honey
> From my seeping breasts;
> I swear I love him more
> Than Floris does Blanchefleur
> And I give him my heart,
> My lips, my mind, my sable tunnel."

Wincing at the licentious blast, the raucous cackle from the others, I tried to concentrate on the pure utterance of Sister Hilaria early this morning:

> "Lovely rose on the thorn,
> Pure dove in your being,
> Glorious sun on your course,
> From you I can never turn away . . ."

And she'd kissed my lips most sweetly.

"Go on, Florine," Lady Faydide demanded angrily, "and this time have the courage to name your sucking swain. Enough years have passed."

Florine grinned at her obvious jealousy, apparently an old rancor.

> "Fair friend, muscle and sinew,
> When will I enthrall you in my chamber?
> Lie soft body to hard
> And open my lips to you?

> I will give and do all,
> Yearn for you rather than my husband,
> But only if you do
> Everything love desires!"

Again the unbecoming hoots from these withered hags, except that Florine wasn't withered; she was round and porous as a mushroom. I was offended both by the sentiment and the source. These women should be looking to God at their age—as I was even at mine. I retreated into my own fantastick cells as the women blethered on about adulterous love in which all apparently had engaged at one time.

Then another argument ensued: should we turn up a brown sluggish tributary of the Vienne or go on a little farther. The queen voted, and we turned. We rode through splashing bogs disguised by marsh grass, across islands of blossoming meads where yellow cuckooflowers scraped our stirrups and hyacinths made Lady Sybelle sneeze. The queen led us to a glade of poppies and silver-backed greensward; now the stream ran sparkling as wine over a weir and into a deep, clear pool.

"Oh, ducks!" squealed Lady Mamile.

We all ran to the shallows above the weir to see six large, brown ducks floating with heads tucked under their wings, apparently asleep except that each had a beady eye exposed.

"As in Scripture, they let God be their rudder," Lady Toquerie said solemnly.

Pleased at her wisdom, I moved closer to her.

"Yes, if God lives in webbed feet," the queen pointed out acidly, "for they're paddling against the current."

The others laughed and I moved away.

Amaria put our wine flasks in water, and the ladies spread themselves upon the grass.

"Come closer, Alix," the queen called. "We want to hear about your inspiration."

Rheumy eyes turned expectantly. I sank on my knees a

few feet from the queen, far enough to avoid comments on my personal odor.

"Why do you bind your hair like that?" Mamile asked.

"And wear that gray rag?" Sybelle added.

The queen stopped them with an imperious hand. "Alix didn't come to defend herself. Amaria, give us each a cup of the red—it doesn't have to be cold—so we may listen in comfort. Go on, dear; tell us in your own way."

She insisted that I imbibe with them as well; the wine was sweet and went instantly to my head—I'd fasted for two days.

"I want to be a nun," I blurted.

From the shocked expressions, one would think I'd declared I wanted to be a whore.

The queen's eyes were viscous tourmaline. "Continue. You don't want to marry?"

I shuddered in the hot sun. "Saint Paul writes that if widowed we should stay like him, that is, celibate."

"He also says that it's better to marry than to burn with passion," Toquerie rejoined sharply.

I'd forgotten that she was the queen's expert on the Scripture.

"But I don't burn," I informed her. *Deo gratias* that I wasn't Sister Damiana.

Sybelle added vaguely, "I think our own rule was that, when a lover dies, the lady should be a widow for two years."

"Exactly," Eleanor concurred. "I planned for you to remain unmarried for two years."

"Two years?" I repeated giddily. I felt relieved—grateful even—though it shouldn't matter if I became a nun. "No, I'll never marry. The only reason to do so according to Father Tertullian would be foul lust."

The crones hooted in derision and made japes in langue d'oc, which fortunately I don't understand.

Lady Mamile wiped mirthful tears. "Oh, Alix, how blithe

your humor, for when you reach our age you'll know that the purpose of life is to spread an erotic net and take whatever fish you pull therein. My only regret is that I caught so few."

"Few!" snorted Toquerie. "You were a fornicating fool until you reached sixty."

"I'm barely sixty now," Mamile retorted haughtily.

More laughter and the argument was lost.

"I'm hot," Faydide announced crossly. "May we take off our boots?"

Suede and velvet shoes were quickly thrown into the bush as the ladies wiggled gnarled toes.

"Go on, Alix," the queen said.

"Furthermore, one can't serve the Lord in his Second Coming if burdened with a husband . . ."

"I meant, take off your shoes."

Reluctantly I tugged on my leather boots. The relief to my hot swollen feet was instantaneous, but even in my religious state I was embarrassed by the sweetish fumes thereby released. Two ladies discreetly moved away.

The queen remained close. "Is that why you affect a slovenly appearance? To avoid marriage?"

"Partly," I admitted. "Tertullian instructs that we should seek meanness of appearance, walk bent over in mourning and repentance for Eve's sin to express the ignominy and odium of human perdition."

The queen held up her cup. "Amaria, I need more wine. Fill all the cups, including Alix's."

"Oh no, Your Majesty, I . . ." But the act was done, so I drank.

"Where do you read Tertullian, Alix?" Toquerie demanded.

Grateful for the question, I explained that Sister Hilaria was my mentor, my ideal, that she was teaching me all the exhortations of the Holy Fathers, all the Scripture except for the Song of Songs because I might think it referred to physical love instead of spiritual. Since no one commented, I continued about Sister Hilaria's wondrous visions, how she confided them to me, then kissed me most sweetly, how I'd had one myself a few nights ago. Now my audience was rapt.

"Give us an example," the queen asked in a strange voice.

Waving my arms dramatically, I described how the vision had come as a fiery essence filled with substance of shining water, burning sun, moon and stars, invisible wind. The vision—shaped like a man with a face like the sun—leaned over me with eyes of flame and a writhing monster on his thigh, then stabbed me with brute matter, which flooded me with ecstasy.

There was long silence when I finished, and I sipped my wine quietly—somehow my cup was still full.

Sybelle cleared her throat. "That's a wondrous *visio*, Alix, not unlike several I've had myself."

"So have I," chorused one lady after another.

I turned scathing eyes on their lechery, but they were beyond redemption.

"And this vision didn't object to your pious body odor?" the queen asked.

"Oh no, he likes it. Saint Jerome instructs us to refrain from bathing, you see, so that we spoil our natural beauty for others and thereby help men resist original sin. However, filth also repels us from ourselves, for our sweet clean bodies can stimulate our own hot desires. It's complicated, but I know that we must destroy our beauty by deliberate squalor and thereby achieve holy chastity."

"Just wait," Toquerie mocked, "and time will ensure chastity."

The queen stood and bent over me, tugged gently at my headscarf. "Did Sister Hilaria never tell you of Saint Ovid?"

"I don't think so."

"He was the first and foremost of teachers, my dear, and

he wrote that young ladies should bathe thoroughly every day, then gown themselves elegantly in God's service. Our Lady deplores rank, goatish armpits and hidden parts that emanate the stench of dead fish."

"But the sleeping fire . . . Saint Jerome warns of the fire in the bedstraw." No, that had been Dame Margery; I poured the rest of my wine into the grass. "I mean the fire in the water."

"Mercy, the fire within our ancient husks has long since been comatose. What say you, ladies? Could a simple douse revive sleeping embers? I think we should test that proposition," the queen cried.

She pulled her own wimple free, then her robes and stepped out of a scarlet slither. Astonished, I noted her pendulous breasts—looking as if they'd satisfied many hungry mouths—her long supple legs, her flat stomach scarred by childbirth, her dark silver-shot hair bright as water spray. Then all the withered nymphs threw garments to the winds and hobbled over the grass to the shallow pool to displace the ducks whom they somewhat resembled. Eleanor went first, sank into a scallop-shaped patch of sun, an ancient Venus returning to her shell. Reflected sunlight zagged across her face.

"Lady Alix, come to the water."

"I'm sorry, Your Majesty, but I took a vow . . ."

"I order you." The voice rang with authority.

Agonized, I turned my back and fumbled with my ceinture, dropped it, kicked my itchy tunic aside. The ladies were playing like children in the shallows above the weir, throwing round globules of liquid sun at one another, laughing and ducking. At least I had enough modesty to seek my own pool; I dashed to the deep pond and plunged.

*Benedicite!*

The cold liquid shocked. I surfaced, trod water, plunged again. Delicious and not lickerous at all. I opened my mouth to clear the wine, somersaulted in cool satin, opened my eyes to the shadowy cerulean world. When I surfaced, I clung to a log extending from the bank and let the weir massage me.

"Did you ever make love under water?" Faydide called.

I'd never thought of such a thing, but I raked memory. Had I?

"Yes." Lady Mamile answered, then elaborated. Outside Vézelay at the beginning of the Second Crusade, when the ladies had ridden as Amazons sporting gold plumes and buskins and with breasts exposed, Mamile had gone forth with the others to rouse knights to valor and had found one called Sir Claude in a water meadow outside St. Père. The two of them had lain in hot salt brine as he . . .

"That knight with the dog face?" Sybelle scorned. "He tried to get me into that hot spring, but I wouldn't demean myself."

The Second Crusade. I knew naught about it except that it must have been forty—no, fifty—years ago. How could they remember it? Or did they make up their pasts? I would believe so, except for the queen; she accepted Mamile's statement without comment, so it must be true. But naked breasts?

I dived again. Now the water found my orifices, gurgling, licking, now the weir's massage centered so that I was transfixed by liquid invasion. Dots of fire clung to the trees. Voices continued in snatches: "Guinevere was lanced-a-lot"; "When he entered, blood dripped from the stars"; "Fireflash in the tip of his tongue." I bit my tongue to choke back my pleasure.

My heart pounded.

Then they were in a row looking down at me. *Deus juva me*, had they seen? Did they guess?

"Our dinner is ready," the queen said.

"Aye, I'm coming."

I waited till they were seated, then ran to the dappled sun. No tunics were to be seen—Amaria must have put them somewhere. I turned my back for modesty, ate lustily and drank deeply, hardly paying attention to the idle chatter.

When we'd finished, I bent my knees and rested my head forward to conceal my sensual parts. Thereby I gazed with wonder down on myself, a pale pink rose with a moist calyx and giving forth a spicy aroma. Confused, I turned to lie on my stomach, watched white butterflies, but my heart still raced.

"Come, Alix, sit by me," the queen called. "You're my golden-haired Iphis again, and I want you near."

I had to obey, was keenly aware that curious eyes watched me. Self-consciously I sank naked beside the naked queen, permitted her to pull my head to her shoulder, kept my eyes averted from her raised nipples.

The ladies leaned forward, their eyes hungry.

"Look at her," groaned Faydide, "and she wants to be a nun."

"That's a vocation for hold-doors, not flowery slits."

"Enjoy your salad days, Alix; the years glide like this moving stream."

"No hour ever returns."

"Don't waste love; learn the technique and use it. I could teach you . . ."

Their voices echoed and overlapped as I gazed dreamily, tranced by the unaccustomed wine, food and bright sun. Indeed, even their appearances altered, for they seemed encapsulated in filmy, shimmering bubbles, like snakeskins about to be shed, while barely visible inside the membranes sat beautiful young damsels, Mamile with vivid eyes and smile, Faydide darkly glowing, fair Sybelle . . . I was seeing them as they saw themselves, as they'd once been, and a frisson took me. Someday I, too, would be inside a bubble, remembering forty—fifty—years ago. Remembering what? Regretting what?

"God help us, Saint Jerome was right," Toquerie

groaned. "Alix is bait for perdition. Who could resist her furry pit?"

"Hush!" Mamile scolded. "Such an expression for Alix's golden furze. Don't listen to the jealous hag, darling; she's forgotten what it is to have such power."

The queen smiled. "Do you have power, Alix?"

"No," I said truly.

"Of course she has," Florine argued. "What other power does a woman have except the seductiveness of her body? You yourself taught us that, Your Majesty."

"I taught you not to throw your power away. A common strumpet spreading her legs under a hedge has the same equipment we have, but she's gulled if she thinks that's power; it's merely the potential for power."

"How do you gain power?" I asked, interested.

"By withholding favors until you've taught your lover the rules and made him obey," Mamile answered.

"But if I never marry . . ."

"Lover, silly, not husband."

"Or have a lover . . ."

"Of course you will. Men prefer stolen passion because of the risk. Don't forget Lancelot and Tristan."

"But their ladies took the risk of being discovered," I argued, "not them." Though I recalled that Lancelot had suffered.

"The pleasure," the queen advised, "came from challenge. The ladies had no duties toward their lovers, only what they would give freely, and therefore could demand a price. That's the source of power."

I was offended. "You mean that Queen Guinevere was a whore?"

"The price was not in money . . ."

"Though to lack cash is vulgar," Mamile interjected.

". . . but in love and respect. Avarice is a stranger to love, but power is an inevitable partner. My rules instruct the woman how to gain that power."

The ladies then pelted me with various rules from the Courts of Love, which my addled wits could only half absorb, though I tried. At one point the queen called for more wine.

"Venus in wine is fire within fire," she toasted.

Fire in my bedstraw.

The talk became faint, and I slept.

When I woke, someone suggested that we wash off the sun's effects before leaving, and we all rolled into the stream once more. It took less time than before to make me pant with sensation—even though I was now sober. Every part of me yearned, burned for I know not what, and I ached to get back to the sanctuary of Hilaria's arms.

When we dressed, however, I couldn't bear the acrid stench of my tunic.

"Lady Alix," Queen Eleanor called from her spot in the shade, "Amaria always brings an extra tunic when I swim in case I get my clothing wet. Would you like to use it?"

Gratefully I accepted the pale shift, which slithered on like a new skin, and mounted Sea Mew.

"I'll take my dress with me, Your Majesty." I reached for it. "Sister Hilaria gave it to me."

"By all means, you'll want to save it as a token of her former kindness."

I heard the faint elegy without comprehension. "She could always give me another."

"Except that you'll not be seeing her again," the queen informed me gently. "Abbess Matilda agrees with you that Sister Hilaria has vast talents and has therefore promoted her to the position of subprioress. Henceforth your religious instruction will be conducted by Sister Ursula."

Tears sprang to my eyes. I should be happy for my beloved Hilaria, and indeed I was, but Sister Ursula? She spoke with a pedantic twang, never received visions and had a long, swart horse-face further marred by a black mustache. Worse, she was cruel—I didn't *like* Sister Ursula.

Saint Jerome was right, I thought morosely, to warn against bathing. I cursed the blithe liquid burbling toward the Vienne for its amoral strokes, cursed the queen for deliberately titillating my fantastick cells with her naked army and their bibulous tales, that wine—heavy as poppy. Wine . . . poppy. A firefly flitted in my brain. The dream I'd had of Enoch when he'd bent from the sky, my vision of the Heavenly Father bathed in fire, the sweet flood entering me . . .

"No!" I cried.

"What's wrong, dear?" The queen turned.

I shook my head. The brook was innocent, the queen the sum of her history, and neither could have influenced Sister Hilaria if she'd been here. I was weak—easily swayed. Or no, like Sister Damiana, I lacked the gift of carnal sacrifice —and for me it would be sacrifice—lacked adequate love for Our Lord. Damiana sought physical release, which was honest; I merely deceived myself and others. I worshipped as most people did, sincerely, when I could stay awake.

And Eleanor had known. I hated her! How cruel! Yet what had she done except reveal me to myself? Watching her back, I gave her grudging credit for knowing character —though I vowed never again to be so transparent.

Reluctantly, I spurred Sea Mew to follow the queen. After all, I had two years of widowhood ahead, time enough to decide on my commitments, and I might yet prove worthy of a nun's vows.

A week later I was summoned once again into the royal presence. Queen Joanna was nowhere to be seen; Eleanor sat alone in her sumptuous chamber with a parchment in her hand.

"I've just received a letter from the Great One, and he reports a sweeping victory. He's taken Tailleburg, Marcillac, Angoulême, Château-sur-Charente, Montignac, Lachaise, as well as three hundred knights and forty thousand men."

"Faster than a Balearic sling," I said politely.

"The barons want to form a peace party and men on our side agree, especially John."

I fought a yawn.

"The king has called a parley at Chinon to discuss the wisdom of such a move. I ride to join him tomorrow."

"We'll miss you, Your Majesty."

"I need company. Would you like to go with me?"

No, I wouldn't. "I would deem it a privilege, Your Majesty."

She told me to pack my new tunics, especially a gossamer silver she'd cut from a private ell of eastern silk, for there might be banquets. I agreed and left. *Deo gratias* I had assurance that I would be a widow two years, or I would fear that Richard might assign me to a husband. As it was, I would eat a little flesh and get an uninterrupted night's sleep.

Fontevrault's song followed us along the lane as we rode out the next morning.

> *"O viridissima virga ave*
> *que in ventoso flabo sciscitationis*
> *sanctorum prodisti."*

# 9

E HEARD RICHARD'S ROAR AS WE CROSSED CHInon's dry moat; the answering roar came from John. Eleanor frowned, tugged her wimple tighter and hurried her steed.

Inside the great hall the two brothers faced one another in the center of a ring of knights, like fighters in a tournament.

"It was the horse-pregnant tactic of Troy!" John shouted.

"God's feet, you're an ass! The Trojans were at war with Greece and should have known better than to take the horse. But you entered Évreux as a friend—*were* a friend to these people—then turned on them most murderously. How can I rule with such a record of treachery?"

Queen Eleanor pushed her way to Richard's side and touched his upraised arm. He kissed her briefly, then described the events in Évreux. In the first test of his loyalty to Richard, John had ridden into the town with a small company of knights; the officials accepted him as an ally of Philip's, not knowing that he'd changed sides. They'd drunk together, made merry; then, with sly insinuation, he'd beguiled unarmed men into halls and alleyways, there to hack them to death most viciously. In the end he'd paraded through the streets with three hundred heads on the ends of poles.

"Don't forget that the town surrendered," John pointed out, "which is what you wanted."

"Not at the price of dishonor to my name!" the king cried in fury. "And what kind of victory did you enjoy? Philip rode the next day and burned the city to the ground, then took the holy relics. His revenge will rest on my shoulders as well!"

Again Eleanor touched Richard and said something in a low voice. He glanced at the door, saw me. Instantly he strode in my direction, as I hastily bowed to the ground. His hand raised me again.

"Welcome to Chinon, Lady Alix, scene of your former triumph." The king's voice, suddenly silky, startled me and I felt my face heat. He gestured to a pulley on the ceiling whence I'd once descended inside a pie to be put on his table, in the days when I'd worked for the jongleur Zizka—the first time I met Richard.

"Hardly a triumph, Your Majesty," I murmured as I bowed once more.

"Triumph of a smooth rump," he teased, "and its flowered winds."

Which was poetic language for the dour event: blindfolded as Cupid, I'd bent and shot my arrow in the wrong direction, struck a dog and farted in the king's face—but hardly with "flowered winds."

"Your gown is most becoming," he continued, "though I prefer your Cupid's gauze. Perhaps you'll repeat your performance."

Struck dumb at the woodly suggestion—at least I'd been only a child the first time—I didn't reply.

He held his intense regard, then resumed his former conversation. Still aghast, I leaned against a wall and counted my heartbeats.

"And you wonder why I don't want to join your peace party?" Richard blazed, as if uninterrupted. "A party devised by you and Henry Hohenstaufen? What is your real purpose?"

John was surprisingly strong in his reply. "Richard, I swear that we're honest in our intent. Philip is terrified of you—you know how he hid in the chapel of Chateaudun when he knew you were riding by—and he needs peace; the country yearns for it. Meet him July twenty-third at Vaudreuil and sign the treaty, I beg you. Your own ally Longchamp has helped arrange it, which should convince you of its sincerity."

"I'm convinced that Philip would like a truce because I'm winning. This is July; by September I'll have Normandy."

The queen intervened once more. The king nodded, turned to me.

"Lady Alix, my page Hamo will show you to your quarters in the sommelier where there's a nice breeze off the river. We'll dine within the hour."

With relief, I flourished and left. In the sommelier, Eleanor's woman Amaria came to help me don the silvery tunic Eleanor had ordered and soon I was sitting at a trestle as the meat courses were put before me: meat with mustard, pork chop, roast curlew, roast pheasant, roast woodcock, roast partridge, roast plover, roast snipe; I skipped the fish except for the roast eels, then ate fulsomely of the almond cream, hot apples and pears, ginger columbine, wafers and the sub- tlety called An Old Man. The king, queen and John contin- ued to talk on their dais, but I paid them no heed. Now if I could get a good night's rest, I would be happy.

After the banquet, the royal party departed first and the rest of us followed. William Marshal, the most famous knight of our time, kindly held my hand as I rose. Outside the salle in the corridor, the queen waited with the king's page Hamo.

"The tunic suits you," she approved. "Better than gray sackcloth."

"Aye, thank you, Your Majesty." I waited for her to move so I could go to my bed, for the heavy food made me sleepier than usual.

For five long days thereafter, the conference about the peace treaty continued and was a most glorious holiday for me. I prayed often, I trowe, but not during the night and therefore regained my animal virtues. I ate very well, en- joyed long walks along the Vienne River and felt more free than I had since Wanthwaite. Finally the parley was fin- ished, and the queen announced that we would return to Fontevrault.

But on the morning before our departure, I was sum- moned to King Richard's chamber. Much puzzled and a little apprehensive, I followed Hamo through the long gal- lery to the royal quarters. Richard, too, looked rested, de- spite the grueling hours he'd kept, and was magnificently robed in deep blue, a most becoming color which he rarely wore because it was French. His clerk, Master Philip, was sitting beside him at his desk when I entered, but the king told him to leave.

"Greetings, Lady Alix." Richard walked around the desk and took my hand to raise me from my bow. "You're fresh as a dewdrop."

His manner was suave and jocular, his movements easy, but his hand trembled slightly as it held mine. Was he angry? He led me to a bench opposite his at the desk, but continued standing himself. A swallow flew in through the open window and perched on a beam above.

"Have you enjoyed your week at Chinon?"

"Aye, Your Majesty, the countryside offers many diversions."

"So it does. I consider Chinon my second home; my first is Poitiers where I grew up."

The bird swooped the length of the chamber seeking a way out; Richard didn't notice.

"I hope you see Poitiers one day," he continued.

"Aye, Your Majesty, I would like that."

"It's close to Fontevrault and has much the same aspect . . ."

As he continued his description of the ducal city and his boyhood there, I studied his face for clues to his purpose, for I knew that the king didn't engage in chatter for nothing. Something lurked under his bland surface, but he wasn't ready yet to reveal it; he was "putting me at my ease," except that the longer he prattled about becoming duke when he was fourteen, going through some sort of peculiar ceremony and I know not what, the more agitated I became. My heart thumped heavily and my palms grew damp. Everything was at odds, sudden pauses, intakes of breath, eyes like firebrands.

Then suddenly he changed his thrust. "Do you remember the first time you were in this chamber, Alix?"

I looked uneasily at the swallow which clung to a beam directly overhead. "Aye, Your Majesty, when you made me your page."

"You were dressed as Cupid, god of love."

Zizka's toty scheme, to put me in flimsy robes and have me sing for the king, though my voice lacked pitch.

"A most enchanting creature." He smiled. "I never forgot your flower face, the sweet curve of your body."

"Aye, you told me how you laughed while in prison," I mumbled, mortified by memory.

"Laughed?"

The word hung there. Neither of us was laughing. The swallow splattered onto a burnt candle instead of my head, *Deo gratias*. The king began to pace behind me, making me exceedingly nervous. I like to face my enemy.

"I demoted a god to a page, most unworthy of me."

I rubbed my damp hands surreptitiously on the bench beside me. His pause required a comment.

"To serve in your household in any capacity is an honor, Your Majesty."

He sat on the bench beside me, his back to the desk so we were facing one another if I'd cared to look, but he was too close.

"I was hoping you thought so, Alix. Would you like to serve again?"

I could swear that the king was as nervous as I was, though I knew I must be reading my own qualms into his thick voice.

"'You mean as page?" I forced myself to smile. "You have rich humor."

"As my mistress."

I knew at once that it wasn't a jape—though it should have been—and my whole insides collapsed.

"I didn't always laugh when I thought of you in my dungeon, Alix. That night when you came into this room changed my life. Your little golden arrow which you shot with such unthinking abandon at the banquet entered my eye, went straight to my heart, just as the legend foretells. I wanted you desperately while on the Crusade, but circumstances . . ."

His large hand touched my back; his palm, too, was damp.

He laughed shakily. "I amuse and amaze myself by my words—I can imagine what you must think—a great holy king, Crusader, fighter, all the rest, talking like a smitten swain to his shepherdess, but there it is. I should need no excuse—your charms are there for all to see—but try to think of me for a moment as if I were your age, for this is my first plunge into love—as the poets say. I'm besotted, obsessed, can't sleep or eat or think of anything else as if I were ill. Is it the cumulation of too many abstinent years? like water bursting a dam? *Heu michi, quod sterilem vitam duxi juveniles.*"

Woe to me that I have lived such a barren youth. Except in my opinion his youth hadn't been barren, just different. I could hardly breathe.

"I'm waiting, Alix."

Waiting for my permission? Hardly. But my response, yes. You have no choice, Bonel had said truly in Wanthwaite.

"It's . . . so overwhelmed I can't . . . honored," I stumbled miserably.

His hand crept upward to the back of my neck, fingers spread and cupped my head. The swallow lighted on the desk, cocked his head quizzically. His golden feathers reflected on the wood as he hopped til and fro.

"To bed with a king is an honor, Alix—my darling Alix —and it will be doubly so in your case. I have worked out the details of our relationship most carefully. The queen will show you the contract."

"Contract?"

I looked at him, looked quickly away. *Benedicite.*

"For your protection. My life is in constant danger . . . someday you'll want to"—his voice became tight—"marry."

He stood to pace again; I let out my breath. My cold bile began to bubble as the full impact of his words hit me. Everyone had conspired to keep his scheme from me, but my fantastick cells had screamed warning from the first. If I could get my hands on Bonel's throat right now, both of his eyes would turn purple! As for the snaky queen . . . I even cursed Zizka for making me into an enticing Cupid, my own father for telling me to dress as a boy, for I knew the root of Richard's attraction.

". . . not easy for a king to be a lover. My war must take priority—whatever my own desires—but now we are close to peace and there will be nothing to stop us. I'll take you with me to Vaudreuil and if we sign the treaty there . . ."

I waited for him to mention a much greater obstacle than his war: the fact that I was still mourning Enoch, still dreamed and thought of him night and day. What would he have done if Enoch hadn't conveniently died? Probably exactly the same. After all, the king had been brought up in the courts of Poitiers and suckled on courtly love; in that lexicon adultery was a prerequisite to love, not an obstacle. The swallow fluttered away in alarm and I knew that Richard was close again.

"You're very quiet."

Hand on my hair.

"I don't know what to say," I whispered. "I . . ."

"What?"

He put his hands to my waist, forced me to stand, very slowly picked me up and held me high above him. Then he smiled, a sunburst of joy. The surprised swallow struck the back of my head.

"My Nelfin Queen."

He lowered me slowly, bringing me close so my entire body slid past his face. He breathed deeply of my hips, my navel, up between my breasts, my beating throat.

"Alix, Alix, God's feet, no man ever felt as I do. If you knew, if I could tell . . ."

He kissed my chin ardently, my cheeks, eyes, lips on mine. Greedy, greedy. His lion's heart shook me, my rabbit's heart fluttered as I tried to escape his devouring jaws.

He held me away. "Now go. My mother will show you our contract. We'll ride tomorrow at dawn."

Very gently, he touched my lips with his tongue.

I staggered backward. When I rose from my flourish, I saw the swallow fly through the window to freedom.

✤               ✤               ✤

THE DOOR to my chamber had no lock, but I dragged my heavy leather trunk to hold it before I rolled out my bed mat. Then, alone and relatively safe at last, I threw myself to the floor and gave way to wrath.

I raged so the whole day as I faced my situation squarely. There was no point in going back to those points when I might have saved myself—such as at the stank—for I was here, this was now.

After the bell rang Haute Tierce and when most of the castle slept, Amaria knocked on my door: the queen awaited me in her chamber. Would I come as soon as I could? Aye, I would be right there. I picked myself up from the floor, ran fingers through my hair and splashed my face. Let her have no opportunity to gloat.

Eleanor sat with her clerk, Fitzroy, whom she didn't dismiss. As I entered her tower chamber, she watched me most quizzically.

"My dear Alix, you've seen the Great One." She approached and kissed my cheek.

"Aye, Your Majesty."

She held my face in her hands and gazed deep into my eyes, as if she wanted to cure me of a fit of yexxing.

"The highest honor in Christendom."

"Aye, Your Majesty," I agreed demurely.

Fitzroy, a dried prune of a man, regarded me without expression.

"Daughter." She kissed me again and smiled, then turned back to her desk, pulling me with her. "If you knew how often I've wanted to say something to you, especially that day by the stream. Remember? A luscious peach ready for the plucking and by what a hand!"

"It must have been tempting," I gurgled, "but you were the soul of discretion. I never guessed. Did Bonel know as well?"

She laughed gaily. "Oh, Bonel is your greatest advocate. He would have you be queen."

I laughed with her at the absurdity, at *my* absurdity for being such a dunce. Bonel with his assurances that I wouldn't be a hostage. What was I then? I could hear him: a hostage of love, Alix, which is quite different.

Oh yes, I would reply, to be the royal whore is different indeed, hardly in the same company as the Archbishop of Rouen.

"Sit, dear, for there are ramifications of this affair that transcend the pleasures of the bed. Did the king mention progeny?"

"No."

"Well, naturally he is so obsessed with the process at this moment that he might think it indelicate, but children are the fruit of love, and in your case children are the only purpose of love."

I caught sarcasm in her voice, studied her brilliant tilted eyes, the conventional turn of her lips. Eleanor was jealous: approving, but nonetheless reluctant to give up power. Momentarily, I savored the sweet sting of revenge. However, she need not worry; I had no governance over Richard.

"Do children come with adulterous love?" I asked. "I don't recall any of you mentioning such 'products' at the stream. I thought perhaps . . ."

"There are ways," she agreed laconically, "but they won't be used in this instance. Richard had months to ponder his situation while he was a captive."

*Benedicite*, had he told his own mother of his mirth and licentious thoughts about me?

"And realized that his first order of business after he became free must be to provide England with an heir. You've heard of young Arthur and his crazed temperament?"

"Aye, Your Majesty." I was now all alert.

"As things stand by the treaty of Messina, Arthur will become our king if anything . . . well, I need not tell you that it would be a disaster. *Vae terrae ubi puer rex est.*"

Woe to the land where a child is king.

"Of course you have Prince John," I said innocently.

Her eyes swam like stagnant water. "Of course. Great blood sometimes skips generations, however; much in John reminds me of my own father. It takes new blood to revive a strain."

Wanthwaite's blood purifying the Plantagenets'; I hoped my "progeny" didn't have yellow eyes.

"Therefore Richard's thoughts flew to you. He had noticed you on the Crusade . . ."

Noticed!

". . . and decided that you would be a fit mother for England."

Fitzroy leaned back in his chair; I could gaze up his hairy nostrils. No swallow flew near; the birds were napping.

"Mother?" I said cautiously as the words took hold. "The king *wants* me to mother a child?"

The queen slapped a vellum impatiently. "He wrote it all here and signed it, a most generous act since he need not give you anything; but Cupid makes his own camps, and Richard is smitten. The situation is unprecedented—that a powerful king should seek a lowly mate."

"Yet King Philip loves Agnes de Méranie—even speaks of marriage," I retorted, wearied by her insults.

"But not Richard—did he mention love?"

"No," I admitted. He'd used other words which in retrospect were not flattering: obsessed, besotted, ill.

"Of course not. As for marriage, Philip is a fool. Richard has no such thoughts, nor should you—I warn you. Don't try to rise above your station."

I looked at her long spread fingers, noted that she'd tried unsuccessfully to paint away age spots on the back of her hand.

"May I read the contract, Your Majesty?"

"If you can read Latin. Otherwise Fitzroy will oblige."

Without answering I took the contract and walked to the

narrow window, there to sit on a ledge. Below me an argument was ensuing between two farmers with longcarts
loaded with yellow summer apples; the pungent fruit scent
wafted upward. I read very carefully, for I knew Latin better by ear than by eye. In the treaty of Messina, Arthur was
named heir to the English Crown unless the king were to
have children of his own, in which case the older (assuming
he was a boy) would be heir and chief to King Philip for all
the Norman territory south of the Channel; the second boy
would hold his share directly of the French king. That was
the first part.

In the second, I agreed to become concubine to King
Richard until two children were produced or for a period of
two years, whichever came first, and to hereby sign away all
claims to such children to the English Crown. The king
promised to recognize said bastards as his own legitimate
heirs and to train them in the royal household to fulfill their
great destinies.

In the third part, I was promised a pension for the rest of
my lifetime and a dowry sufficient to procure a husband or
entry into a convent according to my preference.

I continued to stare at the contract as if still reading
in order to gain time to think. Aye, to think, not to feel,
for if I'd followed my fantastick cells I would gladly have
flung myself onto those apples down below and taken my
chances of surviving. Treacherous, cold, crafted words
to seal my fate for all time. *Think*, Alix. Finally I looked
up.

"I have a quill here," Eleanor said.

"I've never signed a contract before, Your Majesty, but I
have the impression that it's an agreement reached between
two parties."

"Possibly, but only if each has something to bargain. Here
the king is the donor, you the receiver."

"Except that he needs my womb to nurture his seed."

She lay down her quill, her eyes dangerous. "Take care,
my dear, you speak to the Angevins."

"And you speak to the Wanthwaites," I said just as firmly, "though I defer to your wisdom. You taught me that a lady should use her appeal as leverage to her desires."

"In bed, not the nursery! No woman owns her children."

"Not formerly perhaps, but you changed that. You own yours . . ."

"Quiet!" She rose and came toward me like a red comet.

*Benedicite*, she was going to push me out of the window!

"Courtly love has nothing to do with dynasty! You play a dangerous game, Alix."

"I play no game at all!" I cried hotly. "I know how powerful all of you are, but the game is of your devising, not mine! All I fight for is myself and my children. Who else will protect us?"

"You, but not *your* children. *Your* children will come from another man. Later."

"Is there a guarantee? I see none."

She turned her back, looked at Fitzroy, then sat again.

"Let's be done with it. Tell me what you want."

My mind was two words ahead of my lips as I improvised my demands. If one of my royal children were a girl, she should inherit the lands to the south as Eleanor had done. When it was time for me to depart my assignment, I must be permitted to go to Wanthwaite without any interference whatsoever for all time to come. If I decided to take a husband, he must not disparage my rank, but must be at least a baron, preferably greater, and I must have the right to refuse him if he were not to my liking.

"Is that all?" the queen asked with her cynical smile. "Fitzroy, see to it."

"No," I replied. I thought of Bonel's making duplicate records of money owed to Jews. "The contract must be done in duplicate, one for my safekeeping."

"Are you suggesting that you could challenge the Crown?" she demanded, outraged. "You can't fight judge and jury."

"The king lives a dangerous life. If he should die while

my son is in his minority, some unscrupulous usurper might destroy his copy."

A reluctant admiration fretted her brow. "Well, Lady Alix, you have the honeyed visage of Helen and speak with the poisoned tongue of the lawyer Tiberius. I'll be curious to see your sons—my grandsons."

A wrench twisted my heart, so that I gasped aloud. *Benedicite*, if I could feel so for imagined children lost to me, what would I suffer later?

"I hope you'll enjoy them—love them—Your Majesty."

With the promise that duplicate would be done, and when my demands were added, I took the quill and signed.

THE FOLLOWING MORNING a stolid woman called Emma came from the village of Chinon to be my handmaiden; she had all the markings of a spy: taciturn, sulky, sly and pocky. At least she didn't want to talk, and she was strong as a mule. I received my duplicate contract in late afternoon, wrapped it in oiled silk and strapped it to my inner thigh. We left with the army to ride north the next day, and I received a quick lesson in the power of my new position. The knight closest to the King, William Marshal, made a point of seeking me out and spoke graciously of the countryside and the castle of Vaudreuil. Others followed his suit, though ultimately my treatment was decided by Richard himself. Again and again, he turned back to my place in line.

"Is your saddle comfortable, Alix?"

"Aye, Your Majesty."

"I'll have George cover it with a sheepskin. Would you like bells on your bridle?"

"You're most kind, Your Majesty."

"Look at me."

I did so. He touched my thigh, then returned to his place. Within the hour he was back.

"We'll eat together in my pavilion. Do you like red Bordeaux?"

"Yes, if it please you."

"You should know that it does, Alex." He laughed at his reference to my days as page. "I have my personal stock with me."

Most times when he came back, however, he spoke only with his hands. He couldn't resist my hair, my cheeks, my shoulders, my waist; I could feel the hot energy run from his body through his fingertips. He gazed on me with wonder, I would have said adoration if I hadn't been keenly aware of the contract. There was purpose in his love and I felt less an object of worship than a good brood mare. Hadn't he and the queen carefully examined my blood lines? Hadn't he dragged me all the way to Mainz to be sure that his imagination hadn't beguiled him? If I hadn't passed that test, I would be languishing in a dungeon even now. Worse, he had put a limit to our "love"; I'd heard tales of knights going to infinite lengths to extend trysts with their beloved ladies, but never had I heard of anyone signing a scrip for the termination of love. On Monday we would still be in bed; on Tuesday I would be gone. End of obsession, end of illness. How could I feel anything but resentment under such humiliating limits? Even if I could be roused—which I couldn't—the notching off of days on a calendar, the constant testing of my body for conception, would freeze me faster than the teachings of Saint Jerome.

I loathed king and queen both, but my fury went to Bonel. At least they had something to gain by their odious behavior, but he was a toady, a clinging bat, and he'd betrayed a budding friendship. If I were ever in Rouen, if I ever had any influence over the king, I would have Bonel dropped in the nearest stank, there to wallow in swine-murk.

Vaudreuil was a long distance from Chinon, the days tedious and hard. I lost sleep night after night as I thought with dread of what was to come after Vaudreuil. I was also aware that the king paced around my small tent at night, sometimes for hours, and I knew he had the same thoughts.

The castle was an old square-towered structure located in the Eure Valley beside the Seine where the bridge of Portjoie crossed. The far bank belonged to the French and we could see their army spread on the hills. Emma and I were put in a tower for privacy and had a good view of the prospect. The countryside was wooded and scarped with outcroppings of granite, the river smooth. After I'd freshened myself, I went below to walk in the twilight. There I came upon Prince John.

"You should have told me that you were Richard's wench," he accused me. "I asked you, didn't I?"

"And I told you the truth, Your Highness. Please let me pass."

"So he hasn't bedded you yet. You're in for an unpleasant shock—he wears a rabbit's scut to do a man's work."

"If you please . . ."

"However, don't give up hope. I always get Richard's castoffs, his kingdom, his woman . . ."

I ran past him.

"And you'll like my pole, I guarantee!" he called after me.

The parley for peace was scheduled for the following day. From my high window, I watched the French force cross the bridge; a small group turned away from the meeting place and disappeared in a copse. The others, headed by a slender man dressed in blue who must be King Philip, rode along the river toward the field; his army carried blue shields which bobbed like wavelets of water. Directly below us, King Richard appeared in his scarlet and gold and led a parade of scarlet shields after the French.

"Let's go to nearby farms and see if we can find fresh food," I suggested to Emma. "I'm tired of army fare."

Even the King dined on plain salt pork and beef.

Together we wound down the stair and found baskets in the kitchen, then set forth across the meadows. The flowers that had bloomed in Fontevrault had just opened in the north and we waded knee-deep in poppies and cuckooflowers. As we turned toward a thatched hut to our right, the French contingent left its copse and rode toward Vaudreuil Castle. I watched them, puzzled. Did they want water? But there was plenty in the river. One figure in particular caught my eye. From this distance, it was hard to ascertain, but I could have sworn he was a Scot. Well, some Scots favored France.

We had good fortune at the wattle and daub hut, for the crone had fifteen eggs to spare, plus fresh butter and bread. I gave her the few coins Richard had put in my purse. Then we turned back.

Suddenly I couldn't bear to enter that castle. If the truce were signed, this ugly edifice would become my first trysting place with Richard. I prayed against peace, for then Richard would fight and I would go back to Fontevrault.

"You go ahead," I said to Emma. "I'll walk along the river where it's cool."

She hesitated.

"You can watch me from the tower," I pointed out sarcastically, and she left.

I strolled aimlessly, kicking at the flowers, brooding on my unhappy state, until I reached the river where I sat on a rock and dabbled my toes. Certainly I wouldn't bathe in it and rouse my lickerous disposition, though I should clean myself for the coming occasion. I splashed here and there. Then I heard the pounding of hooves behind me and watched the small company gallop from Vaudreuil as if chased by bees. They were close upon me, but veered to cross the bridge. I could see them clearly, including the Scot.

It was Enoch!

"Enoch!" I screamed and began to run after him.

He was already on the bridge making a fearsome racket and didn't hear. Meantime I stopped, less sure. He was thinner than Enoch, rode a different horse. All I could say for certain was that he was a MacPherson. No, it was my fantastick cells, triggered by the costume and dread of the coming night. I'd made that mistake once before when I'd taken the MacPherson at Nottingham for Enoch and . . .

Suddenly the world rumbled and shook under my feet.

Clouds of rock dust rose slowly around Vaudreuil, followed by a mighty crash as the tower crumbled before me. Stunned, I watched a few heartbeats before I understood. The castle had been mined! As the pink dust thinned, I gazed on a low jagged silhouette where my tower had been only a short time past.

"Emma!" I cried.

I started to run toward the wreckage, again heard an army pounding behind me and quickly ducked into the safety of the grass. Philip rode past, slipping and sliding on his saddle, his face a fiendish mask. He and his army thundered onto Portjoie bridge as Richard rode close behind.

"Saddles will be emptied this day!" Richard shouted.

Then he saw the castle.

"My God! Alix was in the tower!" And changed direction.

The French were having difficulty on the bridge which was too narrow to take their horses all at once. Then there was a mighty splinter and the bridge gave way. From the French side, foot soldiers ran to save the sliding knights as they plunged into the waves. Again I saw the Scot as he dived from the sloping rail and swam to the French king. He pulled him to safety.

Shouting orders like a madman, Richard rode back, shot whining arrows at the trapped French and soon the water flowed bright red. He then wielded his deadly crossbow, picking off French on the far bank, as knights hurled lances and curses together at the screaming victims on the bridge. Not until every Frenchman within arrowshot was dead or wounded was the king willing to leave.

He sat on his horse hardly a man's length from me.

"Did Philip go down, Marshal?"

"He wet his britches, but a Scot pulled him out."

"Who mined the castle?"

"I don't know who blew it. The digging had to have been done weeks ago."

"Set our spies on the case. I won't rest until every sapper is dead." He paused. "You know Lady Alix was in the tower . . ." The agony in his muffled voice was heartrending.

"Yes, Your Majesty."

Despite a sense of guilt that the king suffered needlessly, I remained quiet; then, before I could reveal myself, they'd turned away.

"This is the last truce of my lifetime," I heard from afar. "Peace will come only with death, Philip's or mine. Could they have known she was there?"

"They may have been watching us." Their voices faded.

They were gone.

I sat, severely shaken. The castle was now in flames and I could hear men shouting as they struggled to rescue their gear. Poor Emma, a wretched wench but not deserving of such a death. How had I escaped? I looked upward. The sky was still blue, but a slivered moon glowed in the fading sun, was reflected between two rocks in the river's eddy.

And something with the moon. Floating.

I edged along the bank, clung to a sapling and reached. The MacPherson banner. I held the dripping tatter in a trance, my mind sluggish. The banner seemed an amulet of the past, when Enoch had fallen into the Rhône river and I'd thought him dead . . . Richard believed I was dead! *Benedicite, I was free!* I stood to look toward the flames and shouting men. No one was searching for me or calling my name. I'd blundered my escape near Malbysse Manor, missed my opportunity at the stank, but the third time would be different!

Stuffing the banner into my bodice, I bent and began to move through the flowers, then faster on all fours to cross the valley. The ground rose slowly, then sharply until I was on a tree-covered hill. I stood upright and swung through the trunks as fast as I could. Only when I'd reached a dense wood and the shouts were far behind me did I stop.

# 10

BAFFLED BY CLUTCHING BRANCHES AND SUSPIcious breathings in the dark, I shrank into the deep shade of an oak.

Gradually the shouts from the castle were replaced by sounds of the night: a steady low sough in the trees, the tumble of an unseen brook, the shrill chirk of frogs. Groping in the dark, I found a large stone covered with dry moss still warm from the sun, and tried to make a pillow. Too tense to sleep, I watched the pale moon shrink as it floated high on its run. Yet I must have drowsed, for I was wakened at dawn by the melancholy song of a nightingale. Much later, the cuckoo song woke me again and the sun was already high.

There was no motion below; flames had subsided though smoke still rose from pockets. If there were an effort to recover the bodies of Emma or Alix, by the time the bones were exposed I would be long gone.

I walked above the Seine River in the direction of the English Channel on my way at last to England and Wanthwaite and away from Richard. I didn't know how I would cross the Channel, but I would worry about that later. For now, I must stay close to the verge of the forest for concealment and forage for food and water as best I could.

At midday I wasted a precious hour grubbing for a few rotten strawberries under some logs. I picked my way through brambles and fallen trees, dared once to descend to a still pool where I pulled iris spears and ate the roots. By day's end I must have gone three miles or more. I rested on a hill above a field of mustard; a line of poplars cast long shadows across the gold, like bars of a dungeon.

On the second day I found no berries at all and scratched my right calf on a wicked thorn. Now I saw naught but elusive animals: birds just out of reach, a fox staring from the bush, three bold rabbits hopping around me, squirrels, two small snakes that slithered away fast as ground lightning. Late in the afternoon, I caught a single trout in my palms. Carefully I bashed his head and ate him whole, bones, fins, tail and all, relishing every sweet morsel.

On the third day I saw a small red-roofed village on the far side of the river. There were gardens and cows aplenty, all out of reach.

The following morning, I tried to fish again with no luck. A tiny lizard climbed to sun himself on the rock beside me. I slid my hand slowly toward his webbed feet and caught him! I couldn't wait to kill him and he wiggled strenuously against my palate. Relentlessly I crunched him down.

The next day a village was on my side of the river. Surely it would be safe to approach—I was starved. Before I could move, I heard the rasp of arms and horses pounding close. Holding my breath, I curled under a bush and watched. They were mercenaries, whether French or English I couldn't tell, and their objective was a Norman tower standing a half mile in the distance, but they chose to ride through the village first. They increased their pace, raised swords high and cried "Arras!" People and animals fled screaming under the brandishing weapons. The routiers threw torches into barns and huts alike, pounded up and down the narrow lanes slashing at helpless men and women. Back and forth they rode until all was destroyed, the voices stilled. Then they slowed their pace and trotted on to the tower, their jubilant laughter rising with the smoke.

A short time later, the tower began to flame. It burned for an hour, two hours—I couldn't be sure for the bells were stopped—but the soldiers didn't return. Toward dusk, I slid down the hill. Taking a cowpath, I passed an encouraging splatter of fresh dung. A miasma of blue-black flies rose angrily as I walked around the soft muck, then settled back to their feed. I could almost have joined them.

Then I saw my first body, a woman, head struck just above the ear. Both flies and ants feasted on her wound.

The path led to a kinebyre. The torch had not caught here because floor and walls were damp with dung and puddles. Three black and white cows turned expectantly as I entered; they'd been feeding along the forest verge during the melee and now wanted to be milked. I had difficulty finding a bucket and had to stop often to retch, but finally squatted and pulled on their dugs. I slept in the haymow that night and relieved them again in the morning.

Before leaving, I constructed a rude cross of two scorched boards and knelt to pray for the souls of the villagers. As an afterthought, I included the animals for I knew God must love them even if they had no souls. I carried away a skirt filled with root vegetables and a few fresh eggs.

EIGHT DAYS LATER I sat in a heavy rainfall on an escarpment overlooking a walled city. Eelboats sought shelter under the bridge crossing the Seine; farmers, peasants, pilgrims, merchants on top of the busy crossway hurried to the gate. Beside the gate was a pile of rubble and the portal had been repaired with wooden beams. The walls were thick, but pocked with craters as if they'd been attacked. High above the curved walls, two cathedral towers hurled lacy spires.

I found a descending path.

"Hey, you there, doxy!" the keeper called as I tried to slide through the gate. "Show me your license."

"What?" I faltered, my tongue thick from lack of practice.

A monk detached himself from his group and looked around. "She's a country lass, Jacques. I recognize the smell of dung."

"Go fast."

Jacques clanged the gate down behind me.

I followed the monks in the direction of the church, then lost them because they moved too fast, but the two square steeples were easy to discover at each corner. Finally I came to the cathedral square where a vast throng of people crowded the portals to escape the rain. Swept up in their movement, I found myself at the back of an enormous nave, so high and wide I couldn't see the ceiling. I leaned against the wall and began to doze; I woke when I realized that the crowd was leaving.

It was no longer raining. Puddles were blinding patches of trapped sun. I sank by a horsetrough, shaded my eyes and watched people come out of the cathedral. In a short time the square was crowded with vendors, buyers, children playing hide-a-seek among the adults, rich merchants, officials studying everyone suspiciously. Then a commotion rose in the middle and a circle formed.

"Go to, Mad Tib! Thump your jewels for us!"

Curiosity overcame weakness, and I climbed to the lip of the horsetrough. From there I watched as a hefty smiling dame twirled and tossed her clothing piece by piece to a delighted crowd. Swarthy as a gipsy, she grew crops of black hair on her head, under her arms and on her crotch. Her breasts were bellows, her nipples extended like sausages. Rolling her eyes and making lascivious motions with her bosom and hips, she deliberately teased the official who watched. He grabbed for her hair—missed.

"I'll pull your dong!" she cried—and didn't miss.

"Aaauuuu!" he screamed.

"Sodomite!" she taunted. "Naught but a parsnip!"

The crowd howled in approval.

She ran down the street before the officer could take her, and now the people quickly dispersed in the face of his wrath. I noted, however, that a small boy carefully gathered her discarded garments, and that a tall well-dressed merchant strolled after her.

The official now began to harass lingerers and single women on the square. As he approached, I climbed from my perch and ran into the nearest street.

It was a bad choice. Hardly wide enough for one person to pass and with many bridges between houses creating dangerous hiding places for thieves, the way was also an open sewer of human waste. Straddling the worst and becoming hopelessly lost, I finally leaned wearily against a door. In the apartment above me, a couple began to argue. They were so furious and drunkalewe that I couldn't understand a word, and they threw furniture at one another to judge by the sounds. Then suddenly they were silent, followed by laughs and groans.

Courtly love, I thought totily, as practiced by the common folk.

In moonlight again, I saw steps leading down to a space by the city wall where a bench was built into the stone, a perfect bed. I watched it; no one was about. Staying in shadow, I approached it slowly. Suddenly a huge figure rolled from under the seat and rushed toward me! Shouting vile oaths and threatening to kill, he flapped his arms wildly like a giant bat! With my last strength, I leaped up the steps and ran for my life. After another long period on besmirched streets, I emerged into the cathedral square again. No one was in sight. I crouched against a portal.

"You there!" A boy stood before me.

I didn't answer.

"You there, damsel. My mistress says you're to come with me."

The boy was about ten and certainly no threat in himself.

"You're mistaken," I told him. "I know no one here."

"She says you're to come," he insisted.

"Who's your mistress, boy?"

"Sister Tiberga."

He looked unreal in the moonlight and I thought I might be having visions. I tried to rise, fell to my knees, faint and dizzy. He offered me a gritty hand and I took it, feeling he must be my guide in a dream. Soon we were in a tangled maze of alleyways, a web made by a demented spider, crossed several small empty squares, then entered one that was not empty. Women lolled in doorways and hung out of windows calling to men below.

"Rut time, my pretty!" sang one. "I've got a hot, sweet rump for your potato finger."

"Her ling's fat all right and scaled with leprosy," cried another. "Put your knife to my tight lock, guaranteed to relieve your itch without a price!"

"Nay, he's got him an outside copesmate."

*Benedicite*, Sister Tiberga might prove worse than the cathedral square.

The boy led me to a narrow two-storied house attached to a barn. Steps rose at the entry, but the boy pulled me to a second door under the steps and rapped three times slowly, three times rapidly. It was opened from within to reveal a tiny room dimly lit by tallow. A woman rose from the corner. She was swathed in loose robes and smelled of nutmeg; then the flame stroked her thick, libidinous face—it was Mad Tib!

"But—I saw you!" I cried, horrified.

She leered down at me.

"Quite a performance, no?"

"Aye."

"Ditma, bring wine and bread; she's in a bad way," she ordered crisply. "How long has it been since you ate?"

I couldn't remember, perhaps not since the village, any real food.

"Chew well and don't take too much."

"But I shouldn't—I don't want . . ."

"You want food, my pretty, and sleep. We'll talk in the morning."

She snapped her fingers and a mat appeared magically before me; I fell upon it as if in a swoon.

         ᛉ          ᛉ         ᛉ

I WOKE to stare into wicked yellow eyes slabbed with black! Claws clutched my temples; a furry weight choked off air in my throat.

For a moment I didn't know where I was.

Then, "Tib!" I called faintly, fearful of disturbing the lion —for that's what he appeared to be.

There was a rustle.

"Slink, naughty boy!"

She lifted the creature and nuzzled it close to her cheek. It was the biggest cat I'd ever seen.

"He likes you, dear, a good omen, for Slink is never wrong about character. He can smell a rogue at twenty paces, I trowe. I let no one stay without his approval."

Slink made a low guttural sound.

More astonishing than Slink was his mistress. Mad Tib was hard to recognize this morning, for she was dressed as a holy sister complete with wimple, a purity at her neck and a soft violet robe, the pilgrim's color. She called to Ditma who brought bread and cheese, wine and a good apple, then watched quietly as I finished my repast.

"Do you feel better?" she asked.

"Aye." I wiped my mouth delicately with my sleeve. "Thank you very much." I looked into her hard black eyes. "I don't understand why you sent for me though."

She shrugged broad shoulders. "I always notice single women—especially when they look ready to drop, or even more especially when they look as if they might be competition for me."

She grinned to see my face.

"My customer was about to approach you last night. The tall merchant . . ."

The man who had followed her.

"And frankly you looked as if you might be deranged in truth."

"You're not . . ."

"No, darling, but mad women are permitted to solicit

without a licence. I don't like paying the holy fathers and city officials a portion of my ill-gotten gains, since they condemn me so roundly. Of course, I have to pay a little, but the bite is small. Otherwise it would be fifty percent."

I still felt I was in a dream, although my senses had returned.

"Do you wear a disguise by day?"

She looked down at her purity, wiped a few cat hairs off it. "Just the opposite; this robe represents my true calling. I'm a sister in the service of Saint Mary Magdalene."

She then told how she'd worked as a common whore until she'd been reborn in Christ. She'd plied her trade along the lucrative pilgrims' routes, the best leading through Vézelay to St. James of Compostela. She'd been three times in Vézelay, however, before she'd visited the great church of Saint Madeleine. There she'd learned that Mary Magdalene had been a common whore as well; nonetheless Christ had loved her above all women. Obviously He had forgiven her her sin, which was a form of love, albeit it involved profit. Hadn't she been permitted to wash His feet with her hair? What could be more erotic than that? Hadn't He chosen her to be the first to see Him after His resurrection? Furthermore, since she was the sister of Lazarus, He had given her special wisdom for healing the sick.

Tib had been profoundly moved. She continued to ply her trade—it was all she knew—but she wanted to give her money to charity. She quickly learned that an order dedicated to Saint Mary Magdalene had sprung up all across France to serve distressed women of every degree, though the Church looked on it with horror.

"Like the Abbey of Fontevrault?" I asked.

"A little, only that's devoted to Mary and run by the Benedictines, and it's wealthy."

"Where do you send your money?" I asked.

"I've begun a small convent right here in my home. There's a great need in Rouen."

"Rouen!" I forgot her tale completely. "Not Rouen!"

"Didn't you even know where you were?"

No, but I did now. Bonel's home. Richard's ducal capital where he planned to visit. *Benedicite*, I must leave at once.

"What's wrong?" she asked from far away.

I shook my head. "Nothing. I . . . Rouen's the last place I want to be, Sister Tiberga. I must get away."

"Careful, darling, you're upsetting yourself. Are you in trouble?"

I nodded.

"A man?"

Again I nodded.

"Are you with child?"

"No."

"Well, that's something. Want to tell me about it?"

I shook my head.

She touched my shoulder gently. "Don't worry—when you want to talk, we'll find a solution. Can you tell me your name?

"Alice."

"Are you wed?"

"No, I'm a carpenter's daughter from close upon Vaudreuil."

"That's enough for now. Come, let's visit my hospital."

I nodded. Anything to distract me from this dour news.

She wrapped me in a stiff white barmcloth against defilement, though my tunic was torn to a rag and could hardly be made worse.

She started to lead me to the street.

"No!" I hung back. "I mustn't be seen."

"We have to go outside to enter from above; you'll be exposed only ten heartbeats."

With head bent low, I followed her out the lower door, up the steps and into the house proper. Here the wall had been opened to enclose the barn and the whole was whitewashed. It was crowded with twenty women or more, all patients, and the air was heavy with female smells of blood and discharges. Most of the patients lay on pallets, but a few —four I counted—were hid behind red curtains across small dormers. At first their faces were a blur, all sullen with evasive eyes, and the only thing that quickened their interest was Tib's presence; they looked on her with hope bordering on idolatry. She went from one to the other asking about their symptoms as I followed.

I had difficulty paying attention for my mind was still reeling at the news of where I was. Bonel, now a wight to be avoided as much as the king. Aye, wouldn't he like to discover me and return me to Richard? An easy way to gain favor, and what would it matter if I were destroyed? *Trust the king*, his motto in life. For the first time since I'd fled Vaudreuil, I tried to put myself into Richard's head. No doubt he would seek Philip to avenge the mining of his castle, a heinous trick I could agree. But where would Philip be found? Certainly not in Rouen. Yet I knew Richard came here frequently, might come to gather arms or men.

"Don't you think so, Alice?"

"What?"

"Mistress Gilla must give up her babe, for it's dead inside her womb and can only bring corruption."

I looked on a distraught face with dark, shadowed eyes.

"Aye," I agreed uncertainly.

"She's tried clicking her heels to no avail, and the only other way is to attach a horseshoe to her privy member."

The poor dame had a sickening odor and her skin was an unhealthy green, but I couldn't imagine a privy member big enough to hold a horseshoe.

"Wouldn't that be painful?" I asked.

Tib bit her lip. "Yes, but it will save her life. Will you help me?"

Every eye on the room was on us.

"Aye—if you tell me what to do."

Tib placed poor Gilla on her back, spread her legs on a bench, then took a horseshoe from a box and attached a thin rope. I was told to hold Gilla's legs firmly in place. Tib worked quickly and I saw that she hadn't meant the same thing I did by privy member, for she inserted her hand inside Gilla's hole and tied the other end of the rope to the dead fetus. Gilla shrieked with pain, and the whole room chorused in sympathetic keening. The screams increased in volume as we put Gilla on her feet, and something emerged, was stuck . . .

I ran to a wall and hid my face. When I turned again, Gilla was unconscious on her mat surrounded by a pool of blood. Tib pronounced her to be saved and quickly disposed of a small bundle. It was a distressing event, but it gave me a good idea.

Hours later we returned to Tib's room to have dinner. She served fresh chicken and ale which I devoured with relish.

"Do you work all alone?" I asked her.

"So far; the order hasn't attracted many followers here in Rouen," she admitted, "though you can see that there's a need."

"Yes, you do worthy service. Sister Tiberga, perhaps we can reach an agreement."

I then told her that I was being pursued by a brutish squire in my village, a married man who wanted to ruin me. My father was dead, my brother had been beaten badly on two occasions when he'd tried to save me, and I'd been forced to run for my life. But I'd almost perished in the wilderness and saw now that my only recourse was to buy passage on the Seine and go to the coast, and thence to England where I had an aunt who would help me. However, I needed to leave in secrecy, and I needed fare for the journey.

"Why the secrecy?" she asked.

"Two reasons. My—the squire—comes frequently to Rouen to trade. Also he borrowed money for his forest rights from a man named Bonel of Rouen, and Bonel knows me well."

"Bonel the Jew?"

"He converted to Christianity, has a blue Christian Eye."

She shook her head. "Everyone knows Bonel the Jew, but he wears a patch and lives on Jews Street. 'Tis said he owns half of Rouen and he's the king's man."

"It must be the same," I said hastily. "If he's that important, you see my peril."

"I see it, but I don't know what I can do."

"If I give you service in your ward, could you let me have room and board and perhaps pay me a few deniers?"

She pursed thick lips. "Room and board, yes. Deniers, no. I might help you get to England, but I can't spare coin. Why don't you take a man or two? Once in England, no one would be the wiser and it's easy change—especially with your looks."

I flatly refused, but I could stay here and work. As for England, we would have to devise a plan.

SO I WAS ONCE AGAIN a prisoner, now of my own fears, for I refused to go into the street for any reason whatsoever. But I was of great value to Tib. She was very proud of a book on healing from a convent in Germany, but she couldn't read. Day after day, I read her which herbs to seek for various women's complaints and how to use the delivery stool, how to stop madness caused by the moon and other sundry cures. I also became adept at applying the elixirs and we made a laboratory of her kitchen. Ditma, a waif she'd inherited from one of her patients, collected herbs, small animals and birds—river birds were necessary for problems of vision and the liver.

Tib treated men as well as women—thus the curtained dormers—for she'd gained a good reputation for her successes. Shortly after I arrived a man sought her help in having his nose replaced, a most novel and dangerous procedure, but one for which there was an elaborate description in her book. I read it to her twice before she agreed to try, for the case was desperate. The poor churl had a seeping mormal on his nose that was eating deeper every hour and might soon devour his entire face. The man's name was Master Pudlicott, and Tib begged that I help her both with the operation and by reading as she went.

I met him for the first time on the day of the operation. He was a man beyond middle years with streaked hair, a thin frame and a most despondent expression. He had reason for worry: his mormal was unhealthily soft and oozy and smelled of glue.

He raised an agonized face when we were introduced.

"Ye'll be witness to my death, I doubt not," he said in hollow melancholy tones.

"Of course she won't," Tib assured him. "You're a healthy wight, sir, with one small blemish to excise. All you need is faith and patience; Alice and I will provide the skill, won't we, Alice? Now, pull the curtain, take off your clothes and put on this barmcloth. We must have access to your body during convalescence."

With a greater show of confidence than I knew she felt, Tib arranged several sharp knives, needle and thread and a paste on a table with an interested audience peering over her shoulder. I read slowly from the tome to keep her actions in proper order. She cleaned the mormal with a feather dipped in hot salt water—a procedure I'd added from my experience with Bonel—and then had Master Pudlicott drink of the poppy. She applied a paste to numb the area and began to cut a circle around his mormal, then to dig. He struggled and screamed as I struggled just as hard to hold him steady, hoping I wouldn't vomit into his face. When she finished, he had a crater where he'd formerly had a mountain.

Quickly she shifted her attention and turned him onto his side so that his injured nose nuzzled into his own upper arm. Once satisfied that the position was comfortable, she cleaned the arm and cut it open, then buried the nose into the new wound and stitched it onto the arm so that the poor man turned into an instant freak, attached to himself.

Master Pudlicott was in dreadful pain the next morning, but he showed it only by his sweat and deep scratches along his thighs. Tib remarked on his extraordinary courage and several patients wept to see him. He could breathe only through his mouth which was constantly dry and he couldn't avail himself of his own private privy, so he was in agony. Furthermore he would accept only a few ministrations from me, nothing below his waist—for which I felt secret relief. After an older woman had given him the pisspot behind his curtain, I moved to bathe his upper half, to feed him wine and soup, and to talk soothingly to him. I left him sucking a honey-teat, to be alternated with lemon for thirst.

The second day after the operation, I had a rude shock. I was in the ward and Tib was somewhere on the street when the officer Tib had insulted on the square entered the hospital without warning and called loudly for Tib. Before he could see my face, I crowded into Master Pudlicott's dormer and climbed onto his bed.

He was still drugged.

"Wad's wrong?" he asked, much befuddled.

"Nothing, lie still. This is the only way we can be sure you're not infected."

When the officer had left, I climbed out.

"Ab I?" came a plaintive voice.

"Are you what?"

"Infected?"

"No, you're doing wondrously well."

Tib had a great laugh at my expense when she returned. The officer was the man she paid each month to avoid taking a licence. I was much chagrined at my action, but *Deo gratias* Master Pudlicott seemed not to remember it.

Day after day Tib reported that she'd not seen Bonel on the streets and I hoped he might be away from Rouen. I also asked casually about the king, but she had no knowledge of his whereabouts, although his name brought on a volley of curses. Richard's former fiancée, Princess Alais of France, languished in a tower here in Rouen, Richard's prisoner. Twice her brother, King Philip, had assaulted the city in an effort to rescue her. The poor wretch had been seduced by King Henry, Richard's father, when she was only twelve, then kept as hostage for eighteen years, first by the old king, now by his son, Richard. It wasn't fair, Tib complained. I listened to the familiar tale and agreed: all the more reason that I must escape as soon as possible.

The example of Princess Alais, in truth, frightened me more than I wanted to admit. When I'd crept away at Vaudreuil, I'd followed an impulse to escape from an untenable situation and return home, but I hadn't examined the consequences if I were caught. Perhaps I'd thought it was the same as when I'd run from the Crusade, but it wasn't: then I'd been an expendable page; now I was a woman under contract to the king to bear him an heir. There were personal entanglements as well as legal—betrayal and treason—and the king would be justified in wrath if I were discovered. *Benedicite*.

Two weeks slipped by. I grew used to the routine of the hospital, became friends with Slink, who slept on my neck, and saw my first patient recover. Master Pudlicott was ready to have his nose cut free from his arm.

It was a tense moment. What if the graft didn't take? Everyone in the hospital gathered to watch Tib work. We gave him a rag to twist in his hands against pain, and Tib began.

Her small clean fingers moved with incredible delicacy and precision, making several thin slashes here and there on his arm. Almost at once the nose was free. He was too stiff to move, however, so I helped pull him upright, then slapped a poultice on the bleeding arm. We all stared at his nose. I could see no improvement at all. The skin was purple and yellow with deep pits; it looked like a chicken gizzard. Using thin sharp scissors, Tib clipped the excess flesh away which proved it was dead as it looked, for it had no sensation.

Everyone burst into enthusiastic applause.

"It was nothing," Tib protested modestly. "The graft took very well, Master Pudlicott, but I think I can make the nose less flat on the end. While the flesh is new, let me mold it to its former shape."

"Go ahead."

She pressed her fingers to the sides, then clamped two smooth sticks on the bridge. "Wear this a week, and you'll never know you had a mormal."

We all knelt to thank Saint Mary Magdalene for the miracle, but Master Pudlicott thanked Tib as well. Then he turned to me. With much fumbling, he begged me to accept his everlasting gratitude for my ministrations. I demurred that it was naught, for I'd done nothing medical, but I hoped I'd been a good friend. He assured me I had.

A WEEK LATER, Tib announced that my departure for England was secured.

I made her repeat it twice, not believing it was possible after all this time, but she assured me that her plan was perfect, a gift from Saint Mary Magdalene. But she was most mysterious as to her method.

"And may your drunken squire be pooped by a powdered bawd! Alice, pinch your cheeks, rub rose oil in your pits and be prepared to mingle eyes here tomorrow morning."

Her instructions made me uneasy, but I followed them. Still, hours slipped by and I dawdled in the ward, then the courtyard, with nothing to do. Finally Tib instructed me to go to the main house; someone wanted to see me. There was no one in the room but Master Pudlicott. He looked marvelously well, his complexion sanguine, his cod plump as a teardrop, and he was dressed in blue and gold like a French fop.

"I came to thank ye, Alice," he greeted me shyly. "No one ever cared for me as ye did."

"You've thanked me enough already, Master Pudlicott."

He cleared his throat. "I'm soon to sail back to England

and thence ride my rouncy to Norwich where I have a nice cot and a full garden."

"I envy you," I said from my heart.

"Aye, 'tis said that it snows flesh and pasties at my house. I like a good table." His whole face ran with sweat except for his grafted nose. "I have two daughters about yer age, but both be married and out of the way."

"You're to be congratulated, sir."

He brightened. " 'Tis a good situation, none better. But lonely. Plenty of roses but no honey."

I began to be impatient. Would this old fool never go? What if Tib came with the person who was to carry me to England?

Pudlicott suddenly pinched my cheek and I leaped backward. "Ye're a sweet rose yourself, aye, a nest of spicery to make an old bird turn goat, I trowe. Well, to the point: Sister Tiberga and I have settled on terms, and ye'll come with me as my bride. Can ye leave yet this week?"

Flabbergasted, I gaped at his swinish face, suddenly realizing that his mormal had detracted from the evil of other features that no graft could cure. He had tiny rook eyes, a hundred flabby chins where his neck should be, a pulpy gullet and bandy legs.

"Never!"

"I could wait ten days, but no later. Ye mun get used to a husband giving the orders."

A small cloud of white midges hovered around his face, attracted to the sweat and runny nose.

"You don't understand—I can't—won't marry!"

"Don't be coy, mistress; the deal be set. Tiberga has dowered ye with the cost of surgery and I'm in no mood to pay the fee now after we agreed."

"Didn't she tell you? I mean, she doesn't know that I'm wed already!"

In an instant the affable face screwed in anger.

"Ye've made a fool of me! You let me prattle, mistress, to

make gekkis! But ye'll regret it, aye, and that bawd as well. Don't think she pulls the shade o'er my eyes—I know what goes on here. She . . . she . . . I'll report her to the authorities!"

More than ugly, the man was mean. A small mind in a massive rage, and I panicked.

"No! Please, Master Pudlicott, she acted in good faith. It's my fault for not being open with her. Believe me, if I were free, there's no one on earth I'd rather wed than you. You're kind, courageous and very handsome now that your nose is fixed. Please!"

I couldn't have him hurt Tib.

He touched his nose. "Well . . . I can see that ye're disappointed. So am I, to tell truth. Yer husband mun be a clack-dish to put ye away."

Soon thereafter we said goodbye.

I couldn't conceal my disappointment from Tib.

"How could you think I'd wed such a loathsome pocked toad?"

She gazed, astonished. "You're mighty haughty, my girl! He offers protection which you badly need and property as well!"

"He's old, diseased, has no rank!"

"Listen to her! What rank does a carpenter have?"

I quickly sought to remedy my error. "I mean—*Benedicite*, Tib, you befriend women, save them from the ravishing of men."

"Ravishing is not the same as honest wedlock," she said with asperity. "Look you, my bewitching child, you need to understand the world in which you live. You don't want to be a nun—couldn't be, except in my order where you need no handsome dowry—don't want to peddle your wares, have neither father nor husband to protect you. You'll not do better than Pudlicott. Think it over."

I stopped arguing, but I didn't think it over. I recognized, however, that my plan must be changed, for Tib could pay me nothing, and I couldn't spend the rest of my life locked in a single room with her patients. Within a few hours I'd cornered Tib again.

"Have you come to your senses, girl?" she began.

"No, Tib, not if you mean Pudlicott. I couldn't stand to have him near my person."

"Even if I promise that his bellows lack air? That his pump won't make water rise? His trumpet be flat as a trampled horn?"

I shivered in disgust. "Even then, but . . ."

"Don't be such a child, darling. You act as if you're aghast at a man's tool, but how else will you get to England? You can't build a wood hut without trees."

"I'll worry about England later. For now, I must get out of Rouen. What's the next town on the Seine?"

She frowned thoughtfully. "I have a friend who runs a barge as far as La Bouille, though soothly I don't know what you would do there."

"Could I go yet today?"

She put a plump hand on my arm. "Alice, take care, I know you seek a hiding place. Rouen is a great center, and I've found that it's easier to disappear in a city."

"Today?" I repeated.

"Tomorrow at Nones." She stared and gave up. "I can let you have fare and a few pence."

I hugged her fervently in gratitude, then went to seek Ditma. At first the servant boy couldn't comprehend my request; his clothes were old and full of rents, he explained —at least the only tunic he could spare, which was too small for him.

I took the odorous rags and examined them carefully. They would do; once again I would escape in the guise of a boy. The next morning Tib helped me tie my hair with one bandeau, my breasts with another—as tight as she dared— and I pulled on the tights with their suspicious brown stains and stench of boy's sweat, wrapped my lower legs in strips and put on soft wornout shoes, let fall the scratchy tunic over my head and adjusted the billowing skirt at my knees, fastened the hood tight under my chin. Tib's sharp eye assured me that I would pass. I tied my own dress and coins into a sack and cast it over my shoulder. Tib then volunteered to walk me to the wharf.

We started across the empty square under the glaring sun and had almost reached the downward path to the river when we were accosted by a young squire who looked as much like a girl as I did a boy. Immediately I recognized him as one of Richard's army, called Louis or sometimes "Louisa."

I jerked Tib's arm and pulled her into a dark alleyway.

"This is not the road," she protested.

Too panicked to answer, I made her stumble on our fast descent. We came into a tiny airless square and I sighed with relief.

"Now which way?" I asked.

Louis rounded the corner from another path and waggled a finger. "Caughts you!" he lisped.

*Benedicite.*

"You're a pretty kit," he addressed me in jocund manner, "except that your fur looks straggly. I could lick it flat if you let me."

He put a familiar hand under my cheeks.

"Stick your noble post in some other hole," Tib snarled. "This be my son and he's not for sale."

"Everything's for sale if the price is right," argued Louis, "and I'm taken with the pretty perversity of his swaying hips. Soothly, he makes my bodkin pain me."

"Find a Painted Willie to relieve your stretch," Tib snapped. "Now leave us alone."

She pulled me rapidly, and I lowered my chin, but Louis was not to be put off. "Come, sweets, you can pay all your mother's debts with that jolly body."

His lashes curled like houseleek petals; his pursed lips

sucked inward like a moist fud; his small pink snout quivered in anticipation.

"Just a little feel . . ."

He reached his hand and I slapped it smartly.

Reached again and my bandeau slipped to my waist; he saw the bulge of my breasts, instinctively touched, drew his hand back as if stung.

Suddenly he whirled me so I faced him, forced my chin upward. "Damn me for a fool!"

He ran toward the palace as if his tail were on fire.

"Hurry, Tib," I pleaded. "He recognized me!"

She was confounded. "How could he? He's not your squire, is he?"

"Don't ask questions—just hurry!"

Together we scurried to the Seine and the barge that would carry me to safety. We reached a small dock, saw the bark, which was no more than a raft and half sunk at that. Tib had cried out "Bertrand!" when we were seized from behind.

Louis with Richard's mercenary Mercadier!

"What do you think you're doing?" Tib screamed. "We've broken no law."

Mercadier's iron fisticuffs struck her face, and she collapsed with a howl and a spurt of blood.

"Stop it!" I beat his chest with no effect whatsoever. "She's innocent! Take me, but let her be!"

Without a word, he picked me up like a sack of corn and strode up the path where his horse was waiting.

11

CREAMING FOR TIB, I WAS TOSSED ONTO MER-
cadier's steed as he mounted behind me. A
small crowd gathered, awed by the giant
mercenary with his close-cropped hair and
sword-slashed mouth.

"Go to Tib!" I cried to women I recognized. "She's
wounded!"

Mercadier spurred his horse to a gallop as people cursed
and stumbled out of our way. Through the narrow streets
of Rouen we rushed directly to the royal castle. Richard's
guard filled the courtyard.

"Let me be!" I ordered Mercadier as he lifted me down.

He answered by dragging me through a crowded anteroom, into a hall where Hamo and an old crone were standing at the foot of a stair.

"Greetings, Lady Alix," Hamo said, his dark eyes bulging
at my boy's garb.

Mercadier was gone; I was in their care. Hamo introduced
the dame as Mistress Devorgilla and together they led
me up the narrow uneven steps to a small apartment. I
entered first; the door snapped shut and was locked behind
me.

I shouted through the gridded opening. "How dare you
lock me here? Let me out!"

They'd disappeared.

I ran to the window and gazed down on the courtyard
below. *Deus juva me*, I was in a tower. In the distance I could
see the lavender Seine creeping through the crepuscular
light, the same view Princess Alais had. There could be no
doubt as to my situation. I sank to the floor and leaned

against the rough stone, closed my eyes: the image of Tib's bloody face came back and I opened them again. I must devise a story at once and it must be convincing, both for my sake and for Tib's.

Twilight came slowly in my western window, then lingered. A small rat crawled under the corner of the door and looked at me inquisitively.

"You may have room but no board," I told him. "They're going to starve me into submission."

I was wrong, for Mistress Devorgilla appeared with a supper tray as well as a jurdon for my functions. She put both down without a word: I had a fresh venison mess and new-baked bread to be washed down with the king's own Bordeaux. I tossed a few crumbs to my cellmate and ate the rest. I then slept in a sitting position.

At dawn, Mistress Devorgilla came to collect my leavings and said she'd ordered a bath for me; I noted that the bath didn't arouse my lust. After I was washed, she supplied fresh linens and a gaudy Plantagenet tunic, while I folded Ditma's clothes into my sack. If I hadn't seen how Tib had been treated, I would have been less fearful. At least the king was seeing to my well-being.

After another two days in the cramped space, however, I was filled with wanhope. I watched comings and goings below me, twice saw the king, but couldn't understand the delay in our meeting. I changed my story, saw omissions and contradictions, changed it again, then went back to the original. *Benedicite.*

Late on the third afternoon, Hamo came to get me. He didn't speak—possibly under orders—and I didn't force him. Much as I tried to be calm, however, my breath was exceedingly shallow and I tripped twice on the stair. He escorted me to a small chamber where a military meeting was in session. I stood at the back and attempted to be inconspicuous.

King Richard was pointing to a crude map pinned to a

wall and giving instructions for attack. His eyes were red, his voice hoarse. He ignored me, if he saw me at all.

"This is where Philip destroyed the castle—the sappers placed their tunnels along this line, and fired the tower here, using the latest methods. It had been carefully calculated for months. He then rode east, but sent his mercenaries to destroy Fontaine, here"—he pointed to a mark on the Seine, probably the village I'd seen under attack—"which has no strategic importance except that it's too damned close to Rouen. I'm leaving now to strengthen our western fortifications, but pressure must be kept up in the east. Leicester, you'll follow close on France's flanks and harass him; John, you'll divert him by riding to Conches."

There followed a series of questions and comments as plans were honed. In my nervous state, I found the meeting interminable. At last, however, the lords and knights left. Briefly, Richard and I were alone.

"Hamo!" he called without glancing at me. "Bring in Bonel."

The king sat behind his desk and rubbed his temples wearily. I watched the door.

Bonel entered, completely changed. Dressed in gold-shot green silk, he wore a strange golden hat that hung from his crown halfway down his back, jewels of great worth—but no cross—and his Christian Eye was covered with a patch embroidered with gold thread. Furthermore, his hair had been cropped to short curls and he had a small square beard. He was as rich and exotic as an oriental emperor and exceedingly handsome, for patch and beard covered his scar.

He nodded to me; I nodded back. It was a small greeting but, compared to the king's, warm as springtime. He then bowed to the king, and I did so as well.

"You talk to her, Bonel," Richard ordered in a curiously dead voice. He then rose and went to stare out the window as if he had no interest in the proceedings.

"Why don't you sit down, Lady Alix?" Bonel said pleasantly, indicating a small bench in front of the desk.

I sat opposite him.

"We're gratified that you weren't killed in the assault at Vaudreuil."

It was my first test.

"Assault!" I exclaimed with wonder. "I thought it was an earthquake. Or even a volcano such as we saw in Sicily."

Bonel glanced at the king. "So you remember it."

"Not the event—assault?—only before and afterward."

"Suppose you tell us everything you recall, down to the smallest detail."

I then recounted how Emma and I had gone to a nearby cottage to buy fresh eggs and bread, how we'd returned to the castle while the parley took place in the field. Then Emma had declared herself weary and had returned to the tower to rest. I'd sat in the window seat of the great hall on its eastern side, away from the Seine. Suddenly I'd heard a giant rumbling in the earth below and was simultaneously hurled through the air. My tunic was all aflame—though I had no sensation of heat—as I shot high as a tree.

"Her lie confuses Greek fire with a catapult," Richard remarked acidly. "Tell her to confine herself to burning or falling, but not to insult us by claiming she flew."

Bonel tapped his fingers. "Quite so."

"I can only say what I remember," I said humbly, "but if you don't want to hear . . ."

Bonel interrupted. "Perhaps the intense heat underground had an explosive effect. Go on."

By God's grace I'd landed in the castle's fish pond, and the fire had been extinguished. I'd waded to shore, but was injured and disoriented. I'd landed on my head, which throbbed most grievously, and didn't know where I was. My desperate purpose was to escape from the fire. Sobbing and praying, I'd fought my way up the hillside, there to hide.

Stumbling into the wood, convinced that I was fleeing the devastation of Wanthwaite when my parents had been killed, that I was being pursued by their murderers, I'd moved stilly as a fish. Once, I'd watched soldiers destroy a village on the Seine; I'd been sure they were looking for me. I'd lost all memory of recent events, Vaudreuil or—the king. Finally, very sick and near starvation, I'd entered a walled city, not knowing it was Rouen.

"But you must have learned soon. You knew that I lived here, Alix. Why didn't you come to me for help?"

"After Sister Tiberga saw me faint in the cathedral square and took me in, she nursed me for a long time before I was sufficiently myself to wonder where I was. The instant I knew I was in Rouen, I asked for you; she denied knowing you."

The king spoke from the window. "How could she not know Bonel? He's powerful here."

I addressed my answer to Bonel. "Now that I see you, I think I framed my question in a way that misled. I asked for the king's man with a blue Christian Eye."

Bonel touched his beard. "I'm again a Jew, Alix. My conversion was made under duress and the king generously released me from false vows."

At another time I would have been interested, but now all I wanted to know was whether they believed me. I thought Bonel might; I was less sure about Richard.

The king strode back to the desk and sank in his chair.

"If you had the sense to ask about Bonel, you should have had the sense to ask about my whereabouts as well."

"I did, Your Majesty," I replied truthfully, "but Sister Tiberga didn't know."

"No, I'm not in the habit of informing whores of my itinerary. But there is a mayor of Rouen, a castellan in my castle, a bishop—virtually any man on the street could have told you." He was indifferent no longer; his eyes were hot slits, reminiscent of Eleanor's.

I hesitated, not certain whether I should contradict him about Tib's being a whore now or stay with my defense.

"The truth is," he went on in his roughened voice, "that you were running away from your royal duties. You wanted to avoid me, by God, even if it meant becoming a harlot yourself!"

Both Bonel and I were startled by his vehemence. The king was in a rage, but something else as well—agony?

"Oh no, Your Majesty! Soothly, I forgot our bargain—you—for a time! I thought I was in England . . ."

"Don't play me for a fool! I've seen soldiers take direct blows on their helmets and be completely themselves within hours. You tried to escape—just as you did in Acre! And then you worked the streets, fucked with every knave that would buy!"

"No!" I implored. "I was a nurse in a hospital!"

"Quaint terminology for riding the cock. Is it English?"

"A convent-hospital, My Lord, devoted to Saint Mary Magdalene."

"Yes, the whore's saint. Her stewes pock the country's fair face and will be leveled one by one."

"Please, no, they help poor women."

The king went to the door and banged it with his fists. "Hamo, bring the witness!"

Bonel shook his head in warning at me, then watched Richard with growing amazement. Well, I thought grimly, I'd tried to warn him on the road, hadn't I? This was his magnificent monarch who would bring justice.

The door opened and Hamo led Master Pudlicott into the room. I stared in utter astonishment at the churl, then at the king and Bonel. How could this knot-head possibly give testimony about Vaudreuil? How could he be trusted on any subject whatsoever? His very presence was an affront to honest procedure. Richard's face looked sick, Bonel's noncommittal, and Pudlicott preened with pompous self-importance.

His mormal was bigger than ever, purple and pulpy as a

fig, and his clothing would have been comical if the occasion hadn't been so serious. He'd obviously given careful thought to his appearance with the result that he looked like a professional jester: his pointed yellow hat sported a curious vegetable which was supposed to be a feather, his scarlet motley was tied with a sash which had fallen in his soup, his leggings drooped and his new shoes boasted long points that flopped like dead fish when he walked. But just as he'd turned from fair to foul in Tib's house, he now turned from silly to sinister. His small vicious eyes slid in my direction with the cold promise of revenge. *Benedicite*, was my fate to be decided by this scorned fool?

He fell abjectly before the king.

"Yer Majesty."

Richard spoke across his prostrate form. "Is this one of your 'poor women' who needs a nun's care?"

"No, Your Majesty." I tried to hold the king's eye, to plead silently for justice, but he looked away.

"Rise and approach the bench," Bonel ordered crisply.

With some difficulty, for he knelt on his own shoe, Pudlicott sidled forth.

"You know the accused?"

"Aye," simpered the ass, "only she never told me as how she were the king's . . ."

Richard's fist struck the table. "Stay with the question!"

"Oh, that I will," Pudlicott assured him with obsequious delight, "only I wanted to assure yer most glorious Majesty that I meant no offense by what happened, that's all my meaning."

"How did you meet the lady?" Bonel intervened.

Pudlicott smirked. " 'Tis a most fascinating tale if I do say so, for I oncit had a remarkable growth on the tip of my nose, like to a peeled egg only that it seeped most prodigiously and . . ."

"Lady Alix." Bonel interrupted. "How did you meet her?"

Pudlicott bowed and fanned his face against midges.

"Aye, I'm coming to her only ye must know the circum-stances. On the advice of my friend, Taggle, I sought 'Mad Tib' for help in my problem, fer she snipped three carbun-cles offen Taggle's neck and . . ."

"And Lady Alix worked for Sister Tiberga?" Bonel sug-gested.

"Tib had the barber's skills, but she needed young Alice here to read from a sorcerer's book in my case. Alice is wonderful literal."

"And after the surgery?"

Pudlicott raised his brows, licked his blabber lip. "Ye mun grasp my situation afore ye can follow what happed. Tib sewed my nose to my arm so I were fastened like a scorpion to his tail."

An apt image, I thought grimly.

"I couldn't move nor service myself if ye take my mean-ing. Therefore Tib removed all my garb and wrapped me in an apron which covered me in front, but left me with my bare erse showing and no britches between."

He paused for dramatic effect. Neither the king nor Bonel reacted, but I had a surge of dread. Suddenly I guessed the direction of Pudlicott's testimony.

"I were hid behind a curtain in a little box they called a dorter. One nurse attended my functions and Alice here gave me of the honey-teat and stroked me most sweetly, until one day . . ."

He looked directly at me, his splenetic glee plain as his mormal.

"One day as I slept, the wench crept onto my perch and whispered into my ear, 'I mun test ye fer fever. Lie ever so still and let me feel.' Whereupon she trespassed with her tongue and . . ."

"He's lying!" I cried, incredulous. "I never . . ."

"Did you climb into his bed?" Richard snapped.

"No!"

"Go on," he said to Pudlicott.

"As Yer Majesty pleases," the churl sniveled unctuously. "However, I meant no harm. I'm a man as most men and I were in a dangerous position wi' the hussy. If I resisted her, I feared my nose would come unhooked." He paused, but no one commented. "The next day, it were the same, her lips as soft as any snail, but soon the lass proved most supple fer she leaned her buttery bar o'er my head and put my rat in her hole."

"How can you listen to his obscenities?" I cried. "Look at him! Can't you see that he's lying?"

"Are you finished?" Bonel asked Pudlicott.

"Oh no, Yer Honor, the merry swonk went on fer many days and I . . ."

"We don't need details. Please finish with your testimony."

"Aye." The scoundrel turned somberly to the king. "When I were cured and ready to depart, the whore, Tib, presented me with a bill that even a Jew couldn't pay." He nodded in deference to Bonel. "I protested mightily, but the greedy old trot demanded every denier. Then she gave me a way out: she claimed as how I'd seeded poor Alice's ditch with a bastard and I should marry the wench."

"Never!" I shouted.

"Marry her and carry her back to England, where she wanted to go," he finished relentlessly.

"Yes, she's made it plain that she wants to return to England," King Richard said.

"Not like that! Not with him!" I cried.

"That will be all, Master Pudlicott," Bonel said, ignoring my outcry. "We thank you for your cooperation."

"No," I protested, "let me question him. It isn't fair!"

"You'll have an opportunity to refute his statements if you can," Bonel assured me ominously.

Pudlicott eyed me with snide triumph. "Take care of my poor babe, Alice, doomed to be a beggar I doubt not."

"Hamo!" Bonel gestured impatiently.

The page took Pudlicott's arm and forced him to leave the court. The king slumped back, folded his hands wearily behind his head and gazed out of the window.

Boncl spoke to me. "You've heard the accusations, Lady Alix. How do you respond?"

"Every word was a lie," I said bitterly.

"If they're lies, you should be able to refute them."

I quoted back his own words concerning the Jews. "Some lies are so gross, so wild and pernicious, that they defy denial. Yet a reasonable person will recognize them as calumnies." I then turned to Richard and quoted his words as well. "It ill befits a prince of nations to honor such obvious inventions as truth."

His lips twisted. "You were seen by a city official entering Pudlicott's bed."

I lost breath. His steady gaze held me, waited. If I told the truth, that I feared discovery, I would also have to admit that I knew what I was doing and didn't want to be found. *Benedicite!*

"So much for your denials," he said bitterly.

"The curtain often closed behind me when I administered his honey-teats and there was no licentious purpose," I retorted desperately. "I dare say many people saw me enter his dorter, but it signifies nothing."

"Tell us in your own words about your relationship with the witness," Bonel ordered.

I then told the truth, more or less, about the illness, treatment, how Pudlicott had been smitten by love and courted me, how he'd approached Tib for my hand and how she—pitying me for my loss of memory and depressed circumstances—had accepted his offer. Therefore my swift refusal had offended him and surprised her. I'd then determined to leave Rouen, partly to escape his anger and her pressures.

"In short," Richard said, "you corroborate his testimony."

"Not at all, Your Majesty!" I replied. "He's a good liar

insofar as he stays with the theme of truth, but he distorts where it pleases him."

"High praise from the mistress of the art," was his acid comment. "Speaking of a 'distortion,' are you pregnant?"

"I'm as likely to have a baby as you are!"

We both flushed at this unfortunate reference to our former agreement.

To cover my confusion, I turned to Bonel. "Obviously the court will accept the perjuries of a bitter buffoon over my word."

"Why bitter?" Bonel asked quickly.

I glanced at Richard. "Because men of puffed pride and devious motive can't bear rejection."

There was an ominous silence.

I continued. "But my truth need not rest on my words alone. I demand that Sister Tib be brought to court."

The silence deepened before Bonel broke it gently. "That's impossible, Alix. Your friend Tib is . . ."

"I wouldn't listen to a whore in any case!" Richard cried in a rage.

But I hardly heard him. Tib was what? Dead? I stared at Bonel, but he shook his head slightly in warning.

He continued smoothly. "Lady Alix, the king is profoundly disappointed that . . ."

"I'm not disappointed!" Richard contradicted in gravel tones.

Bonel amended his words. "*I'm* disappointed that you took the honor bestowed upon you so lightly but, as His Majesty says, no harm had yet been done."

"But God's feet, it was close," Richard added with a shudder. "To think I might have mixed my royal seed with that villain's . . ."

"As of this moment, therefore," Bonel continued calmly, "your contract with the king is null and void. I'm told you have a copy in your possession. Would you give it to me, please?"

He held out a hand.

"I don't have it," I lied, for it lay in my treasure belt tied to my inner thigh where I always kept valuables. I hardly knew why I concealed the truth, but I followed an instinct.

Richard's whelks were now livid, his hands shaking as the Angevin choler took him. "Lying bitch! Strumpet! Must I advertise to the world that your children are not mine? Is that what you want?"

"On my mother's soul, I'm not a strumpet! And I don't care what you say to the world or anyone else!"

"Where—is—that—contract?"

"I had it on my person when my clothes caught fire. It either burned or it's lying at the bottom of the fish pond—I don't know."

His knuckles were blue-white. "Ger her out of here."

I bowed, then looked up. "If you're finished with me, My Lord, may I go back to Wanthwaite?"

"Criminals are punished in my kingdom, Lady Alix."

"But I wasn't a . . ."

"I speak of treason."

It was the first time that I was truly frightened. Treason was an ominous word and his controlled tone left no doubt that he meant it. But how had I committed treason? Was fleeing from the king's bed an act against the state?

Bonel turned an amethyst pendant as if it were his cross, but I couldn't read his expression.

I flourished uneasily and left with Hamo.

ANOTHER WEEK PASSED in my lonely prison, time for me to pray that Tib would recover from her wound, but not time to relieve my own guilt. I'd done it to her. *Benedicite*, why hadn't I told her the truth? Or escaped on my own? I swore that if I ever had another opportunity I would act alone. There was also time to lay every curse and spell I could recall from the Celts on the head of Master Pudlicott—may his mormal devour him—time to train the rat to eat from my hand.

Then I was informed that I was to leave with the king's party, his prisoner as he made his rounds. I was almost sorry; I preferred the rat to Richard. At least my relationship with the rodent was amicable. Not that I blamed the king entirely for his wrath. The evidence of Master Pudlicott *had* been devastating, and Tib *was* a whore, and I *had* run away. After all, as the king pointed out, he wasn't a fool. He had a reason for ire from his vantage point, but I couldn't fathom the depth of his suspicions. Or his decision to drag me with his army. Why didn't he leave me in Rouen as he had Princess Alais all these years?

Mistress Devorgilla packed a small trunk of linens and changes of garb for me, which Hamo carried down the stair. I felt my first happiness in weeks to see Sea Mew saddled and waiting. A groom offered me his hand which I ignored, but he insisted.

"I don't need . . ."

Our palms met: a small packet was pressed into my fist.

He kept his eyes on my bridle and said through his teeth, "Open alone."

Pretending to adjust my neckerchief, I dropped the packet into my bodice.

We rode at an easy pace, our reins slack, letting the great coursers set the stride. I was close to the end of a line of fifty men or more with Hamo at my side. The August sun was exceedingly hot, but we didn't travel far. Almost at once we came upon another small walled city and entered the fortified castle.

The castle was old, hardly more than a squat square tower, and Hamo pulled my trunk up a steep ramp. The king was greeted by an ancient castellan, William Fitzralph, and we all crowded into a hall to hear a discussion of the ramparts. I stayed near the door, then asked a knight close by if he could show me the garderobe. Embarrassed to be seen speaking to me, he nodded to a door in the corner and moved quickly away.

I entered the foulest room I'd ever experienced. The

gomph stick was a disgrace and I thought the castellan should be mending his privy instead of his ramparts, but I was not using the place for its original purpose, *Deo gratias.* I locked the door and reached for the packet. On a sliver of wood was printed a cryptic message: "Tib all right. Courage."

That was all, no signature, but it must be from Bonel. I didn't understand how Tib could be all right after what I'd seen, but . . .

There was a sudden thumping on the privy door.

"Open at once!" Richard shouted on the other side.

Quickly I dropped the message down the pit and obeyed. His fist was upraised, his face twisted in choler.

"How dare you sequester yourself?" he roared in a frenzy.

Mortified, I peered over his shoulder, but the men behind him pretended to be deaf and blind.

"Your Majesty," I said mildly, "even a prisoner has a right to some privacy."

"You have no rights whatsoever!"

I counted ten heartbeats before trusting my voice. "However that may be, that was my reason."

"For hours? You were trying to escape through the shaft!"

Unfortunately such a thought had never occurred to me.

"Stay in sight henceforth." He strode back to his dais.

The shock of this scene marked the end of fear. My humor changed from melancholy to choler, from wet cold earth to fire; my animal, natural and vital virtues were jarred to action. Whore, prisoner, liar, was I? So be it. Henceforth I would pray to the thieving Mercury to help me steal my freedom, invoke swift summer as my season so I could escape in haste, use my back brain to remember who I was and what I wanted, pray to Mary Magdalene to raise me from this living death. As for Richard, may he be stuck in the shaft of a gardepit for all time.

MY HUMOR WAS SET on course, but my circumstances didn't consequently change. Hamo was assigned as my "handmaiden" and he in turn was under the supervision of Master Ivo the Balistarius, Richard's closest confidant next to Mercadier, both of them ruthless mercenaries. Neither man made any attempt to befriend me, nor did I want to confide in them; we all knew the price paid for protecting any person out of Richard's favor. Indeed, the whole company treated me as if I were a pariah, a role I welcomed: the more isolated I was, the better my chance for escape. So I gave clothing to Hamo for the washerwomen who followed us, accepted my trenchers of food, occasionally had him arrange for baths. Otherwise I traveled in total solitude in the midst of an army.

Only William Marshal still made a point of being courteous at all times. Not that I credited him with a gallant heart; rather I saw him as a canny politician who was keeping my goodwill in case Richard's mood shifted. Still, his small attentions were more pleasant than the ostracism of the others. Great lords and prelates joined and left us according to our location, but a small nucleus moved everywhere. Along with Crusading knights were Petro de Tantentonne and Martino de Nazareth, who were Franks born in Syria, and a swarthy company in strange garb who looked to be Saracens, which must be wrong because they had been the king's arch-enemy on the Crusade. William Marshal, however, informed me that my guess was right; Richard had imported them because of their skill with the crossbow and Greek fire.

Our days blurred into a single pattern. We moved from one castle to another within a morning, for they were placed in a network of lines that covered Normany and were often in sight of one another: furthermore one great castle supervised several small fortifications. The king checked each one, spoke to its seneschal and made such improvements as were necessary from storing more grain in towers to clearing ditches. During the long evenings, the men gathered round the king to drink, tell stories of former exploits, play at bones

and backgammon. Richard liked chess but had no good partner, and certainly I didn't offer to challenge him.

For the first two weeks, I concentrated all my energies in
being inoffensive. Never again did I use the garderobe
within castles—where they existed—but crouched behind
bushes. I didn't speak from one day to the next unless forced
to. I kept myself neat and clean and as demure as I could in
the gaudy Plantagenet wardrobe provided me; I had no
wimples and couldn't braid my hair because of its shoulder
length, but I combed it with pronged sticks and made it lie
flat.

And I watched, waited, learned.

Henceforth I would not be a stranger in this land.

After the second week, I began to cultivate a friend, my
horse. Sea Mew was going to swim the Channel for me
one day soon—at least symbolically—and I wanted to
strengthen our relationship. I groomed him carefully every
day and saw to it that he had the best rations available. Then
in late afternoons, after we'd both rested from the morning
ride, I took him into the field to teach him verbal and hand
commands and close maneuvers—always with the page
Hamo in attendance, of course. Slowly I dispensed with his
saddle, taught him to jump higher and higher hedges as if
they were walls. I bent close to his back, reins loose, for
soon I would get rid of his bridle and guide him with my
knees. Nothing would impede a fast escape.

One afternoon, outside the castle of Bayeux, the king
came to watch me. I stopped the instant I caught his figure
in the corner of my eye, but he called for me to continue. I
pressed Sea Mew to a fast gallop in a wide circle, and once
his pace was set, I let go of the reins, lay flat on his rump
with my hands over my head. After three rounds, I sat
upright, then swung off and landed on my feet. Instantly
my steed came to my side.

The king clapped slowly, a mocking applause.

"Come here."

Reluctantly I crossed the flattened grass, placing my bare feet carefully.

"You've always ridden well," he acknowledged, "but why risk your neck? Why the acrobatics?"

I bowed deeply before I replied. "I need diversion, Your Majesty."

Our eyes met, his cold and calculating, mine as hard as I could make them.

"Your language is still quaint. Do you mean you need to jar your unwanted child from the womb?"

My heart hissed in my ears like waves from the sea.

"Don't look so innocent," he said sarcastically. "We both know you carry Pudlicott's putrid worm, which you no doubt would like to drop."

"You might as well say that I ride to make the man fall out of the moon!"

"You have all the signs of pregnancy."

"What do you mean?"

"We have our ways of checking."

I was baffled. Then gradually a terrible thought took shape: when Hamo gave my linens to the washerwoman, she could check them for signs of blood. Was it possible?

"It will soon be past all doubt." The king verified my suspicion.

And I lost control. "Your search for proof is abominable! Next time you take me to trial, raise my skirts at once! I was bleeding when I came before you in Rouen."

The Angevin wrath rose to meet my English ire. "I need no further proof of your lechery—we have impeccable testimony."

"Aye, the word of a garrulous sod! A liar and snake, a miserable churl, and the great King of England believes him instead of me!"

His face was now bright red, and I expected to be smitten to the ground, but he shouted hoarsely, "I didn't take his worthless word, didn't have to! We had yet another witness.

One of my own knights saw you soliciting on the streets of Rouen! Selling your wares in the company of that other vicious slut!"

Now I was so angry that I lost all decorum, all sense of personal safety, all control of my tongue as I lapsed into my native English, forgetting Richard couldn't understand.

"Aye, one of your knights! You Normans speak so 'quaintly'—as if a knight were the same thing as a man. You mean a lizard with a female face!"

His answer showed he hadn't followed. "You smirked and led his hand astray! Offered your jolly body for cash—his very words!"

"Did he also tell you that I was dressed as a boy? That he spoke to me as a boy? If I were going to solicit, I would do so as a female!"

He grasped the word *boy*. "He knew you were a girl!"

"Oh no, Your Majesty, he didn't know, any more than you did! Remember the song you composed for me in which you admitted that you couldn't resist my boyish charms?"

By his puzzled expression I realized he'd lost the theme entirely, which was lucky for me. He understood my sarcasm enough, however, to raise his mighty fist.

Quickly I brushed my forehead. Sea Mew caught the signal and reared, hooves flailing.

"Careful, Your Majesty!"

He stepped back and by the time he could say more, I'd mounted and was halfway across the field.

A HUGE CONVOCATION WAS gathered at Bayeux to prepare for the offensive against King Philip. I sat sulking on a bench in the cathedral, wishing I could be outside on my horse, but Master Ivo watched me intently. To divert myself, I studied a long embroidery hung on the wall that depicted the Norman invasion of our fair isle, a sad day for England.

I was dozing by the time the meeting was over. As I left in Ivo's company, a hand took my elbow.

"Come with me," Bonel ordered

"Best not talk to me—I'm worse than a leper."

"Master Ivo, I'll accompany Lady Alix back to the palace," Bonel said.

Without a protest, Ivo bowed and let me go.

Bonel hurried me along the streets, then turned into a small garden inn and led me to his quarters. I looked at his room with wonder. It bore no relationship to the timbered exterior of the inn, for it was strewn with thick carpets, cushions and rich embroideries from the orient. Boat-shaped brass lamps stood on small folding tables to make it bright as day even after the sun set, and there were three leather-bound books on one surface, the most I'd ever seen all at once. Standing in the center of this rare splendor, Bonel was a shimmering jewel. His tunic was made of a thousand ribbons stitched together so that every time he turned another hue took precedence, now ruby red, now sapphire blue, now emerald. His turban was deep burgundy edged in the same ribbons. I'd stepped into a strange Byzantine world, rich beyond compare, inhabited by an unfamiliar potentate.

There were four servants, all of them Christian to judge by their crosses. One poured two filigree goblets of dark sweet wine for us, after which Bonel ordered them to wait outside.

"Please sit on a pillow and take your ease, Lady Alix."

I sank onto softness, placed my wine carefully on the carpet beside me, for a single sip had made my head buzz, and I didn't want to lose my senses as I had with Eleanor at the stream.

Bonel rested so close that our knees almost touched, raised his cup, then put it aside as well. When he spoke, his voice was a dagger in a jeweled sheath.

"Let's hear the truth now, Alix."

"Truth?"

"An alien word in your lexicon," he said dryly. "It means the facts and motives for your behavior these past weeks."

I set my jaw to resist.

"It seems to me it's your time for truth-telling, not mine. What happened to Tib?"

"Her jaw was broken, one molar loosened but not lost. I had my physician care for her; King Richard sent a gift of money for compensation."

"Richard sent money?" I repeated with disbelief.

"He's a fair man; he knows she received the blow meant for you."

"Why didn't he hit me then?"

Bonel drank deeply of his wine, poured more from a gold and silver flask. "Do you have to ask?"

I flushed.

"I'm waiting for your answer, Alix."

"Of course I ran away. What did you expect after you'd lied to me over the length and breadth of England about how safe I was? You knew all the time I was going to be the king's concubine, didn't you?"

"Yes," he replied tersely. "Now the facts, and I mean exact facts, My Lady. Your very life may depend on your memory for detail."

There was real threat in his suave voice as well as his words and my heart thumped, though it may have been from the wine.

"Very well. I went to the farmhouse as I described, but I didn't return to the castle. Instead I walked by the river. Therefore I observed the sappers when they rode back from mining the castle—though I didn't have any idea what they'd done—and . . ."

"Go on."

I'd been about to describe the Scot but saw no purpose in revealing my toty illusions, so went on—how I'd seen my opportunity and had run to the woods. He pushed me for a day-by-day description of my survival along the Seine, then my experiences in Rouen.

"The worse mistake I made was climbing into bed with

that noseless toad, but I thought the officer had come to get me. If I'd contradicted Pudlicott when you asked me, it would have betrayed that I was hiding."

"Richard knew you were hiding anyway. If you'd told the truth, he might have believed you. It will be hard to undo now."

"I don't want to undo anything," I said stubbornly. "The king didn't let Mercadier harm me, as you said, and he isn't abusing me now. I can see that he's angry, but his anger keeps him from touching me at least. I prefer this arrangement."

Bonel's brown eye was hard.

"You may prefer it, but I don't."

"It's no longer your affair," I declared.

"It's solely my affair at this point, for I'm the one who must remedy your foolishness."

"Did the king order you?"

Bonel rose and brought another cushion. When it was in place, he faced me again.

"The orders come from me. Alix, you're going to regain the king's good graces with my help, and you're going to give him a son."

"But hardly with your help." I flushed as I heard the implication, but he paid no attention.

"I'll tolerate no more silly rebellion, no more childish trumpery. You'll do exactly as I say at all times."

"You have no hold over me. How dare you threaten me?"

"You're essential to my plans, and I'll brook no misbehavior."

"Is this the way you reward me for the stank?"

"I'll pay that debt in time. You're a mere joist in a large scheme, but placed so you carry critical weight. I intend that you carry it well."

"What plan? What scheme? You tell me the truth 'in fine detail.'"

"You are the linchpin in my strategy to save the Jews."

I sat up abruptly.

"Your first assignment is to produce an heir."

I felt disoriented, as if the drink or the exotic surroundings had robbed me of wits. "You speak in riddles."

"Do I? Then let me be clear. Since the York massacre, it's become increasingly obvious that the Jews have a vested interest in the succession of kings. King Richard is the best monarch in Europe toward the Jews, just as King Philip is the worst, but Richard's health is precarious—partly because of his constant warfare. Therefore he must have an heir of his own, not his brother John."

"I thought young Arthur of Brittany was his heir."

"Possibly, and both Arthur and his mother Constance prefer Philip to Richard. If Arthur becomes king, we will suffer Philip's policies."

I stood unsteadily, weak with rage. "I can't argue about Philip or Arthur or John, but I refuse to sacrifice my life for a group of people I don't even know!"

His brown eye fastened on me like a burr. "Too bad you're not Jewish, I grant you; we would like another Queen Judith. But your bloodlines can't be helped. You're chosen by the chosen people, and your so-called sacrifice is well worth it."

"Worth it to whom? You told me about York; I told you about Wanthwaite. Does it follow that you should give up your home, your friends, your future children to save other families in the north? You're arrogant beyond belief!"

"Not arrogant, Alix, but proud I grant you. The Jews are superior and must be preserved."

"Superior how?" I scoffed. "Richer?"

"We value learning, the law, our families and domestic tranquillity."

"So do Christians!"

"When most kings and all knights are illiterate? When the rule of law is unknown outside of England? Your law is force, and your society therefore ranked with murderous brutes on top. Children are born from rape, abduction or incestuous assignments. No wonder your bloodlines produce so many madmen."

"My bloodlines are better than yours!" I cried, incensed. "Queen Eleanor herself said they were excellent."

"Perhaps you're the exception," he said sarcastically, "but you must admit that your best scholars—popes, bishops and priests—cannot marry, whereas our Talmudic scholars and rabbis are supported by our communes and encouraged to have families."

Dumbstruck by this novel and utterly convincing perception, I sought to turn it to advantage.

"If the Jews are so superior, there must still be some reason they provoke Christian wrath; they can't be perfect."

"True, no one is perfect, but neither are most people massacred because of personal faults. With vile invective, priests perpetrate incredible superstitions and slanders against the Jews—so wild that they can't even be refuted— and incite their parishioners to action. It's a riddle, as you say, in the same manner that it's a riddle why the king selected you as his mistress."

Finally I was on firm ground. "That's no riddle, Bonel."

He smiled, rose and poured us both more wine, then gestured that I should return to my cushion.

"No, I didn't mean to disparage your charms," he said, raising his cup, "but there are other beautiful young ladies, certainly others with more wealth and rank. After all, Richard could have anyone."

I didn't drink. "That's where you're wrong. Why do you think I object so strongly to him?"

For the first time he looked less assured. "I don't know. Some childish loyalty to Enoch or yearning for true love, as you call it?"

"I'm not attracted to sodomites," I said bluntly. "It's my bad fortune that my 'charms' come down to the simple fact

that I'm the only female who can rouse the pederastic king
—if you call that true love."

Now he was dumbstruck. "I don't believe you! He's so
manly, so . . ."

"Aye," I agreed bitterly, "that's what I thought on the
Crusade."

I then gave him a sketchy outline of my relationship to
the king. He drank deeply, adjusted his eyepatch, stared
searchingly with his good eye.

"At least I understand your resistance," he said slowly,
"though I think it's based on a false premise. That he would
be surrounded by boys seeking favor I can believe—the
same is true of all great men—and that vicious gossip would
follow him I can believe as well. I've heard, for example,
that he's an insatiable rapist of women—even nuns—that he
travels with a harem in the Saracen fashion. However . . ."

"I've never seen him with a woman," I continued in the
same flat tone, "and I know he never consummated his marriage. In fact, he indicated to me that what I claim is true,
that I'm the only one who . . ."

Bonel's eye gleamed over his cup; when he lowered it, he
was smiling. "A most illuminating conversation, Alix, and
reassuring. Frankly, I was worried that you'd ruined my
scheme with your selfish behavior, that the king would simply look elsewhere, but you've convinced me that our fish is
firmly hooked. All that's left is to bring him to our net. I'll
console his middle brain by clearing your name somehow—
perhaps by going to England to see Pudlicott—and you'll
convince him that you care."

I rose to depart. "That will be hard to do from England,
where I too plan to go."

His smile broadened. "*In vino veritas.* Thank you for
warning me. Henceforth I'll assign Bok to guard you well."

Damn my waggling tongue. "I still won't help. I'm sorry
the Jews have to suffer but it's not my concern, Bonel."

He stood beside me, still smiling. "Of course it is. Your

spontaneous action at the stank revealed your compassion. I dub you an honorary Jew with all privileges and responsibilities thereof." He brushed back my hair. "Your first responsibility is to alter your perception of the king. Watch him, note his good traits, open yourself to the idea of intimacy."

My hair caught in one of his many rings and he untangled it. "And don't worry about why he likes you. As a man, I assure you that he has good reasons; I can't imagine his accepting any other lady, once he'd seen you."

# 12

WATCHED RICHARD CLOSELY THEREAFTER, though not to obey Bonel; we all watched the king as we would the sun if it rolled in a fiery ball before us.

The whole countryside responded to his magnetic pull. Trumpets sounded and villeins dropped forks where they stood, knights appeared from nowhere to pound across the grapes. Even small boys crept from under the bushes and begged to water our horses, to carry off our slops, anything to be near his greatness. He was a military Midas, turning everything he touched to an army.

Aye, if I were a knight, I might succumb to his glory, but I was a mere woman, an unwanted nuisance to most of the company, though I tried to be inconspicuous. Everyone shot me resentful glances except Richard himself; he seemed to have forgotten my presence, and I might have escaped if it hadn't been for Bonel's Bok at my heels.

We digressed only once from our southern path along the French border in order to visit Constance, Countess of Brittany, and her children, Arthur and Eleanor, the lady known as the Pearl of Brittany because of her fabled beauty. Hamo satisfied my curiosity about this hostile branch of the Plantagenet family: Constance had been married to Geoffrey, Richard's older brother and a rival to John for his irascible, treacherous disposition; she'd hated Geoffrey passionately until, after his death, Richard had assigned her an even worse spouse in Ranulf of Chester, whom the Countess had refused to accept at all because of his brutal nature. The real contention, however, was young Arthur; Constance insisted on being his regent, and Queen Eleanor claimed that power for herself.

The entrance to the castle was through an excessively murky forest, and the gloom cast a melancholy tinge over our company. Ancient trunks leered like hoary giants and reminded me of tales my mother used to tell. The small fortress was also forbidding with its blank thick walls and narrow bridge. Only a few of us could crowd into the tiny courtyard and I was willing to wait outside, but Hamo gently objected, even with Bok to guard me.

King Richard strode through the door first as the rest of us followed. The great hall was narrow and dark, the smell musty and faintly animal; on a dais at the end stood a tiny sinewy woman flanked by her two children.

"Constance, dearest sister, I greet you after a long absence."

"Your Majesty," the lady replied frostily.

Unperturbed, Richard received kisses from Eleanor and Arthur. Eleanor's oval face looked as lovely as reputed, though it was hard to see in the dim light. By chance, a beam from an arrow-slit struck Arthur fully so I could see his hemp hair, his yellow eyes, his large malformed jaw.

"How many of your knights seek hospitality?" Constance asked resentfully.

"None, dear sister," the king replied. "We thank you for your graciousness, but we must ride on within the hour. I came to deliver good tidings to my niece, sweet Eleanor."

The girl glanced at her mother.

"We have arranged her marriage," he finished.

Constance put a protective arm around Eleanor. "You traveled a long distance in vain, Your Majesty. We've long been informed that you gave Eleanor to Leopold of Austria as part of your release from Germany."

I gasped aloud, appalled at the thought of this beauteous young maiden going to that smirking duke.

Richard ignored her mother's chilly bite. "Forget Leopold, my dear; we've caught you a bigger prize. What say you to being Queen of France?"

"France?" she repeated with wonder.

In the babble of joy that followed, Richard convinced Constance that he'd arranged with King Philip to send Eleanor to Paris, there to be wed to young Prince Louis. Puzzled, I looked to find William Marshal, but his face was stoic. Did no one wonder at the effect of this change on Duke Leopold? On Henry Hohenstaufen? Suppose they killed the hostages as a result.

Constance, at least, was skeptical. "This is the third time you've given Eleanor away, Your Majesty, though no assignment progresses once you've achieved your political advantage from the arrangement."

"Because I was waiting for the best possible agreement."

"Best for you, you mean. How do we know that Prince Louis isn't another Ranulf?"

"Even if he is, he'll wear the crown," Richard said, exasperated at last. "As for your hated husband, you must admit he stays far from Brittany."

"Only because my army guards my borders."

"My army," the king corrected her. "And Brittany is my domain."

"Not at all; it reverts to me, its lawful heiress."

"But you do homage to me for your title, sister."

He then announced abruptly that we must leave, though we'd been there hardly a hundred heartbeats, and he kissed first Constance, then her children in farewell.

As Richard bent to kiss Arthur, the boy bit him viciously

on the lip! The act was so fast, so unwarranted, that everyone was thrown into a turmoil. Richard held his hand to his mouth and claimed it was nothing, though his eyes and flowing blood belied his statement, and Countess Constance was stirred to weak apologies. William Marshal muttered under his breath: "A true devil, incorrigible as an asp."

Everyone was glad to be on the road and departing from the dismal pile of Brittany, including me. Yet a shadow traveled with me: Arthur was soothly unfit to be king from what I'd witnessed, his own sharp teeth more convincing than Bonel's arguments. His behavior was beyond that of a naughty or spoiled child; either he was satanic, as Marshal claimed, or he was touched with madness. What a prospect for England. Unless I . . . I glanced at the brooding king.

We continued on our mazy ride toward Mercadier's castle, Beynac, where we would winter, now followed by a pall of smoke and a rear guard of buzzards. More and more perturbed by the king's continued silence, by my increasing isolation, I wondered morosely if I could have been wrong about Richard. I wasn't conceding to Bonel, but to what I observed: if I'd once been the only female to rouse Richard, it looked now as if there were no one.

I watched Hamo with a jaundiced eye. If the king had any amorous yearnings, Hamo would seem the only possible partner with his feminine beauty. I liked him well enough for he was always cheerful and friendly, but I didn't trust him.

One day I put the question as delicately as I could.

"Where are you from, Hamo?"

"The city of Florence," he said promptly.

Florence must produce beautiful men. Hamo's chiseled profile, his grape-blue eyes and dark glinting curls would make any damsel envious.

"And when did you join the king?"

"I was traded with a group of English prisoners by accident. I was fortunate that King Richard would accept me when I . . ."

His olive skin flushed a pale magenta.

"I'm no use to anyone," he blurted. "I'm a younger son and wanted to make my way through the tournaments to glory, as William Marshal did, but then I was captured and . . ."

I bent to hear his whisper.

". . . castrated."

He turned fearful eyes to see my reaction. Quickly I took his hand.

"You can still give the gift of friendship."

"Yes, and will," he said fervently.

From that day on I was no longer lonely. Hamo and I chatted like jays, exchanging histories, opinions about everyone and everything. He had a sharp mind, an excellent memory, and a need to attach himself. To my surprise, Bok tried to join our conversations, as if he too were lonely.

As we came closer to Angoulême, our fighting increased. Although Richard had signed a truce with Philip, he was determined to test the loyalty of his border castles. The pattern was always the same: a contingent was sent to request hospitality for the king and his army; if the castellan resisted, Richard attacked. Rarely did he fight personally in these small skirmishes, and usually the power of his name was enough to bring swift concessions.

I hated the miniature battles and tried to find some quiet, safe spot to wait until they were decided. One day, I climbed to a small hillock to be alone and had no sooner settled in the tall grass than Richard appeared accompanied by Hamo. Had they followed me? No, for I saw the swift start of surprise in the king's eyes. He nodded without speaking, then leaned against an oak. Hamo knelt before him and removed the royal boot.

"It's my calf," Richard said.

Hamo pounded the afflicted area with his fists. I pretended to be interested in the drama below, where the king watched. Villeins ran into the valley with torches and pitchforks; quickly they touched thatches on the chapel and kinebyre and the familiar smoke blew our way. Forks were put to uprooting plants, while hands pulled bark off apple trees.

"That's wrong," the king said with pain. "You're making it worse."

"What should I do?" Hamo asked eagerly.

"If you have a cramp, My Lord, I used to help my father," I offered.

"Then try."

I glanced at Hamo and slid into his place, placed my palms on Richard's hard muscle and kneaded sharply in upward strokes.

"They're responding," he said in a tight voice, referring to the melee.

Confused men ran from the tower, some of them hardly dressed, and fought with bare hands. The villeins torched their hair, and screams mixed with smoke. Now Mercadier released the deadly knights.

"Arras! Arras!"

A few mounted men fought back.

"Alix can finish here," the king told Hamo.

Hamo smiled at me, pleased that I was receiving favor at last.

Knights quickly tumbled the adversary to the waiting villeins, for knights wouldn't kill men of their own rank.

"Higher," Richard demanded.

I worked on his knee. He flexed it forward and I would have fallen back except that his hands held my hair. He slid down the oak until our eyes met, mingled. Women's cries behind me joined the men's.

Richard pulled me to his face and kissed me. Not a gentle kiss, not even amorous, but hurtful, bruising to my lips, a kiss of hatred.

"Don't try to seduce me, Alix. I can see the bloat at your waist and won't be beguiled—take warning."

Then he was gone. I rubbed my lips and discovered blood on my fingers. He and his nephew Arthur were both Devils.

꒦ꙫ꒦          ꒦ꙫ꒦          ꒦ꙫ꒦

THE KING WAS ILL and it was raining. Knights squatted under trees and struck at flies. The heat was suffocating; sweat mingled with rain, horses rolled their eyes, stamped, swished tails. Richard lay in his pavilion with his physician and priest in attendance. No one dared ask what ailed him.

On the third day of our enforced sojourn, a white-bearded hermit entered our camp. Instantly I thought of the hermit at Clifford Tower who'd cried invective at the Jews, but this hermit appeared benign. He was permitted to enter the king's tent. Shortly thereafter, Richard emerged, pale but steady. He disrobed in the rain and knelt before the hermit. His gruff voice carried throughout the quiet camp: he confessed sins of the flesh, carnal thoughts, and swore to God that henceforth he would obey the laws of Saint Jerome and do his duty to God and country.

Well did I remember a similar confession, during the Crusade, of his "strange sin"—made to cleanse himself before he married Berengaria. Then I'd thought he loved me—presumably a boy—and understood his guilt. This time, however, I surveyed the pages in his company with no success. He should feel guilt for the misery he inflicted on me, his toty accusation that I "seduced" him after *he* bit me.

In any case, the change in the king was instant and remarkable. He now joined every fray, no matter how slight, and swept like an eagle onto unwary prey. With his men, he became a saint, tending to their physical needs with humble patience. One day I witnessed him operate on the scorbutic gums of a frightened young squire as the worthy knights sobbed in sympathy.

He paid less attention to me than ever.

WE REACHED Beynac Castle in autumn. The country changed from gently rolling meadows and woods to harsh scarps crisscrossed with wide rapid rivers. We followed the Vézère River through an awesome valley pocketed with caves. The king led us all to view strange scratchings on the walls, executed by ancient people who'd disappeared. The legend was that this was the place where Noah had launched his ark; the drawings had been made by the drowned sinners; the rivers were the vestiges of the flood.

Mercadier's castle was situated on an abrupt cropping high above the Dordogne River. Tall, without depth, it rose forbiddingly against a yellow sky, a thin dun cutout of spires and labyrinths, fit eyrie for vicious hawks, tunnels for scuttering rats. We wound in circles to approach its forbidding towers and crossed its high dry moat with a sense of oppression. No one japed or laughed. Once inside, we looked down on a miniature scape of winding silver ribbon, clouds reflecting in broad water meadows, and castles staring from every cliff around us. I shuddered and stepped back from the sheer drop.

Once inside, I stopped before a splendid apartment to gaze on fine ebony chairs, oriental rugs and tapestries. No one was watching, so I stepped onto a soft rug, twirled in pleasure.

"Elegant, isn't it?" Hamo said behind me.

"Aye. Is it the king's?"

"No, he's expecting the queen."

I stopped in my dance. "Queen Eleanor is expected?"

Hamo avoided my eyes. "Yes, but I referred to Queen Berengaria, Alix. King Richard's confession to the hermit purified him for a reconciliation with his queen."

My heart plummeted to a woven rose on the carpet. I stared at Hamo, not knowing why I felt so miserable. I'd failed in Bonel's assigned task, as I'd sworn to do, but the failure was not my doing. Furthermore, Berengaria's presence contradicted all my theories about Richard and I resented the king for deceiving me. I recognized that I was unreasonable, though certainly my outlook was anomalous. If not a mistress, then what?

"What will he do with me?" I asked.

Hamo shook his head, not answering.

"I can't stay here with the royal couple!" I cried. "Berengaria would never tolerate it—I know her!"

Hamo dropped his eyes and muttered. "You'll stay in the tower."

Then added with obvious difficulty, "Bok is being sent away. You have only me."

Recalling those austere pinnacles as seen from afar, I argued and begged him to help me send Bonel a message. My piteous harangue drew tears to his eyes, but he remained loyal to the king.

Sadly he led me up a circular stair with steps constructed in cunning, uneven depths to tumble unsuspecting invaders, up, and up, and up, across an open parapet where a slip would plunge us hundreds of feet, into the door of a corner tower. From the outside the tower had looked round; inside it was built in a series of short angles, each with a wide deep window that narrowed to a slit—designed to shoot arrows from any position—and overlooking the whole Dordogne to the south, west and north; only the east was partially obscured by the tower's joining to the castle.

"You have your own garderobe," Hamo pointed out, trying to cheer me.

I looked at the large, gaping hole and vowed never to sit there if I had other recourse. No one would ever escape through that shaft unless it was to drop straight to Hell.

Again trying to raise my spirits, Hamo said he would continue to serve me as page and would keep me abreast of the news. After he left, I examined my eyrie more carefully. The space was small—cramped to be accurate—and though the day was hot, the arrow-slits narrow, an icy blast raised my hair and skirts from all sides. I sank to the cold stones, listening. I was inside an organ pipe played by the wind; at the foot of the tower a low guttural growl rose and fell, from the middle came a steady moan, but the updraft was like a baby's scream.

# 13

HE FIRST QUEEN TO ARRIVE WAS ELEANOR.
I watched the royal train wend along the river, disappear for a long time, then come into view at my northern arrow-slit above the dry moat, disappear again. She was a redbird followed by her flock, except one was missing. Not until they were dismounting in the court did I know it was Lady Faydide. I was summoned below to greet them.

The king, tall, serious, handsome, held Eleanor in his arms. Both turned to regard me as I entered. I had to bow, but didn't meet their eyes. Eleanor nodded coolly and left with the king; Lady Mamile took my arm.

"You're out of favor, dear. What happened to upset the king?"

You're a spy, I thought, gazing into her flat pansy eyes.

"I don't know, Lady Mamile. I was struck on the head when Vaudrueil was mined, and befriended by a woman of questionable character. Ever since then, the king accuses me of treason and harlotry."

"What a pity," she replied too swiftly. "But understandable. A king can't be too careful about his line—that's the whole point, isn't it? Even a wife can't survive the accusation of adultery, not the fact, mind you, just the accusation. King Louis put Eleanor aside for adultery when he knew it was a lie."

"What was his real reason?"

"In fifteen years of marriage, she'd produced only two children, both daughters. However, a field lies fallow if it's never seeded. Louis should have been a monk."

And so should Richard, I thought sourly. He must have

cut his teeth on the teachings of Saint Jerome to think every woman a slut.

"Mamile, since I'm no longer in favor—will not live with Richard—do you think I might return with you to Fontevrault? Queen Berengaria won't like my presence here, especially if she suspects the king's former plans."

She smiled brightly. "Why not? I daresay that's exactly what will happen."

And I knew she meant the opposite. My only hope was Queen Eleanor.

In the same brittle tone, Lady Mamile then told me that Faydide was gravely ill. By now I'd learned to read Mamile, however, and realized that in this case she was worried about her friend. Courtesy and courage kept her concerns controlled.

I didn't sup that afternoon with the royal party—wasn't invited—but at last was summoned to the queen's chambers. I went with heavy forboding, knowing that this was my last opportunity to escape a dour situation. Tapers were lit and a fire laid against the short day and early chill. Eleanor embraced me as always, and I breathed deeply of her attar of roses. But that was the last of intimacy; she placed me on a bench by her table, then sat opposite me as if we were adversaries. Only her scribe was missing.

"Well, Alix, you broke your contract."

"Not by design, Your Majesty. I was in a window seat . . ."

"I know the story. I repeat, you broke your contract. I'm both disappointed and offended. Why did you betray us?"

Soothly I didn't know what to say except what she'd already heard. She listened for a time, then rose and paced behind her table in irritation.

"Don't add mendacity to your other sins. You've run away from the Great One twice—yes, I know about Acre—and now play the strumpet's game of tease and withhold."

I, too, became irritated. "I thought that was the game you taught, Your Majesty, the game of courtly love."

"You thought what?" Her brows arched high; her eyes widened. "But I should have guessed. You taunted the king with another lover—did you think to rouse jealousy?"

"I had no lover!" I cried with heat. "And the king needs no impetus to jealousy—he's so afraid of my besmottering his progeny that he's jealous of the horse he gave me."

"Perhaps because he's just placed one unfortunate off-spring—also from a whore. His son, young Philip, was granted lands in Gascony and married to Amelia, a decent damsel. But we need no more such bastards in the family—his mother's bad blood shows."

I had a curious sinking in my cod to hear Richard described as the father of a grown son.

"Who was the mother?"

The queen shot a knowing glance. "A whore, as I said, but a comely wench. Richard seems destined to seek out luscious plums that are rotten at the middle."

"In any case, Your Majesty, I swear I play no games. If you want a contract . . ."

She snapped in anger to match Richard's. "The king has a queen who is neither whore nor adulteress, and his contract with her is sanctified."

"Aye, I know how virtuous Queen Berengaria is," I replied humbly, "and if he truly loves her . . ."

Eleanor laughed derisively. "*Truly loves*, words of a simpering idiot. I invented love, Alix, turned Ovid upside down, in order to tame the wild steeds who would trample us otherwise. True love, as you call it, is the sentiment between vassal and lord, or knights in the field, where the situation demands devotion, or—for a brief time—between children and parents. Love between men and women was born only yesterday in the courts of Poitiers, and then with limited application. Richard needs a son; Berengaria has a virgin's womb. That's the sum total of their 'true love.' "

"I loved Enoch," I said stubbornly, "and he loved me, yet neither of us attended your court at Poitiers."

I awaited further derision, but her attitude changed abruptly.

"Merciful Mary, was that why you fled?"

I thought of the Scot on the bridge and didn't answer, but she read my look.

"It is, isn't it?" She walked swiftly to my side and took my shoulders, her green eyes searching. "Tell me about it, Alix, and hold nothing back."

I looked at her fearfully—could she read my mind? Finally I told her half the truth, that when Emma and I had left the castle to search for food, we'd seen a small contingent from King Philip's army break away and hide in a copse. One of them appeared to be a Scot and, yes, it had set me dreaming.

"Did you tell this to the king?"

"No, Your Majesty." I hesitated. "I thought it would anger him."

She pushed me aside and went back to her desk. "Very wise; it probably would have." She lowered her head onto her hands, then looked up. "Continue. What does the king feel for you now?"

She must know better than I. "He's in ascetic humor—I think he's indifferent."

Her eyes were steady.

"And you?"

I took a deep breath.

"He's—the glorious king."

"And a man. Go on."

I thought of Bonel and the Jews. *Benedicite.*

"I admire him, his generosity, sense of fairness . . ."

"Well said." Her smile was wry. "People followed Henry for clemency; they follow Richard for justice. But I hardly think that's your motive."

No, I followed him as a prisoner.

I gazed at her, drowning in those eyes, and spoke the truth at last. "My feelings are very confused, Your Majesty. I think I won't know exactly how I feel until the king and I are free—if that should ever be—of outside pressures. Now everything is suspect."

She smiled, genuinely. "I'm glad that my trust in your wit wasn't misplaced altogether. You've just stated my basic tenet of courtly love, freedom from convention—especially venal convention—manipulation or ulterior motives. However, having so said, any relationship with a king carries obligations." She rose to dismiss me. "Too bad we'll never know in your case what might have transpired."

I bowed, but didn't leave.

"Your Majesty, if it please you, may I return to Fontevrault with you? I have no further purpose here."

She frowned. "The king will send you away when he's ready."

I bowed and left.

Once again Eleanor sat with Richard to conduct court as runners came from London, from Rouen, from Poitiers, from Flanders, from everywhere. I lived on the edge of the royal sphere, my status undeclared, in the tower by night and most of the day, but permitted to exercise.

Two days later I watched Berengaria arrive, a raven followed by rooks. In the courtyard below, Eleanor hugged her tight, then Richard, his face all smiles. From my position in the tower I couldn't see Berengaria's expression, but I witnessed when she brought forth a pet ape from a cage and wanted the king to kiss it; he stepped back, annoyed, she insisted, he refused. Their irritated voices rose as they walked out of sight.

Queen Eleanor departed within the same hour without saying goodbye to me. I watched her small train disappear with a sinking heart. That night I was summoned to dine with the happy royal couple.

*Deo gratias* we were not alone. Unbeknownst to me, still

another visitor had arrived, Baldwin of Béthune, Richard's favorite companion on the Crusade and the first of his officers to volunteer to be a hostage. I dared not speak to him until invited, but I was most eager to learn what his presence meant. Were the hostages free?

From my position below the salt nef at the most lowly trestle, I looked directly up at Berengaria, now in Eleanor's place, her drab face sans color or animation, her clothing unadorned black, her jaws chewing in rhythm to the music. Richard ignored her for Baldwin. When the last course was finished, Hamo summoned me forward.

King Richard regarded me with remote charity. "Lady Alix, you will be interested to know that the hostages are all well."

"Indeed, Your Majesty, I had many friends among them. Are they now free?"

"No. However, I'm riding north with Sir Baldwin to make immediate arrangements for their release. While I am gone, my dear queen, Berengaria, has volunteered to give you religious preparation for your future assignment."

Berengaria's dun-brown eyes shone with anticipation. "You may serve me as handmaiden, Lady Alix."

"I thank you, Your Highness." She didn't mention knowing me formerly as Alex the page, and indeed she may never have noticed me on the Crusade; certainly I wouldn't remind her.

The king then dismissed me. From Hamo I learned the true facts: Leopold and Emperor Henry had sent Richard an ultimatum to the effect that, if young Eleanor of Brittany were not sent at once to fulfill her marriage bargain, all the hostages would be killed forthwith. The king was frantic and determined to save them at all costs. Sir Baldwin had been trusted with the message to convey its seriousness, and he was ordered to return to Germany with young Eleanor in his care without fail.

So much for her marriage to Louis of France.

Hamo also reported with sly glee that the king had not slept with his queen on the one night they had together.

I was summoned to Berengaria's quarters late the next afternoon, after the king had left with Sir Baldwin. I noticed at once that yesterday's pleasant demeanor had slipped several notches: from bland to baleful, from prudent to prurient, from mellow to mean. She sat in Moorish splendor surrounded by screens and tiled tables in the Navarene style with four ladies, all much older than the queen and all dressed in the same severe black. Her ape, called Pedro, was leashed in a corner where he solemnly devoured apples.

Berengaria assumed a hard caustic tone. "Well, Lady Alix, we meet again—under new circumstances. The king reminded me that I knew you on the Crusade. Such a droll escapade."

Damn the king! Why not remain discreetly silent?

"I'm very grateful, Your Highness, for your offer to teach me."

"And I for your offer to serve me. As you can see, my ladies, Consuelo, Maria, Gabriela and Remedios, are no longer young; you can be most useful."

"I await your instructions."

"Good. First you will dress appropriately and not make a display of your body or hair, for this way lies the gateway to Hell. Saint John teaches us that our beauteous bodies are in fact white sepulchers filled with phlegm, spittle and excrement and should be concealed lest they lure men to perdition. Lady Consuelo will fit you when we finish."

"Thank you, Your Highness." I'd heard the same words from Sister Hilaria, but now they carried ominous connotations.

"Furthermore, I must ask that you bathe, though we shall take strict precautions that you don't gaze on your own body, heeding the warnings of Saint Jerome. But last night I noticed that you carry *foetor judaicus,* no doubt from your long association with a Jew."

Bonel used oil of licorice, a most attractive scent. "What is a Jewish odor, Your Highness?"

"Similar to that of a he-goat," she replied brightly. "However, perhaps the priest at the chapel can spare a few drops from the baptismal font, whereafter you will have a fragrance sweeter than ambrosia."

"I was baptized at my birth, Your Highness. I hardly think such repetition necessary."

Her hard eyes were relentless.

"I asked the king to give me something of your background so that my instruction could be well aimed. You traveled for many months with a Jew."

"Not alone, Your Highness; Bonel was assigned to take me to London, but there were other people with us."

"Nevertheless, the Jews are insidious and infectious, as well as arrogant. It's criminal that a Jew could insinuate himself so high in the court. I shall instruct the king to be more prudent in the future. Only Christians should govern Christians. Meantime, we shall watch for your symptoms."

"Jewish symptoms—if there are such things, Your Highness—must include fetish cleanliness of person, superior manners and knowledge in all things."

"Ah, the first symptom!" she cried. "Your vision is corrupted by the Antichrist."

This time I remained silent; a steely tenor in Berengaria's soft voice alerted me to real danger.

"Your first chore when you are dressed will be to tend my ape."

I started to protest, but again held my tongue. The queen required study, I decided; my former estimation that she was an insipid fool no longer sufficed.

"You will clean his quarters of all filth."

I slid my eyes to the animal; his leavings rivaled a bird's in relation to his size, a cow's in consistency, a human's in odor and shape. It was an odious, lowly task, fit for only a slave or the most churlish villein.

"And you will serve the same function for me. You will empty my jurdon three times a day, and since I am fastidious, I require that you scrub the vessel by hand. Is that clear?"

She defied me to challenge her; I wouldn't give her the satisfaction.

"You will dine with us—since we'll eat away from Mercadier and his mercenaries—worship with us, and in all ways share our station. I shall instruct you as the occasion arises."

Her purpose was plainly to demean me in every possible manner, and she'd been given absolute power by the king, may the Devil roast his tailbone. Well, I could endure Berengaria's childish assignments of the garderobe if that was the worst punishment her small mind could devise.

I followed Lady Consuelo to the wardrobe to be fitted in black with a wimple tied with cruel strips around my jaw that held my teeth so close that I wondered how I could eat. We then walked as a group to the dim chapel to worship silently before the cross, except for Berengaria who whispered ecstatically in Latin. After we'd finished, she told me to prepare her chamber pot for the night. I took the offensive vessel—which, unless the queen were as prodigious as her ape, had not been emptied for days—and staggered into the court, chagrined and nauseated. Afraid that I might be observed, I crossed the moat and sought the nearest pit where I might dump her filth, then wandered around the fields looking for a fast stream. I finally discovered a small falls where the combination of a stick and the force of the current cleaned the pot.

It was almost dark when I returned, and I still had Pedro the ape to attend. At least he was friendly, if not grateful—and wanted to participate. He watched with great interest as I picked up his mess with a small shovel, and then "helped" me by plucking turds from my sack as fast as I dropped them in. The only way I could divert him was to take off my wimple and let him seek lice in my hair. At last I was finished.

The dinner hour was devoted to prayer, the food a simple bun for each lady. Berengaria drew our attention to the fact that each piece of bread was marked with three crosses.

"Before we partake of God's bounty," she pronounced, "I want to hear the significance of the three crosses. Lady Consuelo?"

"The Holy Trinity, Your Highness, Father, Son and Holy Ghost."

I began to bite.

"Wait, Lady Alix; each of us has to speak. Lady Maria?"

"The three crosses of Calvary."

The others followed with the three Marys who visited the sepulcher and the three temptations of Saint Peter.

Berengaria smiled. "The three days Christ lay dead before the Resurrection. Alix?"

They'd said them all. I could think of nothing.

Berengaria leaned forward, her eyes fanatic. "The proud and fell Jews cried three times to Pontius Pilate, speaking of the blessed Son of God, 'Crucify! crucify! crucify him! for He is deathworthy.' "

I gazed at my feet.

"Repeat what I just said, Alix."

"Your own great husband-king was one of three lords who led the Crusade, and surely he represents the highest cross of Calvary, Philip and Leopold the lower two."

She dare not deny Richard his greatness, and I thought I'd won a small victory. But I learned that night that I could never win any point with Berengaria. The next morning, she discovered me as I was cleaning Pedro's corner.

"How dare you remove your wimple?" she screamed.

"It's the only way . . ."

"You're trying to seduce my poor innocent ape!"

"Seduce, Your Highness?" Surely I'd misheard her.

"You think he's a lascivious Jew to be caught in your

wiles! You're full of a thousand evils—vile, detestable, dreadful—and want to insinuate yourself with your luxurious hair."

She grabbed my hair and jerked me across the room as I screamed as loudly as she did and the ape pounded his chest in excitement. Then I was on my knees, my hands wrapped around hers to lessen the pull, when I felt a stabbing pain. My finger had been pierced by scissors as she relentlessly hacked at my locks.

"*Nullum malum impunitum*," she panted.

No evil unpunished, but how had I been evil?

My neck was cut, a lobe of my scarred ear, and I covered my eyes to protect them. My hair fell around me.

"There," she finished, "now see if even a Jew will take you."

I pressed my lips tight. And I'd thought her childish? The woman was a dangerous fanatic, obsessed with the evil of the Jews, the licentiousness of females, and somehow I carried the sins of both.

"Repeat after me: the proud and fell Jews called, 'Crucify! crucify! crucify!' "

I repeated it three times to suit her sense of symmetry.

A small benefit of my delinquency was that henceforth I was excluded from the queen's table. When Hamo brought me fresh game that night, I had him examine my slashes. They were all superficial, but he washed them with wine. He tried to reassure me about my hair—that she'd missed great portions—but I wept even so. I remembered the golden cloud in the mirror at Mainz; it had taken me years to replace my crown after I'd cut it for the Crusade.

The slashing of my hair was the beginning of a nightmare, and each day I revised my opinion of Berengaria downward. I hated to label her a lunatick, though she surely was, for it was too easy an explanation and not everyone could be lunatick: Arthur, John and now the queen. Perhaps Bonel had been right in surmising that Christian bloodlines had degenerated. She must be mad to behave so, and not just toward me. She lashed at her poor ladies regularly, selecting a particular victim each day. Her favorite punishment was to beat the soles of their bare feet with a small steel rod. I'd noted that they all limped, but thought they suffered from arthritis as Lady Mamile did. More ominously, she'd destroyed their spirits; no, even worse, she'd transformed them into shadows of her own derangement. I feared them almost as much as I feared her.

Ostensibly Berengaria's behavior was inspired by God, though, again, my experience with Sister Hilaria had taught me true inspiration; God must be wincing in Heaven to hear His name so defamed. Yet the priest in our private chapel admired her devotion and visiting lords praised her humility and courtesy. Indeed, much as she loathed the carnal act, she looked up to men and hated her own sex as the purveyors of sin. We needed chastisement, had sinned originally and irrevocably, must do penance throughout our brief sojourns on earth. She addressed me as Eve so often that I began to answer to the name.

One afternoon after chapel, she asked me to come to her chamber.

"I noticed that you have an odor, Alix."

Her nose was keen as a dog's and I fidgeted uncomfortably. "Do you refer again to the Jewish odor, Your Highness?"

"No, to a repugnant sweetness. Are you bleeding?"

I admitted that I was.

She leaned forward, eyes avid. "What do you do with your blood?"

"Nothing." I sought to appease whatever disturbed her. "That is, I wash my rags and dry them for future use."

She whispered conspiratorially. "Come now, confess. You save your blood for the Jews."

The blood in my veins promptly congealed.

"Why would I do that, Your Highness?"

"Everyone knows how desperately they need blood. Jews suffer copious hemorrhages and hemorrhoids, and men menstruate as well as women. Many Jews are born blind. All these ailments require blood. That's why they commit ritual murders on Christian children, to draw their blood."

I stared, appalled. "How can you possibly believe such sick superstitions?"

"Do you question my veracity?"

"No," I retreated hastily.

"I was instructed by my priest as you should have been, for all this and more is common knowledge."

She didn't punish me for my supposed sins on this occasion; her insult was to be construed as instruction.

I yearned for Richard's return. Cruel as he behaved on occasion, he wasn't mad. As Eleanor had said, at least he was just, an assertion somewhat tarnished by my trial. Then my yearning gradually abated; if he knew and if he'd deliberately exposed me to his insane queen, I'd castrate him before he could get a child by anyone. Aye, and use Berengaria's scissors to do the deed.

IN LATE NOVEMBER, torrential rains began to fall. Mercadier was the only person delighted by the flood, for he depended on this yearly downpour to restock his cisterns. Beynac had no well nor spring, a serious deficiency under siege, and Mercadier had designed an ingenious way to trap rainfall. All the roofs of the castle pitched toward a small central court which acted as an open cistern. The floor of the court was further slanted to a drain so that excess water ran to a deeper cistern at a lower level, then once again to the bottom cistern. Each chamber was connected by pipes filled with fine stone to filter impurities. Lords traveled long distances to admire and copy his system.

I was the only other member of the household to delight in the storm. Now I could dump Berengaria's wastes where I liked, secure that they would be carried off, then let the rain wash the pot. Unfortunately someone spied me in the act.

I faced the queen's fury. "How dare you disobey my orders?" she shrieked.

I had no idea of my offense.

"You're supposed to clean my jurdon with your hands!"

I lapsed into English in like fury. "You have no right to tell me anything! Your lathly leavings stink like a foul corpse!"

She blanched and staggered backwards, held her gold cross in my face. "*Que turpiloquium loquitur.* The Devil's tongue!"

"I don't speak filth!" I screamed in contradiction.

"*Culpat caro, purgat caro.* The flesh sins, the flesh atones. Consuelo! Gabriela!"

Her demon-women appeared from the shadow.

"I'll show you how it feels to be cleansed by rainfall. Take her arms!"

The women grabbed and I struggled with all my might, not knowing her purpose except that it must be mad. Then Berengaria produced a small Moorish rapier from her drawer and I stopped, horrified.

We walked through the castle, up and down steps, until we reached the floor adjacent to the water level of the inner court.

"Go into the water," Berengaria ordered,

"You can't mean it, Your Highness! It's deep—perhaps over my head."

"Then hold a pillar. Do you need persuasion?"

"It's also my bleeding time and I'll surely chill."

"Or deprive the Jews of ritual blood." She grinned malevolently.

"Do you want to murder me?"

"I trust God to care for you, if you're deserving."

"And I trust to God to spare me your lunatick schemes!" I shouted. The black crows instantly attacked—and won by sheer numbers—so that I tumbled headlong into the numbing drench. Upright again, blinded by the downpour, I sought footing. The women's faint, ghostly faces hung over me, then disappeared.

A sharp cramp made me double in pain. *Benedicite*, I must get hold.

"Lady Alix, here!"

I could barely make out Mercadier's form on the opposite side. He dangled a rope. Holding to the wall, I edged my way around the court till I could grab it. He pulled me upward and I fell at his feet, hardly conscious. Without a word, he picked me from the stones and ran up steps, through more closets, until we reached his private apartment. A charcoal fire glowed on the grate. He lowered me in front of it, then—still not speaking—went out. He soon returned with an armful of furs.

"Remove your wet clothes and wrap in these. I'll be back,"

"Thank you, Captain Mercadier."

I had no idea how long he was gone, but my tunic was dry and I'd dozed a bit.

"Thank you, Mercadier; you saved my life."

"I didn't want my well polluted with a dead body," he said, his face straight. Then he smiled. "That was an ugly show."

"Yes." I shuddered violently.

"How often has this happened?"

"Never in the court before, but the queen devises tortures of all kinds. I think she wants to kill me."

He smiled again. "A reasonable conclusion."

His agate eyes were hard as usual, his scarred mouth thin and cruel, but for the first time I had an inkling of why Richard and Eleanor liked him.

"Tell me of other instances."

Aye, he might be a crocodile, but I poured forth my grievances as if he were my mother. He listened without comment.

"You're ill," he said when I'd finished.

"What? Oh no, I was chilled but I'm all right."

"And should stay in your chamber until I deem it wise for you to attend the queen again."

He avoided my eyes as I tried to discern his purpose.

"Thank you for your concern, Captain Mercadier, but Berengaria hates malingering. Besides, the king gave her authority over me."

"We shall see."

He rose as a signal that I should leave, which I did after more expressions of gratitude.

Berengaria showed neither anger nor surprise at my return, alerted no doubt by her women. On the contrary, she insisted I eat buns with her and her ladies, but her lesson that evening was pointed: *Omnia iniquitas quantum misericordiam Dei est quasi sintilla in medio maris.* Evil compared to the mercy of God is like a live coal in the middle of the sea.

I didn't point out that Mercadier had rescued me, not God, for I knew she would reply that God moves in mysterious ways. With that I could agree.

THE FOLLOWING MORNING I dressed and ate in my tower as usual, but when I tried to go down the stair, Hamo stopped me.

"Mercadier said you were ill and must stay in your closet, Alix."

"Nonsense," I replied nervously. "I'm late to chapel."

I pushed past him on the stair but was stopped again at the foot where Captain Algais, Mercadier's friend, lounged across the step.

"Excuse me, please." I attempted to go around him.

"You have to stay in your quarters, Lady Alix," he said in his thick Brabantine accent. "Those are my orders."

I would rather cross Berengaria than one of Mercadier's mercenaries; I returned to the tower. Within a very short time, I heard Lady Maria demanding my presence in the queen's chamber, followed by Algais's refusal. She then asked to check for herself on my condition and was once again refused. Except for Hamo's occasional ministrations, I was alone for the rest of the day.

The pattern became a new regimen. Berengaria must know that I wasn't ailing, but she also realized that I was a prisoner, which would satisfy her somewhat. It didn't satisfy me, however. My initial gratitude to Mercadier for intervening between me and the queen quickly gave way to frustration and fear. I wasn't suffering, but I was locked away. *Benedicite*, I might be here for eighteen years as Princess Alais had been. Was there no one to help me? Bonel? Aye, when he heard—if he heard. If he were my rescuer, I thought wryly, I could tell him that I now had some small inkling of what Jews suffer, if I could be punished so for simply knowing a Jew.

I occupied myself as best I could, exercised, japed and told stories with Hamo, tried to sing though I didn't enjoy the uncertain pitch of my voice. I recalled how Richard had survived eighteen months of shackles and emerged like a god; I would come out like a goddess—though I had no nation to raise a ransom for me, no one to be hostage. I left crumbs to attract a rat, but none came. However, after two weeks I received another visitor: a large owl decided to make a nest in one of my deep windows. I was flattered that he didn't fear me and I sat like a stone as he arranged his rough home. He was an amazing creature, for his eyes—which until now I'd seen only from afar—were large, liquid and quite beautiful. Then he brought his mate, or she brought her mate, for they appeared exactly alike, and they settled down cozily.

As I reviewed my time with Berengaria, my exercises became pointed. I sharpened my father's dagger on the edge of a stone, then hurled it over and over again against my bench. I developed perfect aim. Never again would I be forced by a rapier.

More than anything else, however, I plotted for my freedom. I was keenly motivated, for I saw a future of slow withering; I planned my escape with utmost care. My former schemes had all been directed to getting back to Wanthwaite, a woodly notion I now saw, for the king controlled all routes to England and Wanthwaite was far away; furthermore, it was occupied by Richard's army. My first step must be simply to effect an escape for freedom, and then go somewhere nearby where the king couldn't follow.

I must go to France, such an obvious solution that I wondered I hadn't thought of it before.

It would be better for me if I could accomplish this before Richard returned. For all her madness, Berengaria had neither the means nor the will to follow me. Somehow I must get back into her service, which offered more opportunity than Mercadier's close protection. When I thought I'd worked out a plan, I had Hamo take a message to the queen: I felt much better and longed to be with her again. Could she persuade Mercadier of my good health?

A week later I was permitted to attend chapel with the queen and her ladies, with two differences: Algais went as well, and I carried my father's dagger where it was easy to reach.

Berengaria studied me with satisfaction. "You look pale, Lady Alix. *Culpat caro, purgat caro.*"

This was her favorite saying, and I wondered if her flesh had ever sinned that she would become so obsessed with punishing others. After the Mass, I was sent to the tower again, but a breach had been made.

There followed several days of uncertainty. A thick fog obscured the court below, but I could hear voices and activity. What was happening? Hamo no longer brought me tidbits from the kitchen, verbal or otherwise, though I was fed by a woman I'd never seen before. I heard muffled voices, the snort and pace of horses, trumpets, twice music in the evenings. On the third or fourth day just after nightfall, Hamo came for me at last.

"You're to sleep with the queen, Alix," he announced happily.

"No!" I shrank back. "I'd rather stay here."

"Queen Eleanor, dear. She and the king are both in residence for the Christmas Court."

"Christmas so soon?" I said, dazed, then pulled away. "I still prefer my privacy and my owl. Bring me a little red and we'll toast together, just the two of us."

"You're to go with the royal party on the Christmas hunt."

I shook my head dumbly.

"Berengaria's been sent away." It was his *coup de grâce* to my fears. "They say her father is dying, but I know that Mercadier told the king what she'd done to you."

I stared, stupified.

"If you come nicely, I have a secret message for you," Hamo coaxed.

"From the king?"

"From Rouen."

"Hamo, please!" I reached eagerly.

I followed him docilely then to the bottom of the stair, through empty corridors to Queen Eleanor's apartment. When he gave me a small rolled piece of vellum, I sought the hiss of a torch and read in flickering shadows: "Pudlicott died of a large tumor on his arm. On his deathbed, he confessed that he'd lied to the King of England; he begged the king's pardon, and yours. You're back in royal favor."

As usual, Bonel hadn't signed.

Well, poor Pudlicott's sinning flesh had atoned highly, I thought; I forgave him the lie, but not the confession. With heavy heart, I dragged into Eleanor's chambers.

# 14

THE LADIES HAD RETIRED. I STEPPED OVER AND around their recumbent forms, barely visible in moonlight, and huddled in a corner. Familiar female odors permeated the dank, night air: wool turned acrid by old sweat, an accumulation of dried urine, wine-laden breath—all overlaid with the refined scents of rose oil, lily-of-the-valley, cinnamon and clove. Once I would have found the emanations comforting, but now I felt alien to my own kind, the residue of my weeks with Berengaria.

The door opened to admit the queen. I hadn't known she was absent. She carried a taper which underlit her face in unhealthy saffron and for the first time she looked old. She placed the candle on her altar and slowly undid her wimple; her hair fell in long braids. Grunting slightly as she bent, she fumbled for a woolen shawl to place over her head, then removed her jewelry. Still dressed in her tunic and furs, she blew out the flame and climbed onto her creaking bed—which she always carried with her—and turned to find a comfortable position.

I sat wide awake. Outside, wolves howled in the hills; an owl hooted—my owl?—and the hounds below answered the wolves.

We woke in the dark. The women groaned at the cold and clutched for support to pull themselves upright. From habit, I offered my hand to Lady Mamile.

"Ah, good morrow, Alix. Where were you last night?"

"Here, My Lady. Careful!"

She swayed unsteadily, then gradually straightened her spine.

"I was told to give you a hunting dress. Will you look in my trunk? It's green, banded in black."

I shook out the garment, quickly discarded my black and put it on. It must have belonged to Lady Castellux, for it fit me perfectly. When the queen had finished her short prayers before her altar, she led us down the steps and across the frosted grass to the chapel, a way well trampled by Berengaria's train. Eleanor had not yet noticed me—or at least she hadn't acknowledged my presence.

Back in the great hall, we hastily ate our sop and hurried back to our quarters to array ourselves with glittering jewels and chains for the Christmas hunt. The queen placed her mirror on the window ledge close to the light and watched as Amaria applied her paint. Soon the grayed flesh glowed pink as petals, fine lines were smoothed as if with mortar, eyes flashed emerald under green-stained lids. When her wimple pulled her chin to a chiseled line, she was ready for the day.

Now she turned to me. "Sweet Alix, words cannot express my joy in having you with us once more."

She embraced me, her semblance of warmth as artificial as her mask—and as cunning.

"Thank you, Your Majesty."

"Mercy on us! Your hair!" She obviously knew how it had gotten to such a sad state. "Amaria, bring me my scissors."

I stood very quietly as once again a queen hacked on my locks, except that Eleanor was determined to rescue my disreputable appearance. Talking to herself and making me turn this way and that, she finally announced that she'd evened the length and that the hair curled prettily.

"Now you lack only a bauble. Amaria, my box."

The queen rummaged in a large casket of jewels and finally held forth a heavy silver necklace set with moonstones.

"Your colors exactly, my dear. Isn't she fetching, Mamile?"

Mamile and Sybelle studied me solemnly.

"She's young!" Toquerie called from across the room. "Everything else is irrelevant."

"Not at all," Sybelle snapped. "Everyone is young at one time, but few have appeal. Alix, you look like a unicorn in moonlight."

Mamile brayed in derision. "Unicorns are bearded, you fool! Alix is a northern wildflower."

I reached for my black wimple.

"No." The queen took it from her hand. "Go as you are."

"She'll catch the ague in her head," Mamile objected.

Again the queen searched in her own effects and finally produced a fur hat of soft gray miniver. With the hat on my cropped head, I followed them down the steps to the court.

Pages carried our gear and truss bags to the court where the men milled around excited steeds, horse and human breath mingling in steamy puffs. It was now fully light, though the sun ran behind dense leaden clouds that looked to be filled with snow. Everyone spoke in high pitch as if the company were deaf, boasting of past hunts and exploits, calling out obscene japes in good humor. Most silly of all were the sly licentious glances at Eleanor's women, the only females available, though the ladies themselves saw nothing comical in the attention. Their own voices twittered like bells in counterpoint to the male bellows, everyone in high disposition.

Towering over the hunters stood Richard, his eyes bright with anticipation. He walked immediately to his mother to embrace her.

"Still queen of them all," he murmured.

"You lick with a honeyed tongue, Great One," she replied, delighted.

He was right. Eleanor defied convention to wear black, which suited her glowing skin. But hers was not the austere black of Berengaria, for her bosom was laden with strings of diamonds which glittered as if sun-struck.

The king turned toward me. Instantly I fell to a low bow,

stared at his soft russet boots. As in Mainz, he reached for my hand and my eyes traveled upward as I stood, but no further than his gold medallion emblazoned with carbuncles of rare worth.

"Lady Alix, lovely as ever."

With a sick heart, I heard the catch in his voice.

"Your Majesty."

Suddenly he bent and kissed my cheek and I looked into his darkened eyes, serious and intent.

"Enjoy your hunt, Lady Alix."

"Thank you, Your Majesty."

He left, *Deo gratias*, but I still must face my panting audience; the queen watched with a cynical smile, Mamile with dewy eyes, Sybelle and the others with undisguised relish.

Grooms brought the blonks forward, saddled and ready. When I mounted Sea Mew, I couldn't help feeling the thirl of wild love and sickness I associated with the hunt. I bit my lip to control my smile, let the melancholy slip away to be resuscitated later. Sea Mew relieved himself, and two snipes landed on the dark turf to peck at his steaming droppings, everyone happy. At a signal from the king, the kennel keepers brought forth yipping deerhounds straining at their leads. Mercadier's horse reared, kicked a hound in the head; the dog lay in a pool of blood until his keeper rushed him to the wall and dropped him over.

Buglers pushed through our ranks to stand at the gates. At their mighty blast, the iron portcullis screeched upward and the beaters took their places at the front. As if the horns had roused the sun, for one glorious moment rays broke through the cloud cover and winter dun was transformed to a glowing Byzantine shawl draped over the countryside, burgundy reds mingling with bronze and yellow against rich browns. We began to move.

The king and his lords followed the beaters, then the ladies, then the archers. We headed away from the river into a woody gorge. We had a hard time holding our eager steeds

who snorted and stamped, impatient to run. Yet I was glad
to move slowly, for I gasped aloud at the beauty of the world
so long denied me in my tower. On the eastern slope of the
gorge a forest of wrinkled chestnuts dropped polished nuts
to attract the boar; the western side was poignantly like
Wanthwaite with its flaming gorse. My home hovered on
the dream-scape, ephemeral and fading.

Now we followed a water course lined with poplars, their
whippets bare of whispering leaves. Deeper and deeper we
progressed into the narrowing canyon, under pale bents and
brambles, birch and beech, until we reached a copse of giant
oaks where even the gray light failed and we rode in mysterious gloom. Richard signaled for us to stop and to spread.
Above us on the slope, the musical bay of the dogs rang
through the hollow.

The king raised his arm. "Uncouple the hounds!"

The excited beasts arched swiftly across the terrain, and
we finally let our horses hit their stride in pursuit.

"War! Ho!" we sang.

Bridle bells jangled! Trumpets snarled in thin golden
rasps! Dogs bayed! Drummers beat! All in a rousing cacophony of joy! Only the curious bleat of the deer sounded
alarm.

"Let the horn go!" Richard shouted. "After the doe!"

Faster and faster, all thinking stopped, only heart and
lungs and wind on the cheek!

"We've got them! Bring forth archers!"

We took sharp arrows from our quivers as the archers
moved among us. We'd come to the verge of a deep, wide
chasm and six deer stood at bay, their velvet eyes stunned
with panic. One doe rose suddenly and tried to leap, clung
for a moment on the far side of the crevice, and fell.

The king shot first. Then everyone. I felt the arrow zing
past my wrist, lost it in the hissing arc in the sky. Foundering, bleeding, braying, the deer sank on their haunches and
gave up their lives. Cheers rose on all sides! Dazed, heart

thumping, I bent and buried my face in Sea Mew's mane, my exaltation too great—or I know not what. I became weak, almost fell.

I was revived by the first flakes of snow which touched the nape of my neck. Men were already hacking at the deer, pulling at the skin and measuring the grease with their fingers to see if they were worthy. Two were loaded on waiting mules, the others left.

We faced into the wind blowing strong from the river. It stung our eyes, took a few hats. Everyone laughed and cried aloud with joy. Never had there been such a merry hunt! "Do you remember when . . ." And stories were shouted in the gale.

Did I remember? Aye, hunting with my father when I was a small girl, then later with Enoch. A rain-bloated leaf lifted from the ground and struck my face.

A hand lifted it off.

"Did you enjoy the chase?" The glowing king, impervious to cold.

"Aye, Your Majesty." The habit of flattery took over. "You are a great hunter."

"I hunt only one deer, for she is my dear." His eyes were hungry.

Habit soured. "You mean you want to slay me, Your Majesty?"

"To capture you."

"But you already have."

"I've caught the ribs, not the heart."

I stopped playing. "To get my heart, you must kill me."

He chose to take my steely retort as more play and laughed aloud. "You English have delicious expressions. Yes, killing and the act of love both stop activity—for a time."

Queen Eleanor rode to my other side. "Are you cold, Alix? I have an extra fur."

Richard answered for me. "I'll warm Alix."

I pressed my lips tight and watched my yellow gloves

where they held the reins. The queen jangled about the deer, the coming feast that night and I know not what. At one point I heard Richard respond.

"*Ponem pedem in aquilone.*"

I will put my foot in the north.

So Berengaria had trained him in the Latin tongue as well.

The world was Christmas-white when we arrived at the courtyard. Richard reached for me in my saddle. I tried to avoid his hands, but he caught me, held me a moment, his body a hot coal through all the fur.

I pulled away and ran into Beynac.

CHRISTMAS DAY, and all must attend the Mass of the Nativity: one year ago we'd been in Cologne Cathedral, and I'd thought I would soon be a hostage. I'd been right as it turned out. The sermon was long, the music magnificent with King Richard joining the choir and raising his hand to keep the singers in meter.

The company assembled after we'd napped and changed our raiment to make merry before the feast of the Nativity. Once again I'd been transformed, only this time I recognized the silk as being from Queen Eleanor's personal stock, not from the wardrobe of Lady Castellux; the queen had kept the seamstress busy at Fontevrault on my behalf—as if she anticipated my change of status. The dress was shaped like an inverted morning glory, tinted in the changing hues of the opal, now rose, now lavender, now green, now gold. I sailed with the other ladies in their brilliant satins to the great hall.

No longer the austere salle of Mercadier's routiers, the walls billowed with Eleanor's rare tapestries hung on red and gold rings, their exotic scenes from Toulouse and Turkistan. King Richard sat on a carved chair piled high with cushions of quilted silk; like a majestic swan, he shimmered in purest white, even his ermine cape being embroidered along the sides with silver and crystal.

We'd eaten only fish on Penance Day, but now the two

deer were crackling on the spit as we took our places at the trestles. I sat with the ladies directly below the king and queen where, if Richard looked at his plate, he must see me. But I didn't have to look upward—and didn't.

"I propose a toast to the hostages!" Richard cried.

Startled, I made the mistake of raising my face and was immediately shot through by marine-blue eyes.

"A runner arrived today from the north with the word that all of our hostages have been freed!"

There was much shouting and clinking of cups, then silence as we awaited further explanation.

"As you know," the king continued, "our niece Eleanor of Brittany was crossing the northern waste to fulfill her part of our treaty for freedom. Meantime, however, Duke Leopold met with an unfortunate accident."

He waited for raucous laughter to die.

"Yes, Leopold ran into a wall and broke his leg badly. Infection set in and the leg had to be removed. But who would face the wrath of Leopold if he should feel pain? No one. He was forced to take an axe and attempt the amputation himself. He failed, bled to death, and that's the end to our tale. Eleanor is returned, the hostages are free!"

Jubilant laughter filled the hall. I was glad that Eleanor had escaped her dour fate, infinitely relieved that the hostages were free—for I'd felt oddly guilty not to be with them —but I didn't find Leopold's death amusing.

"But that's not an end to our good tidings," Richard began when the laughter subsided. "I am delighted to announce that my younger sister, Queen Joanna, will soon be wed to Count Raymond of Toulouse."

Again I looked upward, but the king was smiling at Eleanor.

"I need not tell you how this alliance benefits our Kingdom."

But what about Joanna? Well, she'd wanted it herself, overcome with love. What manner of love? The courtly love Eleanor had invented? The real love I'd known with Enoch?

Simple lust? The royal family needlessly complicated their desires. Another deer into the abyss.

The announcements finished, a jongleur sang from the back of the room and conversation resumed. The venison was removed and other courses were brought on. I awaited my chance. William Marshal went forward to the royal dais and spoke behind the king; Richard had to turn and look back over his shoulder. I excused myself and slipped from my table.

Feeling my way along the walls of the darkened chambers, I was suddenly clutched from behind.

"Mercy!" I cried in panic.

"Hush, you'll rouse Mercadier's guard," the king's voice said.

I tried to bow, but was held upright.

"Come to the window where I may see you."

He led me into a tiny alcove; a winter moon's wan rays caught his snowy form, the glitter of his crystals.

"You should always be seen by moonlight." Again the voice's catch.

I turned my face to avoid his scrutiny.

"I'd planned that we stay here together a few weeks, Alix, but I must ride north tomorrow to greet the hostages in Rouen. You'll follow at a more leisurely pace with the queen."

"Queen Berengaria?" I asked with mock innocence and real fear.

He was silent for a few heartbeats. "With my mother queen. I know what you think—I must talk to you before I ride. Please meet me at the main portal at dawn and we'll walk together."

"As you wish, Your Majesty."

"This is what I wish."

He clasped me so close that one of his crystals hurt my breast, kissed me with the same hungry ardor I recalled from Chinon.

"Until dawn."

"Thank you, Your Majesty."

He let me go.

The owl hunted by night and I sat up until dawn, watching him bring mice to his mate. Twenty all told, better than usual. Their tenderness touched me. Even without souls or brains, they followed their hearts—I wished I were an owl.

THE MOMENT a faint gray lit the winter mist, I slipped down the stair. King Richard waited for me, brown furs draped over fustian. If he hadn't slept, he didn't show it . . .

"I whipped my bed all night with evil desires—did you?" he asked cheerfully. "Clear the amorous heaviness with a brisk walk, I say. Good to get the blood stirring." He took my arm. "Alix, greetings." He bent and brushed my lips.

Without a word I went ahead of him onto the rime-crisp grass of the court, across the bridge and into the snow-laden meadow. Walking was hard, breathing was harder. The king kept easy pace as I wandered I know not where, past the frozen brook—polluted forever, I trowe—that sheltered Berengaria's wastes, into the field where in summer the Domnerie monks put their dark-pointed fawn cows to pasture. I turned downward toward the village.

We reached the river, heavy with white mists, walked beside jagged ice edging black water, came to a deserted longcart half covered with snow. Before I knew what had happened, Richard picked me up and placed me on the cart, his arms around me so I stood level with him.

"Unless you plan to walk to Rouen, we might as well stop here."

Silver-tipped gulls flew in formation behind him. Were we that close to the sea?

"Lovers are supposed to hate the dawn, but that's when they greet it horizontal. In my case, I couldn't wait for the day. I would lie like a Saracen if I didn't tell you that I was ready to break your door if you hadn't come soon."

I gazed balefully into his mercurial eyes. A bit of snow clung to one brow, and his nose was red.

"You wished to speak to me of my experiences in Beynac, Your Majesty?"

He wiped the snow away, became serious.

"Mercadier told me about your immersion in the cistern. I came as fast as I could."

"Only because of Mercadier?"

"Why else? Alix, you must believe me—I knew nothing of your sufferings while you were here. Nevertheless, I am responsible for you and I beg your forgiveness."

His apology was offered with glittering eyes, royal scarlet and arrogant song.

"Why should I believe you, Your Majesty?" I saw his start, but continued. "You had only witnesses in Rouen to refute my word; I have my own ears, for I heard you assign me to Queen Berengaria for instruction. Surely you know your own queen."

"I know her now," he said tersely, "but I didn't before. Believe your king."

"I believe you in exactly the same degree you did me."

"I said your king. My word is infallible."

"In what month should I believe you, *Your Majesty?* In July you say yes, in August no and no again. Are we now back to July? I can't predict the turn of a weather-vane."

His choler rose as I meant it to; I'd grown weary of the Plantagenets.

"God's feet, Alix, I've loved you with integrity for five long years! Be merciful, release me from my prison, my torture, ransom me."

"You play the pretty game of the courtly lover begging for his lady's favors, but there's been no game in my tower. I'm the one in prison and no one *could* release me."

"Pride is the worst prison," he argued, holding his temper. "I've been too proud—too hurt—to admit how desperately I love you. My God, I love you!"

"A strange sort of love that sets spies to examine my undergarments, that accuses me of having a 'thick waist' . . ."

"I never believed you were unfaithful, but as king . . ."

"Oh yes, you believed it, My Lord. When Pudlicott told his lies, you listened like any schoolboy."

"That wretched cur! I'd rather believe a horse!"

"You accepted his testimony as if it were catechism, and you would accept it still except for two things."

"You mean Mercadier's message?"

"I mean the passage of time proved my waist still a reed; Pudlicott's deathbed confession confirmed my innocence."

His face froze. "How did you hear about Pudlicott's death? Did Bonel dare . . ."

"No, Your Majesty," I said hastily. "A washerwoman from Rouen gossiped to my handmaiden. Apparently everyone knows."

"Then let them know as well that the King of England ignores all statements from brutes, whether they accuse or recant."

"Yet you punished me for my supposed sin most grievously."

He took my shoulders. "I told you I didn't know."

"Forget Berengaria. You yourself treated me with contempt when I rode with your army."

He shook his head. "I was miserable to the point of sickness; I wanted you to share my anguish just a little. But, I swear to you on my Crown, I would rather roll snake eyes forever than to hurt you."

I twisted away from his grasp. "You apologize with ease, but words can't remove the damage. Your queen unsexed me utterly, unmirthed me as well."

"Then I must sex you and mirth you again, a task I look forward to with joy."

He pulled me off the cart into his embrace, kissed me so fervently that I trembled for my poor lips. Then he held me close, stroked and murmured endearments, kissed my hair, ears, cheeks, lips again. Over his shoulder I glimpsed the coming dawn as birch wands turned pink, water a pale flesh between coralline ice floes.

He cupped my face. "You're a winter rose. When I look on you, birds sing from the snowdrifts."

I heard only the faint cries of gulls.

Once again he kissed me. "If you've been hurt, it was nothing compared to my pain in leaving you now. I've waited so long, but you'll soon be in Rouen."

"I don't want . . ." I said uneasily.

He put a finger to my lips. "Hush, sweets. If you've learned courtly love, then you know the rule: That which a lover takes against the will of his beloved has no relish. I'll await your bidding."

"And if it never comes?"

He laughed exuberantly.

"You'll bid, and soon. I know you better than you know yourself. When we kiss, we share a darkness in the throat."

He kissed me again to prove his point.

I gave him credit for sensing the fire in my bedstraw—which I couldn't deny—but the darkness was in my heart.

# 15

HE CASTLE OF ROUEN BULGED WITH KNIGHTS and priests, many of them fresh from the chilly forts of Germany, all of them hoarse from their praise of King Richard. The king himself was not in residence—he'd gone to meet Walter of Coutances—but his presence rang to the ceilings. He was the most worthy monarch in Christendom, the most generous, bravest, most honorable. They'd pledged their lives for his release, and he'd kept his word to them. I stared from one besotted wight to another, baffled, for they looked to have all their wits. Yet even the most partial observer must admit that Richard had had nothing to do with their freedom. They should give credit to God, or to Fortune's Wheel, or to Duke Leopold's poor aim with his axe. Yet, the king's massive energies crackled in the air we breathed, and within hours I, too, believed he'd freed the hostages; it was hard to resist his matchless power to fire others' imaginations.

I stayed with the queen and her ladies. A trunk had been sent from Fontevrault filled with gossamer silks and satins for my coming assignation.

AT MY FIRST OPPORTUNITY, I went to see Sister Tiberga. I walked the narrow descent to her house in the company of Hamo and Bok, who'd happily returned to my service, then instructed them to wait as I had Ditma announce me.

Tib rushed into her tiny room and fell abjectly to her knees. "Your Majesty."

"*Benedicite*, Tib, I'm supposed to be the royal mistress, not the queen."

I pulled her upright and peered closely at her scar.

"I rival Pudlicott for beauty, don't I?" she quipped. "Fortunately, my best work is done in the dark."

I put my arms around her. "Can you ever forgive me?"

"We'll see," she said cagily. "I can forgive better than I can understand. Why did you flee the king? He's no common squire as you described. What ails you? You should leap joyfully into his bed even if he had two white eyes, a hanging neck and a sniveling nose. Think of his power!"

"Aye." I then attempted to relate something of Berengaria's cruelty, for which I still blamed Richard.

"That shrunken hold-door!" she scoffed. "She has to pretend to Christian virtue because a man's seedpod deflates upon looking at her. Beware of such women, Alix. They're worse than Saint Jerome and Saint Tertullian combined when it comes to hurting our sex. Let her babble on her beads and you take the king—take his power."

"You misunderstand, Tib. I'll have no power . . ."

I told her that, in any case, I would be with the king only a short time.

"All love is limited, but while it lasts you have power and should set your price high."

"You mean like Eleanor's courtly love?"

"Yes, that's fancy language for the same thing. We're all whores—sex is our only commodity—no matter what our rank. But a smart woman uses her capital wisely."

"You and Eleanor are alike," I said morosely.

"Hardly. She's a hermaphrodite. She gives good advice, but never used it herself; instead she turned into a man, which no one has ever accused me of doing. I've heard that when she walks, you can hear her balls clink. Beware of the queen."

"Richard said he'd sent her away forever."

"Can't you hear? Not Berengaria—Eleanor selected that dead doortree as her son's wife so she could be his queen herself—she would share his bed if she could. Queen Eleanor, Queen Bee, Queen Mother, Queen Queen."

But I wasn't interested in Eleanor. I hung my head, avoided Tib's eyes. She poured me a goblet of wine and waited. We sat in silence a long time before she reached for my hand.

"What are you holding back, Lady Alix? And don't tell me again that it's Berengaria."

I smiled ruefully. "She was as close as I'll ever come to meeting the Devil face to face, Tib, but in a perverse way she did me a service."

"By teaching you religion?"

"By giving me a good reason for refusing the king. If she acted on his orders, then he put himself out of my favor forever. I could never forgive—couldn't be expected to for-give—such treatment."

"And would also never have to state your real objection to his person," she finished for me.

Meeting her bright eyes, I nodded, grateful for her fast wit.

"Do you want to tell me what it is?"

Again I nodded, sipped deeply of my wine, then spoke haltingly of my fears concerning the king's love for boys. I suspected that his vacillation toward me sprang from his own ambivalence—now yes, now no—toward the female sex; that even his rejection of Berengaria must be rooted in his problem.

"Only a blind man eats flies," she broke in.

I disagreed, arguing that a good marriage would serve the king both with the Church and his strategy against King Philip—mostly by giving him a legitimate heir.

Tib remained stubborn. "I'm sure he knows that, but no frog can sing in a cesspool."

I switched from Berengaria to myself. I was neither fly nor cesspool, but he treated me most grievously at times, as if he hated me, which I took as a sign that, when he drew close, he was repelled by my sex.

"It's a time-honored technique," she scoffed. "When wooing doesn't work, a good fight brings the prey to bed. Some women require a beating to release their queint juices."

But hadn't he told me himself on the Crusade—when he thought me a boy—how he'd lost all interest in women? How what had started as a playful dalliance with boys had grown to a pernicious habit? How the master had become the slave? I'd been too young to understand his inclinations, but I followed them now, and as a woman I was repelled, couldn't imagine myself bedding with a man who coveted boys, couldn't imagine any woman doing so.

My voice rose to a passionate pitch, but was stopped by Tib's derisive laughter.

"By my faith, forgive me, dear, but I can't help . . ." and she was off in her guffaws again, wiping her eyes. "I tell ye true, Lady Alix, that if women refused to bed with such men, the human race would end tomorrow. Bless me, darling, if most all of my clients don't bring me posts still hot from the dung hole."

"You're lying!" I cried. "As if that would make me accept the king."

"Of course you should accept him—for his power. But let me put your fears to rest on this other score." She freshened our cups, and we both swilled. "Men can't help themselves, poor dears, for nature has put hot pizzles in their crotches that rebel against reason and religion. A man sits through sermons on carnal sin as his willynilly stands up and looks around for a nice hole to rub. He hears that women are the gateway to Hell, so he seeks a man or dog or anything round and cozy. I tell you that the human body provides more holes than a honeycomb. Priests are the greatest offenders— since women are forbidden fruit—but even the clergy I service admit they'd rather play derry dan on my *belle chose* than dig nightearth with their tools. But what can they do?"

"Tib, you're speaking of terrible sin," I cried, shocked to my marrow. "If priests did such, they'd expire of guilt."

"Or go to confession," she said calmly.

"Surely if they confessed, the Church would expel them!"

"Not if the father confessor shared the sin," she pointed out slyly.

My jaw dropped in astonishment. Was it possible?

"In any case, Richard isn't a priest." I said.

No, she conceded, but soldiers were even worse. Priests were told to love their fellows as brothers, which added the stain of incest to their sins if you wanted to look at it so, and knights were taught to love their lords with all their hearts. The relationship between lord and vassal was probably as passionate as that between Heloise and Abelard, or Guinevere and Lancelot. They lived together, fought together, died together and loved together—all with intense passion. True, they also married, but their wives were little more than material rewards for their services, or a means to establish dynasties.

My tongue was thick, from wine or feeling I couldn't say. "I resent being a brood mare, Tib. I don't want to be a means—I want to be the end, loved just for myself!"

"Oh dear, dear, dear," she crooned, a bit jug-bitten herself, "such a fuzz-brained hare. Love is the rich man's conceit, his song and his poem, which most males haven't even heard of. Yet the rich become poor when they take the sheets, my dear; at best you can expect a few months of hot desire, which I'm sure Richard will provide.

"No, you don't understand. He wants children."

"But not your children, dear."

"I'm the only one he can rise to, Tib; therefore he wants my children."

She put her methier carefully to the floor and refilled it, then peered with shrewd eyes. "Repeat what you said."

I did, elaborating on my first conversations, my contract.

"He's going to recognize your bastards as heirs?" She asked, awed.

"Aye."

"Why didn't you say so at once? Skip all this blether about love! You must get pregnant today—before he changes his mind."

I tried to protest, my tongue now sober again, but she couldn't be stopped. Her own waggling member raced with instructions of how to bring the great event about with seven time-honored positions for conception, none of them the one I knew.

"But once you miss a period," she advised, "you must keep it secret until you're sure, especially with the first child. Desire affects the body in strange ways, and sometimes women believe themselves gravid with good reason, only to be fooled."

"When can I be certain?" Unwittingly I slipped into her theme.

"If you go three months, you're safe. That's as long as any woman refrains from bleeding from other causes, and it's the period when Nature most often aborts. When you begin your fourth month, inform your lord."

She continued her harangue until I was forced to leave; the light was fading. I took her hand.

"I can never thank you, Tib. You helped me when no one else would and now still offer your friendship."

"I'm investing capital, love; I want your help."

"Anything within my power."

"Oh, you have the power." She tossed her black head.

"If I do—and I'm not promising—how could I use my power?"

"By financing me," she replied sweetly. "I want to expand my convents of Saint Mary Magdalene, and you owe it to me, to all your sex. Love is life's leecher, its greatest healer, and that's my theme—if I get the money. Give Richard his treacle from heaven and he'll give you the world."

I wasn't convinced, nor would I offer assurances. However, it was my first political promise.

"And Alix"—her hand held my arm—"I don't want to mislead you, for I'm about to say something foolish. You know I set not a straw on love, believe with good reason that it's a silly parching after fruit over the fence, and yet . . . yet, by my troth, I hear a whisper in my gut soft as any shrift that the king does love you."

I DIDN'T MEET Richard until I attended Joanna's wedding.

Her groom, Count Raymond of Toulouse, was the handsomest man I'd ever beheld. Flawless of feature, perfectly proportioned of body, he flashed glittering teeth, sang forth in musical merriment—all of which masked the character of a jackal. Watching him await his bride in the great Cathedral of Rouen, I caught the discrepancy between his enameled smile and darting eyes; even now he was a ravening beast on the prowl. Aye, he was easy to decipher; the mystery was

Joanna. Heedless of warnings and Raymond's infamous record, she threw herself eagerly into his canine jaws.

Fanfare announced the glorious Joanna who marched to her doom on her brother's arm. Their mutual beauty, their celestial auras, must tempt the gods. They passed close by in a cloud of sweet woodruff and sandalwood, their gold and silver spangles rustling as they walked, their regal chins held high, their smiles set. Then came Eleanor in her royal scarlet, a small diamond chaplet holding her veils to her head; I could see why she emphasized blood lines, for her influence clearly flowed through her handsome, glowing children.

Walter of Coutances officiated in his splendid chasuble of orefois. He finished his Latin prayers to the kneeling couple, then began his sermon in French.

"In marriage, the husband must worship his God which is in Heaven while a wife must worship her husband likewise here on earth, for he is her lord.

"The husband is descended from Adam who was created in God's image, the wife from Eve who was made from Adam's rib and is therefore inferior. Yet a husband must treat her with charity; although she was not taken from his head, which would make her his equal, neither was she created from his foot to be abused and tramped upon. The rib was chosen as midway in Adam's body, yet close to the liver and genitals which made him susceptible to her wiles and led to his fall. Therefore is every woman an Eve in her time, every man again an Adam to resist her temptation."

Berengaria's imprecations rang in my head: "You're the daughter of Eve," and I looked on the archbishop with a hostile eye.

"Above all, a husband must quell his wife's bestiality. Women are wicked, lewd as vipers, slippery as eels, inquisitive, indiscreet and cantankerous, made so by their ungovernable lusts."

Again he echoed Berengaria who had quelled her own bestiality with vengeance, though I couldn't see that it improved her character, and tried hard to smother mine—a more formidable task. Judging from Berengaria's example, lust might be preferable to vicious cruelty.

"However, he has a conjugal duty to satisfy her demands, provided she observe strictly the days of abstinence.

"She must refuse him during all daylight hours, on nights that fall before Sundays and Holy Days, during the forty fast-days before Easter, Holy Cross Day and Christmas, before Wednesdays and Fridays, during menstruation, three months before childbirth and forty days after and the first three nights after nuptials."

I quickly calculated: out of three hundred sixty-five days of the year, one hundred twenty went for fasting which left two hundred forty-five; another fifty-eight must be subtracted for menstruation, another eighty-nine for prohibited days of the week which, not counting myriad Holy Days, left only ninety-eight days to sully the nuptial bed. *Benedicite*, if a woman became pregnant, she'd have to extend the year to accommodate all the forbidden days!

"No matter what her importunities, he must not deviate from those positions according to Nature in his acts."

A titillating command. What might those positions be? The same that Tib had described? Could there be still others? My fantastick cells devised a few possibilities, providing the partners were agile.

"To prevent her from straying outside the nuptial bed, a husband should keep his wife plain and unattractive."

A difficult assignment for Raymond, for nothing could hide Joanna's fair beauty. I waited to hear how she could stop him from straying, which was more to the point, but Walter stayed with his thesis.

"If a wife strays, the lover gets the white bread, the husband the black. Therefore the husband must immediately cast her off lest a child be born of the illicit union, thus depriving the legitimate child of his inheritance."

At these words, Richard stepped to the side so that he

faced the vast congregation. His eyes moved swiftly along the rows until they met mine, where they stopped; his cheeks flushed and he raised quizzical brows.

I lowered my head, twisted my hands, shifted my weight and brought on a whispered volley from Lady Mamile who told me to scratch my itch and be done with it.

THE WEDDING FEAST was held that evening in Rouen Castle for all the splendid lords and ladies of the realm. Gowned in peacock blue with a mantle of shimmering gold, the king sat high on his dais overlooking his minions, his bold laughter ringing joyfully through the hall. I stayed a little behind Lady Mamile as we entered, then chose a trestle screened from the king's view during our dinner. All too soon, the trestles were cleared for dancing.

As the first carole began, the king descended his perch and bowed before his sister Joanna. A perfectly matched couple, they swayed and hopped nimbly to sudden changes in rhythm, exactly as they'd twirled at Richard's own wedding to Berengaria during the Crusade. Only then I'd been drunkalewe on wine and jealousy as I served him in my role as page.

The carole finished; another began. Richard tenderly reached for his mother. Eleanor's natural flush warmed her face as no paint could, and her eyes sparkled like sapphires. Soothly she worshipped her glorious son. I tapped my foot restlessly, the rhythm taking me in spite of myself, yet I felt acutely out of place, a plain white owl in the midst of the gaudy plumage around me. If the king were a peacock, he moved among jabbering parrots of brilliant hue. The ladies had thin brows and high hairlines with tall wimples to extend their foreheads even further before spilling in trails of filmy gauze; their jeweled and embroidered tunics were cut to their nipples, and two young women had open seams along their sides so I could see their naked bodies as they moved. Eleanor had chosen my dress, a plain white tunic sans ornament, albeit it was cunningly cut to flare in layered circles as I walked, and my shoes had silver points. She'd then pinned a few moonstones and pearls in my shorn locks.

Yet it was more than my gown which separated me from this company. My reclusive existence since I'd left Wanthwaite had made its mark and I was disoriented by the gay chirping voices, the constant rustle and movement around me. I yearned for my quiet cell which at least gave me the freedom to be myself. Where could I hide?

The dance changed to an estampe, and the ladies retired for a dozen lusty men who leaped and cavorted dangerously over the waxed stones. Through their flings and kicking heels, I saw movement on the far side of the hall where three aliens now entered: Bonel and two fellow Jews with high jeweled turbans, silk sendal robes and rich furs. With their olive skins and dark eyes, they were magi from the mysterious orient who'd wandered by accident into these strange revels. Or perhaps not by accident; perhaps Bonel wanted to see my behavior, now that I was again in royal favor. The estampe finished; the king spoke to the musicians.

"The king's going to sing," Lady Mamile said with excitement. "Oh my dear, what an honor! He has a surpassingly fine voice."

Indeed, the whole company fell silent as Richard took his place by the violist. The instruments introduced the theme, a searing plaint. The king waited quietly for the passage to end, then raised his eyes and searched the room.

And found me.

Instantly I slid a little further behind Lady Mamile and fixed my own gaze to the scratched pavement at my feet.

> "As warrior I soar to splendid deeds,
> But as lover I serve my lady's wishes;
> I'll kiss and stroke, do acts delicious
> If you confess your intimate needs."

He moved as he sang; his bright blue tunic was hemmed
with gold orefois as it fell to the floor before me. His hand
reached to take mine.

"Will you honor me with this dance, dear Alix?"

I couldn't speak—my heart bounded painfully. In front
of all these people? Lady Mamile pushed me gently, and I
held forth my trembling fingers. Deftly, the king turned so
we stood side by side, his arm at my waist. I breathed his
sweet woodruff, knew he gazed down at me as we swayed
to the music's reprise.

"I beg to be your slave, Alix," he said in a low voice. "Tell
me how to please you, how I must follow your own rules of
love's craft."

He bent low to hear my whisper. "How can I teach you
of love, Your Majesty? You know more than a hundred
damsels such as I."

He laughed softly, then sang again for the company.

> "A hundred ladies may seek my love—
> Leave lands and gold for my caress—
> To them and the world I here confess
> That I give my heart to this sweet dove."

Again he laughed and turned me so I faced him. The
audience joined the merriment and clapped as we danced
backward, dipping and gliding in intricate patterns that
Richard led with a firm hand. I felt myself floating in a
dream, watched my silver slippers peek and disappear under
my glistening swirls.

"You are my dove, Alix, the bird of true love," the king
said over his shoulder.

I joined the game giddily. "Your praise exceeds my merit,
Your Majesty. I'm earthbound, have no wings."

"Your smiles have wings that fly straight to my heart."

"How can that be, My Lord? Birds are free as the wind
and I am in a cage." I dimpled archly to soften my words.

"Given freedom, the dove seeks its master," he countered.
"Or its home."

A faint frown fretted his brow, but he laughed gallantly.
"I am your home, Alix, as you are mine."

We returned to our first position, only now he pulled me
close so that my lowered face rested against his shoulder.

> "So completely does she have my heart—
> Her beauty and worth so beyond compare,
> I swoon and hope her bed to share
> And swear that we will never part."

The music carried me into my own arabesque, and I
whirled in the center of my bright skirt, bent and moved my
arms to the yearning rise, aware always of the king's ardent
gaze. Then he stepped forth and held me close as the delighted guests whispered "Ahhhh."

"I can't resist you," he murmured. "Please give me some
sign, a word, a glove, a ring, a token of love . . ."

I arched back, met his flame-blue eyes, lowered my lids
demurely. "I have nothing to give, Your Majesty, no treasure."

"Then I'll steal my token I want above all else."

He kissed me—the crowd burst into applause.

"You swale my heart," he whispered as he released me.

I swayed slightly—he held me steady—and I bowed to
the floor. The king gave my hand to Lady Mamile, and left
us for the eager hostages and wedding party. That lady plied
me with comments.

Still watching Richard as he talked to Joanna, I hardly
heard her.

"Never such a beautiful couple, my dear!"

"You don't think it was an unseemly display?" I asked.

"As a fish must have water," she returned sagely, "courtly
love must have gossip. The king is master of the game."

Master of the game, of the hunt; I recalled the frightened
deer just before she leaped into the abyss. Then forgot as

Richard turned and looked in my direction, his lips parted for words that never came. The brilliant company faded to a blur of color, their voices a distant chorus; Richard and I gazed, alone in the world.

"Lady Alix."

I jumped slightly and faced Bonel. The other two Jews stood slightly behind him.

Bonel's face was transfigured by a well of emotion, his brown eye shining, his lips very red. I wondered if he'd had another vision for he seemed under a spell.

"Greetings, Alix," he repeated. "I would like you to meet my friends, Vives and Aaron."

Aaron? I stared at the young man who'd escaped from York with Bonel. There was little now to indicate his former suffering; he was draped in blue silks, his neck entwined with heavy pendants of great worth. Yet his heavy-lidded eyes were somber.

Bonel stumbled over his words. "You look like an angel."

"Thank you." The compliment was innocuous, but his intensity gave it significance. "Except that you don't believe in angels."

"I believe in one."

I laughed lightly, out of my depth, and glanced uneasily at the other Jews. "Not in me, Bonel. Don't forget how I looked when I was attacked by the eagle."

His urbane mask split asunder, revealing a Bonel I didn't know. He spoke so softly that I had to bend my head to hear. "You're fair as the moon, clear as the sun, terrible as an army with banners."

There was no answer to his strange statement, but I couldn't look away from his hypnotic eye. *Benedicite.*

"Bonel, greetings."

Richard's silent approach made me turn guiltily; Bonel bowed with the other two Jews. By the time he stood, his mask was in place.

"Greetings, Your Majesty."

Vives and Aaron added their salutations.

"Are you enjoying the celebration?" the king asked, placing a possessive hand on my elbow.

"A most auspicious occasion, Your Majesty. I hope your sister will be as happy as she deserves."

The king grinned. "Be generous and wish her joy beyond her deserts." He glanced down at me. "What think you of our northern wildflower? She's come full bloom at last."

"She's equally lovely as bud or bloom," Bonel replied with formal courtesy, not looking at me.

"She dances most charmingly, does she not?"

"With you to guide her steps, Your Majesty, she does passingly well. Now, if I may beg your permission, the hour's late and we have an early appointment with Flanders tomorrow."

Richard's manner was jocular. "I'm sorry to see you leave, but appreciate your devotion to duty. How goes the collection?"

This was not the time or place for such discussion, and the answers were cursory.

After the three men had left, Richard squeezed my arm. "You made another conquest, dove."

There was an implicit question in his comment, which I was quick to quash.

"Oh no, Your Majesty. Bonel condescends to be my friend, but he's gone to some pains to let me know how inferior I am."

"Then he speaks against his heart; I know the symptoms." He lowered his voice. "Spend tomorrow with me, Alix. I have meetings, but I want you near."

The urgency in his voice offered no choice. "I would be honored, Your Majesty."

"If you should bid me that you are ready for love, I can leave my duties in an instant. Put your hand to your forehead as a signal—I'll be watching."

He kissed my hand, leaned his cheek briefly against mine,

and left. The rest of the evening passed in single heartbeat. The company danced until dawn. Penciled brows disappeared and wimples slipped askew to reveal plucked hairlines; paint dripped down noble chins, a fight was stopped between two young squires; and the old people fell asleep in the corners. The cock was crowing when I finally dropped to my bed.

ALMOST INSTANTLY I was wakened by my door slowly opening. One glance at the familiar feet approaching my mat told me that it was the king. I pretended to sleep and began to pray, for this was the end. After all he'd promised about awaiting my bidding, he was going to rape me most cruelly. His hand touched my cheek.

"Alix, wake up."

I opened dazed eyes. "Is something wrong, Your Majesty?"

Noises all over the castle told me that there was—and the king was armed.

"That She-Devil in Brittany has raised a rebellion against me. I have to ride."

Our eyes mingled. I didn't know what to say. Nor did he.

"Are you her ally?"

Not kenning what he meant, I continued to stare, speechless.

"For it's the only thing that could make me leave your bed. God's feet, your scent . . ."

He buried his face in my neck, breathed deeply, then kissed me. No courtly kiss this time, but real. Tender. Moving. *Benedicite.*

"I'll write you," he whispered.

"Aye, thank you . . ."

He pulled me so tight against his mail that the impression lasted for two days.

Thus Constance of Brittany ensured my chastity for the weeks to come.

A runner had arrived not an hour ago to inform the king that Constance had raised an army against him, provoked because she resented young Eleanor's being sent to Germany —though the maid was now safe in Rouen—and Constance herself had been abducted by her hated husband, Ranulf of Chester. The Bretons had managed to release her from the brutal Ranulf, but she swore that the King of England was behind the plot; worse, she had joined forces with France. Even now young Arthur was with King Philip in Paris and fighting raged in Brittany.

I quickly forgot the war in Brittany in the heady freedom the occasion awarded. I was no longer in a tower, no longer policed at all hours of the day—though carefully guarded— and could therefore do as I liked.

The following day, therefore, Bonel and I walked down to the Seine even though it was snowing. The river was reduced to a narrow black trickle by banks of ice. Bonel stamped his feet for warmth as I finished my description of Berengaria's tortures.

"So you need not tell me more of the suffering of the Jews," I finished bitterly. "I've learned by experience."

"I'm sorry. I hate for you to suffer because of your association with me." He gazed through his frosted breath.

"*Benedicite*, it's not your fault, only . . . Tell me, Bonel, are there many lunaticks like Berengaria?"

"Religious zeal is not considered a sign of lunacy," was his sardonic reply. "Ignorant priests inflame even more ignorant louts to brutal acts. Since the Third Lateran Council called for tolerance to the Jews 'on the grounds of humanity,' you rarely find such behavior among the upper hierarchy of the Church—or among the royalty. However, Berengaria is such a rarity and so is King Philip."

"But not King Richard?"

"If I thought so, I would have snatched you from his arms the other night," he blazed.

His vehemence surprised me.

"You have no cause for anger—I danced only for you."

"For me?" The catch in the voice was like Richard's.

"Aye, I thought it was what you wanted. When the king asked me to dance, I was aware that you were watching, so I smiled prettily and accepted. You must have noticed."

"Everyone noticed." He skipped a stone across the ice, then turned back. "You glided like a swan. No one in the room could look away from you."

All the words were right, but the humor behind them was skewed. We stood in morose silence.

"At least I have a little more time, thanks to Constance of Brittany. And I could have more—it's my decision."

He glanced up quizzically. "What do you mean?"

Embarrassed, I explained the rule of courtly love about waiting for the lady's permission in order to relish love.

It was one of the few times I'd heard Bonel laugh outright, and the sound grated. Mortified, I waited for him to finish.

"Try to put him off when the days of abstinence are past."

"What days?"

"You should know better than I. Isn't this a period of abstinence among Christians, the period of the Nativity? And then Lent, which is early this year."

I felt like a knot-head. "Is *that* why?"

My tone drew his surprised stare. "Why else? By my faith, you don't think the king would restrain himself on *your* account, do you?"

"Of course not. I never said . . . "

He touched my flushed cheek. "But you thought. Alix, Richard is the king. He'll do what he likes when he likes; it's not only bred into his bone as his divine right, but he's also been taught to deny himself nothing."

Gulled again. I'd been impressed by his concern for my feelings. When would I learn?

Bonel tactfully ignored my chagrin. "I'm happy that your

waiting period is to be spent in Rouen at least. We'll have many good talks."

"Aye."

Suddenly he stepped close and his face assumed the same wonder I'd noted at the ball.

"Alix, I wish you didn't have to go to the king at all. When I watched you dance last night, circling and dipping as if you had wings, I thought . . . you don't know . . ."

I waited.

"I've never been in such conflict, Alix, dear Alix; I promised to protect you, promised to help the Jews, thought I could do both, thought . . ." He struggled, his face shadowed, then turned back to the river, threw a stone viciously. "I thought that you and Richard were Greek gods, superhumanly beautiful and perfectly matched."

"Yet you would like to spare me."

"Yes."

His back was turned; I touched his fur with my glove, but he didn't feel it.

BONEL WAS RIGHT; we had many happy talks during the weeks that followed, but we carefully avoided the subject of my approaching assignation with the king. I learned more about the Jews, their customs and beliefs, learned about Bonel's own background, but mostly we laughed and played all sorts of games, from chess to bones, as if neither of us had a care in the world. But it wasn't until he taught me to skate on the ice with shin bones tied to my boots— slipping and lurching as if drunkalewe, leaning on his strong arm—that I realized that we played a more serious game.

Never again would I forget that he was a man with a man's feelings. By unspoken consent, we set limits on our behavior, but there could be no limits on awareness.

Tib proved the more innocent distraction. I helped her in her hospital—though not with her male patients—and stewed animal brains and herbal concoctions in her laboratory.

Hamo took me fishing on the Seine where we talked away idle hours. Meanwhile, the days grew longer, the air milder, as winter gave way to spring.

FIGHTING IN BRITTANY was fiercer than expected, thanks to the intervention of King Philip on Constance's behalf, but Richard sent daily reports that he was gaining. He also sent private missives for me. His words were brief and to the point: he missed me most grievously and lived only to see me. Poetic—exaggerated perhaps—but repetition gave the words credibility. I began to look forward to the small rolls of vellum, tied them carefully together.

Then one day he missed. I took small note until the second day, then the third. Was he forgetting me? Had he met someone else? Queen Eleanor summoned me to her chamber.

The instant I saw her, I knew something was wrong. No amount of pink paint could hide the waxy pallor of her face. My own heart began a heavy thud.

"The king's been wounded," she said without preamble.

I cried aloud, clasped my lips to control myself. The message echoed ominously and I was back at Nottingham, learning about Enoch.

"Is he . . . ?

"We don't know." Her voice was drained. "I'm going to the cathedral. Would you come with me?"

I joined her ladies to walk through heavy rain to the church. This became a daily ritual as spirits fell ever lower and the days stretched to two weeks. My animal virtues were in turmoil. If he should die, what would become of me?

One night I had a most terrifying dream about the king. I forgot the details but not my horror. From that time on, I began to think of King Richard differently. I recalled his laughter, his courage and, aye, his devotion to me. What he felt might be woodly, but it was constant; all of his angers and vacillations had sprung from uncertainty. If only King Richard lived, I bargained with God, I would accept my fate.

Then one day the queen had news. "He was struck in the knee!" Her eyes filled. "A foolhardy assassin crept inside the inner court—no one knows how."

"Gangrene?" I whispered.

"No. He wanted you told, but said not to worry." She hugged me and whispered, "He asks that you join him in Poitiers."

I began to protest but quickly changed when I saw the queen's earnest rapture. She loved him more than her own life, assumed that everyone did the same. Now that I knew he was safe, old doubts returned. But I'd traveled a spiritual distance these last weeks, and I didn't see how I *could* refuse.

I left for Poitiers the last week of March in Bonel's company, for he was returning to England to collect money and deviated a few miles on my way. Before we separated on the road, I was inspired.

"Bonel, you have many contacts. Could you get a message to my friends at Wanthwaite to say I'm all right? Then ask how they are, especially Dame Margery."

He listened carefully to my list.

"There are no Jews left in the north, but perhaps through the Exchequer or the Church. I'll try."

He smiled, the sweet smile I always tried to invoke, then turned away.

"You go first," he said. "I'll watch till you're out of sight. And, Alix—I want you to be happy."

I nodded, suddenly choked. To my surprise, he leaned forward and kissed me gently, then stared as if memorizing, his eye suspiciously bright.

When I looked back from the crest of a long rise, he waved in farewell.

# 16

NE OF MY MERCENARY GUARDS RODE AHEAD TO inform King Richard of my arrival, and I watched the main portal of Poitiers with a mix of excitement and apprehension, expecting him to ride out to greet me. Instead, the guard returned with the news that Richard had not yet arrived. The castellan thought he would surely be here today, tomorrow at the latest, for he rode from nearby Chinon.

Peter Bertin, the mayor of Poitiers, had been alerted to our arrival and met us as we crossed the last bridge. He greeted me most courteously and he led our party past Notre Dame la Grande, a small elegant cathedral that opened in three parts across its portal—an intricate ivory triptych made large—and finally dismounted before the ducal palace. The small company of knights who'd escorted me were instructed to ride further for their lodgings; only my guardians, Hamo and Bok, entered with me.

Peter Bertin showed me to my apartment, the best in the palace as it belonged to Queen Eleanor. Awed, I stood inside a chamber with walls frescoed to look like an aviary filled with colorful birds of rare plumage and a dais with a huge bed. A curved canopy draped in Spanish lace topped a mattress as wide as my entire floor in Beynac tower.

"Soothly, Mayor Bertin, I don't require this much space," I said. "Doesn't King Richard use this room?"

His smile made me turn away in embarrassment. *Benedicite*, the king *would* use it.

I tried again. "I prefer someplace where I may have privacy."

Unsure of my authority to change his instructions, he

finally led me to the adjacent room where the Countess of
Champagne had stayed. It was smaller, but exquisitely appointed, and I pronounced myself satisfied. Before he left, I
asked if the streets of Poitiers were safe, as I would like to
explore them until the king's fanfare was heard. Surprised,
he assured me that they were.

Nevertheless, Bok and Hamo stayed close as I walked til
and fro on the gay sunstruck avenues.

I insisted on visiting Notre Dame la Grande, and Hamo
came with me, but Bok leaned, yawning, at the main portal
to wait for us. We stood inside a prism of light, different
from all other churches. In contrast to St. Paul's or Rouen
Cathedral, it was small in compass; unlike Fontevrault
Chapel, it was infinitely complex instead of being simple;
unlike any of them, it shimmered and moved in a shower of
jewel colors, as if it were alive.

"*Benedicite*," I breathed, "we've found the rainbow."

The source of the light was the moving sun, but the effect
was created by man. Light entered through stained-glass
windows in gule shafts and fell on a series of round pillars
which formed the side aisles; each of these pillars was
painted in gaudy geometric designs which altered as the sun
moved from one window to another. At the end of the nave
sat a glorious Madonna with her Son on a high throne of
gold illuminated from all directions, so that she moved and
smiled as well from her glittering eminence. The illusion—
if it was an illusion—was uncanny.

Hamo and I moved toward her in a trance, fell to our
knees. Suddenly a voice thundered behind us: "Beware! The
end of the world is at hand! The Lord will avenge in blood!
Bring forth a great earthquake and the sun will be black as
sackcloth of hair!"

Frightened, we both looked over our shoulders to see a
fully armed knight of huge proportions striding toward us
in a rattle of steel. He stood directly over us, blocking the
Virgin, his crazed face furious.

"The moon will swell with blood and stars will fall to earth."

He pointed an iron finger to my face and Hamo raised an arm.

"The day of His wrath will bring fire in the air and who can stand? All will be silence!"

"Get away from her!" Hamo piped in terror.

Suddenly Bok ran down the aisle and took the giant knight from the rear, pinning his arms to his side.

"The star is called Wormwood! Beware!"

After this bellow, the knight suddenly became docile as a lamb and permitted Bok to lead him to the door. Hamo and I quickly followed, waiting till Bok said it was safe to emerge into the blinding sun. Much perturbed, I returned to the palace, there to lie on my bed and gaze at Venus and Cupid painted on my ceiling. Had the knight been an omen?

I ate my supper alone in my apartment. Then a bath was sent—again I blushed at the implication—and I sank against linen covers which lined the tub and almost fell asleep in its warmth. My handmaidens, Agnes and Hulda, put their mats next to my high bed, and soon all of us closed our eyes.

Fanfare woke me in the middle of the night. Bright April moonlight spilled over the strange room and I didn't know where I was. Then I heard the king's voice, jubilant greetings around him, and I sat up. After a long time, he passed my door, his tones now muted; I lay back on my pillow, to sleep no more. The sky gradually turned a deep, clear blue. I rose, selected a tunic of pale viridian embroidered along the hem and neck with a border of leafy flower entwinements. Agnes went for my bread and wine. I rinsed my mouth with mint, let Hulda dress my short curls with a flower chaplet which matched the tunic and waited.

Richard summoned me almost at once. The king sat by his trestle surrounded by arguing monks and knights. Unseen, I studied him a few heartbeats. He was thinner, worn, his eyes shadowed, his voice rasping in frustration, and he was dressed in a short tunic of dark red and blue, as if he planned to ride. Then he saw me. A smile brightened his face and sparked his eyes; he shed ten years.

"Lady Alix." He tried to rise, had difficulty until his page offered an arm. He limped around the table to greet me.

I bowed low, stared directly at a bandage and leather brace on his knee. He took my hand.

"Are you in pain, Your Majesty?"

"Not when I look at you. Welcome." He bent, kissed me decorously on the cheeks. "I'm here, and so are you—that's all that counts."

He then gestured that I should sit on a faldstool until he finished his business. His talk resumed, a plan of strategy for the fighting season which would begin in June. His principal concern was the Bishop of Beauvais, whom he wanted to defeat at all costs. Never mind what the Pope might say, this bishop was no man of peace, but a rapacious killer hiding behind priestly robes. I listened with interest, then growing morbidity. How odd, to consider a bishop as an armed enemy. Again I thought of the lunatick man in the church and wondered about the king's knee. Was the wound also an omen?

The conference continued—Richard put his hand to the nape of my neck. Finally the men rose after their meal and one by one said farewell to the king. William Marshal spoke to me kindly as he passed, as did Baldwin who'd left his new bride, Hadwisa of Aumâle, to support the king.

At last we were alone.

"Each time I forget you," Richard said. "I can't recall those eyes, lips . . ." He smiled. "Are you well? Glad to see me?"

"Aye, Your Majesty."

He laughed aloud.

"Are you hungry?"

"Aye," I admitted.

"Will bread and an apple suffice? I'm tied in knots and want to get away."

He made the order. Both of us were reserved—almost shy.

Quietly I nibbled at the edges of my bread—it was too dry to swallow—and ate half of my apple. The other half was wormy. *Wormwood.*

I looked up, down again. "Where did you take your arrow?"

"Dinard," he answered shortly.

"Did you see the man who struck you?"

His silence made me look up again; he was frowning.

"That's an odd question."

"Aye, Your Majesty, but I wondered because . . ." And I told him of the strange, mad knight in the cathedral.

"I'll have Mercadier seek him out." He said lightly, then took my hand. "I have to survey land in a valley I'm purchasing from greedy monks. May I show it to you?"

"Aye, Your Majesty."

"Good, we'll have real privacy. Go change to something simpler; I've duly noted how pretty you look in your new finery."

When I returned, I helped him rise and hobble to the court. I was shocked at the severity of his wound—he had difficulty getting on to his horse—but his manner was offhand, even debonair.

Soon we'd crossed one of the many bridges fanning from Poitiers and rode almost alone along a rutted lane, for Mercadier stayed at a discreet distance behind us.

"This is it." The king pulled his horse up short and looked around him. We were beside a thin copse with a pale green meadow beyond. "Get off first, dear girl, and help me so I don't put my weight on this damned leg."

I stood where he told me, felt him use my shoulders as he slid to his good leg.

"How bad is your knee?"

"I'll be all right for fighting. I may lose a little flexibility."
He ruffled my hair. "But not enough for you to worry,
sparrow."

Moving very slowly, he limped with my assistance
through the wood and into the golden field of daffodils
flocked with blue lupine. An invisible meadowlark sang
sweetly above us; the air buzzed of bees seeking honey; the
sky floated in ever-changing formations against the vast
steeps. I could feel the king's body become less tense.

"This is Poitou, Alix, my only home. Do you like it?"

"It's heaven."

"Yes." He closed his eyes, breathed deeply, opened them
again. "See if you can find a few sticks as markers."

Happily I ran into the field toward the opposite hedge
where there was much dead wood. The low clink of cow-
bells alerted me to a small herd of kine grazing in the corner,
a single black and white goat in their midst. They turned
their heads in one motion and gazed with bland curiosity at
what I was doing, then resumed munching. I called aloud to
them, waved to Richard, broke off a half-dozen branches.
Then, hopping and twirling in circles, I danced back toward
the king. He was slowly limping to meet me.

"A glorious day!" I shouted.

"My God, you're alive," he said when we came together.
"I've been the arbiter of death so many weeks that I'd almost
forgotten."

He then described for me the plan for the field where we
stood. He was going to build a large fortress with a town
around it as part of his defense system between Poitiers and
Toulouse. I tried to picture ugly stone walls amid the daffodils—only there would be no flowers—crenellations for
archers, battering rams and the rest. No wonder the king
seemed depressed; what a grisly occupation to be king.

He limped and talked; I stayed where I was. Here he
would dig a moat, using the bogs in this field and the next
for water; here he would bring in dirt and rocks to build up

the wall. I watched and listened; so did the cows. One lowed softly and walked in his direction as the others followed. Here he would place a monastery, which the monks required as part of the purchase price. The cows were near to him now. He raised an arm and pointed to the road, telling how he would have to change its direction. The black and white goat was close enough for him to pet. Then, as he gestured back again, the goat took a mouthful of his sleeve.

"God's feet!"

"Careful, Your Majesty!"

Richard batted the goat with his strong right arm, but was put off balance by his injured leg and had no leverage. Meantime the goat ripped at the fine linen and chewed it down. I dropped my faggots and ran to help. By the time I got close, the slab-eyed beast had taken a good portion of the royal breeches and the king was swearing in a steady stream.

The scene was so ludicrous that I stopped to stare. Then began to laugh.

Richard called in fury, "Stop braying like a she-ass and come help!"

Staggering with mirth, I approached the goat from behind and grabbed his filthy tail. Great patches of Richard's bare skin were now exposed, and I let go to clutch my cod, stamped in circles as I whooped in glee. I knew I shouldn't —knew my humor was warped—but there it was. I couldn't stop. The more the king raged, the more I howled in mirth. Tears coursed down my cheeks.

The king carried only a dagger, which he couldn't get from its sheath because of the goat's interested probings, but he ripped it off his belt and beat the animal about the head until it finally moved back. Standing in shreds, his parts plainly hanging free, the king glowered at me.

"Now I see your true feeling for me! Sorry he didn't get my cock so you could have a real cackle!" He lurched toward me, and I raised my arms in defense.

He grabbed my shoulders, shook me hard as I laughed ever harder, fell against me and I tumbled onto my back with his heavy weight pressing me into ooze.

"You wallydrag!" I shrieked. "I'm lying in mud!"

And he started to bellow like a banshee! Tears gushing, his body shaking against mine, he gave way to laughter. "See how the gods revenge? Mud with muck! That will teach you to mock your lord."

I tried to push him off so I could clean myself, to no avail. His weight was an iron effigy. He rested on his elbows, wiped his eyes with his bare arm for he had no sleeve, took a handful of daffodils to complete the task.

"You'll have to look for a stream to wash yourself."

I could hardly see him through lowered brows.

"But what will I use for cover? A figleaf?" And he was off again, now laughing at himself. "I swear that goat did worse damage than the crossbowman."

His body shook in hard gasps—now I was aware of his motion, his nakedness.

So was he.

He looked into my eyes. "Am I heavy?"

"It's all right."

"What's all right?"

His tongue moistened his lower lip.

I didn't reply.

He glanced from right to left to find a clear patch, then stretched by my side, pulled me so I lay on him, threw my besmottered cape off my back.

"Do you remember?" he said softly, and put his hand to my hipbone.

I began to laugh again.

"Tickle-Bones, that's what I called you, and you said I was like your father."

He lifted me easily so I dangled above him. "That day on the Crusade, and you had a special kiss for your father. Do you remember?"

"Aye."

He lowered me slowly to his chest.

"I'm dirty, Your Majesty."

"And I'm naked as a jay. Give me the kiss, Alix."

I slid upward—heard him gasp—kissed his right eye, his left, his chin . . .

His lips.

Almost swooned at their sweetness. Felt his nakedness through my thin tunic. My liver flamed as it never had before, and this time my stomach boiled.

He rolled again, looked down on me. Reached his hand to my hip, tickled gently as I gasped with delight, then—fingers still moving—touched the inside of my thigh and over . . .

My breath short, I stopped laughing, gazed into his gray-blue eyes and the wild-moving clouds behind him. His fingers continued—I know not what—the sensation incredible. I tried to move, couldn't, didn't want to really.

"Oh no, Your Majesty, we mustn't . . . someone will see."

"Mercadier? The goat? I personally wouldn't care if Berengaria, my mother and Saint Jerome were lined at my shoulder, I want you so badly. But if you say to stop . . ."

But I was beyond saying anything. A vast wave raised me into his embrace as I closed my eyes, put my arms around his neck, my legs around his moving hips. Yet it was so strange, the act of love, the first time since Enoch, and it brought him back as nothing else had. I turned my head, opened my eyes, saw an ant climbing up a lupine, felt the thrust as he entered—the most natural sensation in the world as if it were yesterday, but also foreign, for this was King Richard—and tears filled my eyes. I was happy, my heart bursting with joy, yet distraught by such grief, longing, guilt, that I felt I must cry out. I tightened my grasp on the king.

He was murmuring my name, words of love, kissing, then gripped my cheeks and watched me fiercely as we both gave

in completely to our mutual race. Oh, oh, oh—biting one
another as the flood spread its honey and our delight was
surpassed by the wonder—the miracle.

Slowed.

Lay atop me, his cheek against mine.

"Tears?" he said with wonder. "Were you that moved?"

I nodded, new tears rising.

He touched my eyes with his tongue, drinking my tears.
"Christ, Alix, you make me so happy . . . relieved. I've
been so afraid you didn't care . . ."

I traced the contour of his brow with my finger, too full
to speak.

"You never say anything, no endearments." He kissed my
hand. "I've even thought you might hate me. You're like the
will-o'-the-wisp, silvery and elusive; I despaired of ever
catching you."

I dug fingers into his ears—he grinned.

"Do you know how much I love you?" he asked seriously.

My voice was thick. "You're good with words . . ."

"No, I'm dreadful. Why do you think they call me *Oc e
Ne*, Yes and No? I'm terse, inarticulate as that braying goat
when it comes to my deeper feelings. I can quote the poets
but, from the heart, it's simply that I love you. But, oh God,
I do love you, love to say it. My life, my Alix."

He kissed me anew with mounting passion and moved
again—not entering for he'd never left—for a longer time
and with breathtaking savagery. This time I looked at no
ant, thought no thoughts, just abandoned myself to sensation. Finally, shuddering, awed, we were quiet again.

After a long silence, he nibbled my ear. "I'm cramped
holding myself here, but damned if I want to roll into a bog.
Should we continue our play in Poitiers?"

"But you haven't placed any of your sticks, Your Majesty.
Don't you want to . . . ?"

"I could have sworn I've placed my stick a hundred times.
Are you never satisfied?"

We laughed as if we were daft, everything comical in our giddy entrancement.

Getting free of our muck-puddle took ingenuity, and we were both stained before we succeeded. From the corner of my eye, I saw Mercadier walk to his horse. The king and I gazed at one another, torn, filthy, ecstatic. Before our amazed eyes, Richard rose again and had to slap himself hard in order to pull his shreds forward for decency. We laughed all the way back to the city, but attracted no attention—such was the king's power—except from disrespectful flies. We rode in a miasma of the pests until, still laughing, Richard ordered baths and food to be brought to his chamber.

WE STAYED IN his giant canopied bed for four days, suspended in love. We ate, bathed, cared for other animal needs, did everything except sleep. Several times I went into a comatose swoon from weariness at the same time that I was being loved.

"Pudendal things befall the sleeping maid," Richard whispered.

We were both naughty and solemn by turns, delighting in irreverence. We tried to imagine every position prohibited by the Church and wrenched my back, Richard's poor knee again and again, as we contorted ourselves into strange shapes and combinations.

Once, when he gave his knee a particularly bad turn, I repented. "It's because we're sinning."

"*O felix culpa!* God wouldn't have made us flexible, Alix, if he didn't want us to flex."

Which could well be an excuse for any sin we were capable of devising. Then Richard whispered soldiers' jokes into my ears until I collapsed again in mirth, whereupon he "took advantage" of me, for he loved my laugh—though he needed no excuse.

He loved my hair—all my hair—my teeth and throat, all

openings into "my heart"; he memorized the shapes of my fingernails, toenails, the dimples at the base of my spine, my breasts and the various moods of my nipples. Never had I been so examined, so caressed by lips, teeth, tongue, every part of him on every part of me. He pronounced me a miracle and a mystery—the more he delved, the less he knew.

He, too, was a mystery, but he wanted to unriddle himself. On the third day—I believe the third—he tried to talk. In darkness, he confessed the passion that convulsed his soul: he was consumed by his deadly hatred of King Philip. He dreamed of him by night, thought of little else by day, and recognized the paradox that his inner obsession was defeating him, though he won most of their overt battles. The only thing that displaced this morbid fixation was his love for me, the only emotion equal in force. Did I wonder that he sought me so avidly? That he needed me? I was literally life in the face of death, the face of Philip.

He wanted to talk more than he wanted to listen, which was just as well. What could I confess? I had no absorbing hatreds; even Berengaria ceased to exist once she left my life.

I dared not speak of Enoch.

The only shadow in my tryst was the memory of Enoch. It waxed and waned, *Deo gratias,* or I would soothly have suffered. Richard and Enoch were nothing alike, even though the love act—despite our variations—was always much the same, probably as it would be with anyone. But Richard had intruded into my most secret reaches, where I belonged to Enoch. I knew it was woodly, but I felt guilt, as if I'd betrayed the Scot. I also missed him, so poignantly that I could hardly bear it. Things I thought forgotten—had tried to forget—came back with vivid immediacy. Never had I been so loved, had I so loved, as with Enoch. Richard loved me, I believed now that he did, but his love was dark, Byzantine, full of hidden places and frightening intensity. Nor could I approach him with the same innocent open

heart I'd offered to Enoch. Oh, I knew that there's only one
first time, only one first love, and I was slowly being coaxed
into a new relationship of great power, perhaps the greatest
of my life, but I wasn't ready to let go of my innocence. Not
yet.

It was hard to hide my feelings. I felt guilty toward Richard as well as toward Enoch. I tried to compensate with
excessive tenderness and passion, memorized his magnificent body as he had mine, tended his wound with poultices,
listened raptly to his confessions.

Another guilt that haunted him was his rebellion against
his father. (Indeed, *Oc e Ne* was a turmoil of raw emotions
under the surface brilliance.) He'd hated Henry with the
same deadly animosity he now had toward Philip, but when
he looked back—when it was too late—he believed that his
paternal hatred had been frustrated love. He'd been brought
to Poitou when still a small boy, had not seen his father
during his childhood and youth, had bitterly resented the
neglect. As a man, he knew that Henry and Eleanor had
been estranged; what he'd construed as neglect toward him
was probably Henry's reluctance to see his queen. In any
case, Richard's rage at rejection had led him to dreadful acts.
His voice faltered, not enumerating his foul deeds.

I felt the weight of his trust. He was giving me himself. I
was flattered, grateful, fearful. I didn't think Bonel would
ever regret his confidence about York; I was less sure of
Richard. If his love changed to its opposite, he might punish
me for knowing him too well. Once Richard had loved
Philip. Secrets were dangerous.

Our skin became raw, our eyes shadowed, and Richard
could count my ribs from the hard work of love. God knows
what might have become of us if we hadn't been stopped on
the fourth day by a pounding on the door. Prince John was
here and demanded an audience at once: he had wonderful
news from Bristol.

Before we left our bed, Richard buried his face in my

neck and whispered shyly, eagerly, "When will you know, Alix?"

"Know what?"

He laughed softly. "Silly pixie. What's all this about? Whether you've conceived?"

A cold wind crossed my naked body.

"Two weeks, My Lord."

He sat up. "I like to think of sowing my seeds in Poitiers. I can tell that we succeeded, can't you?"

More and more alienated, I gazed on his glowing face. This frantic love had an end and would end when that end was achieved. Didn't he grasp the irony? A tangle of feelings stopped my tongue. But he didn't require an answer. Quickly he slipped on his tunic, splashed his face and prepared to meet John. I followed just as quickly.

# BOOK THREE

# Shalom

Set me a seal upon thy heart,
As a seal upon thine arm:
For love is strong as death;
Jealousy is cruel as the grave;
The flashes thereof are flashes of fire,
A very flame of the lord.

—SONG OF SOLOMON 8:6

# 17

ICHARD, CLEAN AND REFRESHED IN A FLOWING white tunic, limped into the great hall where his brother was supervising the placement of heavy casks on the floor. I stayed in the shadow of an arch, not wanting to hear the coarse innuendos John was sure to spout when he saw me.

"Heigh ho, King! Who's your best friend and ally now?" John cried in greeting, his swinish face wreathed in smiles.

"I take it you refer to yourself," Richard responded coolly. "Have you found some magical method to restore the heads of our friends in Évreux?"

"Forget Évreux!" John's elaborate shrug indicated that he done so already. "Forget warfare, dear brother. You have the wherewithal within these boxes to make your final victory over Philip. I tell you, his days are numbered! Normandy is yours, the Vexin, all of France if you so desire!"

"Then you've found a magic elixir after all," Richard commented dryly. "Do show me. I expect Merlin's books and wand at the very least."

John, his henchman Louvecaire and two squires began to pry at the casks with the sharp edges of their battle-axes. One by one the tops were wrenched free.

His face sweating, John stepped back. "See for yourself."

Richard bent over the first cask, put his hand inside, then looked at John. "Silver? All of it?"

"Every mark pure sterling. At least ten thousand pounds English."

Richard was impressed, but wary.

"Where did you get it, John?"

"It's yours, I promise, given to you by a loyal Englishman."

"In a will?" Richard's skepticism was open. "But who has that much treasure? And who died?"

"Aaron the Jew bequeathed it," John replied triumphantly.

"Aaron of Lincoln?"

"No, of Bristol—but he's just as rich."

The Jews had made such a magnificent gesture? Richard's suspicions mirrored my deeper worry. Since Berengaria, I was forever a Jew, at least in my sensibility.

"Did he die?"

For the first time, John's arrogance edged to irritation. "What does it matter? He gave it."

"It matters to me, John," Richard declared. "Tell me how you collected it."

His brother's familiar whining tone returned. "Richard, listen to me. You know that the Jews are richer than princes, thanks to us, but why should they withhold their bounty when we need it?"

"They pay twice what Christians do to the Exchequer, but go on."

"Yes, but they also stand between us and honest revenues. As I see it, we should collect on defaulted debts directly and bypass the Jews."

"Even though the Jews do the lending?" Richard pointed out acidly. "What's their incentive to risk money in the first place if we're going to collect?"

"Henceforth, we'll make the loans," John argued, "but until we do, we should take what's ours and get rid of the Hebrew scourge."

"That sounds familiar," Richard replied with ominous calm. "Doesn't King Philip have a similar philosophy?"

"So you heard!" John exclaimed brightly. "Yes, Philip rode into Champagne to the town of Bray, a Jewish commune, and slew every Hebrew therein. He had a good excuse, of course, for he'd heard of ritual murders of Christians."

As I had heard of them a few months ago.

Richard's voice began to rise; the cords in his neck stood forth. "His excuse, sir, was that Count Henry of Champagne was fighting with me in Jerusalem and couldn't defend his people. Going strictly against papal edict, against God, against all honor among princes, he destroyed an innocent people for their money! And you want me to emulate him?"

He finished in such a roar that his knights and sergeants ran in from all directions, much alarmed.

John stood his ground. "I didn't slaughter all of Bristol, for God's sake. Don't lose your temper until you know the facts!"

"Very well, give me the facts. How did you get this silver?"

John looked at his audience, grinned proudly. "I offered the Jews an honest choice: give me your silver for the king, who needs it, or I'll put you in a tower."

Clifford Tower, my heart squeezed.

"They desisted; I did so. Then I plucked Aaron as an example and took him to the lower court in full view from the window of the tower. My surgeon pulled one of Master Aaron's front teeth as his brethren watched and listened to his cowardly shrieks. Each day I pulled another, ten in all, before Aaron agreed to pay; by that time his screams for mercy convinced his onlookers to do likewise. But he still lives."

"I never want to see you more!" Richard bellowed in a rage. "Get out of my sight forever or I'll not be responsible for your life! Do you hear me!"

"With the soul of our own father as my witness, Richard . . ."

"Out!"

John's lips twisted to a sneer; he strode to the door. "You're a hard man to please, Richard, but you'll see me again. God damn you to Hell if you don't! Yes, and welcome me too. Meantime, use the silver!"

"No more of your schemes! You'll ruin me!" the king shouted at his back.

There was a rattle of arms and clatter of hooves as John's knights left the palace yard. William Marshal walked to the boxes, examined each one.

"This is a great amount of treasure, Your Majesty, and needs to be guarded. Should we escort it to Chinon?"

"Yes," Richard said tersely, after a pause, "and thence to Rouen. I'll turn it over to Bonel to return to its proper owner, if he still lives."

My aching heart thirled with pride. He talked earnestly with his men, making arrangements, then turned again to me.

Back in his chamber, Richard ordered sweet Bordeaux and drank two goblets quickly as I sat on the floor and watched.

"God's feet, is there anything more vexatious than a family?" He filled his cup a third time and sipped morosely. "Am I anything like my brother, Alix? Tell me the truth."

"No," I replied honestly, "neither in appearance nor temperament. Are you sure he isn't a changeling?"

He laughed wryly. "My mother doesn't deny him, unfortunately—though she would if she could—and my father doted on him. Made him Lord of Ireland, Count of Mortain, promised him Essex, arranged his marriage with Gloucester —the largest and richest marriage coup in England—then jokingly called him 'Lackland.' He even tried to give John my own duchy of Poitou."

"Then he was spoiled."

Richard's gray-blue eyes brooded on mine. "Perhaps, but does that explain such an incorrigible nature? I don't believe that a parent's indulgence breeds godless cruelty, sensuality, treachery and cowardice, or I would desist at once from rewarding my own lords. No, Alix, the stars cojoin at our births and our humors are fixed for better or for worse. In John, we've bred a viper."

"Aye." I moved closer, leaned on his good leg. Instantly he spread his knees and pulled me between them, tangled his fingers in my hair. "All we can do is find an elixir for his sting."

"I pity the Jews."

"And me, pity me as well."

I pushed back his tunic, kissed the smooth hard skin of his inner thigh.

"*Deo volente*, you will protect both yourself and your empire, My Lord. But what recourse do the Jews have? What will Aaron of Bristol do?"

"You heard me say I would return the silver."

"Yes, now that you know, for you are the opposite of Prince John, *Deo gratias*; the stars leaped in joy at your conception." Our eyes met at the word "conception," breaths caught; quickly I looked down again to force myself to stay to my point. "But when the persecution first began, was there nothing the Jews could do? No local court to protect them?"

Richard pulled me closer still and explained the situation, though his mind was no longer on it. The Jews were under the direct protection of the king—which I knew—and, in the king's absence, of the local authorities, mayor and bishop or priest, which was why Jews always lived close to the centers of cities. If they had serious grievances, they presented them to the justiciar of the Jews who in turn reached the king.

I wound my arm around his good leg and rested my cheek. "Is the justiciar a Christian?"

"There are usually two—usually Christian—but I've not appointed them yet."

I pulled away and looked upward. "Then why not appoint a Jew? Why not Bonel?"

His cheeks had red spots, his eyes swam. "Don't go so far

away." He bent and kissed me, then struggled out of his chair and pulled me upward against him.

"Bonel would be perfect," I persisted between his rapid kisses.

"Bonel it is," he muttered, "and now come to bed. I've wasted too much time."

We fell across the tangled covers as if returning from a long, tiresome journey. Love revived both our bodies and spirits as we embraced avidly, whispered idiocies, gave in to sweet rapture. I'd forgotten John entirely when sometime in the night I lay half asleep on top of Richard, my cheek against his chestspoon. I counted his heartbeats, rose and fell with his breath.

"Alix? Are you awake?"

"Mmmm."

"I meant it when I said I would make Bonel justiciar of the Jews."

"I'm sure it's a wise decision, My Lord."

"And your wish—your first request of me."

I opened my eyes, saw the yellow moon setting like a disappearing thumb. "Aye, thank you."

"But it won't be the last." There was a faint hard edge to his dulcet voice. "I love to indulge you in all ways. However . . . take care."

I raised my head. "Did I do something wrong?"

His eyes were black wells. "Bonel was once handsome, he's young . . ."

"But I swear that . . ."

"No, don't swear. I can see his empty socket. More important, he's a Jew. Even if you harbored some misguided, perverse sentiment toward him, he would no more covet a Christian woman than I would Berengaria's ape."

I sat up, righteously offended. "If you don't trust me, don't want to . . ."

"Heed me, Alix." He pulled me down again, put a heavy hand on the nape of my neck. His heart increased pace. "I'll never share you with another man, even in thought. If you ever make plea for any man whatsoever, that man is dead. Do you understand me?"

My own frightened beat mixed with his.

"Yes, I understand."

I UNDERSTOOD as well that I'd entered a new world of emotional bondage. Nothing in my former life had prepared me for the assault on my body and heart that Richard now waged. Warrior, son and king subsumed to lover, and I was recipient of all his violent energies without competition or relief. We were constantly crossing the stormy channel again, experiencing the highs and troughs of ecstasy, beginning with physical contact but building to ever wilder peaks until we transcended our bodies and entered a spiritual delirium, floating and gasping beyond pleasure, beyond life.

Calm seas were rare and when they came I gained fleeting insights into the nature of my lover and myself. For Richard, rage was never far from the surface. So far I hadn't felt his rage, but I saw glints. The pounding on the door in Normandy typified his irrational possessiveness. He must own me, body and thought, night and day, and was jealous of my slightest interest. He himself gifted me with a bouquet of jonquils, then grew jealous when I buried my face in their petals to devour the scent, tore them from my hands and fell into a gigantic pout until I assured him that the flowers meant nothing to me compared to what I felt for him.

I, too, suffered a dark undercurrent, though it was harder for me to define. When I'd first loved Enoch, I'd noticed how the love of my dead parents transferred to the Scot. Now something of the same sort applied to my feeling for Richard, but the transference carried with it the awareness of mortality.

One bright afternoon we walked into the palace garden to enjoy the summer warmth. Golden laburnum tumbled down walls, bees hummed in happy occupation, a single frog twanged from a hidden pool. I dragged bare toes through silky new grass as I stumbled with half-closed eyes beside Richard. We wandered hand in hand, joyous and mindless, breathing the bay bush, listening to the throstle, through overgrown paths toward the fruit orchard where pink and white froth made brides of the ancient, gnarled trees. A sudden gust of western breeze took the blossoms and showered us with petals. Uncannily, I was back in Wanthwaite, walking through our fruit orchard with my mother on the day before she died.

I turned to Richard. "Make me go 'round!"

"What?" He laughed at my urgency.

"Take my hands, so, and turn as fast as you can."

He pretended to bow. "Anything my lady desires."

Soon he was whirling, leaning back, and I flew in circles, undulating up and down until I was toty. He stopped; we staggered against one another, giggling as if we were drunkalewe, and collapsed on the breathing turf.

As I lay gazing upward at black branches etched on the paschal sky, the delicate tracery blurred and I had an overwhelming sense of my mother being with me. She had entered me in the act of love, never to depart again.

Or with Enoch. Perhaps it was Richard's wound that evoked him as well as our lovemaking. I know only that one night when Richard undressed me and I watched my own clothes fly against the silvery light, I gave forth a sudden sharp cry of recognition. I pretended it was desire, but it was the memory of my first time with Enoch, and it *seemed* that Enoch entered me in the dark. This time I wept openly as Richard comforted me.

As for my father, he'd always been a part of Richard's attraction for me, but now he didn't so much live in Richard as he surrounded Richard with the aura of death. On the occasions that Richard had to leave me a few hours, I could hardly bear to say goodbye, seeing again my beautiful father as he turned thrice on his horse in Wanthwaite's court, hand upraised in final farewell.

The beginning of love, then, contained the end as well. I resisted happiness for the cruel sadness it anticipated.

RICHARD WORSHIPPED ME outrageously. Indeed, he idolized me to the point of making me want to confess every sin and vice I'd even thought to do, so fearful was I of being discovered and despised for what I really was. He was charmed, delighted, amused, and begged me to repeat each episode in detail. My life at Wanthwaite was comical preamble to my true existence with him and he relished my fey, barbaric mother, my quaint nurse, my childish escapades with Maisry, my imperfect instruction under the guidance of Sister Eulalie and Father Michael, accused me of making up the whole thing to test his credulity. Meantime, he stroked me, wondered at my innocent sweetness, my open passion, my person, which he could never fathom any more than he could grasp the ultimate mystery of God—an awesome comparison.

Yet he could surprise me. As I soon discovered through my own gluttony, he was capable of compassion that had nothing do with the highs and lows of love. He sent runners to Bordeaux to ply me with rare edibles, and one day a shrimp proved my undoing. I woke in the middle of the night writhing in agony. For two days thereafter, the king bathed my fevered brow, quenched my thirst with wined water, supervised my cleanliness in unseemly ways, much to my distress. When I began to recover, however, I saw that I'd given him pleasure bordering on the ecstatic by my lowly needs; he wanted me to need him as he claimed he needed me. He was a prism with many sides, each capable of myriad lights.

He also surprised me when I failed to conceive. He talked of "his son" over and over, yet seemed indifferent that he would have to continue trying. Indeed he japed, called it God's gift to extend the assignment.

Daffodils gave way to poppies; throstles sat on their nests; crickets added their shrill overtone to the froggy chorus, and

I gained a rival: Richard's need to fight Philip. Every day he and his knights rode to the fields on the far side of the boggy outer moat to hone their skills for the battles to come. With his usual resolve to keep me in sight at all times, Richard took me with him as mascot. Teasing, he dressed me in green cloth of Tars, placed an oaken wreath on my head and dubbed me chaste Diana to his warlike Mars. Certainly I no longer resembled the cold virginal moon, nor the huntress here on earth, but I recalled my mother telling the tale of Diana's underworld guise as Proserpina, and I felt like Proserpina as I watched the games of death.

Horses and weapons were prepared first. The great war destriers with hearts of steel and hooves that flashed fire pounded new grass to dust as they turned, reared and rolled on command. They didn't wear the parements and brouding of parades, but carried armor as tough and heavy as their masters did. If knights loved anything better than each other, they loved their foaming steeds, each worth his weight in gold.

Points were nailed to shafts to create spears; shields were gigged with leather straps; spurs sharpened with files and hammers; heavy steel-thorned "morning stars" attached to long chains for swinging; battle-axes—called sparths— edged to killing sharpness to match their twenty pounds of weight.

When all was prepared, the men took their places. They submitted to brown fustian to protect their bodies, testers for the head, then the donning of steel mesh fresh dipped and oiled, the buckling of helmets, the lowering of nose-pieces, the lacing of breast-pieces, the donning of heavy gloves. Skinned in steel, they sat stiffly with lances in hand, spears in their rests, maces and axes according to preference. Richard always worked with the lance first, but his favorite weapon was the murderous mace, followed by the two-edged broadsword, which he could hold with one hand.

Now pipes, drums, trumpets and clarions evoked the real battle as opposing forces faced one another. Then the signal and they were off! Sharp spurs pricked the coursers to action, heads were lowered, shoulders hunched as a forest of lances reached for the chestspoons of the opponents. Men tumbled in heavy, bruising crashes, rolled to their feet to foil with truncheons, short swords and knives in hand-to-hand combat. On the third day, a wight called Sir Lavanne had his helmet knocked fore to aft and had to be led to the town blacksmith to have it removed.

At night I worked on Richard's knee, now cured for normal purposes but too weak for his pleasure. I flexed it and rubbed it as long as he would let me, but ended by giving it exercise in a different manner. He loved with the same frantic concentration, but I felt we were already once removed. I was amazed at my anguish. If Richard was an empty vessel as he claimed ("a sailor in a seaport after a lifetime at sea," "a nomad before an oasis," "a knight stumbling upon the grail"), then I was the flood which filled his void; I gave him substance, he gave me form. I would be chaos without him.

Yet the day came when we rode out of Poitiers for the season of fighting. Richard and his army were escorting me to nearby Fontevrault on their way north.

He took my rein and pulled Sea Mew next to his horse.

"I never thought I would regret going to battle," he said softly. He turned full, bright eyes. "How can I leave you?"

"Easily. You'll be too busy to even think of me."

He shook his head. "Separation's like death."

Startled, I studied his face with new awe. He felt it, too, as I did, though when Bonel had said it about Enoch I hadn't understood.

"We'll meet often at Chinon," he promised, "but don't come unless I send a guard." He hesitated. "Bonel was right to give you Bok, but I'll add Algais to your arsenal, and stay close to the buildings. Do you promise?"

"I have no enemies, have I?"

"No, but I have," he replied grimly, then added, "but not for long. I've assigned Mercadier to kill him."

I knew he meant the assassin who'd wounded his knee.

Queen Eleanor rode out to meet us and she and I exchanged guarded greetings. She must have seen in my eyes
what had transpired between Richard and me; I could see in
hers conflicting reactions, which she fought in vain to conceal. On the surface, approval, then pain, resentment, envy,
speculation and I know not what. He made no effort to hide
his radiant happiness, but walked with his arm around me
to her royal quarters where we would spend the night.
However, they had a long conference alone.

The summer thereafter was life on a trapeze for me, now
up, now down. I met Richard four times at Chinon for brief,
glorious interludes. We swam in the Vienne River, took our
falcons to hunt, frisked like children in the gardens and
woods. At Fontevrault I again entered the scriptorium to
learn the art of copying. The nuns were still working on
Psalters for lay use and I copied their letters, the illuminated
traceries that reflected the art of the Romanesque buildings
with strong solid colors and sharp angles. I liked the work
and had more natural talent for it than I did for singing,
which I'd tried to do for Zizka and his jongleurs of yore. Or
maybe painting is easier. However, whether in Richard's
arms or within the tranquil halls of Fontevrault, life was still
a trapeze, still dangerous. Neither my mercurial lover nor
his mother made any move against me during the long summer months, but I was always aware of how high I was,
how far I could fall.

AT LAST the deadly season was past, and I was summoned to
Rouen, where the king would winter. I left Fontevrault
without regret, though Eleanor and I had developed an easy,
friendly rapport on the surface, and headed to my favorite
city a much happier lady than when I'd left it. I was now
heavy with the scent of love both given and received, aching
for Richard's embrace. As I rode through the faintly russet
countryside, I couldn't restrain my smiles.

Then we came to a scorched field, then another and another. I tried not to breathe the acrid fumes or look at the ravaged huts. We ate at the edge of an untouched forest, when suddenly Bok's sword flashed.

"Wait!" I stopped his slash.

A dull-eyed waif, only a few years younger than I, stood in the shadows gazing at us.

"Don't be afraid," I called. "Come, have something to eat."

She tottered from the shadow on scratched, swollen feet, her legs like pipes, and sank wordlessly to the grass. I gave her bread, cheese, a pork pie. She ate them slowly and silently, taking care not to choke. Then she tried to speak.

"The little 'uns?"

"You have brothers and sisters?"

She nodded dumbly, but gradually I coaxed out of her that her parents had sent the children to the woods to escape the fighting, only that was days ago and she hadn't been able to find any adults since then. She brought from the bush three urchins with vast, frightened eyes who accepted food with the same quiet courtesy. I invited them to ride with us to the next village where we would seek help from the priest.

When we stopped at the church, we learned that her village had been decimated, her family destroyed, but she was fortunate in that she had an aunt in this village who would take the children.

Richard himself rode from Rouen to meet me. He leaned to kiss me, lifted me to his horse's back and pulled me to the curve of his body. From that point we were oblivious to our surroundings and Algais had to lead us.

The king basked in his triumphs in the field, which he attributed to the inspiration of love. He'd just taken the seaport of St. Valéry where he'd burned the town and carried away its sacred relics.

"A triumph," he explained jubilantly, "for it's the center of the Duchy of Aumâle."

"You took Duchess Hadwisa's town?" I'd met her that

summer in Fontevrault, a formidable lady, unhappy bride
to Baldwin of Béthune.

"I thought I told you. Philip managed to find a husband
for his ruined sister Alais, and he captured Aumâle as part
of their wedding portion. I'm trying to get it back for Duchess Hadwisa."

He'd demonstrated in the neighborhood of Gournai, hoping to rout the Bishop of Beauvais . . .

"Did Mercadier kill your enemy?" I interrupted.

He stiffened. "What enemy?"

"You mentioned a special enemy when we were at Fontevrault—I assume it's the man who shot you."

"You're a shrewd wench, aren't you?" He turned solemn.
"No, he hasn't had an opportunity yet—but he will. Philip
hired a crafty bastard."

He then began enumerating the prisoners he'd taken.

"How many did you kill?" I asked, thinking of the hungry
children and their parents.

He was surprised. "None. Why would I kill valuable prisoners?"

"I meant the villeins and burghers who live in the vil-
lages."

"Oh, them. Naturally they must be slaughtered and
burned out in order to starve the castles, but they don't
count."

"Not count as people?"

He became irritated. "Of course they're people, tender
goose, but they don't count for ransom. The purpose of
taking prisoners is to force payment."

"But they have souls," I protested. "We're all alike in
God's eyes."

"Did you take your vows in Fontevrault? God wants us
to win, and in His Holy Name I do the best I can!"

I put my hand to his cheek and he quickly kissed my
fingers.

"I am a most magnanimous lord, Alix."

"Don't I know that?"

I turned my head; our lips met.

With his cheek against mine, he continued to describe his strategy against Philip, whom he hated with a ferocity livelier than ever. He was making devastating alliances in the north, had already stolen Flanders, and of course I knew he had Raymond of Toulouse in the south. Even more important, he had found a site for a magnificent fortress from which he could launch new aggressions in the Vexin. It was on the Seine River close to Les Andelys; he need only persuade Walter of Coutances to sell him the riverfront, for it belonged to the Church, but he foresaw no difficulty as his castle would protect Rouen. Incidentally, had I heard that Robert of Leicester had been captured in an effort to defend Rouen?

I listened happily to his talk, loving the scrape of his cheek, his wine-sweet breath, the warmth of his massive chest. I leaned against his shoulder and watched the approaching outline of the city, the bridge, walls, spires of the cathedral. When would I be able to see Bonel? He was now justiciar of the Jews and had the ten thousand marks of silver from Bristol to return. I wouldn't tell him of my role in his appointment, but I wanted to hear that he was content. I also looked forward to his pleasure in my situation. He'd worked hard to get me here, God knows.

My trunks were carried directly to Richard's chamber, for the palace was too crowded to pretend I had separate quarters. The first important man I saw was Archbishop Walter of Coutances.

"Welcome to Rouen, Lady Alix," he said stiffly.

"Thank you, Your Grace."

He avoided my eyes, the first rebuff I'd received in my new position. It was slight, but Richard noticed it as well.

"Alix will attend our meeting about our land negotiations," he said in a hard voice. "In all matters, she is my queen."

"Except that you have a queen," Walter answered coldly. "You know well, Your Majesty, the Church's rule on taking a *superduxerit;* you are living in sin. If you don't care for yourself, think of this poor child."

"I need no urging to think of her," Richard replied just as coldly, "since she is my very life to me. I use the word 'queen' advisedly; she is my other half. Perhaps you're the one who should think."

He then pulled me with him up the stair to his closet, an ample room though in no way as luxurious as his quarters at Poitiers. He left for a brief period, then was back accompanied by the ewerer with refreshments which we never touched. Almost at once we were on his bed engaged in frantic love. We'd noticed often how our need grew at each meeting, rising to such feverish intensity that we were almost frightened. Love was a third person between us, a master to whom we were both slaves.

Richard chose to blame me. "You're worse than Philip in your demands, Alix. Well, the Church warned me about women and all I can do is find new weapons, beginning with a ramming rod to go deeper."

He illustrated.

"A longer lance," he panted. "Oh God, remove your spell or I'll surely expire. There, there, there, damn it. I'm not a growing boy, Alix, and I stretch to my limit."

He then "did siege" to my breasts, pretending my nipples were castles to be "nibbled away."

He lay his head on my shoulder. "Have I told you I loved you?"

"Aye, My Lord, your lance speaks for you."

"In a different language, I do love you."

Two languages to make a simple statement, lucky king, whereas I could not separate my body's fervent responses from my middle brain's cautionary words: careful, Alix, passion is distorting judgment. The king's "I do love you" was addressed to the future mother of his child. But how would he feel when the battle was won? Success would be an end to carnal love, the beginning of paternal pride, an end for me. So I fought my own private battle against the seduction of my fantastick cells.

Fought hard—and lost.

# 18

HE INSTANT BONEL RETURNED FROM ENGLAND, he sent word that he wanted to meet with me.

"Greetings, Bonel," I said shyly when he entered Rouen Castle.

We gazed at each other, pushed by people milling in the gallery.

"You've changed," he said abruptly.

Indeed. Since our last farewell, I'd become the king's mistress. Did my happiness show? I felt heat rise in my face.

"Aye," I admitted, lowering my eyes.

"I'd like to escape the crowd. Are you dressed warmly?"

"My cope is fur-lined."

I followed his brisk stride into the street and down the path to the Seine, where we often walked. I began to sense that something was seriously amiss.

"Did you receive the ten thousand marks of silver?" I prattled with false cheer.

"Yes, and returned it to Aaron of Bristol."

I then described the scene, omitting only that Richard and I had been in bed when John arrived, and told of John's cruelty, his admiration of King Philip's abuse of the Jews. Either Bonel already knew what had taken place or he had other weighty matters on his mind, for he didn't respond.

I changed the subject. "Were you able to send messages to Wanthwaite as I asked?"

"I didn't get word to the north, but I learned something about Wanthwaite, yes." He hesitated.

"Tell me."

He took my hand. "I met with Bishop Hugh of Durham while in London. You remember him?"

"Yes, I do." There was a pause. "What did he say?"

He didn't answer.

"*Benedicite*, Bonel, what's wrong?"

He squeezed my hand. "Your nurse—what was her name?"

"Dame Margery?"

"Yes. I'm sorry, Alix, but she died. Some time ago . . ."

But I no longer heard. Transported back to Wanthwaite, I saw her face as she handed me my father's dagger, heard her say that we'd see one another no more. Margery gone? Then so was Wanthwaite, childhood, everything.

Bonel pressed my hands sympathetically. "I'm sorry, Alix."

"I knew she would die," I wept. "But knowing isn't the same as being prepared, is it?"

"No, it isn't. We're never prepared."

We continued on our way, both of us now deep in thought. Not until we turned at the wharves and walked into the wood upriver was I able to speak again.

"What else did the bishop report? How does my household fare under Richard's occupying force?"

We'd reached the spot where we usually conversed, and Bonel picked up a stone to toss into the current.

"Richard doesn't hold Wanthwaite."

"What?" I gasped. "When did he withdraw?"

"He never took it." He threw a rock viciously at a floating stick and missed.

"But you said . . . you told me in Winchester. Don't you remember? When I wanted to return to Wanthwaite after I'd learned that Enoch was dead and you said that the king

must hold it because of the Canterbury . . . the Canterbury . . ."

"Quit claim. Of course I remember."

He squatted with his back to me so I couldn't see his face.

Rain the previous night had brought down the last of the
leaves, and the Seine now carried a brilliant flotilla toward
the sea. Bonel seemed absorbed by the dizzy rush of water.
One crimson maple leaf lying in the shallows of the river
was the same shade as his brown eye, an angry russet under
the murky liquid.

I grew impatient with his morbid truculence. *I* was the
one to be upset.

"Then why did you say he took it?"

No answer.

I left him, lifted my tunic so it wouldn't trail in the mud,
then curled atop a large flat rock.

"If Richard doesn't hold my castle, then the King of Scotland must have taken it," I said. "Is that what you mean?"

He glanced fleetingly over his shoulder, paused. "Yes, it's
occupied by Scots."

"Does Richard know?"

"Of course he knows."

"Then . . . then . . . I have no place to go." I'd thought
Margery's death the end of Wanthwaite? That was senti-
mental; this was the real end.

Bonel rose and walked to my rock.

"Unless Richard takes it back for me, I have no home?" I
asked with foreboding.

"That's right." He hesitated. "And I don't think Richard
will fight in England for a long time, if ever."

The dank vapor off the river was giving me a megrim, and
the gaudy leaves hurt my eyes. They were floating to the
Channel and England—where I would never go again.
Never?

"But Bonel, if Richard never held Wanthwaite, then why
. . . I don't understand."

"Don't you?" he asked wryly.

Of course I did, had suspected since the first day, and now knew for certain. Richard had wanted me by fair means or foul. I'd long since forgiven him, except—to lose Wanthwaite?

Bonel sat beside me on the rock and again held my hands. "You have to believe me, Alix; I didn't know the truth myself, told you what I was told, but Richard . . ."

He stopped tactfully.

"Wanted to keep me as hostage for himself," I finished for him. I tried to recall that bleak afternoon in Winchester, the gray clouds scuttling across Bonel's Christian Eye. "Why are you telling me the truth now, Bonel? Wanthwaite's been lost for years—what's changed?"

Bonel leaned close, his eye shot with light like pine needles floating on black water. "You're very sharp. What's changed is that Bishop Hugh told me a secret beyond the loss of Wanthwaite, a fact of such dire consequences that even to know it is to invite death. I'm glad I know for your sake, but I can't tell you. I'm not lying, Alix, just withholding truth."

The very trees held their breath as if trying to hear the message below his words, but it was elusive. The chilly emanations were no longer from the river, but from Bonel himself.

"Then I don't want to know," I said, frightened. "I have nothing to do with court politics."

"You have everything to do with policy," Bonel contradicted me bitterly, "thanks in part to my own schemes, but I'm determined to save you, Alix."

"Does it also concern Richard?" I asked, thoroughly terrified.

"Yes, and that's all I'll tell you."

But I thought I'd guessed. It had something to do with the mad knight in Poitiers and his ominous prophecies.

"Is someone trying to kill the king?" I asked.

"What makes you think that?" Bonel was startled.

I told him about the knight, but he dismissed him. "No, Alix, the fellow is dangerous, no doubt, one of a new class of self-styled prophets who wander the countryside, knights, hermits and Mendicants. I'm surprised he didn't turn on the Jews."

"But Richard himself told me that the wound he received came from an assassin."

This intrigued Bonel more, and he pressed me for details, took the incident very seriously and conceded that it might be connected with the secret. Then he echoed Richard's words.

"His enemy is apt to seek you as well, in order to hurt the king. Be very careful."

More and more dismayed, I waited for worse revelations.

"Alix, we must rethink your future. You won't have Wanthwaite, and this new problem is an added complication. I must ask you a few questions, so be patient."

I nodded.

"Has the king given you gifts?"

"Aye, many," I said eagerly. "He spoils me every day with new surprises, seafood from Bordeaux, rare wines . . ."

"Anything of tangible value?"

"Flowers every day, ells of silk to make new clothing, a fine silver mirror, sachets, an ivory comb . . ."

"Jewels? Property?"

"No property, but all the jewels I want. Diamonds, opals, garnets, gold . . ."

"The Crown jewels?"

"Aye, I can wear them anytime I like."

"So long as you return them to the chest. Do you have nothing of your own?"

"I don't need anything," I cried defiantly. "Richard is generous to a fault."

His silence contradicted me.

"You sound like Tib," I said sullenly. "I don't want fancy gifts; I have faith in him."

"Say rather that you depend on his charity. You are utterly dependent on his goodwill and largesse, and he's contrived to keep you so."

Again my voice rose in hot contradiction. "He controls everybody around him—not just me—and his knights don't ask for jewels or property!"

"No, Alix, you're wrong. He rewards his knights with rich gifts—look at the marriage to the Duchess of Pembroke he made for William Marshal, the match of Hadwisa of Aumâle for Baldwin of Béthune. They give loyalty; he gives material gifts, which make them rich beyond compare. He's afraid you would use wealth to seek freedom."

I could hardly get the breath to speak. "I suppose—when the time comes—he'll find a rich lord for me as well."

"No, he will not," Bonel said flatly.

It was the first utterance he'd made that I absolutely believed, though I didn't know why.

"You don't think he loves me?"

"Love! Love! In God's name, forget love! It means nothing!" he cried out savagely, as if I'd insulted him.

The trapeze I'd mounted this summer was swinging wildly, and my vital spirits flew from sorrow to rage. "Perhaps Jews don't love, but Christians do!"

"What do you call love?" he shouted just as wrathfully. "To be wooed, beaten, discarded for a richer wife? That's the way Christians love!"

Silver ripples from the corner of the river filled the corner of my eye like the glints of swords in Richard's war games; aye, both love and death were defined by intricate rules.

"You once had a contract with the king, didn't you?" Bonel continued, straining to control himself.

I nodded.

"I always wondered about it. Whose idea was it?"

"Queen Eleanor's," I managed to reply. "No, she presented it—Richard devised it."

"Why?"

"She said because he cared about my future, wanted me to be safe."

"That's what I hoped," he said grimly. "At least he has some conscience."

I forgot my agitation in my surprise. Bonel was criticizing Richard? I couldn't believe it.

"What were the terms?"

*Benedicite*, what were they? All I could remember was the time limit of two years—the end of love—the fact that I would give up my own children, but Bonel waved these aside as unimportant. What about Wanthwaite?

"I was to return there."

"As a married woman?"

"Aye," I said uncertainly. "The king was going to give me a dowry"—how could I say the hated words?—"and find me a proper husband. Or I could go into an abbey."

"Think carefully, Alix. Were these terms merely spoken or were they written into the contract?"

"They were written. Why?"

"May his heart turn to stone!" He slid off the rock and went back to the river, clung to the trunk of a sapling. I jumped down and followed.

"You confound me, Bonel. Have you changed your mind about the king?"

"Yes, where you're concerned."

"But you always said to trust the King," I protested.

"Very well, I've changed. Trust me instead."

"I do," I murmured, "but I trust him too. He protects me wondrously well. He . . . he has to love me."

"He has to have a child, you mean, and that's our weapon. If he wants you, he must pay. I'll write a new contract for you."

"No!"

"Yes. He'll provide a new home for you, now, before he discards you, and an income for life."

"He would do it—*will* do it—for love!" I cried. "But no law could enforce a contract!"

"I'll have Archbishop Walter witness it; if he doesn't honor it, he'll face the Church's wrath."

"Please, Bonel," I implored, "I know you mean well, but it's taken so long for Richard to trust me. I don't want to jeopardize that."

He paid no attention. "If he refuses, then you must withdraw all favors. Do you hear me? You explained that he loves you exclusively, and why. That's our strength. If he wants a child, he must concede."

"No, I can't!"

His face whitened. "Are you so enthralled then? If you knew Alix . . ."

"I'm already pregnant!" I cried, and burst into tears.

Bonel froze in shock, then belatedly reached for me.

I ran up the bank, into the wood, but Bonel caught me easily.

"My God, Alix, why didn't you tell me at the first?" He held me tight, forced my face onto his shoulder and patted my back. "Hush, dear, it's all right, will be all right, you'll see. I'll take care of you."

"I wanted to tell you, but . . . I thought you'd be so happy. For the Jews . . ."

"Yes, yes, of course I'm happy." He pulled back. "You want to be a mother, don't you?"

"Aye." I smiled shyly. "I know I shouldn't under such circumstances, but I can't help it. It's a miracle, isn't it?"

He placed the back of his hand against my cheek, a gesture of curious intimacy. "Always a miracle. Richard must be overjoyed."

"He doesn't know." I explained that Tib had warned me to wait three months, a period only now finished.

"Then do as I say," Bonel said sharply. "Don't tell him for a few days. Give me an opportunity to press your contract."

"Please don't . . . I'm afraid."

He grimaced. "You have reason to be. I promise you, dear, that I'll be tactful, won't reveal that you know anything about it. Trust me."

"I have no choice," I said, evoking my situation at Wanth-waite.

"Good girl," he replied, not catching the irony.

WHEN WE REACHED the palace gates, we were forced to stop by an unexpected host of soldiers in the courtyard.

"Who could it be?" I asked.

Bonel spoke with grim disbelief. "The prodigal brother returns; Prince John is with us again."

I began to protest, then saw Louvecaire.

With great difficulty, Bonel led me til and fro to the door and inside. A jubilant roar echoed in the anteroom as every-one crushed to the great hall to hear the proceedings. With unspoken agreement, Bonel and I joined the horde. Rough soldiers gave way to Bonel's splendor and my female pres-ence so that we could see the dais from our position against the wall.

King Richard was listening with bent head to his brother as John spoke with intense animation, making his points with his hands as well as his words. On John's far side stood an angry wight with a small head, a goat's beard, and a heavy body, which ran downward in a triangle to huge spraddled feet. Dressed in dirty fustian and bits of armor, matted with dried blood, he was obviously a fighting man; however, his heavy cross and embroidered vest hinted that he might also be a holy father.

The tableau was provocative, and I was as curious as the rest of the company, but I was also absorbed in studying Richard. How could Bonel distrust him? His flashing smile turned this way and that, his blue eyes sparkled with joy and his infectious laugh broke forth again and again; it was a face to trust—and to love.

I tried to take a step backward in my fantastick cells to the day I'd left Wanthwaite, still myself, neither hostage of love nor a mother. But how could I retreat to the past? How could I bear to be a solitary person again? Even if by some miracle Bonel was still able to secure my contract, no parchment could give me Richard's enduring love, which was what I craved. *Deus juva me,* I'd fallen helplessly in love myself—I couldn't face a future without Richard. The magnificence, passion, power, constant excitement had finally bewitched me, along with his tender underside of compassion, uncertainty and need. Watching him now, with his child inside me, I was a grown woman at last.

He was ready to speak, and the crowd hushed.

"My brother John has just presented me with the greatest coup of our long struggle with King Philip!"

John smiled at the crowd and waved at someone in the back.

"He has brought me as prisoner the Bishop of Beauvais."

The triangular man scowled and tried to inch away, but he was shackled. Richard continued with glowing praise of his brother's daring and acumen, for Beauvais was a war prize next only to King Philip himself, worth a king's ransom. In one blow John had filled Richard's coffers for fighting, and deprived Philip of his fiercest general. There were no honors, no treasure with which the king could adequately reward his dear brother, but he would start by restoring John's friend, the Bishop of Nunant, in his favor and put his former treachery to the Crown aside.

William Marshal and Mercadier were called forth to share Richard's gratitude, for Marshal had distracted Philip at the castle of Milli in the north while Mercadier joined John's forces at Jumières.

Bonel squeezed my hand and we gazed at each other, both sickened by the spectacle. So much for John's treatment of the Jews. In favor, out of favor, *oc e ne,* all because of derring-do on the field. Both of us quietly eased our way out of the hall.

I tried to be cheerful. "At least one good thing came out of John's perfidy: you were made justiciar."

He caught my reminder. "Thanks to you?"

I smiled happily. "I'm sure the king would have thought of it himself in time."

"In the future, perhaps it would be best to let him make his own appointments," he said dryly.

"But what's wrong with . . ."

"I don't want to face Mercadier's strong hand."

Of course I knew what he meant, recalling Richard's woodly jealousies. "The king said he didn't mind in your case, because . . ."

"Because I'm a Jew?" he finished when I came to an embarrassed stop.

I couldn't reply.

Bonel turned bright red with choler. "Tell your smug, all-wise king that the Jewish faith does not affect the *gonnades!*"

"But Jews don't love . . ." I was going to say "Christians."

"Yes, my God, yes! More than any Christian from what I see, for we honor our wives, accept responsibility for our families! Tell your king that love is accepting responsibility for those we love."

He left me abruptly, then turned and shouted back, "And you should remember that as well!"

# 19

OHN'S VICTORY OVER BEAUVAIS MIGHT PLEASE Richard, but Pope Celestine was incensed. He sent a runner from Rome protesting the arrest of an anointed, peace-loving bishop, protected by canon law from civil abuse. Richard was ordered to release Beauvais at once or the pope would put all England under the interdict. In reply, Richard sent Beauvais's bloody armor to Celestine as damning proof that the "peace-loving bishop" was a murderous soldier to be dealt with as any fighter taken in fair combat; let Philip pay the ransom if he wanted his bishop-general freed.

While the king awaited the pope's reaction, Walter of Coutances quietly lay the interdict on Normandy. He, too, was appalled at the capture of a fellow bishop, but his main reason was Richard's persistence about Les Andelys. Richard braved his wrath and continued with his plans, but the people suffered. Without the Church, there could be no more baptisms or funerals, that was the worst. Bodies were piled in their coffins on the far side of the Seine awaiting Christian burial and when the wind was from the east, the stench was sickening. Worse, for it was a double tragedy, were the children who died without baptism; they could be buried later, but there could be no postmortem baptism to promise their souls to God.

Indeed, I became obsessed with the fate of children. I watched every mother on the street as she scolded or caressed her babe. How utterly sweet it would be to hold my own child so. I spent hours touching my own stomach, finding the outline of the life inside me, trying to imagine how he looked. I thirled with joy. Once I laughed aloud and startled the king where he lay beside me. We were now a triangle of mother, father and child, only Richard didn't know. Perhaps we were designed to be pairs, always one person excluded, and at this stage it was the father. For a short period, my babe and I belonged exclusively to each other. I was delirious with bliss, and I knew that my son— or daughter—was too.

I was amazed that Richard noticed neither the subtle changes in my body nor in my disposition, but he was much occupied with his castle. He didn't neglect me—in fact, his love seemed to expand in proportion to his occupation—but he was oblivious to my responses.

Hamo was aware that my regimen had changed, though he never questioned why. I was grateful for his preparation of more food and his solicitude when I was tired.

In late November, Richard summoned Queen Eleanor to work her magic on Walter of Coutances. She swept into our dreary hall like sunlight from the south, her red robes glowing, her attar of roses evoking spring gardens, her green eyes gleaming confidence. All of us succumbed to her charm. Her old friend and counselor Walter of Coutances lifted the interdict, presumably so the Nativity could be observed; Richard talked enthusiastically through the night to his queen of his massive structural plans; my spirits became more animated.

And she noticed at once that I'd changed. When she kissed me in greeting, she held me against her shoulder and whispered, "What's your secret, dear? Have you found some wondrous love potion to turn you to a goddess?"

I couldn't tell her the truth until I'd informed the king, but I trembled in gratitude to have an astute woman in residence.

Richard could now go forth with his schedule at Les Andeleys without impediment and planned to ride out to his site with his principal engineer. The day before he left, he was in conference and I slipped up to our bedchamber to nap. I was wakened when he sat on the edge of the bed and leaned over me.

"You look lonely in that big bed." He kissed my cheek. "May I join you?"

"Lonely and cold." I pulled him close for another kiss. I'll tell him now, I thought, just as soon as we're finished. I can't wait any longer for Bonel to settle the contract—and it doesn't matter.

"Then I'll warm you as well."

Indeed his body was a hot gleed beside me and I gave myself gratefully to his ardor. He'd never been so tender as he caressed me with leisurely wonder—as if it were the first time—building slowly to his climax of passion. I was so happy, so carried away by our mutual love, that I couldn't wait to match one ecstasy with another, the news of our coming child.

But we both fell into a deep sleep.

When we woke, I was shaking with cold.

"Should I warm you again?"

"Aye, but first I want to talk. Would you get me a robe?"

"Tell me where it is."

"A soft green wool, on the bottom of the trunk under the window."

He slipped on his own tunic against the chill and walked barefoot to the casket. As he picked up the garment, a bunch of dead flowers fell to the stones.

"What's this?"

I laughed giddily, hardly able to hold my tongue. "The jonquils you picked for me in Poitiers. Remember?"

"Of course." His eyes shone with love, for he recalled only the gift, not his jealousy. "I'm touched. Do you have other mementos?"

"I've saved everything you gave me." I didn't add that in Bonel's opinion, that wasn't much. "Please come, I can't wait to tell you a secret."

"May I?" He was already rifling through the trunk. "More jonquils?"

"No, those are daffodils from the field where the goat . . ."

We laughed together.

"This glove—did you think it strange that I gave you only one? It belonged to my sister Marie, a wonderful woman, my favorite sister. You'll meet her one day. The mirror is from the Holy Land."

At last he turned and walked to the bed.

"What's this? Should I recognize it?"

He held up a piece of tattered yellow silk. My heart froze within me: it was the Scottish banner I'd fished from the Seine when the castle had been mined and it completely contradicted my claim that I'd known nothing of the attack until I'd been blasted into the fish pond.

"Just a rag—my handmaid must have put it there."

He started to toss it aside, and my heart beat once more. Then he frowned. "It looks Scottish."

"Uhhh . . ." I cleared my throat and reached for the robe, which I slipped on. "Aye," I said brightly. "It's a banner of the MacPherson clan."

No longer besotted with love or bewitched by my own babe, my middle brain charged like a destrier, except that it went in circles.

"Why did you say it was only a rag?"

So you wouldn't react as you're now doing, I thought dumbly.

"That was Enoch's clan, wasn't it?"

I took the cue. "Aye. He gave it to me to remember him by when he went to the Orkneys, many years ago. You can throw it away if you like."

His lips pursed, he sat and smoothed the rag across the bedcovers. "You always told me you didn't love him. Yet you kept this?"

The familiar ring of jealousy. How could I have been so stupid? The banner meant naught to me since it came from a stranger. Soothly, I'd simply forgotten I had it.

"I don't recall saying that."

"At the wedding in Sherwood Forest, you admitted hating him."

"No, my lord." I knew my danger, but my cheeks heated; I wouldn't deny Enoch. "I said I hated him before we wed, not afterward."

"And this is still afterward, isn't it? Do you think of him often?" His voice remained almost casual, but I saw the tremble in his hands as he continued to stroke the banner.

"No," I answered honestly. "My mind and heart are too full to dwell on the past. I want to tell you . . ."

"How do I compare to him in bed?"

My mouth hung open.

"Oh, don't look so amazed. You loved him only after you

bedded, and I've noticed how you covet my dagger and pouch. I ask you again, how do we compare?"

His manic disposition, the coarseness of his tongue both hurt and frightened me.

"I never thought of such a thing."

"No, perhaps you close your eyes and pretend that I'm the Scot? Ah, I see a telltale flush. I've hit the mark, haven't I?"

"No!" I fought for control, not wanting to lose this opportunity before he left on the morrow, not wanting to inflame him further. "We love each other too well for jealousy, My Lord. Please lie beside me, put your arms about me so that I may tell you something you want to hear above anything else."

"All I want is the truth: do you still love the Scot?" His face was pale, red whelks showing.

"I loved him, love his memory, but he's dead. I live in the present, but can't deny the past."

He rose to pace. "How can you call it the past when you still think of him? Or is that all you do?"

"What? I don't understand."

He sat on the bed and grasped my hands, squeezing my knuckles till I cried aloud. "Yes, you understand."

"Please let go. You're hurting me."

"Serve me right, choosing a traitor to elevate. You don't know the meaning of loyalty—you're filled with greed, not love!"

My control broke, and I jerked my hands free. "You dare speak to me of greed? All you want is a mother for your sons! You care nothing for my person or my happiness!"

"What would make you happy, Mistress, aside from my speaking with a Scottish brogue? What do you want beyond the finest court in Europe, gowns and riches beyond your feeble imagining, and—yes, God help me for a fool—the love of a king?"

"I live in the finest court as a lap dog, eating crumbs and fawning for the smallest favor, except that even a dog can expect to live out his life with his master. Your 'love' goes by the calendar—once I'm pregnant, out!"

"You appear to be sterile," he interrupted. "Or do you use the strumpet's impediments?"

My breath caught in pain. To think I'd been about to tell him!

"Perhaps my womb is more intelligent than my heart. Perhaps I'll conceive when I know it isn't my own death warrant."

"Death?" He guffawed in derision.

"A form of death, to be without my son, without a home, husband, or any form of support." To be without you, was what I meant.

"Ah, now it comes! You're harping on Bonel's contract."

My heart stopped. When had Bonel approached him?

"I don't know what you mean," I whispered.

"Don't you? He demanded all the stars in the heavens for you! What's his share of the spoils?"

"Please, Richard, you know that I never . . ."

"As if you couldn't trust me after I've showered you with gifts!"

"All I ask is love," I implored.

But he was beyond reason. "God's feet, you are a harlot! What's your price? Banners of gold to go with this shred?"

*Benedicite*, I didn't want anything except to wipe out the past few heartbeats. What had happened?

"At least I'll give you a whole one—not rags." He tossed the silk contemptuously at me, but it drifted to the window. He went to pick it up, stopped, his back toward me, rigid. When he turned, his eyes were dull, his lower lip forward. "Let's begin again, My Lady. Where did you get this?"

"I already told you . . . "

"But you lied. This banner has seen battle. It's not old, but damaged."

"Yes. Enoch's father carried it at Dingwall Boggs against the Danes. It's a clan heirloom."

"Strange, since banners were not in use in that time, especially in the barbaric north. Try again. Try the truth."

"I've told the truth." I forgot everything but fear. What was in his mind?

He walked close. "What was your assignment? To stab me while I slept? To put poison in my wine?"

"Who would assign such woodly things?" I cried fervently. "Why do you accuse me?"

"Because someone gave you this banner, someone in Philip's army, and recently."

Inspired, I shouted in righteous indignation, "I can prove I've had it since Wanthwaite!"

"How?"

"Ask Bonel. When I fell into the pool outside Nottingham, Bonel saw everything I carried. He'll remember this scarf."

His eyes fixed on me coldly. "I'll ask him."

And I'd reach him first to warn him.

"Meantime, consider yourself my prisoner."

"But not your bedmate!" I cried bitterly. "Never again! You think I have a fire in my bedstraw? You'll learn that it's a snowdrift instead!"

Before he could stop me, I ran from the chamber. He dashed after me, shouting my name, but I was hidden on the stair leading to the tower. After he'd run down the steps and I could hear him asking everyone where I was, I slowly crept upward to join my old friend, the rat.

I GROPED MY WAY along icy stones, past the barred window with its keen gale off the Seine, and stumbled on something soft, a greasy mat left by the last occupant of this grim tower. I sank to the floor and pulled the matting over my head, tried to warm myself with my own breath. Below me, the shouts diminished; I heard steps on the stair, whispers and murmurs outside the door, then silence.

They knew where I was.

But no one came. No doubt Richard was satisfied that I'd crawled voluntarily into the cell where he planned to put me anyway. Tears of self-pity and disbelief filled my eyes. What had changed him so radically in the last hour? He'd turned into the raging monarch of my trial with Pudlicott, accused me of preposterous acts as if we hadn't been lovers for months, hadn't confessed our innermost secrets, hadn't shared wonders that no one else could know or understand. How could he now call me a harlot, a traitor and liar?

All because of a meaningless banner? No, not the banner, I amended, but my lies about the banner, my toty contradictions that it was my handmaiden's rag, a gift, a relic, as if I were concealing some dire significance. How could I ever explain?

I wiped my eyes and nose on the mat, tried to make myself into a tight ball against the draft, which struck from all sides, and cursed myself for the fool that I was. I was a born liar, that was the truth, even as a child at Wanthwaite when Dame Margery had whipped me many a time for the fault; then later with Enoch, who'd pelted me with Scottish curses and a few befts on the behind for the same sin when he still thought me a boy; and now with Richard. I wallowed in self-hatred and castigation for I know not how long, but until I was thoroughly frozen and miserable.

And yet . . .

Dame Margery had still loved me, as had Enoch, for they knew that my lies weren't venal, just self-serving. Did my silly lie about the banner justify the king's making me a prisoner? Calling me a traitor and worse? No, I'd behaved foolishly under duress but had committed none of the offenses of which Richard accused me. The lie had sparked his rage, but it hadn't caused it. Some dormant suspicion lay ready to be fired. What could it be? Why did he have so little faith in me? And how could I tell him of my condition under such circumstances?

Again I traversed through mental tunnels that ended in

blank walls. Then gradually, in one speculation, I saw a glimmer of light. Bonel had warned me that Richard's support was not to be trusted, that something was seriously wrong. Aye, a secret he'd called it, that he'd learned in England. *Benedicite*, I wished now that I'd insisted on knowing what it was. A secret that undermined love?

Another woman?

The thought appalled, but what else comes between a man and a woman? No, it couldn't be. I knew how Richard spent every hour of the day and night. We were never apart except during fighting season, and then there were no women, only his lords, knights and pages . . .

Thought stopped.

Started again.

Was it possible? Aye, it was, and it would explain why Bonel was so secretive. He knew I would be outraged with the king if I thought I had a male rival. It would also explain Richard's mercurial changes, for he would put the onus on me for his own delinquencies. Enoch had taught me long ago that men often attack to cover their own guilts.

*Deus juva me.*

Suddenly I was too hot and threw the odorous matting away, walked to the window to let the wind rake me. Richard loved elsewhere, loved a man but still needed an heir. No—he must love me as well. I couldn't be wrong about that!

Curious, his "strange sin" as the Church called it, was also the source of my lies, beginning with my disguise as a boy and all that followed. I breathed deeply of the hurtful air, tried to clear my fantastick cells.

And decided to tell the truth at last. I loved Richard too well to continue with a shadow between us. Immediately I felt better, though frightened. How could I broach such a delicate subject? My eyes grew grainy as I stared into the dark, trying to think. I mustn't betray Bonel's warnings, that above all, and, indeed, there was no reason to. What did I actually know? Nothing except the history Richard and I shared. Aye, stay with that, and let it lead where it would.

The window became a gray smudge. I looked out on a bleak dawn with tiny snowflakes whistling on the updraft of wind. Then—familiar footsteps on the stair—I turned as the door swung open.

"Alix!"

Richard swept me into his arms as if I were a babe, wrapped me close in his warm furs.

"Forgive me, say you forgive me," he whispered desperately between kisses. "Some demon took my tongue, I swear. I didn't mean a word."

I breathed deeply of his sweet woodruff, melted in the heat of his body and caresses, forgot wild fancies and resolutions—night thoughts fell away.

"Thank God you mentioned Bonel. Of course he remembered the banner, told me it had been in your drafsack all along."

And night thoughts returned. Dear Bonel, loyal even when he didn't know the issue. And Richard, still with the demon's tongue, for it had taken hard refutation to change him. My fantastick cells flew in erratic gusts like the snow.

"Are you as exhausted as I am? I'll never spend another night apart from you, will never . . ."

He kicked the door open to carry me down the stairs.

"Wait, Richard, I want to talk."

"Later, sweets," His voice was thick with love. "First, let's lie before the fire, make up properly."

"No, I can't until . . . I must confess."

Bemused, he rubbed his nose against mine. "There's nothing to confess. As I said, Bonel confirmed . . ."

"Bonel doesn't know what I'm going to say. You were right, Richard; I did lie to you."

His eyes became puzzled, wary. "Alix, I've already admitted that I was wrong and apologized. The fault is entirely mine, and I wouldn't believe you if you swore on the bishop's robes that you were a harlot or traitor."

"Would you believe that I deliberately ran from you when we were in Acre?"

His lip thrust forward, and I thought I would faint. There was still time to retreat—I began to take back my words.

"I thought you wanted to talk about last night. If you must repeat our entire history together, at least let's be warm," he entreated, his jocund tone strained.

"The events of last night began on the Crusade," I insisted, "where we first played this scene."

"Nonsense!"

"Is it nonsense? In your tent—that last night—you accused me of deliberately deceiving you, of being in the employ of your enemy in order to stab you in your bed. Now —years later—you still repeat the same theme."

"Very well." He sighed deeply, as if indulging a silly whim. "Only make your point quickly, love. The place is dank and I long to . . ."

But he placed me gently on the mat, sat beside me as we pulled his furs across us.

"That last night in Acre, we had an assignation, a young girl and a mighty king."

He laughed. "And there was a wind storm, the candles blew out and you poured wine on my naked stomach. Do I remember it accurately?"

"I wonder. I came as a young girl, but you thought me a young boy."

"Never!"

"You thought me a young boy," I repeated, though my voice trembled, "and when your searching hands discovered otherwise, you reached for my throat to kill me."

"God's feet, Alix!" he exploded. "Your reason has been addled by this melancholy tower! I knew you were female —haven't I said so a hundred times?—and I would never kill you."

"Only my plea that I hadn't deceived you—that I'd believed you knew my true sex—saved my life. You knew I told the truth."

"Alix, I refuse to play the lovers' game of yes I did, no you didn't. You were only a child in Acre, hardly capable of understanding the facts."

"I agree," I said candidly. "In my innocence, I didn't know what was happening. You see, I'd never heard of love between men and boys, couldn't conceive of such a thing."

He chided me lightly. "I thought kings were exempt from inquisitions."

I took a deep shuddering breath. "Then I beg you to remove your crown. If we are to continue as lovers, I must be frank."

There was a pause. "Go on."

"I lay that night terrified, confused, not knowing what had transpired. Yet, gradually, remembering all that had already happened between us, and listening to your own transparent denials, and seeing the evidence . . . I knew that you could be carnally roused for the boy, not for the girl."

"By God, this is absurd! You impugn my chivalry if you can't see that my inhibitions were your tender years and the fact that you were my ward!"

"Yet you invited me back the following night, though I was still young, still your ward."

"But you didn't come," he agreed bitterly. "Do you know that I postponed my march to wait for you?"

"I didn't come because one of your pages caught me in Acre and put a knife to my throat. He claimed I'd replaced him in your bed, that he'd murder me if I dared . . ."

"That hairless lackey called Sir Gilbert," he scoffed. "Every great man has to contend with ambitious toadies, Alix, but it means nothing."

"After I escaped Sir Gilbert," I continued, "I went to your troubadour, Ambroise, and asked him to find me passage on a ship."

"You will note that, because he helped you, he's no longer with me."

"Be that as it may, My Lord, he confirmed that you'd loved me as a boy, that he himself had sought me for your pleasure."

"Yet you've admitted that I knew you were a girl that second night."

"Aye, that seemed to contradict what I'd learned," I concurred, "until I recalled a ditty you'd composed for me after your wedding to Berengaria. You couldn't love your queen, and you thought it was God's punishment for your pederastic preferences." I felt his body stiffen and added hastily, "Your words. You could love only boys. Only me."

He forced me to look at him. "Only you. Did I lie?"

"No," I admitted again. "When you sought me in Mainz, and later told me in Chinon that you needed an heir, I realized that sometime during that first night in Acre you'd discovered that, with me, you could be roused even knowing I was female."

"Absolutely true," he said bluntly, then searched my eyes. "This is a most strange confession, in which I'm asked to defend myself. What is your point?"

"Well," I foundered, thrown by his casual admission, "I felt insecure, as if I possessed a unique quality I didn't understand, like a magic ring or spell, which had nothing to do with myself. Sometimes when you're angry, I think you resent this quality, might prefer . . . might still prefer . . . to be with men."

There, I'd said it. I waited in dread; he seemed to wait as well for me to say more.

"That's all?"

"Aye."

His relieved laughter made the rat scuttle from his hole in terror.

"And that's the reason you ran from me?"

"Aye."

"The only reason?"

"Yes, my lord."

"Then you haven't grown up at all. God, where can I begin? Well, to answer your fears. Have I dallied with boys? Of course. Have I loved boys? Never! Men do love men, have to for our common weal, sometimes carnally as you put it. Or sometimes they dally without love—as in my case."

"Every man?" I asked. He was confirming Tib.

"Every fighting man, to some degree. Most marry, of course, but that doesn't stop affection. Look at Baldwin of Béthune and William Marshal, both happily married but still lovers."

I gasped with shock. William Marshal was rarely seen without his wife, the Duchess of Pembroke, and was considered a doting husband.

"As a man, of course I sought release, but I never loved, a lack which used to worry me. In fact, as time went by, I became less and less interested even in lust."

His hand reached for my breast, rested there.

"Then I met you. Did I think you were a boy when we went to bed the first time? Yes, Alix, I did."

He must feel my racing heart.

"But, as I said, you remember incompletely. The error shocked us both, but the real loss was love. I knew, lying there in the dark with the wind howling around the canvas, that I couldn't bear to give you up. Boy or girl, it didn't matter, I loved you."

Like a flower opening, I did remember, our wet cheeks pressed close as we'd thought we must relinquish love.

"What had begun as carnal attraction quickly changed to something new in my experience." Again he put his cheek against mine, placed a gentle hand to my throat. "Alix, I can never tell you how . . ."

Gently he pushed me down so that we lay on the mat, under his furs.

"You're right, you place me under a spell, but the magic isn't outside you, it's the essence of you. Before you, I was only half-alive, half a person—you make me whole. Sometimes I think I'm mad because I'm in such a constant state of frenzy for you, but it isn't madness, it's sanity. To lose you would mean madness."

He kissed me deeply, slowly. "I'm glad you're female because you can give me an heir, but otherwise it wouldn't matter. Whatever the link between us is called, for me it's life, a form of *hubris*—if ever God punishes me, it will be for loving you too much."

I closed my eyes, gave way to his kisses. But he wasn't finished.

"Now that I've 'confessed' in your place, suppose you answer me."

I opened my eyes, met his hot probing gaze.

"You lied about the banner. What is the truth?"

I opened my lips to tell the honest tale of Vaudreuil, when I remembered Bonel and the lie I'd forced him to say.

"You know where I got it. What else do you want to know?"

"Simple, Alix. Obviously, I'd had considerable carnal experience before we met, but I'd never loved. Yet you did love before me. Do you still . . . love Enoch?"

The question disturbed me for its present tense, and I struggled to find the truth.

"You were my very first love," I said slowly. "I worshipped you as only a very young girl can while we were on the Crusade. Then there was an interim in which I was wed, and I did love Enoch. Now, however, I love you, Richard, more than I can ever say. You were my first love, my present love, and you will be my last."

"Ah."

And we loved on the cold stones of the tower, our bodies almost as incompetent as our words to express the poignant, transcendent need we felt for each other.

When we were finished, Richard pressed his cheek against mine. "You'll never leave me again. I'll keep the banner myself, just for giving me that assurance."

Too moved to speak, tears rose to my eyes. Then he carried me down to our chamber, but we didn't need the fire's crackling warmth.

"I had your handmaiden pack for you," he said jubilantly. "I want you with me in Les Andelys, want to show you my giant rock."

Transfixed, I hardly heard him. Something like moth wings beat in my womb.

"How high is your rock, Richard?"

He pointed upward. "High as Heaven."

I laughed giddily. When we were close to Heaven, I'd tell him about our child.

Our happiness would be complete.

IT WOULD BE the largest, most expensive castle ever built in Europe, stretching for miles along the Seine and standing as an impassable obstacle between Paris and Rouen. Richard talked enthusiastically as we rode across the long plain to Les Andelys.

I sat with a perpetual smile, hardly able to respond appropriately when his voice rose in question, so engrossed was I with the faint moth wings inside me. My baby slept, he waked. Did he enjoy the rocking motion of the horse?

Richard had made a devastating error in returning the Vexin to Philip, which gave France a direct route to his ducal capital, but Château Gaillard—Saucy Castle—would remedy that.

"A piquant name for a castle," I managed to comment.

"But just right. Wait till you see the setting."

He was joined by his engineer, called Sawale son of Henry, who farmed the issues of the Vexin and held a sergeanty in Northumberland.

"I'm from Northumberland as well," I said. "Do you know Wanthwaite?"

He glanced keenly from pale-lashed blue eyes. "Know it well, though not for a few years. Baron William . . ."

"My father!"

Before I could ask if he knew its present condition, Richard cut in quickly about his castle again, describing the curved walls of the Krak in Syria which deflected arrows. Sawale listened attentively and asked a few questions as I sank into my reverie.

The king took two days to reach Les Andelys, wanting to arrive in midday; the snow melted, and the ground was slippery with a mix of ice and mud. The Seine River moved along the plain on our side, but the other bank was a steep cliff rising like a wall before us. Outcroppings of granite jutted over the water and the angle of the cliffs made it difficult to see what lay atop them, another plain that dropped into nothingness or a series of mountains. Slightly to our right, and in line with an island in the middle of the river, rose a behemoth of a rock, the highest I'd ever seen, a sheer crag.

"That's it," Richard boasted. "From the top, you can view river traffic in both directions because the Seine loops here. What a locale!"

Sawale was stunned to silence.

"But how do you get to the top?" I asked.

"You can't see it, but there's a horse path through the bushes that goes about halfway. From that point, we'll walk. He glanced at me. "You can wait below if you prefer."

"Never!" I laughed totily. "I want to be as close to Heaven as possible when . . ."

We took a ferry that crossed at the island, waited for our horses, then began our climb. At first it was easy, but soon we reached a small plateau where we had to leave our mounts and climb on foot. Richard walked with Sawale while I used Hamo's arm. Again the climb began easily, but soon became more steep. We pulled ourselves up by the bushes, a difficult task made more so by the treacherous mud. Then we reached a bare spot.

"You stay here, Alix. I'll go ahead and reach down for you," Hamo instructed.

He made several tries before he found a rock. I dared not look behind me at the steep drop, but kept my eyes on trickles of melting snow on the bank in front of me.

Hamo leaned as far as he could; our hands locked; he pulled and I dug in my heels. My feet slipped from under me—I fell with a hard thump onto an invisible stone. I lay with my cheek in the mud, unable to speak or to move because of the pain. Only Hamo's grip saved me from falling. I heard him shout for the king.

Richard lifted me easily up the slope.

"Are you all right?"

I forced a smile and nodded.

"Sure?"

I nodded again.

He laughed gently. "You remind me of your fall in Poitiers—remember?"

I tried to look into his eyes but all I could see were two blurred outlines of his body. The rest of the climb was done in a foggy limbo, and finally I sat on a flat rock at the summit with Hamo beside me. Richard walked til and fro, pointing at this approach or that, explaining his engineering. I leaned forward until my head reached my knees and saw something alien, a thin red drip at my foot.

"Richard!" I screamed.

His huge figure ran in a mist.

"God's feet, what's wrong?"

"I'm losing my baby!"

His white face hung like a wild-eyed moon.

"What baby?"

I pointed mutely at the dreadful red spot.

"My God, why didn't you tell me?"

No answer.

"How long have you been bleeding?"

"Just started."

"Then there's hope! Hold on, Alix, don't let go!" His eyes pleaded.

I lay across his chest as two knights supported his elbows for our descent.

"Are you in pain?"

"No," I whispered, except that my heart was breaking.

"How long . . ."

"July."

"My God, why didn't you tell me?"

I couldn't remember.

We slid down in no time, were on the ferry, There, Richard knelt before me and gently slid his hand up my tunic.

"I think the bleeding's stopped. Do you feel anything?"

I shook my head, meaning I had no pain, but I was trying to feel something else, the faint flutter of wings.

He improvised a litter between horses so I wouldn't have to straddle, rode on one while Hamo took the other. We went forever in gray twilight.

Why didn't my baby move? Did the rock of the horses put him to sleep?

I began to sob. "I'm sorry! I'm sorry!"

"Hush, sweetest, you'll hurt yourself. Besides, it's not your fault. You tried to tell me, didn't you? Only my damnable temper . . ." His voice broke.

But I wasn't apologizing to him; I was apologizing to my child. I closed my eyes, pretended to sleep, but I was bargaining with God, offering Him everything if He would only revive that sweet flutter again.

# 20

HEN WE REACHED ROUEN, I WAS JARRED FROM a deep lethargy by Richard's angry shouts. "That's not enough!"

Father Orlando, the King's personal physician, was gazing down on me with barely concealed distaste.

"I can bleed her from the great toe which may help."

"And it may not," Richard replied wrathfully. "I want her examined, cared for as you would a knight in the field. Now will you do it or not?"

Father Orlando stroked his iron-gray beard, eyes moving furtively to Father Nicholas who stood beside him. "No. Holy Scripture prohibits the examination of women's bodies, especially in childbirth. Best find a midwife."

"Tib," I whispered, but no one heard.

"I would be happy to pray for her, Your Majesty," Father Nicholas soothed Richard. "Or even to exorcise an unfriendly demon."

"You call my unborn child a demon?" the king roared.

"Tib."

This time he heard me. "What did you say, dearest?"

"Take me to Sister Tiberga. She's a—midwife."

Richard straightened, his mouth a hard line. "Hamo, go get Bonel. I'll have the Jewish doctors attend her."

"That's not necessary, Your Majesty," Father Orlando protested.

"Or wise," Father Nicholas echoed. "She must have Christian attendance in order to save her soul and the infant's."

"I agree," Richard said caustically, "only not yet. The

Jews are more interested in curing bodies than transporting souls to Heaven."

I recalled that he'd sought a Jewish doctor on his way to the Holy Land. I closed my eyes again, much relieved.

When I opened them, the priests had gone; Bonel was talking earnestly to Richard. As soon as he saw I was awake, he took my hand.

"How do you feel, Lady Alix?"

I didn't answer.

"The king has agreed to put you in my house. Our doctors don't like to treat a woman in your condition without total control of her regimen."

"Thank you."

I was transported by litter to Jews Street, entered a large stone house, more airy and better furnished than any palace. Lying on my back, I watched the tops of myriad doors as one ceiling gave way to another. At last we stopped. Carefully, I was lifted onto a bed of clouds, was supported to a half-sitting position by mounds of cushions. A fire warmed from the grate, boat-shaped oil lamps illuminated the corners though it was still daylight; thick, soft carpets decorated the stone floors. There were no rushes, no wind from open windows, no darkness, and the air was redolent of sweet cinnamon.

Richard and Bonel left me; a thickset maid appeared. Dressed in russet and dull blue with a scarf tied low over her forehead, she was as remarkable as the room in her way: she was scrubbed, her breath was fresh, her nails clean. Deftly she removed my crusted garments and left me naked under soft woven covers.

A second maid appeared, taciturn and efficient. She placed a bowl of warm water on a table and indicated that she wanted to bathe me. I was willing until she reached my crotch.

"No!" I groaned. "No—careful!"

I needn't have worried; her hands were gossamer. She gave me a blue spun robe to slip over my head and departed.

The king returned.

"Are you all right? Comfortable?"

"Aye, except . . ." My eyes filled. "I want to be with you. I could stay in the palace. I'm not sick, you know."

He sat gingerly on the edge of the bed. "I'll visit you as often as I can, but it's essential that you remain quiet—perhaps for the whole nine months. Obey your king." He tried to smile.

Our eyes held.

"I was going to tell you on the summit of your rock because it was close to Heaven. I was foolish, wasn't I?"

"Don't look back; concentrate on the fight ahead. I tell you as a man who can judge an enemy that we'll win, all three of us."

"Is that what the doctors say?"

He stroked my hair. "They have to examine you before they give an opinion, but I'm your real doctor. Trust me."

"Aye, I do."

"I'm leaving now—I have to tell my mother, attend to court business—but I'll be back." He leaned forward and kissed my lips. "I love you."

"I love you."

I fell into a profound sleep. When I woke, it was dark; the lamps cast deeper shadows and there was a night quality to the silence. Then I realized that I'd been disturbed by voices in the outer hall. The door opened and Bonel entered, followed by two men, a strange woman and the two maids.

"Greetings, Alix. I believe you look better already." Bonel stood at the foot of the bed. "May I present Doctor Solomon of Montpellier? Doctor Clarice of Salerno?"

A rotund man in an outsized robe lined with fur stepped forth, his kindly face concerned. Slightly behind him stood a gaunt, heavy-jawed woman, Doctor Clarice, her eyes like garnets, the lines from nose to the corners of her mouth deeply defined. Both seemed to have stepped from stained-glass windows with their rich reds and blues, dark golden skins and shadow-black outlines.

"So you had a bad fall, Lady Alix?" Doctor Solomon intoned. He took my wrist and began to count my pulse. "Good strong beat. You're a healthy young woman, aren't you? Isaac."

His surgeon stepped close to take blood from my finger, which Doctor Solomon rubbed on a shard, then examined carefully.

"What do you see?"

"Nothing to worry about yet. A good dark color, a fresh odor. Now, Doctor Clarice."

Doctor Clarice replaced him and gestured for the maidservants to lift hangings to screen her procedures.

"I want a sample of your urine," she said with an accent.

She gave me a small clear jar in a wicker basket and insisted that I fill it at once. When I'd complied, she dipped her finger in the liquid, sniffed, held it to the light.

"No blood, a good sign" she comforted me.

She then reached under my blanket and quickly ran her hands over my body, pressing gently and asking my sensations. Finally she put her ear against my stomach.

"Is he alive?" I asked anxiously.

She stood, answered evasively. "They turn in the womb. It isn't always easy to tell."

The curtains were lowered, and Doctor Solomon asked me my zodiacal sign and my last date of menstruation, then pondered a long time.

"The moon was against you. The crab runs backward on the earth's rim in August, puffing foul winds onto the moon. We may have to bleed you, but not yet. Right now I want you to promise me to think only happy thoughts, to eat well and to sleep. My colleague can teach you the Salerno rule."

Doctor Clarice smiled. "Use three physicians still—first, Doctor Quiet, next, Doctor Merryman and third, Doctor Diet."

They all left except Bonel who pulled a faldstool close.

"That's good advice, Alix. Try to relax." He stroked my hand. "Do you have pain?"

"I did. Now I'm just afraid. You're wise about medicine, Bonel. Am I going to keep my child?"

"You're in your fourth month and not bleeding at the moment. There's a good chance."

"What can I do?"

"Pray. God creates and God takes away; all we do is to facilitate the process. Ask Him for mercy."

I turned to the wall.

"Alix, don't be afraid. You're not the only one praying." He stood to go. "I'll send your supper to you; then I want you to sleep. I've put my mat just outside your door and if you need anything in the night, call me."

He bent and brushed my lips as Richard had an hour before.

In the middle of the night, God refused our prayers. A knife plunged into my middle—I shrieked in agony!

I FLOATED on the mists around Andelys with pain as my rudder. From my giddy heights, I observed the scene below, saw myself lying in a coma as Bonel shook my inert body and called to me.

Others entered, the doctors and strangers, and the shouting increased. The farther I drifted, the less pain I felt and yet. . . . Pain was life now, and when I stopped feeling it, both my baby and I would be lost. The paltry shouts below were no match to the heavenly pull above, but I tried to respond.

"No! No! No!"

"She can hear us. Alix, it's Bonel. Speak to me—keep talking. Where's the pain?"

I thrashed til and fro, pointed.

"Get a basin—she's bleeding."

"No! No! No!"

My hips were raised, hands reached.

"Don't go!" I cried to my child. "Don't let them take you!"
"Drink," Bonel ordered.

THE FAMILIAR POPPY SYRUP ran down my chin.

I lay in limbo, no longer able to scream or sob or speak. Fear departed along with pain and I was swept into a world I'd never seen before. A lavender radiance sucked me to its center, like a deep hungry flower, and I heard whispers, laughter. Then I saw my father and mother suspended in the light, younger than I remembered them, and my mother held a golden-haired baby in her arms.

"Mother!" I ran toward her on bare feet, past the root garden where old Robert knelt digging. "I'll race you!"

"You can't win," she cried in her Celtic cadence.

Her dark hair blew across her dimples and she stepped back to force me closer.

"Give me our special kiss," my father whispered.

I felt his lips.

The glow darkened, and I heard hoarse sobs beside me. King Richard sat on the floor beside my bed, his face buried in the quilt, his shoulders shaking.

Had he kissed me or had it been my father?

When I looked again, Richard had turned into Bonel, his shoulders shaking, his black curls resting on my wrist. Much as I wanted to comfort him, the effort was too great.

I closed my eyes to seek the violet light again; I wanted to see my baby. I drifted on a long voyage before I saw a small circular glow in the abyss and heard my mother summon.

"Mary Alix, this way."

And I was with them, again the little girl of youthful parents. This time I wouldn't leave.

"Is it a boy or a girl?" I reached for the cradleboard.

"Come closer if you would see, closer, pretty wench," my mother teased. She took my hand and pulled.

Someone else held me back by my other hand. The person squeezed, and I whimpered.

"Don't you dare die yet," I heard.

"Let me go," I whispered. "It's beautiful."

"Not yet. I order you to stay. You still have work to do here."

That carillon voice was familiar but I couldn't place it. I opened my eyes to a scarlet slash that wavered across my vision.

"That's better," Queen Eleanor said. "Now, say my name."

"Eleanor."

"*Alia-anor*, they called me at home, because I was from Anor, my mother's name. Say it."

I didn't care about her mother, only mine.

"Say it!" Her green hawk's eyes bent close as if to rip me apart.

"*Alia-anor*."

"Good. Now repeat after me: my name is Alix and I'm going to live."

"No!"

I closed my eyes and tried to find my parents, my baby again; the brilliant hot light faded to red, the color of my eyelids. The bones in my hands were pressed till they cracked together. I glared upward.

"Say it."

"My name is Alix and I'm going to live. I hate you!"

I could see her mouth curl. "Good, hate all you like."


WHEN I WOKE, Richard lay on top of the cover beside me, staring upward. I watched him without his being aware. For the first time, I saw lines etched in his forehead, at the corners of his eyes, counted a few white hairs at his temples.

I must have made a sound, for he turned his head. Then tears came. We were no longer a triangle; we were back to man and woman, but now incomplete. Without speaking, he put his arms around me, and we wept together, children ourselves, forlorn and inconsolable.

"I had her baptized Marie; she had a Christian burial."

"Thank you. I'm so sorry."

"I'm sorry too."

We comforted each other as best we could.

"At least we know we can conceive," he said.

But I couldn't look ahead, couldn't desert Marie yet.


"*SHEM'A YISRO'EL!*"

I was staring into a black void.

"*Shem'a yisro'el!*"

A clatter of sticks against shutters and doors began the day, then chanting and wailing in minor keys as the Jews started their ritual prayers. I waited for the smell of raisins baking in bread.

My door opened, and the first maid who'd undressed me entered with kindling in her hands.

"Greetings, Rebecca," I said shyly.

"Peace be with you," she replied with a grin of perfect teeth. She knelt, cleaned the hearth and lit the logs.

No sooner had she left than the door opened again to admit Bonel, a tray of fresh bread and fruit in his hands. "I'm playing maidservant today. Can I tempt you?"

"I do feel hungry," I admitted, eyeing the nuts and dried fruits.

"Good." He arranged my tray and pulled his faldstool close. "You want to build your strength."

I ate greedily as he watched.

"King Richard is coming today to talk to you."

I looked up. "Where's he been?"

"He took another trip to Les Andelys before summoning his Christmas court."

Christmas so soon? It seemed only yesterday that we'd ridden on our Christmas hunt in Beynac, yet much had happened.

"How long have I been here?"

"Almost two weeks. Do you like it?"

"Under different circumstances, I would love it. It's odd, but civilized." I tried to smile. "Unlike Wanthwaite."

"But it was nice in its way."

"Hypocrite! You thought it barbaric, hardly better than an animal's lair."

"Except for its owner, yes. You were enchanting."

"*Benedicite*, Bonel, have you been drinking the poppy? I recall well that you looked upon me as if I were a monkey swinging in a tree."

"Perhaps I like monkeys. They're wild, free, independent."

He hesitated. "You need diversion. There's a young woman living in our commune from England. She'd like to meet you and converse in her own tongue."

"Oh yes, I'd like to meet any friend of yours." At the same time I felt a woodly twitch of jealousy.

"Good. Her name is Muriel."

Muriel must have been waiting in the hall, for the instant Bonel left, she knocked on the still open door. My jealousy vanished when I saw a child clinging to Muriel's skirts, a little girl who was the image of her mother, or vice versa, for Muriel was a childlike woman, despite a considerable height and girth. Her eyes squinted in perpetual mirth, her full-lipped mouth smiled moistly, and her fine baby hair flew in an unruly cloud.

"Greetings, Lady Alix," she said in a high squeak. "I'm Muriel and this is Margaret. Say greetings, Margaret."

Margaret immediately retired to the safety of her mother's skirts.

"We're sorry for Margaret's rudeness. However, you may be fortunate; she jabbers like a jay when started, and this gives us a chance to become acquainted."

"Please sit down, Muriel, there on the faldstool."

She drew close with Margaret settled on her lap; the two of them gave warm sparks like a Yule log.

"I'm very sorry about your accident," she said without preamble. "I lost my first baby, so I know how it feels."

Margaret sucked her thumb and reached with her other hand to her mother's lips.

"You have a beautiful little girl now. Did it take long?"

"Not at all." Muriel then revealed her own personal travails of conception as openly as if she'd been Tib.

I listened, fascinated and perplexed. "How did you come to the commune? You're English and . . . aren't you Christian?"

"I was until I married Jurnet."

"You converted?" My shock wasn't flattering, but soothly I'd never heard of a Christian becoming a Jew.

"Jurnet didn't want to become Christian, so there was no other choice," she twittered, then laughed.

"But . . . wasn't it difficult?"

I meant to give up her religion, but she took it otherwise.

"Dreadful. My father promptly cut off my inheritance, and Jurnet had to pay the king six thousand marks, which is a great amount." She smiled slyly. "Though not as much as Jurnet was willing to give, if the king had known."

She was so frank that I dared continue. "But are you happy?"

"With Jurnet?" Her eyes widened and she wet her lips. "We're still like two doves, Lady Alix. It's shameful to be so smitten after years of marriage."

"No, I meant as a Jew."

"A happy Christian makes a happy Jew. I don't see much difference."

But she'd given up Our Lady and Our Lord, a sacrifice in my opinion. However, I pointed to the material differences. "I find this house very different from Christian abodes."

"Better. Aye, Jews live better. It would be hard for me to go back, especially if I had to take a Christian husband. Jews honor their wives and provide for their families, whereas I remember my father, a good Christian, beating my mother, and many Christians discard their wives for a better-endowed woman."

"But don't you ever worry?"

Her pale eyes didn't flinch. "About the riots? Of course. Jurnet is from Norwich where the Jews were terribly persecuted. We're not completely safe anywhere."

We both fell silent.

"However," she continued brightly, "I don't dwell on it. After all, my chances of survival with Jurnet are better than they would be with a Christian husband. We have good medical care and sanitation and our men don't fight. Did you know that most knights are dead by the age of thirty?"

A cold wind blew over me; Richard was forty.

I became aware that she was studying me.

"Do you love Bonel?"

I jumped under my covers. "I'm . . . the king . . ."

Her steady eyes waited.

"Is it possible to love two men?" I asked. I depended on Bonel almost as much as I did on Richard, if dependency be love.

"Not for me, but I'm sure there are those who do."

She felt her question had been answered. *Benedicite*, would she tell Bonel?

"Muriel, please . . ."

She took my hand. "I wasn't sent to ask, if that's what worries you, and I could never tell Bonel anything he doesn't already know. He's our wisest man. Now, I'm going to call for the maid and supervise a bath for you—you'll find it marvelously refreshing."

As the bath was administered, I ruminated on Jews and Christians. What would it be like to give up the Virgin Mary? And did the Jews believe in Heaven? I could never forsake my parents, my baby . . .

"Farewell, Alix," Muriel said. "I'll come again if I may."

As she left, King Richard swept in, still dressed for riding. Muriel dropped to her knees, then quickly exited. Just as quickly, I was in Richard's arms.

"You smell like a rose," he murmured, "and I must smell

like a horse. I didn't go the castle to change—couldn't wait to see you."

We exchanged news, he of his castle, me of my progress, embraced, stroked, comforted. Finally he rose, promising to return the next day.

"Who was that woman just now? Do I know her?"

"Her name is Muriel, and you may. Her husband, Jurnet, paid you six thousand marks in order to marry her. She was a Christian."

"Yes." His eyes narrowed. "They appeared before me just before I left on the Crusade. What did she want from you?"

"Nothing, except to offer friendship."

He waited, frowning. "Go on. What did she say?"

I elaborated, omitting only the fact that Christian men die young. I thought he would be amused at the differences between Christian and Jewish husbands, but he wasn't.

"Does Bonel know this Muriel?" he asked curtly.

"Aye, he suggested she come talk because we're both English."

"I see." His eyes were fixed as if in anger, and I feared he might mention the odious contract again, but he bent, kissed me warmly as ever in farewell.

TIB BUMPED AWKWARDLY through the door, scarring the sills with a heavy wooden case she carried.

"May my hothouse go up in smoke if that's not the handsomest king in Christendom!" she cried. "And to think he plays billiards on your sweet dish!"

I held out my arms. "Thank you for coming, Tib."

She placed her box by my bed and leaned over to embrace me. Dressed in her violet and white pilgrim's garb, she smelled strongly of fish scales, meaning she'd been working in her laboratory.

"What's in the box?" I asked.

"A few elixirs to bring back your blood," she said, as she gazed avidly around the room. "By my faith, what a lot of objects the Jews collect! They must be richer than kings or popes, I trowe."

"I believe they have a religious purpose, though I couldn't say exactly what. How is your hospice?"

But she had spied a shining golden box close to the window and rushed to pick it up. With the swing of her ample hips, her billowing barmcloth toppled a delicate stand with a fearsome crash.

"*Benedicite*, Tib, take care! Did anything break?"

She glanced indifferently over her shoulder. "No harm, sweets." She breathed on the box, polished it vigorously on her apron and held it to the light. "I'd say twenty silver marks, and all for a no-good box. What a waste."

"You could say the same for gold crosses," I reminded her. "When faith is deep, it's fitting to use precious metals."

But she was already holding a crystal dish to the light; rainbows flew around the room. Then a filigree tray took her eye and another table smashed.

I sat up in dismay. "Please, Tib, watch yourself. You act as if you're drunkalewe."

"No, sweets, I'm only a drab who's found a feast."

"Come, talk to me."

"Here you are lying in a treasure vault, and you don't even appreciate it," she said enviously. She ran her fingers lightly down a tapestry, plumped a pillow on a bench. "I wish the Jews would take me into their quarters; if I were sick in your place, this gold would restore my vital juices faster than the spurt of a man's honey."

As she walked toward me, her skirt wiped two other tables clean. Trying not to show my alarm—I must get the maid here at once—I opened my arms to urge her on.

"I do appreciate where I am," I assured her, "though in ways that can't be carved in gold or woven into a picture: the Jews are a kind people, generous . . ." I was too close to my illness to speak of it.

"Jews are all very well when it comes to sorcery and black

magic," she said scornfully, "but if your womb is to flourish in the future, you need the wisdom of experience, and that means a fizgy well acquainted with the female parts."

Relieved that her attention was finally distracted from Bonel's riches, I agreed eagerly, though I defended Doctors Solomon and Clarice.

"Forget all they said. I'll examine you."

Before I could demur, she'd popped her head under my cover and pulled my robe high. Her delicate fingers poked as I clenched my teeth. *Benedicite*, I'd prefer she went back to the gold objects.

She emerged, triumphant. "I'll wager the Jews didn't tell you that you carry the mark of Mars on your queint, did they?"

Embarrassed, I shook my head.

"That's Richard's sign, honey-hair, sure as I'm sitting here. And, since you were born under Venus's sign . . ."

"Taurus," I corrected her. "I'm the stubborn bull."

"Then you were born on a Friday."

Startled, I admitted that I had been.

She continued that we'd conceived under Cancer, which controls the organs of love, which meant that our signs were all in the ascendency.

"But I lost my baby," I pointed out, suddenly dispirited.

"Because it was begot under an ill moon," she said casually. "Most first conceptions abort or, if they live, die in infancy. The body has to practice; childbirth is no easy thing. However, the next will be different because we'll make it different."

She dug into her box and produced a jug. Rancid, pus-colored slime oozed under its cap.

"What is it?" I asked uneasily, thinking of the entrails and chopped snakes lying in Tib's laboratory.

"An elixir to warm the cold winds in your womb. A secret concoction of lupine, mercury and panax. Where's a cup?"

Before I could stop her, she'd knocked at least three other fine objects to the carpets and handed me a rare gold cup embossed with rams.

I put it aside. "I'll drink it when I sup." And after I'd checked with Bonel.

Tib promptly returned the cup and picked up other objects from the shelf.

"Is that all I should do?"

She returned to my side. "Oh no, dear, we must replace lost blood by churning your spleen."

She produced a second jug, which she told me contained wormwood, gladiola and mother's milk.

"Where did you get mother's milk?"

"You remember Cuxette? She used to work the streets, but discovered that she pumps milk like a fountain, which brings a better price."

Unfortunately, I did remember her—a sluggish dame with rheumy eyes and warts to rival Pudlicott's mormal.

"Though I admit I added a bit from Bique, my she-goat, to make the proportions right. I can't insist too much on this brew."

I told her hastily that I would drink it later, to keep her from seeking another cup.

"Most important, darling," she said solemnly. "You must keep the king from pissing his tallow too soon. Your soil needs to lie fallow before seeding."

I flushed painfully, not seeing how I could control the situation.

She read my thought. "However, a little pinching in the tube matters less than preventing the root from taking. Get yourself a few linen squares, soak them in warm tar and insert them before the act. He'll not notice, may even love the yield."

Her final gift was the jasper stone, to insure conception and happiness.

"For I see that gleam of sorrow."

I thanked her again.

"Mercy!" she cried suddenly. "What a mess this room be! Does your maid never clean? I'll straighten it before I leave, dear."

Quickly she moved around the crowded space, straightened tables, polished and replaced objects, then returned just as briskly to close her case and take her leave.

"Farewell, sweets. I'll check again."

With the same sweating effort, she lugged her heavy box toward the door.

I looked sadly to the window where the sun was lowering —noticed something different. The crystal no longer reflected on the ceiling.

"Tib!" I cried.

"Yes?" She turned a scarred, bland face.

"Why is your case still so heavy? You left the jugs!"

" 'Tis made of oak, heavy as iron."

"Let me see inside it."

There was a long pause.

"If I have to walk to you, I may hurt myself," I warned.

Sheepishly, she came back to my bed and removed one precious object after another, so many that I wondered how I hadn't noticed at once.

"Tib, how could you?" I cried, appalled.

She didn't apologize. "I could because I see all this wealth rotting on the table of an infidel's house while my poor patients starve and go without treatment for lack of cash," she said wrathfully. "Everyone hates the Jews, Alix, for their wealth. It isn't fair!"

"Nor is it fair to blame them and rob them for a situation we put them in," I said with equal heat. "Return everything at once, and I'll watch."

Sulkily, she emptied her case and prepared once again to depart.

As she opened the door, I relented. "Tib, I'll ask Bonel to contribute to your convent. I'm sure he will."

She smiled slyly. "That will be wondrous, dear. Meantime I've taken a wee offering on account."

She flashed the gold box, and slid out of sight.

MY DAY ENDED as it had started, with Bonel. We sipped hot wine together.

"Did you enjoy Muriel?"

"Oh yes, such a twinkly lady. She's an elixir herself." I watched his face to see if Muriel had quoted what I'd said about him, but there was no evidence that she had.

"Her situation here is excellent," he commented. "Her husband adores her and so does everyone else. There was some opposition at first, but her sanguine disposition soon dispelled any fears."

The words were innocent except that an unspoken significance hovered. Bonel, for once, was transparent. Not knowing what to say, I pressed his hand.

KING RICHARD filled the room. Lines and shadows under his eyes had completely disappeared and I could feel energy radiate from every pore. He laughed aloud when he saw me, kissed me with ardor as of yore, laughed again as if in manic disposition.

I glanced enviously at his magnificent purple robes, wished I had something splendid to wear for Christmas, but he immediately told me how becoming my blue cover was against my ivory skin—he would have a blue tunic made for me at once. Finally he sat on the faldstool and took my hand in his. Seen closer, his face had changed almost imperceptibly; the shadow of Marie was still there.

"My darling Alix"—he kissed my hand—"good can emerge from suffering as we all know, especially in this season of Our Savior's birth. I've taken comfort from Him, as I know you have."

"Aye." I watched him.

"In our case, your illness has . . . " His voice choked. "In Chinon, I offered you a contract."

My stomach tightened. I couldn't bear another quarrel.

"Yes, My Lord."

"Which was destroyed in Vaudreuil."

I kept discreetly quiet. *Deo gratias*, my copy of that old document hadn't been in my trunk the night he'd found the banner. I'd left it at my copying desk in Fontevrault, fearing just such an accident.

"Now your Jewish watchdog demands another, but of course I told you that."

I nodded.

He rose and paced nervously, too agitated to sit still. "I didn't sign it because it didn't conform with my own plans. I've known since the beginning . . ." He stopped, gazed at me. "Can't you guess?"

"No." I could barely say the word. What a woodly time to discard me, cruel beyond measure.

"I'm going to marry you, Alix." He rushed back to my side, clasped me in his arms.

His voice rambled on, thick with emotion, about his imperishable love, his need for domestic regularity, the throne, the coming peace and I know not what. I gazed over his shoulder, one strand of his hair cutting my vision like a golden bar, traced the top of a screen in one corner with its pearly dragons breathing fire, waited for him to come to the point of his jape. He sat upright, my vision became whole. His eyes were clear; no lurid creature lurked in their depths.

"Our little Marie changed my life," he concluded. "When I knew that . . ." He couldn't go on.

"I'm sorry," I said anew.

"No, no, don't be sorry. I mean, of course we're both sorry, but without her, Alix, I might never have recognized the depth of my love for you. Or not until it was too late. What do you think I felt as you lay here closer to death than life? Grief for an infant not yet formed? No, I faced existence without you and knew it wasn't possible. It isn't possible."

Now I must respond, but warily.

"I'm overwhelmed, My Lord, but—forgive me—not convinced. You have a queen already and I know that it's not easy to discard a wife. Hasn't King Philip tried for five years now?"

"The seige may be long and difficult," he admitted, "but I'll plan the strategy carefully. I have something the pope wants in exchange."

"The Bishop of Beauvais?"

"No!" he snapped. "Not that hypocrite. Celestine wants me to stop my war with Philip."

"You would give up fighting?"

He grinned wickedly, more like his old self. "After I've gotten France into a position favorable to me. However, I'm close, Alix, I'm close."

More and more: Bonel would have to raise money quickly, for Richard would buy allegiances now to secure his borders; he must finish the string of fortresses with Château Gaillard as their centerpiece, and there were key castles yet to take. Then and only then, he would sue for peace and send a proctor to the pope about his annulment.

"How long will all this take?" I was caught by his excitement.

"Two years."

"Two years?" A lifetime.

"That may be optimistic, but I have both skill and will. Alix!"

His embrace promised friendship, partnership, marriage. Queen Alix. I fought to control laughter—was it from joy or disbelief?

"You'll go to Fontevrault to recuperate—we're coming into Lent in any case—and I'll winter at Les Andelys. You'll join me in mating season."

Warmth flooded my chestspoon as he continued. He soothly loved me as I did him; finally all doubts, suspicions, anxieties about an uncertain future dropped away. For the first time since I'd left Wanthwaite, I was completely happy.

After a long period, we were joined by Queen Eleanor,

who'd waited tactfully for me to absorb the news of my new status.

"Welcome, daughter," she said as she kissed me.

I couldn't yet say "mother," but I held her with my arms. "Thank you for saving my life."

"You hated me at the time," she reminded me.

"No, I didn't hate you, but death attracted me."

She stood, straightened her robes, kissed Richard as well. "You may hate me yet, dear, when I become your task-mistress. Richard wants me to teach you the arts of queen-ship."

Queen? To be like Eleanor? Dazed, I looked from one to the other, thought of my life on the Scottish border, felt a keen pang of regret for its loss, then reached for Richard's hand. The queen reminded him that Hubert Walter of Can-terbury awaited him at the palace, and soon they took their leave.

BONEL BROUGHT ME my supper.

"Bonel, King Richard and I are going to wed!"

I saw blood drain from his face, his scar stand forth, but couldn't stop myself.

"He said that he couldn't bear the thought of losing me and he's going to sue for peace so the pope will give him an annulment and oh, I can't remember everything. *Benedicite!*"

He still didn't answer, so I babbled harder to fill the si-lence: I promised to protect the Jews throughout my life-time, to train my sons to do likewise, to succour the sick . . .

"You don't believe me, do you?" I ended in accusation.

He moved away so rapidly that my tray tumbled, and it took him several heartbeats to right it. Then he called for a maid to clean the carpet and bring more broth.

"Do you?" I repeated.

He sat on his faldstool, head in his hands, then straightened. "I'd like to, since it's what you want."

"Forget what I want—no one asked me—and answer my question."

He stared a long time, his irridescent patch glimmering in firelight, his brown eye dead. "No."

"Do you think he's lying?" Anger welled inside me.

"No. I believe that he wants to marry you. That doesn't surprise me."

"But he'll change his mind?"

"No."

"What then? You don't want me to marry him, do you?"

"I wasn't asked what I wanted," he echoed me sarcastically. "Richard has an impressive imagination when it comes to what he wants, however. He's a visionary or a fool—or worse, a hypocrite without peer. In any case, you mustn't believe him."

"I didn't ask an analysis of his character, just a simple answer."

"This is your answer and it's simple: he dreams, he acts, but where does he succeed? He didn't take the Holy Land, hasn't defeated—and won't defeat—Philip, and he won't marry you. The odds are insuperable."

"How are they insuperable? I won't fight him."

"Others will, and so far they've thwarted him. Remember what I said by the river . . ."

"Aye, that contract. If you knew what trouble you caused between Richard and me, how angry . . ."

"He wasn't angry about the contract! Have you forgotten the banner?"

*Benedicite*, I had. "I'm sorry, Bonel. I never thanked you."

"Where did you get it?"

He watched me keenly, as Richard had.

I described again what I'd witnessed at Vaudreuil, only now I included the Scot and my woodly reaction to him. Bonel became extremely agitated.

"Did the sappers see you?"

"No."

"Could they have known you were in the castle?"

"That's what Richard asked William Marshal. I doubt it,

though I also doubt that my presence would have changed their plans."

"That's not what I meant. You must never be alone, Alix. I'm going to assign Bok again."

I protested that Richard guarded me sufficiently well and would do so even more now that I was to be England's queen, but Bonel was adamant.

"I'd like to press the contract."

"Marriage is a contract—the best!"

"How long does he estimate it will be before your wedding?"

"Two years."

"So I'll get a contract for the interim."

And I lost my temper. This was now my affair and I would brook no interference, did he understand? To ask for a contract under such a circumstance would be a breach of fealty and love. I wouldn't do it, wouldn't permit him to do it. Besides, Bonel's motives were more suspect than Richard's. All that talk about secrets. . . .

"Not talk, damn him!" Bonel shouted. "And I can't tell you the truth, but you'll learn." He rose to go. "Our business isn't finished, Alix; I'm still your guardian. When this hoax is exposed, remember that."

Then so suddenly I couldn't avoid him, he knelt by my bed and kissed me passionately, again and again. I smelled his licorice, felt his dark curls on my cheeks still imprinted with Richard's golden waves, saw his searching look as he pulled back after kissing me.

Then he was gone.

# 21

HE QUEEN AND I TRAVELED WITHOUT EVENT and found Fontevrault as hectic as ever. Lady Faydide still lived, albeit in pain, and Lady Mamile was still euphoric, her excuse now being that I was to wed the king, for which she took complete credit.

"Remember how I insisted that you wear the rose and silver at your first meeting in Mainz? I saw his eyes then, my dear, tranced as a bird with a snake."

An unfortunate comparison. Besides, Lady Mamile could hardly claim to have dressed me as Cupid, my first costume before Richard when I'd descended in the pie at Chinon.

I slipped back into my old routine at the scriptorium, adjusted anew to waking every three hours during the night for prayer, took long solitary walks along the waters where I permitted melancholy tears to flow for my lost Marie, or, when she was free, talked with Hilaria of my coming bliss. Alone with my secret thoughts, I compared my future and past husbands, Richard to Enoch: Richard was cast in the heroic mold, a magnificent warrior-king, whereas Enoch had been more rounded as a man, capable of heroics but not of taking himself too seriously. I could still hear his guffaws ringing in the hills, for he had *de gustibus* for life, amusement at others' pretensions—including mine. I must teach Richard to laugh like that.

My routine differed, however, in that Queen Eleanor had meant it when she'd said she would prepare me for my new role. A formidable instructress, she imparted first a basic knowledge of the outlines of the Angevin empire. It stretched from the Scottish border in the north to the Mediterranean in the south. Angevin authority rested on the monarchy in the islands, but had less power on the continent, where the English kings were merely dukes of Normandy, Brittany, Anjou, Maine, Poitou and Aquitaine with connections to Toulouse and Navarre. As dukes, they did homage to the King of France for their lands, a system established by the great Charlemagne, from whom King Philip was a direct descendant.

"Of course, I'm also descended from Charlemagne," Eleanor noted with asperity, "but my influence doesn't count because I'm not a queen by blood. In fact, my duchy of Aquitaine is larger than either Britain or France, if that were all that mattered. Remember how I asked about your bloodlines?"

Indeed I did.

She then defined the holdings in terms of their inhabitants: the Irish and Welsh were superstitious and anarchic, but also weak, so fortunately they remained irritants rather than threats to political stability; the English were rich, stolid, dependable, a graceless race who stoked the coffers; the Normans comprised the heart of the empire, exemplified by Walter of Coutances, loyal, shrewd, principled; the Bretons were mercurial cousins to the Welsh, except that their geographic position made them dangerous enemies; the dukes of the south were unruly devils who created constant havoc in the realm; neither Henry nor Richard had been able to quell their ebullient rebellions, for they fought for fun and glory instead of gain and changed sides on every Tuesday.

"I'm one of them," she admitted, "and in my youth took perverse pleasure in pricking staid old potentates, but they're formidable foes when you're trying to maintain the peace."

The primary duty of the royal family was to travel constantly over this vast territory in order to establish its own transcendent power and to settle disputes which cropped up everywhere; it kept the peace by legal means preferably, but by arms if necessary. This was as much as Eleanor cared to transmit by words; I must learn the rest in the saddle in the manner she'd learned from her father.

In early March, therefore, we made a short *chevauchée* to Angers in the company of Eleanor's ladies so that I might observe the queen in action and discuss her methods. Our first stop was at a Benedictine monastery devoted to Saint John, Eleanor's favorite apostle because the dying Christ had appointed him to look after His Mother Mary. Yet, when we met Abbot Anselmo and talked with him, I observed her manner to him to be abrasive, even rude.

Keeping my voice low, I remarked on my surprise to Lady Mamile.

"That cotquean," she scorned. "Your Majesty, explain to Lady Alix why you excoriated the good abbot."

The queen turned her green eyes, still baleful from her recent exchange. "He's applying to Rome for lands I recently purchased for Fontevrault. It's pure thievery."

"But how is that possible? If you already bought . . ."

"Our queen supports Fontevrault virtually alone," Florine said, "whereas the Benedictines have all the wealth of Rome at their disposal. It isn't fair when she donates and buys . . ."

"I love Fontevrault," the queen interrupted, "so don't make me a martyr. I'm used to neglect, but not attack."

"Surely the pope appreciates Fontevrault," I commented.

The queen's words were bitter. "He's the general in a vast war, Alix, against all women. Skirmishes in the bedroom are sufficiently odious without taking the battle to convents."

"But what can he possibly have against convents? They do such good."

Certainly Fontevrault was a small Eden.

"The issue is power."

"The issue is always power," Lady Toquerie commented, "and the lines unfairly drawn."

"That's just it," Eleanor agreed. "You've seen the desperate need for ladies of quality to have a refuge from abusive husbands, or from cruel fathers if they cannot wed . . ."

"And there are many more females in the world than men, Alix," Lady Sybelle informed me, then turned puzzled eyes to the queen. "Why does God make so many of us?"

"What do you think the ratio should be?" Lady Faydide asked from her litter. "A hundred men to one woman? Perhaps even we could find lovers."

"Lovers but not husbands," the queen said grimly, "and especially since your rank forbids marrying just any churl. Yet the clergy won't marry, the military—mostly common roughs seeking their fortunes—can't afford to, or get killed before they can. Ladies are excess kits in the litter, good only for drowning. Yet the Church refuses us sanctuary, preferring to pamper catamites in rich living and sloth. Need I say more?"

"No, Your Majesty," I murmured.

The queen carried an elaborate folding altar with her at all times and was strict in her devotions, but I'd noted before that she was bitter toward Rome.

"The problem takes on particular piquancy for a queen," she added significantly, "for the Church's land system is a kingdom within a kingdom, a potentially dangerous situation. As queen, I maintain a delicate balance between wooing Rome's support and putting down its presumptions."

"When will you make your next trip to Rome?" Faydide asked wistfully. "I think I could tolerate a journey into the sun."

"When I go to plea for the Great One's annulment." Eleanor reached and patted my hand.

My heart thirled with pleasure. Someday I might journey to Rome on Richard's behalf.

We were forced to turn off the main Roman road into a narrow lane.

"Mercy!" Florine puffed, battling low branches. "I wish I were a squirrel. I could leap all the way to Bordeaux without touching ground, I trowe."

"With your girth, dear, best wish to be a slug and creep under the wortes," Sybelle said innocently.

The queen still brooded on Rome. "By the time I go," she added as an afterthought, "I hope that the matter of the Bishop of Beauvais has been settled."

"In what manner, Your Majesty?" Surely Beauvais had naught to do with me.

"Pope Celestine clings to his contention that Beauvais was wrongfully taken. He's bound to prove stubborn to any other cause so long as this situation rankles."

A frisson ran along my spine. "You mean that Beauvais's imprisonment could stop the annulment? Our marriage?"

"Don't be apprehensive, child. Surely Philip will ransom the bishop, or Richard will reconsider his capture. After all, Richard knows Celestine's mind."

"But he said he would never release Beauvais," I commented miserably.

"That's true and with good reason. Besides his illegal support of King Philip, Beauvais influenced Henry Hohenstaufen when Richard was a prisoner. The emperor treated Richard as a brother-king until Beauvais intervened; henceforth he was maligned as a lowly, dangerous criminal."

My heart sank: whatever his other virtues, Richard was not a forgiving man.

When we reached Angers, Eleanor stopped our train outside the walls and insisted that we groom ourselves for an entrance.

"Time for the sweet chicanery of rouge!" Lady Mamile cried, pinching my cheek.

"As the queen said, we must compete with Rome however we can," Toquerie added. "They have their great processions of relics; we have our royal pomp."

Trestles were erected in dappled sun and handmaidens brought out the paint pots. Faces were stretched so that jowls and extra chins could be pulled to the side like soft cheese and fastened with gauze bands; foreheads were similarly smoothed by tugging hair upward until the ladies cried "mercy"; delicate brows were then etched on plucked skin, high and arched in perpetual surprise. Magnificent wimples hid the various skin-stretchers, and jewels held wimples firmly in place.

Then the painting began. Egg white mixed with alabaster powder transformed flesh to ivory masks, with daubs of scarlet high on the cheeks to indicate bones; eyes were out-lined and shadowed to match the gowns; lips, which the ladies deliberately pursed and sucked in to make as small as possible, were touched with coralline. The effect was arrest-ing if not exactly alluring, and the ladies didn't so much appear younger as they did ageless. I didn't know what the effect might be on the rabble, but there could be no doubt that the women themselves were entranced by their mirrors; Lady Mamile straightened her arthritic back and smiled to show off her perfect teeth; Lady Faydide thrust out her high bosom, also banded, and hid her gout under a magnificent silk robe; Lady Toquerie tied her waist so tight that her face burned red through her white powder, and she kept her mouth firmly shut to conceal her snags. Of course Queen Eleanor outshone everyone. Her impeccable red tunic was cut to trail the ground when she sat on horseback, and her proud profile was the prow of our wobbly ship.

I, too, was gloriously gowned in a blue and gold tunic to contrast with the queen's scarlet, and she lent me strands of chains and jewels. My place directly behind her made me a mysterious new star in her constellation.

Then jongleurs pranced before us singing and strumming, our trumpets sounded in a merry display, and crowds ap-peared as if conjured. I studied their faces covertly as we ambled past their awed eyes and concluded that the queen was right: they gazed with religious fervor. Indeed, it oc-curred to me that they might well confuse us with a holy procession, for the ladies had the unsettling appearance of mummified saints, lacking only the gilt coffins.

That night we gathered before a fire in Angers Castle,

where King Henry had been born, to discuss our day and our strategies, much as Richard gathered with his knights when he traveled. We too held jeweled goblets of wine, and Faydide and Sybelle idly rolled dice. Heat crackled egg white like old enamel and eyes were dark smudges, but spirits were merry.

"To gain power, you must have a firm understanding of human nature," the queen began.

"Pardon, your Majesty," I interrupted, "but isn't one born with power? Or failing that, marry power?"

The resounding guffaw from the ladies made me blush. What was so comical?

"Of course it helps," the queen said calmly, "but you still have to assert your rights."

"Which means," Florine explained, "that you must recognize toads who toady, snakes who sneak."

"How can you tell?" I asked. "Everyone I know seems very nice."

Again the cackle.

"Restrain your mawkish winds," the queen ordered, "and let me speak. First, human nature. The Church's view is that we are born sinners who must repent in order to save our souls, but you will note that it flaunts its wealth in order to attract the penitents. For all the talk, few are drawn by sackcloth."

"Horse flies and blow flies live on carrion!" Sybelle said absently as she tossed the dice.

The queen winced, but continued. "The Church is correct, however, in calling the rabble sheep, for human society is comparable to a herd of sheep and follows a leader whatever his worth."

I thought of Bonel. "But they can distinguish a good king from a bad."

The raucous hoot persuaded me to stay silent henceforth.

"As you know, the motto of our house is, 'As you are seen, so are you esteemed.' Appearance over substance, paint over Nature. Of course we try to rule well, but we have no illusions as to the source of our power: the mobs demand a good show. They like to believe we are demigods, above common concerns."

"Above common morality," Toquerie finished. "Tyrants succeed where saints fail simply because they grasp this principle."

"I see," I said, though I wondered which of these ladies had ever known a common person intimately, as I knew Tib. "Is 'appearance' how women gain dominance as queens?"

"It's the public tool, one of many, but of course it doesn't prevail in the back corridors of power."

"Where you have to confront the pride of bobtailed black-guards," Lady Mamile finished. "No woman can rule except through a man."

"That's correct," the queen concurred. "I never tried be-cause I had the example of my mother-in-law, Queen Ma-tilda. She was the heiress to England's throne, but she was forced to rule through my husband Henry, despite her val-iant efforts with an army."

I studied the queen earnestly, now too wise to speak, but I wondered if she were suggesting that I should rule through Richard. It was a provocative thought.

Instead I asked, "And this is where courtly love enters? You govern your lord by withholding favors?"

"When you're a queen," Lady Mamile snorted, "you put cutworms in your cut and snip your lord down to size."

Eleanor smiled cynically. "Not so simple, Mammy dear. Again, Alix, you must look to the Church, for it dictates the hierarchy of power for royal families as it does for the com-mon: God the Father is worshipped by man; woman wor-ships man in parallel fashion; animals are at the bottom. However, the Church made one error which we've been quick to exploit."

Cynicism was sliding quickly into heresy and I sipped my wine uneasily. I hoped there were no spies among us. "How, Your Majesty?"

"They gave us Mary. She was once a minor character in the Birth and Passion, but we've tried to change that in our time. Now she's been made a saint and is exalted everywhere."

I so loved Mary that it was inconceivable that she hadn't always been worshipped, but I didn't argue.

The queen leaned forward: "Mary's power comes from her Son; she gives us our example for the attainment of power. Our sons, Alix, learn to love and obey us before they learn to deride; God gives us power over them, and only them."

She took my breath, since she obviously referred to my unborn son. I leaned back on the cushion and thereafter lost the drift as they argued how to separate slanderers and cuckolds from honest men. They spoke of the humors one is born with, the signs of the zodiac, pondered the effect of geography, for there seemed to be national characteristics. Finally, I drifted asleep.

The next day we put on different finery and attended a local fair. This was no accident; that night the queen gave me a list of the mercantile fairs in the kingdom and told me to memorize the dates. They were prime places for exposure.

My final lesson was a small court in a nearby village where the queen sat as judge. The contenders, a butcher and a barber, offered no real evidence except their own vitriol. Therefore, they were a classic case of character determining the outcome. I favored the barber, but the queen ruled for the butcher.

"You watched the eyes, whereas character is revealed in the more mobile organ, the mouth; you heard words, not the tone in which they were delivered—the sweetest of compliments is sometimes intended as a curse; lastly, you must study walks, the set of shoulders, the movement of hands."

She then pointed out that she'd made her decision in the name of King Richard.

"Never forget that you are his extension, his presence

when he's absent. No one person can be everywhere, and he'll depend on you to rule both for him and with him." She hesitated. "I need not say that he loves you dearly, as I believe you do him, but of course there will be differences between you."

I started to demur, but she waved an imperious hand.

"You must never show your differences even to your closest associates, or they will exploit you for their own ends. Most court intrigues begin by the gleeful exaggeration of hairline cracks in the facade. You and Richard are one person in flesh, soul and policy. By necessity you will be frequently apart, but this rule must never waver."

I thought wryly of what I knew of her history with her own husbands.

"Of course, such problems need not concern you for a long time to come."

"Never!" chimed her ladies anxiously.

"I don't understand." They all watched Eleanor with fervid regard.

"They refer to my death," she said pleasantly. "For, of course, I am queen."

And her ladies achieved power not through men, but through their beloved queen, Richard's queen. He had a legitimate queen in Berengaria, but she languished alone in an obscure castle in Maine; soon I would replace Berengaria—but not Eleanor.

Her bright eyes followed my thought. "Your time will come, sweet thing. Meantime I'll continue to instruct you, and you can be privy to my acts."

"Thank you, Your Majesty," I murmured uneasily. Belatedly, I saw that the son she referred to was not my unborn heir, but her own son Richard.

LATE IN MARCH, before Palm Sunday, a runner came from Richard demanding that Eleanor and I travel north at once. He'd had alarming news that the Black Death had devastated portions of Marseilles and other ports on the Mediterranean. He wanted us both far from the southern sea, and inland as well. Lady Mamile, Sybelle and Florine rode with us to stay with the queen in Rouen.

I had only one day in the capital, no time to contact Bonel or Tib. Bok, Hamo and three knights from Eleanor's retinue rode with me to join Richard in Les Andelys the following morning. As we crossed the bridge outside the city gates, we were joined by three new knights.

"Lady Alix of Wanthwaite?" One of them addressed me courteously.

"Aye."

"My name is Sir George. King Richard sent me and my companions to escort you safely to Les Andelys."

I thanked him most graciously.

"Are these your knights?" He eyed the men from the queen.

When I explained, he said that their presence wouldn't be necessary; I dismissed them, but naturally kept Bok and Hamo.

I rode in a daze of delight; I would soon see Richard. After an hour or two, Bok reached for my arm and said something in his native argot.

"Speak French," I ordered.

His small eyes slid significantly to our escort and I knew he didn't want them to understand.

"Then more slowly." After all this time, I grasped most that he said, for his language was a dialect rather than a separate tongue.

"The sun is in the wrong place."

I glanced upward: it was at my left shoulder. We were traveling due north, and Les Andelys lay to the east. Hamo had noticed the direction as well, I saw by his worried face. *Benedicite*. Sir George hadn't spoken a word after his first greeting and the other two knights were equally taciturn. Now that I looked at them closely, I realized I'd not seen them before. Richard would never send complete strangers. My cod turned to ice.

"Sir George!" I called. "I need to stop a moment."

"Of course."

I slid off Sea Mew; Bok and Hamo also dismounted as if to relieve themselves. The knights courteously averted their eyes. I deliberately sought a bush as far distant as I dared go. Hamo stood on the other side.

"We think you're being abducted, Alix."

"Aye. What can we do?"

"Go as slowly as possible; Queen Eleanor's knights may alert them in Rouen."

I dallied until Sir George had called three times. When I emerged, I smiled prettily. "I'm so sorry; I should never have eaten shrimp in this season."

Within half an hour, I begged to stop again, and again. Sir George looked suspicious, but didn't challenge me. At Haute Tierce, I ate nothing, then gripped my stomach and doubled as if in pain to give Hamo and Bok opportunity to steal what weapons they could. We'd decided to fight rather than go much further. Bok managed to relieve one saddle of its battle-axe, but the odds were formidable against us. I put my father's dagger into my belt. When we started again, Bok told me he'd been bending branches and moving stones, when possible, to leave a trail.

We heard a church bell ring Nones in the distance, our signal to each other to flee. Without warning, Hamo and Bok struck the knights' steeds with stones and whips and shouted "Arras!" Instant havoc—one horse running away and curses from the knights! Then Bok spurred his own horse forward. A knight chased him while I whirled Sea Mew in the opposite direction. Sir George came after me as soon as he controlled his steed, but I had the lead and took him on a twisting chase. Sea Mew feinted and turned, dashed up hillocks, stopped on a pebble and reversed direc-tions. I screamed as loud as I could.

"Help! Help!"

I would surely have been caught except that there was an answering shout. Sir George stopped, cried to his men.

"Richard!"

The name was enough—the knights fled for their lives.

Around the next curve, I rode headlong into a company of knights led by Richard and Bonel.

"To the side, Alix!" Richard shouted.

Pulling his visor into place, he spurred his great charger and hurled past me, followed by a cloud of dust and scarlet shields.

Bonel reared to a stop and helped me dismount. "Are you harmed?"

"No! *Benedicite*, Bonel, who were they?"

He hesitated. "King Philip's men, no doubt."

"How did you find me? The king . . ."

"Was on his way to meet you. In my position, I keep a network of informants and. . . . My spies at the gate told me they'd seen the exchange of knights. I rode with the palace guard when we met Richard and . . ."

The king and his company rounded the bend on their way back. Richard pulled beside us, hurled his helmet to the brush and dropped to the ground in a clatter of arms. I was crushed against steel and hot lips.

"Alix, God help me, if anything had happened . . ."

"It didn't—I'm all right," I managed to gasp. "Did you catch them?"

"I could have, except that I wanted . . ." He pulled me still closer, stood silently with his head bent over mine.

"Did you find out who they were?"

"No. Did you?" He pulled away, searched my eyes.

"Bonel says King Philip's men."

"Then we'll take his word." He smiled, touched my face. "Sure you're not harmed? Come, sit with me."

He lifted me lightly to his horse and mounted behind me.

He kissed me again before we started, held me so close

that I felt I was inside his skin, talked incessantly into my ear as we meandered happily back to Rouen. I forgot the threat to my life, forgot everything except the mix of mail and hard flesh enclosing me.

A long time later, he lifted me down inside the courtyard, and I was face to face with Bonel. His suave mask had slipped to expose raw jealousy.

"Bonel, I haven't thanked you . . ."

He whirled and galloped back to Jews Street.

Guilt shadowed my joy briefly, and I fought an impulse to follow him. He would never understand that I cared for him, when it was plain that the king and I loved with equal passion. Then Richard took me to his bed, the first time since my fall on the rock, and I forgot Bonel.

THE CHANGE at Les Andelys was awesome. The granite behemoth that had formerly been an austere marvel of Nature was being chipped and altered to a new conformation. From a distance, we watched tiny men scurry up and down ropes, perch perilously on ladders, thousands of them scrambling over the inert body, like ants atop a dead destrier. As we came closer, we were assaulted by the ring of anvils, explosions from tunneled cliffs, the thunder of raining stones. Closer still, a fine white dust covered our clothes and saddles, went up our noses. I groped for a shawl to tie over my face.

We pushed our way through throngs of sneezing, spitting churls who hacked, sawed, wheeled, threw, heaved in a dense cloud of chalky powder. Finally we reached a long swaying bridge that took us to the island, and I glimpsed the octagonal outlines of the house Richard had built for us, a miniature fortress, slightly reminiscent of Orford Castle on the Channel.

Immediately I asked Richard to take me onto the rock and explain his plan. Flushing with pleasure at my interest, he quickly agreed. We met Sawale, the engineer, as we left the house. He greeted me warmly and asked especially about my health; I'd forgotten that he'd been with us on the day of my near-fatal fall. He sought the king because one of his masons had been picked off by an arrow as he'd dangled on the cliff's face.

"God damn Philip!" Richard swore. "Did you see the man who did it?"

"The same one as before; he didn't look French."

The king called for his shield-bearers to escort us across a series of bridges, and walking behind our moving wall, we left the island to the castle-side of the Seine, across what Richard called the Tête de Pont. Instead of reaching the wild shore I remembered just a few months ago, we were in an embryonic town with streets and low structures, surrounded by water off the Seine; Richard's creation, it was named Petit Andelys. The large town, Grand Andelys, was at the end of an inlet, fortified and ditched, on the opposite side of the river. Between them, the towns formed the primary land defense, leaving only a promontory of land on the south by which to approach the castle.

What I saw thereafter was a jumble of unrelated activities, as if grown children were set loose in a stone quarry, but what I heard from Richard's lucid description was a breathtaking design emerging from chaos. The basic castle would be elliptical in shape, with its main tower on the apex of a jutting triangle with walls ten feet thick. Before an invader could approach the curtain wall, however, he must scale seventeen concentric semicircles of bastions set only two feet apart. When we reached the first courtyard, Richard held me tight as I leaned over vast black cellars being excavated on piers of solid rock to be lit by lancets; most of these would be used for storage, but one was to house prisoners.

"There seems to be someone there already," I said. "Or is it a workman?"

"No, that's the Bishop of Beauvais."

"Shackled to a rock?" I looked up, startled.

"Exactly the same treatment he decreed for me. In fact, I'm more generous. Twice a day, I unlock his irons, permit him to walk and do his functions."

"But . . ."

"He's about to get company," Richard continued. "As you just heard, France is harrying my masons unmercifully and we've captured valuable knights in reprisal; they can be Beauvais's cellmates."

My mind was racing, but I didn't say more about the bishop.

"I'm surprised that King Philip can get close enough to harm you."

"That coward!" Richard pointed to a row of cliffs to the north. "He's found a few suicidal archers to operate from there. However, I've sent for three thousand Welshmen to guard the workers, which will give us one soldier per man."

At the top of the hill, the layout emerged in clear outlines. Here two other engineers, Robert, son of Hermer, and Matthew, son of Enard, became our guides. They were supervising a ditch being dug on the vulnerable south side of the castle, only this was no ordinary ditch. Working in solid rock, the sappers had dug forty feet down along perpendicular walls. On the river side, Robert pointed out that the natural cliff had been engineered so that arrows or stone balls from above would ricochet with double force as they fell. Furthermore, there were no dead spots, that is, places not accessible to our missiles when the enemy approached below.

Our attention was deflected when the body of the dead mason was heaved up the cliff's side in a basket. I looked away, but Richard knelt and pulled out the arrow.

"Same markings as the other," he said tersely, "and a perfect shot, incredible from a crossbow at that distance. I'll reward the man who gets that murderous bastard."

It took three hours to cover all the area under construction, and that didn't include smaller fortifications along the

Seine from Vernon to Gisors, a project which compensated for Richard's disastrous decision to give up the Vexin or, as he pointed out, put him in an excellent position to regain the Vexin.

"I thought the purpose was to seek peace," I protested.

"Of course. That's what I meant."

At that moment I stepped backward and stumbled on a large rock, the one I'd been sitting on when my bleeding commenced. I felt myself grow faint, felt Richard's arms about me as we clung together in a wave of fresh grief.

DURING THE YEAR that followed, I grew used to living inside a kettledrum and softened the interior of my little fortress as best as I could. It was easier than I thought, for I was already a queen in my power to demand. If I told Richard I wanted brass boat-shaped lamps, a runner was sent to Rouen to secure them; if I craved fresh fruit, another was dispatched to the south. Soon I sent my own runners, without the king as intermediary. I grew toty with power and took delight in testing my limits; the boundary, I discovered, was inside my own domicile. If I wanted to influence policy, I must approach the king crabwise, and I had much to learn in the skills of indirection.

As for Château Gaillard, progress showed every single day. The Saracens Richard had brought back from the Crusade, plus the English engineers, gave skilled impetus to the project and gradually the lumpish mass took on the shape originating in Richard's fiery imagination. Sawale told me that the king was a genius, that posterity would judge him so on the basis of this single work. Richard himself was surprisingly modest; he gave credit for his innovations to the Syrians, though he admitted that he'd put them in new combinations and introduced them to Europe.

The ferocity of the French attacks, however, grew as well. We were all relieved when the Welsh arrived, looking like tree dwellers with pieces of shaggy bark attached to their crude hides, and hair twined with leaves. They spoke the Celtic tongue, told stories and recited poems, sang songs of bird flights and sea monsters when they weren't fighting either against the French or among themselves. The workers disliked them intensely, but I enjoyed their gaiety. They reminded me of home.

As summer waxed hot, ominous rumors came of the encroaching Black Death, a particularly hideous way to die with blood-engorged buboes oozing in the neck, armpit and groin; vomiting, fevers, severe pain and an odor so foul that the victim finally welcomed death.

On a particularly hot afternoon, I carried a flask of cooled wine up the rock to Richard. Halfway up, I rested where the dungeons had been hewn and was arrested by a familiar voice.

"Wormwood! After a thousand years the dragon that is old serpent and Satan will be loosed on the world, and evil shall befall us!"

I walked to where a circle of workmen were crouched, hypnotized by the old knight I'd seen in Poitiers.

"The sign of perdition is in the Black Death, born in the mouth of the unholy Jews as frogs come from the jaws of the serpent. The Holy Spirit prophesied that a king would fall into evil ways and that king is France."

One workman applauded until fiery eyes stopped him.

"He expelled the Jews, but now he lets them return and verily you see his reward. They carry the foul pestilence from Hell . . ."

"Get out of here!" I shouted. "How dare you speak such vicious words! Go now, before . . ."

He stepped close, his iron finger pointing. "And the second king is made drunk with the wine of fornication. You ride the scarlet beast with seven heads and ten horns, and verily I say . . ."

But we never learned what he was going to say, for Richard smote him from behind and he fell in a swoon.

I waxed to a frenzy. "He's the same one I told you of—in Poitiers." I wept uncontrollably. "I'm afraid . . ."

Richard held me close, spoke over my head.

"Send him away."

I closed my eyes.

When I opened them again, the mad knight was gone as well as his audience of cheering workers. But not his words: they seemed to echo in the rocks.

"What's this?" Richard lifted my chin. "Your teeth are chattering. You must be the only person in Normandy who isn't melting with the heat."

"I'm so frightened," I managed to say.

"Of a lunatick? Come now, where's my brave girl who hurled herself into a pool to save Bonel? Who rode to the Crusade when only a child?" He smiled tenderly.

"Aye, but those were real problems. This is . . . uncanny."

"Not at all. The man is deranged, probably took a blow to the head in battle, or picked up a brain sickness in the Holy Land."

"Bonel says that fanatics aren't deranged," I contradicted stubbornly. "The man is a religious zealot, and dangerous."

"I bow to Bonel's superior wisdom," the king said lightly, "but only in this matter. I know what's best for you, and I say you should come back to the rock with me and we'll share the wine you carry."

Gratefully I walked upward on the cobble ramp, now graded for horses to carry heavy burdens, through a series of gates and walls to the pinnacle. Château Gaillard was a finished fort except for the installation of various weapons. The only construction remaining was the long wall along the Seine to connect the subsidiary forts and towers.

"You sit here, and I'll be back."

Richard lowered me beside the rock where I'd fallen, which we'd left as a shrine to our lost Marie. I was enclosed by high walls but they were based lower on the hill, so I was cooled by a breeze, which always blew at this height. My inner quaking ceased, though I was left with a melancholy residual. Jews and foul pestilence . . . wine of fornication. I looked at the jug of wine I carried in a wicker basket. I knew that Richard was probably right to dismiss the incident, but in ancient times God had sent prophets warning of man's sins. Before the flood, for example, and I thought of the empty caves in the Dordogne, of the rushing rivers.

So many "mad" men now wandered the countryside, all with the same message, that the end of the world was at hand. Next year was the last of this century, and perhaps the Antichrist would appear. Oh, I recalled that Bishop Hugh had said it meant naught, that no one should worry until the year 2000. But suppose he were wrong?

Richard returned and sat beside me, then opened the wine.

"You first."

Under his insistent gaze, I swallowed the sweet Bordeaux, then watched as he drank deeply.

"Do you think the end of the world is coming, Richard?"

"Unquestionably," he replied cheerfully, "but not in our lifetimes."

Except that the end of our own lives would be the end of the world in a way.

"It's hard to believe that all of this could disappear," I said slowly.

"You mean Château Gaillard? By God, I've shaped the walls so cunningly that they would hold if made of butter."

"They will hold so long as you're here to defend them," I said loyally.

"And I'll always be here." He bent and kissed me lightly.

Richard was a practical man, not given to eerie ruminations, a quality I'd noted before but never fully appreciated. He now took my hand and insisted I come to the river side of the castle to view a remarkable sunset. We stood at a

crenellation and looked out on the long sloping plain to the
west, which was gradually disappearing in a dense, rising
mist. Above, the sky was startlingly transparent, as if all its
clouds and vapors had settled on the earth. Gradually the
air turned an intense carnation red and the mists reflected a
roseate turbulence, as if they rose from a cauldron.

"It looks like Heaven, doesn't it?" Richard commented
enthusiastically.

I agreed, though I'd thought just the opposite, that it
looked like Hell. I must be still in the grip of the mad knight.

"Would you like to sleep up here?" he asked. "It will be
cooler."

"Oh, yes, and an adventure!" Anything to avoid passing
the spot below with its echoing rocks.

Richard brought forth a cache of cheese and crusts he kept
in the grain cellar of the tower, which with the wine made a
fine supper. We watched the sunset shade from scarlet to
peach, to clear green, to violet, when the evening star appeared.

"Venus, the star of love," Richard said.

We found a patch of clean grass for our bed.

"We're on the deck of a ship made of rock," Richard remarked, "floating through unknown mists."

"Floating through the stars," I amended. "See how they
move."

Never had I seen so many stars, small, large, red, blue,
white, yellow, even green, pulsing or steady, occasionally
shooting in long tails.

"What are the stars, Richard? Are they God's sheep, as
I've heard?"

"Or bits of hard crystal as the Arab astronomers claim?
Or genies to guide each of us here below? Archbishop Walter says that they're the shining souls of the dead, still alive
and awaiting the Second Coming, when they will assume
their bodies once again. I agree with him."

"Aye," I breathed, much pleased at the revelation, for it

made the Second Coming less ominous, more an occasion for rejoicing. The stars seemed so close, so friendly, but also so numerous. I could never find my mother, father, Enoch, baby Marie or Dame Margery in that vast horde of souls.

"Do you feel better?" Richard asked, the familiar thickness of love in his voice.

For answer, I put my arms around his neck, raised my lips eagerly.

It seemed no time before the busy sun had made its round and rose confidently in the east. Reluctantly, Richard and I prepared to descend.

"You took me on a wonderful journey," he said smiling.

"No, you took me," I insisted. "You're the captain of our fortress ship, and I'll never be afraid again."

He kissed me gently, put his fingers to my eyes.

"Glistening dew, your eyes. I'll never see morning without thinking of you."

And your eyes are full of stars, I thought; you are my firmament, my heaven, my very existence for all time.

And I forgot the mad knight.


BUT NOT FOR LONG.

Richard sent two thousand Welsh to check the border along the fortifications before he sent workmen to begin the walls. On the evening they were expected back, a single badly wounded drummer crawled into camp. All two thousand had been trapped in the Vale of Andelys and brutally massacred. No cry for mercy had been heeded; the French had hacked and stabbed with unparalleled viciousness.

Our entire work force was stunned. Whatever the men had thought formerly of the Welsh, they now wept and wailed in rage.

All except Richard.

The next day we assembled on the top of the rock as Richard had three French prisoners dragged from the dungeon. Trumpets blasted a war charge to get the enemy's attention. When Richard saw the French gather on the opposite cliff, he pushed the prisoners to their death. We heard the inhuman screams, the ricochet of bodies against the cunning angle of rock, then silence.

The following morning Mercadier blinded fifteen more and sent them back to the French camp.

"It doesn't even the score," Richard told me grimly, "but it's all I can do."

It wasn't all the French could do, however.

Unfortunately I was again on the rock when they retaliated.

"Your Majesty, quick!" a mason shouted.

Richard leaped up a series of stone steps that connected the towers. As the mason pointed, we watched a man bring forth three Englishmen on the French side.

"Is it King Philip?" I asked.

"No. Get back—out of sight!" He pushed me toward a stair.

No, of course it wasn't. Kilts blew around the man's knees; he was a Scot, probably the same Scot I'd seen at Vaudreuil, though he was too far away to tell. He shook his fist at us, then deliberately pushed three prisoners off their cliff, the cries reaching us uncannily after the bodies were stilled. Richard shouted every curse ever invented at the small distant figure, knowing well he couldn't hear. The Scot—if he was a Scot—didn't move.

I watched him intently. *Deus juva me*, he was a monster for what he'd done, but he stirred memory. Then he stopped moving, stood with his legs spread, raised a fist—no, a hand, as if in greeting.

"Alix, didn't I tell you to go to the stair? I don't want you hurt."

"Aye, I'm going."

I took one last look; no, he wasn't staring at me, couldn't be. He was watching the king.

"Who was the man who pushed them?" I asked the king later.

"I think he's called Cadoc," he replied tersely.

"Where's he from?"

"Straight from hell! He ambushed the Welsh."

I didn't blame Richard for being angry; I would be too. And I was relieved to hear the enemy named. I shouldn't care if he were Scottish, if he were the Scot I'd seen at Vaudreuil in fact, but I was still relieved.

Fifteen blinded Normans arrived the next day, led by a woman. It began to rain, and the workmen said the drops were blood.

Richard's wrath made him redouble his pressure on the workmen who now labored by torchlight to extend the days, but we faced a new problem. The men took pride in their creation and loved their king, but they weren't willing to work for nothing and Richard had run out of money; in fact, it was difficult to get food from the countryside on credit. I didn't know the cost of the castle nor did I ask, but I knew it was greater than all other castles combined. I wondered if Bonel were collecting and borrowing to finance it.

Richard wasn't deterred, however. He sent Hubert Walter, Justiciar of England as well as Archbishop of Canterbury, a demand that all lords and bishops of England send three hundred men at their own expense to work for one year or until they were killed or crippled; if they refused, Walter was to seize their lands. Hamo told me that a knight had told him that such an order had never before been given by any king; Richard could expect strong resistance.

Strong and swift. He had word almost at once that the bishops of Lincoln and Salisbury refused to obey, and on the heels of the message came Bishop Hugh of Lincoln in person. When he arrived, we were in chapel.

The intrepid bishop followed us there. Richard, sitting beside me at the back of the apse, kept his eyes stonily ahead as the choir chanted: *Ave, inclyte praesul Christi, flos pulcherime!* The words, I thought, were prophetic: Hail, illustrious pontiff of Christ, flower of spiritual beauty.

Hugh, a lanky, sweet-faced man with deep-set eyes and a white beard, made obeisance at Richard's feet, but the king looked at me.

"My Lord," Hugh asked quietly, "won't you give me the kiss of peace?"

Richard kept his face averted.

The bishop took hold of Richard's mantle and shook it. "I've made a long journey; I have a right to the kiss."

Richard gazed at him coldly. "No, you refused my order to send men; you don't deserve it."

"Yes, I do." Bishop Hugh shook Richard til and fro like a naughty boy until the king began to laugh, as I did, too.

Then Bishop Hugh joined Richard at the altar where they both knelt with their eyes fixed to the ground during the *Agnus Dei*. When Richard received the *pax brede*, the tablet to transmit the kiss of peace, instead of passing it to Bishop Hugh, he leaned forward and kissed him directly upon the cheek.

My eyes filled. Was this my influence? Was Richard becoming more tractable?

After Mass, we walked together to the king's chambers, where Bishop Hugh presented his objections to the king's orders. He then pointed out that, since Richard was born in Oxford, he was in Hugh's diocese. What was the state of his conscience? Rumor had it that the king refused communion or the confessional.

"My conscience is clear," Richard said firmly, if a little less warmly, "except that I hate my enemies."

Hugh's brown eyes bored from under bushy brows. "You'll overcome your enemies when you're at peace with yourself. Your only foe is sin."

Richard stared back with equal intensity. "To what sin do you refer?"

"Keeping the Bishop of Beauvais in unlawful imprisonment," Hugh replied.

"Thank you for reminding me," Richard replied coldly.

"I fear that the dungeon here may be insecure; I'll increase his chains."

Hugh was undaunted. "And you continue your infidelity to your wife."

I gasped in dismay and Richard's face turned ashen.

"You will apologize to Lady Alix at once if you don't care to join Beauvais in his dungeon."

"Threaten me as you like, Your Majesty; you can't change the truth of what I say."

"You don't know the truth! I have never cohabited with Berengaria and seek an annulment to our union which is no union," Richard answered evenly. "Lady Alix is now and will be forever more my true wife."

"If you want the pope to respect you in this matter, I advise that you free Beauvais forthwith; you can't commit a crime against God and expect friendship from the King of Kings."

"Beauvais loaded me with so much iron when I was a prisoner in Germany that I couldn't move. I'm more Christian than he is by far. And I shall wed Lady Alix, despite your opinion."

Hugh didn't deign to look at me. "I'll pray for your soul."

Richard then gave the bishop permission to go in God's name, for which, if he'd known Richard better, he should have said a *Te Deum*.

I was grateful for Richard's bold assertion of my position, grateful that he'd shown the bishop clemency, but I was also disturbed. Queen Eleanor's thoughts on Beauvais and Bonel's dire opinions began to haunt me. Beauvais was my serpent in Paradise.

A week later, Richard and Mercadier rode out to survey the vale where the Welsh had been massacred. When they returned, we discovered that the Bishop of Beauvais had escaped.

# 22

THE KING'S WRATH BROUGHT FORTH A CLAMOR and yowl of proclaimed innocence that rang through the whole Vale of Andelys. No one had witnessed the escape—no one had helped. How could he suspect anyone's loyalty?

Robert, who held the only keys except Richard's, wept as he jangled the key at his waist to prove it had never left him. Then Richard's priest, Father Milo, thought to look for the king's key. When we searched in the chest where he kept it, it was gone.

"How is that possible?" the king cried, incredulous. "How could anyone enter my house unseen?"

The guards wailed that they'd been on their posts all day and seen no one pass. I'd taken my accustomed nap after dinner and heard no one, though the cask was in the chamber next to mine. Yet the irrefutable fact remained that the Bishop of Beauvais was gone.

Richard grasped my arms. "Think, Alix; you must have seen the thief unaware, perhaps a washerwoman or strange priest. Try to recall."

"The laundry was returned by two or three women. I didn't notice them in particular."

"Or a noise while you slept?"

"I dozed soundly, My Lord, for two hours," I admitted. "Because . . ."

"Never mind." He pulled me roughly to his embrace. "Forget the bishop. But I hate to think that anyone could get that close to you."

To everyone's surprise, he then dropped the search for

the culprit. He delivered a mild lecture to the guards to be vigilant henceforth, asked Robert to have a second key made to replace the lost one, and dismissed everyone.

That night as we lay together, he told me why.

"I know who did it and I can't punish her," he said quietly. "She thought only of my good."

My heart literally stopped beating. Did he think I'd done the deed?

"My mother has been urging me for months to reconsider my position."

My poor organ throbbed once more. I marveled at the queen's boldness as well as her ingenuity. I also silently thanked her.

"But how could she do it, My Lord?"

He laughed indulgently. "You don't know the queen. She probably has a spy right here in our bedchamber."

"Still, I feel guilty," I said honestly.

"Why, Tickle-Bones? What could you have done?"

"Guilty for sleeping so soundly. I doze round the clock these days, much as before when . . ."

Now his heart bounded.

". . . I was with child."

He sat upright; moonlight caught the lower part of his face, his spreading grin. "God's feet, why didn't you tell me at once?"

"This is at once; I've known only a few days."

"Alix—my God." He leaned to kiss me. When? Was I sure? His voice choked. *God's feet*, he repeated again and again, for once inarticulate.

"How do you feel? I couldn't bear it if . . ."

"Never better," I assured him. "Hungry, sleepy, contented as a cow."

"Now we must have peace. I want time with my son."

The Bishop of Beauvais was forgotten.

DESPITE HUGH OF LINCOLN'S WARNINGS and Bonel's jaundiced view, events suddenly moved in Richard's favor very rapidly, as if our unborn child turned Fortune's Wheel. The first two were acts of God.

Henry Hohenstaufen became ill while fighting in Sicily and knew himself close to death. He begged Pope Celestine to lift his excommunication so that he might die in peace; the pope agreed to do so only if Henry won Richard's forgiveness for attacking a Crusading king. Henry asked and promised to return all the silver England had sent as ransom money, if dear Richard could see in his heart to have mercy. At the prospect of so much silver, Richard's heart readily absolved Henry of his sin. It was an unexpected coup for the king's treasury and made his push for peace more possible—and thence his push for an annulment.

Henry's death also benefitted Richard insofar as his favorite nephew, Otto, now became Emperor of the Holy Roman Empire, which in effect secured all of northern Europe for Richard. Peace was another step closer.

The second act of God was of even greater import: Pope Celestine himself soon followed Henry to his grave and with him went animosities that had been built over the years. Pope Innocent III quickly took his place, and every king in Europe prepared a proctor to seek the new pontiff's favor, foremost among them Richard. Accompanying the proctor would be Eleanor, going to plead our cause.

The third event was completely Richard's doing. He and Mercadier accompanied by a small force went to reconnoiter and came unexpectedly upon King Philip and five hundred men. Although Richard was outnumbered two to one, his trained eye told him he could win, and he swooped down like a hungry lion onto his prey, routed the French and chased Philip all the way to Gisors. In his haste, the French king tumbled from his horse and would have been captured except that one of his own knights saved him.

Richard was euphoric: it was a "second Jaffa," and if the caprice of Dame Fortune hadn't raised the dust, he would have captured the whole army.

Now he was ready to sign a truce.

✤          ✤          ✤

WE RODE TO Vernon to meet with King Philip to make the peace. The French king appeared on the far side of the river on his famous old war-horse, Morel, Philip's favorite because he was easy to ride. Even from here Philip offered an astonishing contrast to Richard, and it was hard to fathom why he was such a formidable foe. Dirty and unkempt, squat and stooped, his hair matted, one eye gone milky, notoriously cowardly, how could he match the greatest warrior-king of our time or any other? Richard himself had posed the question and answered it as well: sly, treacherous, niggardly Philip might be, but he lived for one purpose alone, to extend France's borders, and he wasn't inhibited by chivalry in his pursuit. It's hard to win at a game where your opponent refuses to abide by the rules of warfare.

Philip came to the river's edge while Richard entered a small boat. An oarsman took him to the exact center of the Seine, no farther, and dropped anchor. Now the two kings could hear to parley.

The courtesies were brief, the bickering long. I studied the knights behind Philip, knowing I sought the Scot. I found him, but he was in the second row, partially covered by two knights in front of him, his face a blur under his tall fur hat with horns. He was a MacPherson, no doubt, and by his age he must have known Enoch. Had he fought with him on that last battle in the Orkneys? I wished I could talk with him. I continued to look until again I had the uneasy feeling, almost uncanny, that he was watching me with equal concentration. I nudged Sea Mew behind the horse next to me, out of view.

Negotiations bogged on the issue of Gisors Castle, once the stronghold of King Henry and later Richard, now in Philip's hands. Finally it was settled by a marriage contract between Philip's son Louis, the same who'd been promised before to Eleanor of Brittany, and Richard's niece, young Blanche of Castille; Philip would bequeath it to them as a wedding present.

Richard was victorious. He'd won all the castles he'd lost while on Crusade, controlled the Vexin if he didn't own it, had made strong alliances on all sides of Philip. There remained only two things to do: to pay for his forts, his army, his alliances, which depended on gifts, and to get his annulment.

We left Château Gaillard to ride to Chinon, there to take stock of the depleted treasury. When we arrived, the Lenten season was upon us and Richard told me that immediately after Lent his mother would ride to Rome.

Bonel met us in Chinon just as Richard had learned the full extent of his financial crisis. Henry Hohenstaufen's restoration of the ransom had proved illusory, and there wasn't a penny in the coffer. Bonel was blunt: both poor men and rich in England were in revolt, feeling they'd been drained thrice for Richard's exploits. Normans likewise were close to insurrection.

"You must face the facts, Your Majesty. Dismiss your army, retrench your spending until we can replenish the coffers."

"Philip has already broken the truce four times since Vernon," Richard commented wryly, "and you want me to dismiss my army? You ask the impossible."

"I ask nothing," Bonel retorted, "except that you be realistic."

*Benedicite*, he spoke to Richard as he did to me, as if we were dreaming children.

"Very well." Richard jumped from the stone bench, for we met in the garden. "I hereby revoke the great seal of England. I'll design another with the three lions of my shield on one side, myself on my horse on the other. That will automatically cancel all treaties and gifts made by the old seal and I can sell offices once more."

Bonel argued hotly against the unfairness of such a trick, but to no avail, for the king pointed out that all the officers had grown fat on their collections and could well afford to share. Furthermore, he would now permit tournaments in England, another rich source of revenue.

On the third day, Bonel and I managed to be alone while Richard rode to visit Eleanor in Fontevrault.

"When are you expecting?" he asked quietly.

"How can you tell?" I looked down at my tunic, only slightly rounded.

"By your face."

"September or October, I'm not sure." I bit my lips with happiness, tried to contain my smile.

"And the queen goes soon to Rome?"

"Aye, after Easter."

He stared steadily. I gazed back, smiled in spite of myself.

"And you still think the king will ask for an annulment?"

My smile faded, and I turned away, vexed. "If you're going to start on the king's intentions again, please leave me. I know him better than anyone."

He touched my arm, pulled me around until I faced him.

"Of course you do, Alix. You've gone far beyond my ability to sway you on that issue. However . . ." He groped inside his robes. "However, I admit that I'm still worried, call it my weakness. Therefore I want you to take this to protect yourself, no matter what happens."

He presented a small box.

"Wait. Before I open it, I have something for you as well. I'll be right back."

When I returned, I gave him a thin square wrapped in a scarf.

"Open yours first," I begged, smiling again.

He unfolded the scarf: inside was a thin volume I'd been laboring over for years at Fontevrault.

"I made it myself," I explained. "The copy is clean, but I wish I were better at illumination."

He opened to the first page as I watched anxiously.

" 'In the Year of Creation, 4952, in the city of Aborak, I, Bonel, lived with my father Benedict, my brother Isaac, my mother and sisters . . .' " He looked up at me, his brown eye bright with tears. "Alix . . ."

"You said that the *Memorbuchs* of Germany had saved lives, and you knew that books helped . . ."

He put his arms around me, and we stood together, quiet and close, under the spring froth of trees along the Vienne River.

"I love you, Alix," he whispered.

He stepped back, his fingers against his lips, then he wiped his eye.

"I love you too," I said.

"As well as Richard?"

I shook my head hopelessly. "And Enoch. I love all of you, can't seem to fall out of love."

"Then you should learn." He looked at his book again. "It's the best gift I've ever had or will have. I'm afraid mine's poor beside it, but go on."

I broke the wax on the box and pulled it open. On a black velvet bed lay Bonel's staring Christian Eye.

"It's . . . it's . . ." I couldn't go on. Obviously just an enamel artifact, albeit cunningly devised, the eye still evoked the sorcerer's skill, whether Evil Eye or Second Sight. It also evoked Bonel himself as I'd first seen him.

"I knew you wouldn't understand," he said quickly, "but remember that I told you that the eye could do miracles."

"Aye, see evil in the human heart." Was this a subtle reminder that Richard's heart might be evil? I put it in my drafsack.

"It did that for me, yes, but it will perform for you according to your need. Now listen to me, Alix, and listen well: if ever you're in dire difficulties—and they must be dire—you're to press this eye hard. Do you understand? Press it and say 'Help me, Bonel' until the eye responds, which it will."

I nodded. "You mean it's a talisman."

"More, it's magic."

I nodded again. "I do thank you. It's—it's very pretty."

He laughed aloud. "There speaks Alix of Wanthwaite, who claimed my scar didn't show. Just do as I say."

When we returned to the castle, Richard awaited us with his own miraculous news: a Gallo-Roman treasure of great worth had been found on the lands of the Duke of Limoges, at a small castle called Chalus. Limoges had offered half to Richard as his overlord, but Richard was claiming the whole thing. If he were right in his estimate, the treasure would solve his financial problems once and for all.

"Mercadier and I are riding at once to take it."

"May I go with you?" I asked.

"No," Bonel answered sharply.

Richard looked at him quizzically. "Of course you may, Alix. There will be no fighting to speak of and I want you with me at all times, especially now."

Bonel's scar was red against his pallor, but he remained prudently silent.

APRIL IN THE SOUTH is a season when new life springs everywhere. I listened to busy birds as they built nests, noted tiny wildflowers along the verge of our track, felt the moth wings beat below my own heart. Richard shared my bliss as he held my hand and sang softly the troubadour airs of his youth.

The instant we saw the castle of Chalus, we both knew that we had too great an army with us for the task. Hardly more than a walled house, Chalus contained a few peasants and burghers from the tiny village, two knights if any, and they had no arms. However, the few people who were there hid in the tower and refused to open the gate. Mercadier ordered his sappers to start digging to undermine the walls while the king and I set up our household. There were many empty wattle and daub cots in the village, but we preferred Richard's large linen pavilion. The only gnat in our ear was his priest, Father Milo, who prophesied terrible results if the king fought during Lent.

For three days the sappers worked. Richard didn't bother to fight, but he rode out at dusk each evening to see the progress. There was no action at all unless his men ventured too close to the wall; then the people inside dropped stones, but couldn't dent the shields. Mercadier's knights shot arrows from the crossbow to apply pressure, but it wasn't necessary.

On the third and last night, before the tunnel was set afire, Richard permitted me to ride with him. The sun was set, the twilight long. We rode through quiet gray oaks in the valley approach to Chalus.

"I want you to see a remarkable sight," Richard said jocularly. "There's a youth who stands on the wall and deflects our arrows with a frying pan."

We rode close, Richard wore a helmet, but I was completely covered by the rectangular shields carried around us. Richard ordered one of them lowered that I might see.

Sure enough, a black silhouette stood on the perilous rim with his bow and alternated between deflecting arrows with a round pan and gathering them to shoot back. One whizzed toward us.

"Good shot!" the king called, as the shield went up.

"Too good," he added quietly. "I want to get you back."

We rode slowly in Mercadier's company to our tent.

Richard turned affably to his priest and two knights who came after us. "No, I'm tired. Only Alix and Mercadier, please."

We went inside together.

"I'm hit," Richard said hoarsely. "Alix, get a light and let Mercadier look."

I held back a cry. It couldn't be serious—he hadn't made a sound and he'd ridden back. As Richard stretched out on his stomach and Mercadier bent over him, I went outside and casually took a firebrand.

Once inside, I held it low. The feeble glare revealed a wooden shaft—half of the arrow—protruding from the nape of Richard's neck where it had entered at a leftward angle.

"I'll pull it out." Richard reached behind his own head.

"No, let me," Mercadier said. "The angle's wrong for you. Do you need drink?"

"God's feet, no! Take it!"

Sweat soaked Richard's tunic. I offered my hand, but he held to the sides of the bed.

"I'm going to work it."

Mercadier put one hand at the flesh, the other higher, and turned the arrow back and forth a little. Richard groaned through clenched teeth.

Suddenly Mercadier jerked.

The shaft broke in his hand right where it entered.

"Did you get it?" Richard asked in agony.

"We'll have to cut. I'll get my surgeon." Mercadier dashed out of the tent.

I knelt beside the king. "It's going to be all right, Richard. I can see that it will hurt, but . . ."

"God's balls. It's deep and close to the spine."

He closed his eyes.

Mercadier came back with a rough-looking mercenary who held a box of sharp knives such as a barber uses. *Benedicite*, if only Bonel were here. I went for two more torches.

The men outside the tent were told to move back; the king wished privacy. I daresay they thought he referred to our lovemaking, but he wanted the luxury of screaming without alarming his army. I held the flambeaux until my arms ached as Mercadier and his surgeon began to cut into the king. Fatty flesh was rolled back, blue muscle hacked, white strings laid across his back and blood spilled everywhere. Richard howled in excruciating pain, drank deeply of the liquor I gave him. Through half the night they dug. If the king could survive their ministrations, he would survive the arrow.

Finally they reached the bolt with splinters of the shaft still attached: it was barbed lead, big as a man's hand. By the time the wicked object was out, Richard had a crater in his back.

"Use wine," I begged them.

"Do it," Richard whispered.

Without a word, Mercadier poured wine into the gaping

hole, then herbs and finally a poultice to draw infection. The surgeon cleaned his instruments on his tunic and returned them to the box. Richard lay in a red pool.

"I'll clean you," I told Richard.

"No, lie with me."

Startled, I looked up at Mercadier. Using his palm, he swiped the worst of the mess off the bed and threw a cover over it for me. He then took the torches and left.

Carefully I stretched beside Richard.

"Touch me," he whispered.

"But . . ."

Toward dawn, he slept fitfully.

Then the screams began again. Only Mercadier, Father Milo, the surgeon and I were permitted entry into the tent, and it took all of us to hold Richard to his bed. His agony was like all things he did, heroic in proportion, awesome to watch.

And he insisted upon making love to me.

Father Milo protested vehemently that he was killing himself with unholy lust, but Richard replied grimly that he knew the best weapon for battle.

So it went for three days. The priest was now scandalized by our open lovemaking and often walked into the tent when we were in the act. I was killing the king, he insisted; the king was killing himself.

Richard and I knew better.

Our eyes locked as of yore, as they had in the field outside Poitiers, on the riverbanks, in the castles, in towers, on the rock of Andelys. Richard's cure lay in his will to live for me. Living intensely in the present, we confirmed faith in the future. Yet our frantic confirmation was bred of numbing fear.

On the third day he sent for Eleanor.

"It isn't necessary—I'll take care of you, my darling," I protested, wiping his fevered brow.

"Take a deep breath, Alix. What do you smell?"

"A dead rat somewhere. I'll have the servants find it."

His smile was eerie. "That dead rat is commonly called gangrene."

My ministrations halted in horror. "Gangrene? But . . ."

"Remember how I sneered when Leopold of Austria died of gangrene?"

"And Enoch had . . ." Hated myself for blurting his name.

Richard's pain-darting pupils stilled for a moment.

"Do you love me?"

"I love you!" I cried desperately. "You have to live for me! For our baby!"

"Let me feel it again."

I guided his hand up my tunic to my bare abdomen.

"There—like wings."

"All I feel is a turn of your stomach."

"No, soothly, there it is again."

For a moment his face was transfixed. Then pain took him.

MERCADIER CAME to announce that there was no treasure in Chalus, but at least he'd captured Richard's killer.

"Bring him in," Richard ordered.

Stumbling over his ropes, a sallow youth was dragged by Mercadier's men into the king's tent, followed by a crowd of knights, who by now knew the king's plight.

"What's your name?" Richard asked when the boy stood at the foot of his bed.

"Pierre de Basile."

He had terrible teeth, angry eyes that stared malevolently from under a forelock. He was bony, as if hungry, and his voice broke from youth.

"What harm have I ever done you, Pierre, that you would kill me?"

"You slew my father and two brothers with your own hand and you would have slain me. Do whatever you like with me. I don't care if you torture me to death so long as you die as well! You've done naught but inflict evil on the world!"

A faint frown fretted the king's forehead, but his voice remained calm.

"I forgive you my death," he said simply. "You may go free."

Pierre de Basile's scowl deepened at the words of pardon, as if he dreaded freedom more than death.

Richard smiled tersely. "Take a hundred shillings and live on, Pierre de Basile; you, at least, will behold the light of day."

He nodded to Mercadier who dragged the boy out.

When the company had left, I sat on his bed. "You showed true Christianity, My Lord, except . . ."

The blues of his eyes had faded into the whites. "Except what?"

"How can you forgive him your death when you're going to live?"

He took my hand. "I'm finished, Alix. I have no more talent for love. Which is life."

"Of course you have! You're tired, that's all. I'll show you. Please, let me . . ."

"No. If I could, I would; I need no stimulus."

"But I . . ."

"I still love you, Alix; that's God's irony. More than ever."

He released my hand.

"I must ride pain a few more days, long enough for me to prepare my death. Go now, and send the priest in."

I couldn't believe him. Only yesterday, only this morning, we'd . . .

"You're not saying goodbye, are you?" I cried. "I can't just . . ."

"No, Alix." Even now his smile tried to reassure me. "I'll send for you."

I stumbled out of the tent and ran through the crowd of somber knights—many more than we'd brought with us— into the wood. There I threw myself on the cool damp earth, tore at new flowers in a fury at their life and sobbed like an animal.

❧             ❧             ❧

WITHIN HOURS, we were crowded into his tent again. Dazed, I recognized William of Briouze, Thomas Basset, Peter of Stoke, Gerard of Fonival, Geoffrey de la Celle and two new chaplains, as well as Richard's own priests. Richard was propped as high as he could endure on pillows, was dressed in white and wore a small gold crown. Tapers had been placed on several tables and their amber light made the king look waxen; the increasing stench of his wound was almost disguised by strong rose oil.

I no longer had the place of honor, but must sit in a corner alone, deeply aware that I was a woman attending a sacred male ritual: the death of a king among his knights, a brotherhood stronger than family or even the Church. The priest made the sign of the cross over Richard's forehead, murmured a few Latin words, then stepped back to make room for Richard's clerk, Philip, who held vellum and pen to record all that was said hereafter.

Richard's low rasp carried throughout the stilled tent. "I will soon face my Maker and therefore must divest myself of all my worldly possessions." The effort exhausted; then he continued. "The most valuable of these is my crown. My intimate friend and intended wife, my . . . Lady Alix of Wanthwaite, now carries my chosen heir, who will be born early this autumn." Despite his control, his voice broke. "I designate this child, whether male or female, to wear my crown and hereby appoint as regents until he or she reach his majority my mother, Queen Eleanor, Walter of Coutances, Archbishop of Rouen, and Hubert Walter, Archbishop of Canterbury; Lady Alix of Wanthwaite will care for the child.

"Let it be known that all previous statements, treaties or rumors that either Arthur of Brittany or John of Mortain might take the crown are hereby declared by me null and void. Any challenge to this decree is to be met with force of arms. *Teste me ipso.*"

No one spoke, but a faint rustle revealed shock.

He then signed the document, had it stamped with the royal seal and instructed that the seals of Rouen and Canterbury be affixed as well; it was passed so that the knights could sign as witnesses.

When the king held the finished document, he said, "This, the most original and foremost, shall now be passed to the mother of my child, Lady Alix of Wanthwaite, as her own copy to hold for my unborn son."

Father Milo accepted the vellum and walked to my corner; all heads turned to witness my acceptance of the testament.

King Richard closed his eyes briefly after the act, then continued. A second copy was to be written and signed for Queen Eleanor, and a third for Hubert Walter, Archbishop of Canterbury. The contents of the will were to be kept private until the king's funeral at Fontevrault; then Queen Eleanor would make public that his unborn child was to succeed him under the regency of the aforementioned persons.

The tent was very quiet, with only the scratch of the pen to be heard. No one looked in my direction.

He continued with the disposal of his goods: his jewels and three-fourths of his treasure to go to Otto of Germany, the rest to be distributed to the poor at the feast of his burial; his horses and arms to a long list of favorite knights, his three hundred or more rich gowns and furs to be distributed among friends.

At last he was silent. His weeping knights rose in respect and, one by one, kissed his pale lips.

When they'd finished, the king turned again in pain. "I'll make my confession when I've rested, then take communion. Leave me, please—except for Lady Alix."

Father Milo cast me a withering look, but the rest filed out without a glance. As soon as they were gone, I rushed to Richard's bedside.

His transparent skin revealed faint veins of yellow-green; the infection was everywhere. Surely such a rapid alteration could change just as rapidly in the other direction, couldn't it?

He turned his tortured face.

"My confession begins with you, Alix. I've deceived you and beg your forgiveness."

"When you've just acknowledged our child? Made him your heir? Rather I should thank you—and I do!" I put my wet cheek against his.

"If only I . . . it won't be easy, Alix."

I clutched at his wistful tone, a sign he still valued life.

"Tell me what to do."

He pushed me gently away. "I must confess my sin . . ."

"No! You've been nothing but kind. Please talk of our child."

His eyes stopped my protest. He was already a long step on his journey, inacessible to me. I became quiet.

"I loved you from the first moment I saw you, loved you during the years we were apart; only you could be the mother of my heir. But I didn't anticipate . . ."

He was sorry he'd wrenched me from Wanthwaite as a hostage? It had long ceased to matter. He continued before I could tell him.

"I hadn't expected that you loved your husband."

Aye, so I had, I must admit. But once Enoch was dead . . .

"Or that he would prove adamant about keeping you."

The rasping words penetrated slowly.

"You mean what my household said when Bonel came? When Enoch was in the Orkneys?"

"I mean when I first contacted him, as soon as we landed in England, again from Nottingham, again . . ."

He watched me struggle.

"But he was dead!"

"We told you so, yes, bribed a Scot to verify our tale."

"Bribed a Scot?" I heard myself repeat vacuously. I couldn't think, couldn't absorb. Perhaps Richard raved in his last delirium.

"We offered every reward possible—gold, position, your castle and others. I had no choice but to order his death."

"You had Enoch murdered?" Stunned, I began to believe. "How? When?"

"Never. He went to France. But we tried, Alix. I assigned Mercadier."

My heart raced, my breath became shallow; the Scot at Vaudreuil, on the cliff, in Vernon. *Deus juva me.*

Richard's icy fingers entwined in mine. He forced me to look at him. Over and over the Scot had been approached on the subject of an annulment—in my name, as my wish —and had refused. He'd promised to follow Richard's proctor to Rome to fight the issue if necessary.

"But why? He must know that we're lovers."

"Oh yes, he knows." A trace of his old cynicism. "My guess is to thwart me. He may grant it once I'm gone."

Richard had been prepared to renounce Berengaria, but his spiritual advisers could think of no way to resolve the dilemma of my living husband.

"So there was to be no annulment?" I begged him to contradict me. He couldn't have lied about that.

"Not until we persuaded the Scot, either with words or a well-placed arrow. But I wanted it, Alix. I didn't deceive you on that score. I would give anything if . . ."

The moth wings inside me beat wildly, and I had to stand in order to breathe.

"Do you still love him?" Richard asked with dread.

"How can you ask?" I walked away, came back. "He's a phantom to me. I can't grasp . . ."

"I loved you too much," he said simply. "That's my sin."

I looked down on my lover of the past four years, the dying father of my child. He'd forgiven the man who'd killed him; I could do no less.

I bent and kissed his dry lips. "I forgive you, Your Majesty."

For the first time since he'd been struck, tears filled his eyes.

"Thank you. Pray for me, Alix. I deceived you most foully for which I'm sorry. But when I face Our Father, I know He'll put my love for you on the positive side of the ledger. You redeemed my life. Now go."

I turned at the door to look at him once again. Then backed out slowly, holding his eyes as long as possible, then seeing only his body, then the tip of the bed we'd shared so often.

And no more.

I LAY on the carpet of flowers again. Bees moved widdershins among the blooms and one lighted on my open palm.

*The king is dead! Long live Enoch!*

It wasn't Enoch who'd had gangrene, it was Richard. And I'd been lied to and lied to and lied to. Bonel had known: that was his "secret."

Bonel had advised me to learn how to fall out of love. Excellent advice. As excellent as my telling Richard to live. Who wouldn't do the impossible if it were possible?

I closed my fist over the bee, hoping he would sting so I could have honest feeling again.

He waited till I opened it and flew away.

For two days I hardly moved.

WHEN I WALKED through the forest gloom among the knights, I heard fragments of Richard's progress toward death. He'd made arrangements for his corporeal shell: his body was to be buried at the feet of King Henry at Fontevrault in perpetual penance; his entrails were to be given to the lords of the south for their infidelity; in "memory of love," his heart was to go to Rouen.

On 4 April Queen Eleanor arrived. We heard a woman screaming and keening long before we saw her, but it wasn't the queen; it was her daughter Joanna. Very pregnant and unhealthily swollen besides, her face was bloated and twisted with grief. She was maddened by frustration. She howled her lament for all to hear: Raymond of Toulouse had abused her most wickedly and her brother king must live to release her from the savage tyrant.

She was not permitted to see Richard.

Eleanor was silent as a stone. Drained of all life, she walked inside her stoic shell to the tent of death and didn't emerge until two days later.

Across the silent dell, her clarion voice carried like birdsong. "The Great One is no more. I have lost the staff of my old age; England has lost her beloved king."

Long shadows cut her red robes. It was seven in the evening, 6 April, and Richard's life departed with the day.

Cries and sobs rent the air. Then everyone started. What was that? Above the keening rose an unearthly shriek, as if the Devil himself passed over us.

It was Richard's assassin, Pierre de Basile. Joanna had ordered that he be flayed to death. Mercadier complied, then had him drawn and quartered.

The king was dead: his orders were no longer obeyed.

# 23

HE FUNERAL BELL TOLLED.

When his body was carried forth on a large platform, his hair flowed in shining waves under his thin crown, his face was painted to the same glowing hues as his mother's and looked serene, his body was draped in rich fluttering silks of soft rose, green and blue from the Holy Land, his folded hands were encased in jeweled gloves.

The long cortège formed behind Richard and his unmanned horse, Fauvel, whose stirrups were hanging backward. As we walked close to Chalus, a song reached across the field.

*"Viris, avaritia, seelus, enormisque libido,*
*Faeda fames, atrox alatio, caecca cupido,*

*Annis regnarum bis quinis, arcabalista*
*Arte, manu, telo prostravit viribus ista."*

"Venom, avarice, crime, unbounded lust,
Foul famine, atrocious pride, blind desire,
Have reigned for twice five years. An archer
With art, hand, weapon, strength did all this overthrow."

It was a second shaft shot into this shaded valley of death.
My eyes filled with pain, with anger at "unbounded lust."
What a cruel depiction of Richard's love for me and how
unjust, as all the other descriptions were, yet no one else in
the cortège reacted. Eyes straight forward, heads high, the
queen and her followers moved with dignity through the
green twilight.

Two days later we were in Fontevrault. Our small party
had grown to a vast throng, as great men from all over the
kingdom rushed to pay homage to their departed lord.
Prince John was here, fresh from Brittany, where he'd been
visiting young Arthur, where—I heard in passing—he'd
been plotting with Arthur to overthrow Richard. Berengaria
had been notified but hadn't come, whether because of my
presence and the forthcoming announcement, I couldn't tell.
Bishop Hugh of Lincoln had sped hither to deliver the funeral oration.

Foremost among the mourners was the pope's legate, with
word that Pope Innocent sent his special benediction for the
dead king and was offering Mass in Rome for his passage
into Heaven. The legate also brought the sobering report of
a new papal bull, to the effect that the Jews were charged
with killing our Lord, that all Jews presently living and
forevermore carried their ancestors' guilt for the heinous
deed against God.

I wondered if Bonel had heard the bull, for it confirmed
the Edmundsbury cross that was a presager of more serious
acts. My breath grew short. What would it mean? I heard
snatches of conversation evincing satisfaction but no dismay,

or even surprise. I was glad that I might have the power in the future to offset the devastating proclamation.

Richard's body now lay high on a bier for the edification of the living. His still-dazzling remains mirrored the future of us all, what even the greatest of this world must come to, the way of all flesh. I glanced fleetingly at his waxen glow and then turned away. That hollow effigy in its splendid silks had nothing to do with my Richard, the most vibrantly alive of men. His soul had ascended to Heaven; his flesh remained, not in that discarded shell, but inside my womb.

The funeral was called, the crowds pressed to enter the chapel. No longer in a position of honor, I leaned against the back wall, unable to see the altar of Bishop Hugh. But I could hear.

Richard had passed as a mighty river through the kingdom, bringing nurture and glory and honor with his tide. We would not see his like again, for he swept with him the flower of chivalry, virtue and deeds of surpassing glory. But a great king, even as the most lowly man, is created to gladden Christ, and Richard had heard the trumpet of bliss heralding from the skies. Therefore his living current had joyfully passed to the great sea, which is our Eternal Father.

The earth mourns and fades at his loss, the people languish in sorrow. We approach a new century with hope, but also with sadness, for we weep for our king.

Indeed, quiet weeping throughout the chapel grew in volume as knights fought to control their anguish.

Except that he left a son. I felt a quickening in my womb; Richard was reminding me of what I must do. I glanced at the wet-cheeked men around me who didn't yet know of what awaited them, that Richard had given them an heir of his own valor, a prize without peer.

"I say, enough of these pompous clichés. Let's eat."

John's querulous voice jarred me from my reverie, brought a murmur of anger from the congregation. Low intense words from Bishop Hugh stopped the interruption, then he continued the sermon.

A king who loved peace, without fury, yet who would set briars and thorns against him in battle? He fought for God, was the first to take the cross against the infidel in the Holy Land; his righteous sword thrust a flaming blade against the unfaithful . . .

"Your sermon is windy, Father, and the food will spoil."

John's rude words now brought an open reproach from the crowd, and the funeral threatened to disintegrate.

*Deo gratias* that my son existed to defeat this boorish prince, and the diabolic Arthur as well.

Bishop Hugh continued: Richard, glorious ruler and defender of the faith, was also a man with a man's failings, but he loved God more than corruption, put his sins behind him before he faced his Maker, would surely enhance Heaven even as he did earth, would become a bright star in the firmament.

The stars above Château Gaillard, Richard now among them, so near, so far. Tears flowed down my cheeks, my throat and into my bodice. I couldn't bear the loss.

Then there was a steady jangle of metal from the front, and again Bishop Hugh stopped his speech and spoke sharply to John, this time for all to hear.

"You mock your God and blaspheme against your brother king who is expired," he warned.

"I'm only playing with my gold," John argued. "I must do something against this numbing speech, or I would expire from boredom myself."

Queen Eleanor's quiet tones chastised her son, and the funeral was ended with a psalm; "Lo, though I walk through the valley of the shadow of death . . ."

WE WERE IN THE COURTYARD, and the food was being distributed. The clamoring poor were admitted from the road to partake in the feast in accordance with Richard's instruction. Soon the momentous announcement of the succession would be made, and I would be elevated to a high position forevermore. I sought the queen to see what I should do, where I should stand, but she was engrossed in conversation with Bishop Hugh and the papal legate.

From a small platform next to the bier, Faidit, a famous troubadour, began a mournful strain:

> "Ah God, the valiant King of the English
>   is no more . . .
> Of all the *preux chevaliers* the first . . .
> A thousand years shall not see his peer,
> So openhanded, noble, brave and generous."

The haunting words were the most appropriate I'd yet heard. I bit my lip, left the main courtyard and sought a seat under an arch in the cloister, there to fight inner torture. Also to relieve the hard kicks of Richard's son, true offspring of his energetic father, whom he would never see until he, too, went to Heaven. Then I had a marvelous revelation: Richard was with Marie! Together in that glorious violet glow, father and daughter, to love and console each other. I bowed forward with new desolation.

And touched a red robe.

"You have my heartfelt sympathy, dear Alix," Queen Eleanor said, "I know your loss."

"Thank you, Your Majesty. We share the most dreadful . . ." But I couldn't finish, couldn't even meet her eyes, for with both faces glossed with the same paint, she and Richard were cruelly alike.

"I've arranged with Abbess Matilda for both you and Joanna to give birth here at the abbey."

"Thank you, Your Majesty."

She bent and kissed my cheek, her rosewater now redolent of Richard's death.

She left, her slow progress through the crowd the perfect performance of a perfect queen, grieved beyond solace, but retaining her majesty.

At last she mounted the platform vacated by Faidit and

prepared to make her momentous announcement in the shadow of Richard's corpse. John stood beside her, and the crowd fell silent. I rose and straightened my skirts, prepared to respond to her summons.

Her carillon voice carried easily across the hushed crowd. She began with a touching acknowledgment of mutual grief, her gratitude for expressions of sympathy in this trying ordeal, her hope and belief that the great lords would remain loyal to the Crown, despite the terrible loss.

"King Richard of England, the Great One, died in my arms. On his deathbed, he commissioned me to announce his choice of heir and successor on this occasion." She paused dramatically. "He most specifically abjured his nephew, Arthur of Brittany, and chose instead his brother and our last son, John, prince of the realm and Count of Mortain."

John grinned at the audience and raised his hand in salute.

A collective murmur of surprise rippled through the crowd, then a belated cry, "Long live King John!"

I, too, cried out in horror, but my words were lost as the cheer for John gained momentum. Dazed and disbelieving, I fought my way forward to correct this ghastly error. Did the queen suffer from shock? Did she have a lapse of memory?

A hand held me back.

"Best stay here," Mercadier warned.

"But it's a mistake, Mercadier!" I gasped. "You were there when Richard said . . . you heard . . ."

"It's not a mistake."

Hard gray eyes held me as his message sank in.

"But you yourself heard that my son . . . and Father Milo signed and . . ."

That knight, and that one, a score or more knew the lie. Would no one speak up? Cry for justice? What stopped them?

Mercadier continued to stare, his blank expression telling

me that they did know, all of them. I was the only person kept ignorant of the facts, the conspiracy.

"Let me go," I whispered to Mercadier. "I feel faint . . ."

He released me and turned away. Like a wraith, I floated through the crowd and into the fruit orchard, now in full bud, stumbled blindly past the pears, the cherries and to a hummock under an apple tree. Could I have mistaken the words? Did the queen mean for John to rule until my son was of age?

"No!" I cried aloud. Not at the infamy, but at my own gullibility. When would I resist illusion?

A most awesome suspicion halted my fantastick cells. Was it possible that Richard had changed his mind on his death bed? Or been persuaded in his weakened state?

"No!" I cried again, more vehemently. Richard had lied to me, but there was a truth between us beyond mere words. Falsehood came from too much love, never too little, and he'd adored both our children whom he would never see on this earth. No! No!

I was not alone. The queen appeared with John at her side, their stroll purposeful; they were seeking me. Before they found me, I studied their casual perfidy. Eleanor had instructed me that a queen rules only through her son, and she had one son still living by whom to extend her power, even though he was a freak of Nature. Did she think she could control him? Even she had more to learn "in the saddle," for this new king was as tamable as a poisonous adder.

John saw me, broke from his mother and sauntered to my tree, where he squatted before me. At least his face didn't remind me of Richard.

"I've been looking for you, plum." His lips dripped pork grease, and he held a cup of Richard's favorite Bordeaux.

"I felt a little oppressed, Your Majesty, but I congratulate you. England is honored that you are king."

He smiled lasciviously. "I told you once that I get my brother's leavings, his crown, his wenches."

He reached for my breast, but I moved easily away from his grasp.

"Too soon, is it?" Over the cup, his cold eyes contradicted his jolly slur. "Still pine for that painted husk? Or is it his whelp in your belly that stops you?"

"With your permission, Your Majesty, I would like to return to my dorter."

He stood and offered his hand.

"By all means, and while you're there, be so kind as to take a document that belongs to me and return it here forthwith. A silly statement that Richard dictated when he was delirious."

His iron fist released me.

"You'll find me by the wine. Make haste."

I bowed until he'd retreated. In the corner of my eye, I saw the scarlet slash move to her son.

I began to run.

"Wait, Lady Alix!"

I turned to John once more.

"You have nothing to worry about, pigeon. I'll take care of Richard's brat."

Followed by his wine-laden bray, I flew past Eleanor with her sly secret smile, across the familiar herb garden and into my dorter where I flung myself across my mat. My brain brimmed with panic, and my heart pounded with shock. Take care of . . . aye, I could envision the care—in a tower or dungeon or worse. *Deus juva me*, what could I do?

Inside my womb, my infant prince echoed my dread as he flailed and kicked. I sat upright to relieve the discomfort, put my hands where he turned.

"Rest thee, bairn," I crooned desperately. "I'll not permit them to harm thee."

Voices and laughter floated in the soft air as grief gave way to celebration. While they were occupied, now. . . . With shaking hands I put my few valuables into a trunk and pushed it under the bed. Then I slipped back into the garden.

⚜     ⚜     ⚜

I HID BEHIND the heart-shaped leaves of a lilac bush.

"Hamo!" I whispered.

Moodily watching the carp in the fish pond, he didn't come to me until I'd called twice.

"Hamo, I want to leave Fontevrault without anyone knowing. Will you help me?"

His sad face brightened. "Where are we going?"

"Not you, Hamo. I flee for my very life and . . ."

"Your life is mine," he said fervently. "Tell me what to do."

There was no time to argue, so I gave him instructions. He stood by the pond until I'd skirted the fruit orchard, then began a leisurely stroll in the direction of the stables. I waited until he was out of sight, listened to the grating hoots of the bibulous mourners—John's shrill bleat uppermost—and then ran across the herb garden to the administration house, there to seek Subprioress Hilaria.

Her response to my blunt recital was exactly what I'd expected; she well knew Fontevrault's debt to Queen Eleanor, but its higher dedication was to God. Praying briefly and to the point for my welfare, she then gave me what I needed. Furthermore, she walked with me to my dorter to protect me from John if he sought me. In brief time I was packed and ready.

Hamo came almost at once, lifted my trunk to his back and led the way to the lower gate. Hilaria waved from the porch, my last image of Fontevrault.

No, not quite the last. When I mounted Sea Mew, I was able to see the quiet figure of Richard as he lay in state on his high funeral platform. From here, he might have been sleeping.

My throat tightened; I looked away and rode through the gate. Bok waited in the lane.

"No, you mustn't . . ." It was hard to speak. "Danger . . ."

"We're your vassals, Lady Alix," he responded, "and will protect you."

I pressed my lips and nodded. Then, without pause, I spurred Sea Mew off the lane and into a dense boggy wood where we might find immediate cover.

*BONG! BONG! BONG!*

The king's faint death knell was his dying voice and would ring in my heart forever. Oh God, how could I live without him? Hot tears stung my eyes. What had Bonel once said about Enoch—that separation was like death? If only death could be like separation, if I could believe that Richard awaited me now in Chinon or Poitiers or Rouen or Sherwood Forest. Aye, that's how I would think of him, riding close in his hunting green, his hand reaching for mine.

I sobbed aloud, lay my wretched face against Sea Mew's mane.

It had rained the night before, and wet branches struck my cheeks with monotonous regularity, despite Hamo's best efforts to spare me. I welcomed their flagellation as fitting for my unremitting despair. Oh Richard, Richard, don't leave me! Without you, how can I survive the queen's serpent cunning, the villainy of King John? How can I even want to? If it weren't for the doomed bairn riding within me, I wouldn't try.

Sea Mew stumbled badly in the fetid swamp; foul bubbles rose, and slitherings whispered below as shrill bird-shrieks protested above. Hamo sought higher ground where twisted vines and fallen trees gave way to pines.

Pine needles increased my welcome torture, and I noted that the long-needle pine was filled with tears, one per needle, hanging in a single shining drop ready to fall.

"Do you have a plan, Lady Alix?" Hamo asked softly over his shoulder. "Which direction should we take? North?"

To Rouen, the comfort of Bonel and Tib—and their sure demise if they were caught harboring me.

"No. Go as you are."

Whatever that direction was.

So we plashed through the drear black greenery as the death bell tolled. Were we descending ever deeper? Or did my fantastick cells conjure the abyss of despair? The wood was filled with charnel stench, rotting wood, mildew and animal flesh.

Sew Mew whinnied and jerked his head to the side. I'd ridden him directly into the flank of Hamo's steed.

"We've reached an end, Lady Alix," my "knight" said.

I thought he read my thought, but no, he meant an end to the wood. I blinked against a long bright blear of new grass and gillyflowers bending in the steady breeze, the dapple of fast moving cloud shadows.

Damn the landscape, which must haunt me forever! In this very meadow last summer Richard and I had rolled most merrily. Eleanor had wanted me to know the empire? I could have given her a lesson on the sweet clove-laden nooks, the shelter of hoary trees, caves, rills—all the places that conceal lovers in their bliss.

"We can move more swiftly here," Bok suggested, "and there's cover on the other side."

I slid to the ground. "Let me think a few moments."

There it was, the very place, and he'd made me a chaplet of poppies for my hair, called me his elixir of drugged honey.

"They'll send a search party as soon as they notice your absence," Hamo reminded me.

"Aye, but we must disguise ourselves against spies. Here, put these on."

Fortunately Hilaria had given me two outfits for a man, since we hadn't time to worry about size, and soon Hamo and Bok would both appear to be common villeins.

"Keep your weapons, but conceal them," I ordered, "and remove any revealing insignia from your saddles. I'll change over here."

I took a novice's coarse haircloth tunic and wimple for myself and walked purposefully into the swaying grass. As soon as I was sure I was alone, I threw myself onto my beloved flowery turf, as if it would bring Richard back to me.

A hard rock bruised my hip.

I sat up to change position, but no, the rock was inside my own drafsack. I reached to remove the offensive stone and found Bonel's Christian Eye.

It gazed up from my palm, reflected the moving clouds much as it had that day outside Winchester, seemed alive. Aye, Bonel had said it was magic, that I should use it only when in dire straits. What could be more dire than my present circumstance?

Feeling slightly foolish and glad that I was alone, I pressed the eye hard between the heels of my palms and repeated, "Bonel, help me. Bonel, help me."

The eye broke, and I opened my hands in dismay, expecting to find them full of blood from the shards. Instead, the eye wept for me, was filled with tears. It was the final confirmation of my doom, and I almost dropped the miraculous shatter, then looked closer.

Each teardrop had a hard surface which caught the sun in a thousand angles.

The tears were diamonds.

I ENTERED A TRANCE.

My rent heart pounded, my breath grew shallow, and my tunic was damp with perspiration. Sickened almost as if I were under the influence of the poppy, I looked through mist at an altered world. As snow had once seemed apple blossoms to my drugged eyes, so now the rain-strewn landscape glittered with diamonds. A single frond of grass crossed my vision, its underside coated with rain drops, and they were neither water nor tears, but a caterpillar with diamond feet about to transform itself into a butterfly.

The marvelous world of the caterpillar in its royal cocoon slipped away with a wrench, became memory. I'd loved and been loved more than any woman before me, and that could never be lost, but I was no longer held in my silken trap. I was free to fly in the wind, under the clouds, free for the first time in years. The prospect frightened, but couldn't be denied.

Bonel. I'd lost Richard, but not Bonel, and Bonel had given me the world. The diamonds could be turned to silver, the silver to freedom. At last I had a choice!

Magic indeed.

I'd lost the vaunted power I'd never had, lost the real title of concubine, the promised title of queen, but I was still myself. Again myself. That was the miracle of Bonel's gift, to give me back to myself. Inviolable.

Eleanor had taught me the rules of deception and betrayal, had taught me, in short, to know her heart. But her toty rules couldn't change me. I rejected them all, had always rejected them. As she said, bloodlines give us our birth and I was still the daughter of my wondrous parents, still the northern wildflower. Her perfidy meant nothing. Or yes, it did: her betrayal was also a liberation, for I owed her nothing, need not live under her rose-scented rule.

And John's villainy? He still threatened my life, no doubt, but he'd been unwittingly kind in sending his signal so early. He'd given me the opportunity to escape.

Richard's death. Even diamonds couldn't turn his loss from tragedy to hope. I would love him forever, would happily throw a million diamonds into the sea to have him back.

And yet . . .

We'd lived under a shadow, which descended each day. How much longer could he have pretended that we were to marry? That Eleanor would go to the pope? That our child would have a wedded mother and father? This was one lie that must be discovered as surely as my disguise as a boy. Would the intensity of our love have proved equal to such betrayal? His death had accelerated a revelation that was inevitable.

His death made it easier to forgive.

Terrible thought, but true. We were now not so much finished with love as frozen in time at the height of our bliss, and memory could only enhance perfection. Richard had been released from an uglier confession; I had been released from the demise of love.

I straightened and looked at the distance across the meadow with a calculating eye. My babe complained of my shift with a hearty kick.

"Easy, sweets," I whispered. "I must make an important decision."

To escape, that was my first order, for I didn't doubt that Eleanor and John wanted me dead, as well they might. They were formidable foes, but right was on my side, and I could feel Richard's gaze from above as if he rode a cloud. I touched the will where it lay safely against my thigh. I would bide my time, but let the Plantagenets beware.

I slipped on the rancid tunic and black mantle, tied the wimple firmly under my chin. This disguise could not serve me long with my fatherless bairn growing with each heartbeat. Fatherless, but he had a mother.

Fatherless?

He was no more fatherless than Our Lord had been fatherless. God who is in Heaven fathers us all. And Richard might be dead, but he'd declared himself to be my babe's natural father on earth; a dead father is still a father. Then there was Bonel. He'd told me how the Jews love their wives and protect their children; we might not be wed, but Bonel cherished and protected me and my child. His love was boundless. Of course Our Lady had an earthly husband in Joseph, while I . . .

I stifled a cry! I was still a married woman—Enoch was the babe's legal father.

Enoch. Suddenly the very name was a sunburst in my

soul. I'd dwelt so completely on the fact that his death was a lie, that Richard had lied to me, that I hadn't been fully aware till this moment of the portent of that lie. Enoch *lived*, that was the miracle, as remarkable as if I'd learned that my father and mother awaited me at Wanthwaite. Oh, I knew he must hate me now, be filled with spite and resentment, and he had every right. Yet—no matter how bitter and twisted—he was still Enoch, just as I was still Alix. And he didn't know that I'd thought him dead, that I'd never repudiated him in my heart, nor would he believe it simply for the saying. There was a long hazardous road ahead with Enoch, and I wasn't ready to ride it yet.

Meantime, it was enough to know that he breathed the same air I did, knew dawn and sunset, hope and despair. He might hate me forever, but I was still glad he lived.

Now I must face the physical dangers at my heels. I walked to Sea Mew and mounted. Hamo and Bok, dressed as gardeners, mounted as well.

Had the death knell stopped ringing, or were we beyond its reach? Above, an invisible lark trilled its song.

"What is the closest port where we might sail with safety?" I asked Hamo.

Surprised at my purposeful tone, he thought a moment. "Bordeaux. It's the queen's favorite city, but she rarely goes there, nor is it threatened by Philip or Duchess Constance."

"Which way?"

He pointed directly toward the sun, where it already rested at a blinding angle on the topmost branches, and beyond to the long slope to the sea.

"Stay low as we cross the mead," I ordered.

Once again the world transformed itself, not from rain to tears or to diamonds, but to sunstruck sea spray.

I bent and whispered to Sea Mew. "It's time to swim the channel, darling. Hoyt!"

Ears raised in joy, he flew fast as a bird toward the radiance that was England.

# acknowledgments

~~~~~~~~~~~~~~~~~~~~~~~~~~~~~~~~~~~~~~~~~~~~~~~~~~~~~~~~~~~~~

Of the many books which informed nearly every page of *Banners of Gold*, a few were essential. For the narrative line, Sir Maurice Powicke's *The Loss of Normandy*; for the life of fighting men, *L'Histoire de Guillaume le Maréchal*, translated from old to modern French by Paul Meyer; for the interaction of Church, knights and women, George Duby's *Le Chevalier, la Femme et le Prêtre* are three such works. Abstracts from "The Anglo-Norman Anonymous" and correspondence with fellow members of the Haskins Society contributed needed details in that same area. For the sections concerning women, Doris Mary Stenton's *The English Woman in History* and *The Medieval Woman's Guide to Health: the First English Gynecological Handbook*, edited by Beryl Roland, gave special information to add to innumerable chapters and works by other authors. For the characters of Tib and Sister Hilaria I also referred to *History of Magic & Experimental Science*, vol. II, edited by Lyn Thorndyke, and the life and writings of Abbess Hildegard of Bingen. The seminal works on the Jews were the *Chronicles of the First and Second Crusades*, *The Devil and the Jews* by Joshua Trachtenberg and *English Jewry under the Angevin Kings* by H. J. Richardson.

Aside from military and social history, I am also indebted to a long list of works for their aesthetic value. In the early stages of writing, I was stimulated by an unfinished novel about the children's crusade, *Feast of Fools* by the late Gene Kearney. For language and the essence of medieval thought,

I immersed myself in Ovid, Chaucer, William Langland's *Piers Plowman*, the Gawain poet's *Sir Gawain and the Green Knight* and *The Pearl*, the music and poetry of the troubadours and medieval lyrics; for form I studied Northrop Frye's *The Secular Scripture, a Study of the Structure of the Romance*.

Though most of the research and writing was a solitary occupation, I am also indebted to a number of people who helped me. Carla Nino accompanied me on a difficult winter trek through Normandy and Brittany where we gained first-hand knowledge of the chill of castle life. Many individuals were of aid in Rouen, Bayeux, Angers, Poitiers and Fontevrault, the most notable being my excellent guides at Château Gaillard and Château Beynac. Then, when I discovered I'd overlooked needed details, Shirley St. Leone furnished further crucial photographs from the Dordogne; Jacques Épain and Laurie Tuller of the University of Poitiers sent additional materials; Bruce Coy gave finishing touches to military history.

When the manuscript was almost completed, Julian Blaustein of Stanford made valuable suggestions, and Beatrice Rosenfeld gave a second professional reaction. My secretary, Damiana Chavez, contributed thoughts based on deep involvement in the material. Eli Boyer was my liaison to the National Foundation for Jewish Culture which, in turn, furnished me with a list of books to begin my enquiry into Jewish history. Harry Horner lent me volumes from his private collection on Jewish history, art and religion.

Rabbi Joel Rembaum, formerly associate professor of Jewish History at the University of Judaism in Los Angeles and a specialist in the interaction between medieval Jews and Christians, also guided me to proper research on the Jews. He then gave a critical reading to the final manuscript for accuracy in the Jewish characters and history and was able to hone the finished product, even to the kind of Hebrew which would have been used in the period.

At Crown Publishers, my editor, Lisa Healy, followed the book during its entire writing, sent me research from New York upon request and, when the pages were finally submitted, scrutinized every word with loving care. Indeed, all the people at Crown who've worked directly on the making of the book have shown themselves to be extraordinarily devoted to the creation of an accurate and appealing tome.

To all these authors, strangers and friends, I am grateful. To my family who've permitted me my strange journey through the twelfth century at the expense of missed holidays and celebrations, I owe special thanks. As with *Shield of Three Lions*, however, my husband, Charlie, has been my staunchest supporter, my most exacting critic. Charlie has read every page with a sharp professional eye, has alternated high praise with constructive suggestions, but always with love, always with a sensitive understanding of the material and the author. Therefore, *Deo gratias* for Charlie.

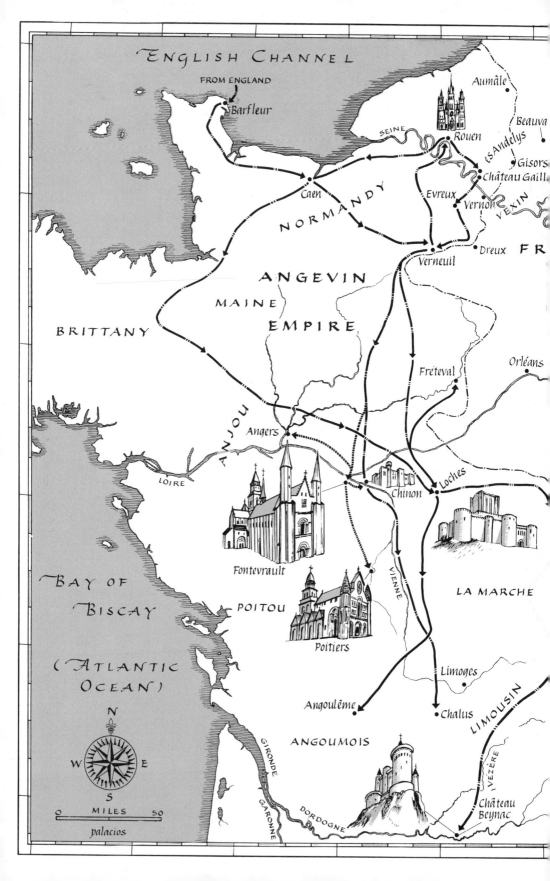